THE NOSTALGIST

First Published in 2012 by M P Publishing Limited
6 Petaluma Blvd. North, Suite 6, Petaluma, CA 94952
12 Strathallan Crescent,Douglas, Isle of Man IM2 4NR

ISBN: 978-1-84982-164-3
The Nostalgist
1 3 5 7 9 10 8 6 4 2

Cover Design by Matthew Tanner

Book Design by Maria Clare Smith

Hansbury, Griffin, 1971-
The nostalgist / by Griffin Hansbury.
p. cm.
ISBN: 978-1-84982-164-31.
New York (N.Y.)—Fiction.   2.   September   11   Terrorist   Attacks,
2001—Fiction.   3.   Mental   illness—Fiction.
4.   Interpersonal relationships—Fiction.   I. Title.
PS3608.A721 .N67 2012
813—dc23

A CPI Catalogue for this title is available from the British Library

THE NOSTALGIST

BY GRIFFIN HANSBURY

MP Publishing
WWW.MPPUBLISHINGUSA.COM

Dedicated to the neighbor
(d. 9/11/01) I knew only in passing

Part One

"The city, for the first time in its long history, is destructible. A single flight of planes no bigger than a wedge of geese can quickly end this island fantasy, burn the towers, crumble the bridges, turn the underground passages into lethal chambers, cremate the millions. The intimation of mortality is part of New York now: in the sound of jets overhead, in the black headlines of the latest edition."
—E.B. White, *Here Is New York*, 1949

1

When Jonah Soloway stepped out of his building on the morning of March 11, 2002, he had no idea that the day would end with a terrible lie. Already, it was taking shape inside of him, the way most lies take shape, from the coupling of shame and hope, from the humiliating and impossible wish for everything to be different. Looking back, he would wonder if the lie had been fertilized, at least in part, by the unexpected smell of smoke.

He stopped on the sidewalk and thought about the kitchen stove. Had he checked to make sure it was turned off? He checked it every time he left the apartment. Why, today, should he forget? Every morning, before he headed to work, he pointed his finger at each knob on the stove, in turn, and whispered the word "off" five times: "Off, off, off, off, off." There were five knobs (four for the burners and one for the oven), and five times five was twenty-five, the golden number. He thought of it as the "golden number," but in truth, five times five just felt right. If he failed to check the stove this way, something terrible would happen.

Jonah wasn't certain what that terrible thing might be. He used to be afraid his mother would die, but since September he must have been afraid of something else.

He closed his eyes and took a deep breath. The air was cool and fresh with the smell of the greening earth, mixed with the usual urban odors of car exhaust, cigarette smoke, bacon frying in a nearby diner. But there was something more—he could barely taste it yet—a sharper note tingling underneath, a distraction growing stronger as Jonah groped toward it, trying to hold it in his nose, to name it. It couldn't be. But there was nothing else like it. Somewhere in the otherwise spring-scented current, there wafted a familiar, malodorous aroma. Jonah hadn't smelled it in months, not since the weather had turned cold last fall. Before then, every time the warmer winds shifted, they brought the smell with them from downtown, from the still-smoldering ruins. Between September and December, the odor had served as a barometer of the weather. Upon waking, Jonah knew it would be a warm day if his apartment was dusted with the particulate tang of smoke. Then, as winter came and the chilled air sat low over the wreckage, physics held the odor captive at Ground Zero. *Hot air rises*, Jonah reminded himself now. But the television news said there was nothing left to burn. So it must be something else, he reasoned—a dry cleaners on fire, a torched trash can. He listened for sirens and searched the blue sky for smoke. Nothing. Had he checked the stove?

He suspected that he might be imagining it altogether. He inhaled again. This scent was subtle, not the acrid, overwhelming stink that had hung in an invisible cloud over the city for so long after the attacks, a powerful mix of incinerated synthetics—office furniture, computers, asbestos, Xerox equipment—and all the other things that burned that day and went on burning for far too long. If he let himself think about it, the list of the lost seemed infinite: potted ficuses, plastic forks and spoons, reams of paper, boxes of extra-thick rubber bands, Zip disks and CD-ROMs, photographs of families and fishing trips and weddings push-pinned to cork bulletin boards, vases of fresh flowers, reading glasses, neckties, shoes, and, of course, somewhere in that tortured symphony of smells there quivered a human strain, one that Jonah and the rest of New York City's remaining citizens had tried desperately, unsuccessfully, to tune out, day after day.

He looked at his watch. If he didn't get moving soon, he would be late for work. Jonah prided himself on his punctuality, but lately he'd been dragging his feet, losing minutes here and there, as if the sidewalks beneath his thrift-store wingtips were gradually turning to a sticky bitumen, a tarry resin that slowed him down as it hardened into the amber that would eventually trap him. He took another deep breath. He wanted to be sure about the smell. It drifted up his nostrils, tickling the 10 million receptor cells of his olfactory epithelium, which then sent their signal to light the main olfactory bulb in his brain's cortex, where it branched out to his most ancient core: amygdala, hippocampus, hypothalamus, the nooks and crannies in which his emotions curled alert, like half-napping cats. At this signal, the singular memory designated "9/11" began to stir, and Jonah felt its rough, familiar sadness brushing up against him.

He set off at once for the subway, past the many Indian restaurants that lined his block, still shuttered against the morning; and the brittle, colorless vines of Heavenly Blue morning glories that clung—even in death—to the sycamore trees, flowers he looked forward to seeing bloom again, now that spring would actually be arriving. In September he'd had his doubts.

He walked past the MISSING poster, the same one he'd walked by every morning and again every evening for the past six months. Scotch-taped inside the window of the front door to the apartment building next to Jonah's hung the smiling face of a young woman: Rose Oliveri. Thirty years old. Her hair dark with a streak painted midnight blue, her heavy-lidded eyes brown beneath high-arched brows. She stood 5'2" and weighed 120 pounds. She wore a small silver stud in her left nostril wing and her upper right arm was wrapped in a thorny bramble of tattooed roses.

In hand-printed letters, the poster read, "Rose is my daughter. She works at Omnisphere Technologies on the 89th floor of Tower 1. If you find her, please call us right away." And then a phone number.

After six months, it was no longer a missing poster. It was a memorial. Every time he passed it, Jonah felt a twinge of shame for possessing such intimate knowledge of a woman he did not really know. Before 9/11, he and the woman passed each other every morning as he walked to the subway and she walked her dog, a cream-colored pug that sniffed around the squares of dirt surrounding each sycamore along the block. Jonah never once said hello to Rose Oliveri, and Rose never once said hello to Jonah Soloway. They barely made eye contact. That was New York, Jonah told himself, no time for good mornings. Who was he to presume, anyway, that she would say "good morning" back to him? She was stylish and pretty and Jonah was bald, bespectacled, and stooped.

He had begun losing his hair at the delicate age of seventeen, just after an orthopedist had freed him from the clunky Milwaukee brace that had kept his scoliotic spine from curving into a sine wave, and just before an optometrist had declared him myopic. Crooked, near-sighted, and bald, he'd just turned thirty and already felt like an old man. He dressed for the part in vintage suits and skinny ties, thrift-store wingtips, and a moth-eaten porkpie hat that he rarely removed from his bare and shining head. His horn-rimmed glasses were glass-brick thick. For these reasons, he was certain, even if he had said good morning to Rose Oliveri, she would not have said hello back. This, of course, was no excuse. On each of those mornings, as he slouched past Rose (who, then, remained unnamed to him, was just the Woman with the Pug), Jonah mostly cast his eyes down—at his worn-out shoes, at her more fashionable footwear (size seven, he now knew), at her dog, or at the scruffy garden patches filled with winter's rime of snow, autumn's fallen leaves, cigarette butts, bottle caps, daffodils, shifting with the seasons. But there were also times when Jonah did not look down as he passed the Woman with the Pug, times when he looked at her face, for just a fleeting moment, and he would see that she was pretty in a not entirely intimidating way, that she wore little make-up, that she was tired, and that she seemed lonely, too. She reminded him of the office girl in Raphael Soyer's 1936 painting "Office Girls," the one staring straight at the viewer from beneath a soft felt hat, a girl with wilted flowers in her lapel and red lipstick half bitten off. She had the look of a young woman caught by surprise, as if by an intruder's gaze. It was a wide-eyed, open-mouthed look, as though she might be about to say something. Rose sometimes looked this way, a bit startled, about to take offense. The resemblance didn't stop there. The girl in the Soyer painting had that hat, not a cloche and not a fedora, but something in between, and so did Rose. Jonah liked that about her—that she would wear such a nostalgic object, in an age when the only hats people wore were baseball caps. She had a half-vintage aesthetic, sort of Depression-era, post-flapper punk turned adult and disguised in quasi-corporate drag. But even in the rarefied offices of the World Trade Center, Rose sent a changing streak of color through her hair, sometimes blue or green or pink.

Just once, they touched. Or almost touched. Jonah couldn't be sure. It was winter. Rose stopped to let the dog investigate a yellow patch of snow and Jonah stopped, too. He bent down as if to tie his shoe, watching Rose as she removed one red glove from her hand, replaced it with a plastic baggie, then leaned over to pick up after her dog.

"Good dog," she said, standing up and turning toward Jonah. He grew warm at the sound of her voice, imagined for a second that she was talking to him. "Good dog." He stood up, straightened himself, then folded back into his customary slouch, a cloak of invisibility he pulled over his shoulders. That's when he saw it: the red glove, fallen on an untouched bank of white snow. He pointed to it.

"Uh," he managed to say, clearing his throat, "Ahem." And then, without thinking about it, he was moving forward, bending over again, his fingers touching the fingers of Rose's glove for just a moment.

"I've got it," she said, snatching up the glove with her bare hand. And then it happened. The tip of her index finger touched the tip of his thumb. Jonah jerked his hand back and jumped, as if from a shock of static electricity.

"Oh," he said, his mind scrambling for something more, something graceful and gallant to say. But Rose was already walking away. Maybe she hadn't seen him, Jonah reasoned. But she did say, "I've got it," so she must have seen him. Unless she was talking out loud to herself. But even if he had been invisible, she would have felt him. Their fingers touched. Or did they? It might just have been the air he felt brush against his thumb.

The next day, they passed each other as usual, with no words, no touching, and no look in Rose's eyes to tell Jonah that she recognized him as the man who'd stooped to pick up her glove. Their gazes met for an instant, as they always had, but nothing was changed. He wondered what she saw when she looked at him, and imagined himself as a flash of gray, a smear of human shape passing by, an almost imperceptible ripple in the air. A ghost. (If Rose was the girl in "Office Girls," then Jonah was the man standing behind her in the crowd, a watching shade she'd never see.) And every time their eyes met, in that nanosecond of recognition quickly followed by disavowal, Jonah thought of a quote by Thomas Mann.

He had never read a thing by Thomas Mann, except for this quote. He'd committed it to memory from the moment he found it at the Whitney Museum's 1995 retrospective, "Edward Hopper and the American Imagination." The words were stenciled in large type on the wall next to "Summertime," Hopper's painting of a girl in a sheer white dress and broad-brimmed sun hat, stepping down the front stoop of her apartment building in what was probably Greenwich Village (her dress so transparent, Jonah could clearly discern the pink flesh of her thigh where it pressed against the fabric). In his sketchbook, next to his cartoonish renderings of Hopper girls with their Hopper legs and arms and breasts, he copied down these words:

> "There can be no relation more strange, more critical, than that between two beings who know each other only with their eyes…and yet by some whim or freak of convention feel constrained to act like strangers. −Thomas Mann."

He thought of those words now as he crossed Second Avenue. The breeze washed over him, rushing up the long canyons from downtown, carrying to him again the smell of burning, stronger than before. The smoke lingered in his nose, reaching deep down into his neuro-circuitry, into the tight little vaults where he had locked away his most potent memories of those days in September, the days of white masks and worry, when the city was shrouded in a shimmery curtain of dust, bracing itself for whatever was next. He was back there now. He saw the florid explosions, the litter of paper, the metal bracings bent like tinfoil. And then, as in a dream, the images shifted to a stretch of roadway just outside the city, on a rise with a vista of downtown. It was the same day. The same moment. A shock and a swerve. Nobody saw the SUV when it came to crush his parents in their little emission-conscious car. Nobody paid attention to what was, by comparison, an insignificant plume of smoke on the Newark Bay Extension of the Jersey Turnpike. They were all looking at the city.

Jonah tried not to inhale, tried distracting himself with the pleasant, everyday sights of his morning: the Met Food grocery store where boxes of fat red strawberries waited on the sidewalk to be carried inside; Moishe's Kosher Bake Shop with its window filled with poppyseed-stuffed *hamantaschen*; Seventh Street (where he turned again) and the Qi-Gong Acupuncture Center ("Help to Relieve Stress Pain Tension Insomnia Fatigue Poor Digestion Car-Accident Sequela Etc."); the lace-curtained church basement windows where old women would soon be rolling out thousands of pierogi in preparation for their annual Ukrainian festival; McSorley's Old Ale House, whose handlebar-mustachioed proprietor was just opening the door, letting out the bar's yeasty breath, sprinkling fresh sawdust on the floorboards while a fat orange cat dozed in the window above the coal-chute grate. He thought about stopping to make a sketch, but he had not yet outrun the smell. It followed him, drifting on a thin current up Third Avenue, undiluted by the opposing aromas of bagels, cigarettes, perfume, the fresh shampoo on girls clicking past. Did anyone else smell it? He regarded his fellow pedestrian commuters. They appeared not to notice, putting one foot in front of the other, dodging, bumping, being bumped. At the DON'T WALK, one of them stuck his briefcase briefly in the tender spot behind Jonah's left knee. As the lights changed, another stepped in front of him, cutting him off, breaking his stride. Didn't they see him, he wondered, as he was forced out of the crosswalk by a large, angry man who was shouting into his cell phone, "Don't fucking hang up, don't fucking hang up, bitch, don't fucking hang up."

It occurred to Jonah that, while he felt a deep and often painful compassion for the many anonymous men and women who died in the World Trade Center, if he had ever shared a sidewalk with them, he probably would have despised the majority of them. Alive, they would have been like all the rest: hurrying, pushing, shoving, not watching where they were going. Deceased, they were saintly, so quiet and still, even heroic. But surely, Jonah thought, some of them were a bit more human—angry drunks who beat their wives, cold-hearted women who cheated on their husbands, ungrateful children, greedy thieves, unrepentant liars. They weren't all angels, like the newspapers and memorials would lead you to believe. In death beloved and mourned by much of the world, in life they would have been no different than those in the throng he now fought his way through. Just more hungering, hurried bodies in the already over-swollen crowd—scowling, striving, consuming, shouting into cell phones, stepping on his heels. Maybe even Rose Oliveri. She never once smiled at him. When he bent to retrieve her glove, she didn't say thank you.

The odor drifted across Astor Place, swirled up in the pedestrian rush. An odor, he reminded himself, is a physical thing, a collection of molecules that, when inhaled, literally enter the nose and are absorbed by the cells within the nasal cavity. Unlike a sound or a sight, a smell becomes a part of your body at the very instant you perceive it. He thought then about carbon atoms, how they are forever recycling, never destroyed. A blade of grass today, the digestive system of a dairy cow tomorrow. And then a carton of milk. And then a cup of coffee. And then. If a carbon atom in a cup of coffee possessed consciousness, could it remember the supernova that birthed it so many millennia ago? Unaware that he'd stolen the idea from Primo Levi's *The Periodic Table*—assigned to him by a high school English teacher and gladly mistaken by his astrophysicist father as hard science—he felt original as he traced the possible journey of a single carbon atom, from its endless days drifting through space, where it hitched a ride on some hell-bent comet streaming toward the fiery, early Earth, and then the long, hot years it spent waiting for the planet to congeal, to cool, to begin its ecstatic creation of life.

"At last," Jonah narrated inside his head, in his best public-television narrator voice, "the carbon atom embarks upon the unending joys of travel: from ancient protozoans to sweaty ferns and giant dragonflies of the Carboniferous forests; into the reptilian eggshells of the Permian age, through Jurassic sea lilies, spiraling ammonites, *Tyrannosaurus rex*; through the body of old Lucy, who left her footprints in the proverbial 'sands of time;' to the tempting apples of wild, prelapsarian gardens; to the smoke that rose above the first campfires, in the flickering light of which language, art, and music were born. On and on, a single carbon atom travels, until: blade of grass, dairy cow, carton of milk, cup of coffee."

He swiped his Metrocard and passed through the turnstile of the N/R station at Eighth Street and Broadway to wait on the gum-stained platform for the train to Times Square. And from that cup of coffee, he imagined, on a Tuesday morning not like any other, the atom is swallowed into the body of a database administrator on the 103rd floor of One World Trade Center. Then the carbon atom takes a coffee break. It waits inside the woman's body. But not for long. Sometime on the morning of September 11, 2001, struck loose from the database administrator's piteous and beloved body (recently held and kissed beneath dark sheets of a rainy summer night), through its terrible combustion at 2,000 degrees, the carbon atom bursts into carbon dioxide and, with its billions of compatriots, drifts on the winds from Bayonne, across Tribeca, Little Italy, the Lower East Side. Some of the atoms are soaked up by the gingko trees lining the streets. By the geraniums on the pre-war windowsills of old Sicilian ladies. Others pepper the non-fat, sugar-free frozen treats of couples walking hand in hand out of Tasti-D-Lite on Second Avenue, to be lapped up like candy sprinkles. And some of the atoms are breathed in by Jonah Soloway as he sleeps fitfully through September's nightmares, in his bed with the window open just enough to allow an entire galaxy of invisible particles, dust from the thousands lost, to flow discreetly into him.

The train arrived in a rumble of noise and Jonah stepped aboard automatically. Somewhere in his body, even now, building the stuff of his bones or stitching together a new brain cell, he was certain, there lived an assortment of carbon atoms from the estimated 2,801 lost receptionists, executive assistants, mailroom workers, ladies' room attendants, bond brokers, accountants, computer programmers, vice presidents, security guards, elevator operators, grill cooks, sommeliers, brass polishers, hoarders of Post-It notes, collectors of giant rubber-band balls, closeted artistes, saviors of stray cats, Elvis Presley fans, former debutantes, snowboarders, mothers, fathers, lovers. Maybe even Rose Oliveri. She was a part of him. He knew this now as a deep and unassailable truth.

2

"What's *your* excuse?"

Keith Starling, Jonah's pod-mate, slapped him on the back as he was waiting in line for coffee at Mediacom's Outpost Café.

"You know mine," Keith continued, not waiting for Jonah's answer. "Same as every other day."

Without apparent repercussion, Keith was often late for work. He got away with it, Jonah understood, because of his good looks and boyish charms. And because his name was Keith Starling, which mnemonically (and ornithologically) brought to the minds of their thirty-something female bosses the honeyed memory of Keith Partridge, played by David Cassidy in the long, hot *Partridge Family* summers of their girlhoods. A freelance copy editor, Keith was partial to t-shirts printed with retro brand insignias for all-American products like Mr. Bubble, Wonder Bread, and Nestlé Quik. Today Bob's Big Boy emblazoned his chest, forelock glistening, cheeseburger held aloft like an icon. The Big Boy somewhat resembled Keith, whose everyday expression was that of a young man to whom nothing bad had ever happened, who truly believed that, no matter what, everything was going to be "just great." His hair was shiny and thick, shampoo-commercial robust. His long torso was genetically programmed, without the assistance of protein shakes or weightlifting, to adhere unerringly to the coveted V-shape that *Men's Health* magazine said was the male physique found most desirable by women—pear-shaped being the least. (Jonah learned this important fact from thumbing through the magazines he found in the bathroom stalls of the office men's room.) Jonah felt a vague sense of embarrassment for himself whenever in Keith's presence. He wondered if other men felt this way when faced with Keith Starling, and if, in that situation, they too felt their own physical flaws more painfully than usual.

When Keith turned to flirt with the woman standing behind him, Jonah, feeling at once relieved and abandoned, pretended to be deeply interested in the decorative objects displayed on the shelves of the Outpost Café, a collection of Wild West wagon wheels, cacti in terracotta pots, and taxidermied desert rodents perched among the wares. Though the Outpost harkened back to the past in its décor, it was definitely a product of the present, having dubbed its coffee sizes with vaguely European, Starbucksian titles. As he did every morning, when his turn came, Jonah rebelled by pointedly ordering a "*Large* Sumatra Mandheling." And, just as she did every morning, the cashier responded by shouting into her walkie-talkie headset, "Molto Sumatra!" correcting his order for the barista who poured the coffee not ten feet away.

"They call it Molto here," Keith said.

"I'm aware of that."

"It's confusing, right? Because usually a large is called Venti."

"I can't utter that word," Jonah said. "I hate Starbucks."

"How can you hate Starbucks? It's so good. I wish they'd put one in here."

"Hating Starbucks," the woman behind Keith interrupted, "is so unoriginal. And misguided. They're a totally ethical company and, like, really good to their employees. You should try hating something else."

Jonah just blinked at her. He didn't know her, but he knew her type. She had the sort of vacant, equestrian bearing of a Marketing Girl, flinty and mean, pawing the floor with the chocolate-brown toe of her knee-high leather boot. She dismissed him with a derisive lift of her upper lip's leftmost corner and a gust of air from her throat, a sound that was somewhere between a laugh and a scoff. A *loff*, Jonah thought as he grabbed his coffee and hurried out, telling Keith he'd see him upstairs.

The cup, he soon realized, was burning hot. To punish him for his rebellion against Molto, the cashier always "forgot" to give him a textured cardboard sleeve to protect his hand from the steaming paper cup, and Jonah, running late and shoved along by the crowd of caffeine-thirsty Mediacom Networks employees, always forgot to ask for one. It was usually not until he was through the security checkpoint and into elevator bank G that the coffee's heat seeped through the paper cup and began to sting the palm of his hand.

He had rushed out of the Outpost hoping Keith would be left behind. For reasons Jonah could never fathom, Keith considered him a friend, or a potential friend, and was forever trying to rope him into some social event, a party or a show that Jonah could not have cared less about. Furthermore, he didn't want to hear the inevitable story "about last night," which always involved the sort of woman and the sort of activities that Jonah could never hope to enjoy—nor, he told himself, did he want to. As he stepped onto the elevator, he cursed the cashier under his breath, gently passing the coffee cup back and forth between his heat-reddened hands. Keith appeared just as the doors were closing. Two of the women in the crowded elevator raced each other to press the OPEN DOOR button. Nobody ever raced to hold the doors for Jonah. How many times had he watched his fellow elevator riders look down at their watches and magazines as he hollered at them to hold the door?

As Keith squeezed into the space made for him, Jonah noticed that his coffee cup had been lovingly snuggled into a protective cardboard sleeve. Through Keith's fingers, he could just read the car advertisement printed on the sleeve with the slogan: "DO UNTO YOU AS YOU WOULD HAVE OTHERS DO UNTO YOU."

"Wait'll I tell you about last night," Keith whispered seductively in Jonah's ear.

Jonah flinched. After working there for nearly a year, he still got the jitters every time he rode the elevator up to the forty-second floor of the Mediacom Building. As they zoomed skywards (the digital panel above the buttons reading "EX" for express), Jonah noticed Keith's ease—even pleasure—with the ride. Jonah could tell he was the sort to enjoy rollercoasters and snowboarding, the sort who had always believed that his body was an efficient, capable machine on which he could rely. Jonah, on the other hand, felt his body cringe. He was acutely aware of the floor pressing against his heels, the solid earth receding far beneath him. He listened to every sound as the hurtling metal box moaned and roared, rocking from side to side. The cables slapped against the outside of the car, snapping like rubber bands. Now and again, a lone chirp sounded from inside the walls, as though a bird were trapped in the mechanism. Jonah's ears popped and he yawned to clear them, braving the heat of the coffee cup with one hand

and gripping the handrail with the other, as the car shook and shimmied, threatening, it seemed, to break loose from its track, to sink like a plumb line toward Earth's center of gravity. He hoped Keith could not see his sweat.

At the forty-second floor, he let go of the rail, leaving behind a faint sheen of perspiration in the shape of his palm, and stepped swiftly across the gleaming metal threshold, the dark gap where the elevator, bobbing slightly in a way that Jonah found particularly anxiety-provoking, lined up with solid floor. As he leapt across this dividing line, a whoosh of wind from below riffled his pant legs, reminding him that he was held dangling over the gaping blackness of empty space. He slipped his ID card into the security scanner and opened the door. Somewhere in the building, a computer kept track of his time.

"Maybe they'll finally fire us," Keith said, right at his heels. "And then we'll be free."

At his desk in the office of one of Mediacom's less-visited web sites—www.PinwheelKids.com, an online magazine for parents of preschool-age children—Jonah settled into his $700 ergonomic Herman Miller Aeron chair, one of the last leftover perks from the ebullient E-conomy. Slow to warm to new technologies and lacking the confidence to get into illustration, he had toiled in print for years as an assistant editor for a small-circulation trade magazine called *Boxboard Today*, providing the global cardboard box industry with crucial information about the latest in flexo-folder gluers, flexographic die cutters, and barcode printing. When he realized that *Boxboard Today* would not enable him to retire at forty and dedicate himself full time to his comic-book art, he knocked on the door of the Internet boom, lying his way ("Yes, I know HTML") into what he imagined would be days filled with free bagels and many flavors of cream cheese. He was too late. Within a few months of working at Mediacom, the economy faltered. The free bagels were discontinued and he was forced to take a 25% pay cut. While he watched his laid-off coworkers fly away to Hawaii or graduate-school writing programs, generous severance packages footing the bills, Jonah sat in his Aeron chair, reading and revising articles that gave helpful tips to young mothers on how to decorate Easter eggs like syndicated cartoon characters, how to make a papier-mâché piñata in the shape of an octopus, and how to be a better parent through the use of interactive puppetry. "When you've got something difficult to say, let puppets do the talking! A bird and a bee puppet, for instance, can educate your kids about the facts of life!"

Jonah had trouble taking his job seriously. This might have been why he was so often late. The office had been designed to be "fun" to appeal to the stunted inner children of the Generation X-ers who filled the warren of its many workpods. The decorators had intended to give employees the impression of working in a high-tech tree house, carving green sheets of Plexiglas into the leafy shapes of treetops and drilling them to the cubicle walls. Along the painted-on "trunks," synthetic woodpeckers pecked and lifelike robins laid their plastic eggs in steel-wool nests. Instead of a conference room, the staff held their meetings in the Pool Area, a kidney-shaped section of blue carpeting surrounded by Adirondack lawn chairs and porch swings swinging from the ceiling on lengths of chain. For poolside tables, they had giant toadstools and fake tree stumps, underneath which Philippe Starckian garden gnomes grinned with blushing cheeks.

Easily distracted by intrusions, Jonah kept his desk neat and spare, avoiding the practice, popular among his coworkers, of covering every available inch of space with toys. Keith's desk, a quarter inch of plywood and Plexiglas away, was decorated with *Star Wars* action figures, a lava lamp, Pez dispensers, plastic chattering teeth, Chia pets, canisters of Play-Doh, a *Welcome Back Kotter* lunchbox, and a Nerf basketball hoop—the clutter of a generation still clinging with desperation to the popular culture of its past. Jonah wasn't interested in memorializing his own past. He preferred the pasts of previous generations, the imagined pasts he never knew.

"I've got to tell you about last night," Keith said, booting up his computer and checking his AOL Instant Messenger. Keith loved to IM. If only the minds at Apple would invent a miniature, handheld computer that could enable him to carry his AOL Instant Messages everywhere he went, Jonah thought, Keith would be a happy man. Not that he wasn't already happy, grinning into the screen's soft glow. Jonah knew his cubemate would be distracted for the next several minutes and he could take the time to indulge in his own morning ritual.

Though he avoided the clutter, Jonah did keep two personal items in his cube: an "expanding universe" Hoberman sphere and a telescope—the same one his father had promised him years ago when Jonah won first prize in the fifth-grade science fair for his project, "Is It Possible for Planet Earth to be Engulfed by a Black Hole?" An astrophysicist, Daniel Soloway only bonded with Jonah through this narrow lens. He had helped him build the classic Newtonian reflector from a length of PVC pipe, a couple of mirrors, and a few bolts and wingnuts. Actually, "helped" was not the right word. Jonah's father, after quickly getting frustrated with his son's wandering attention and lack of dexterity, took over the construction of the telescope himself. Jonah, relieved he would no longer be yelled at for failing to hold the terrifying electric drill straight, withdrew into a Twinkie-sticky issue of *House of Secrets*, where ghosts and ghouls prowled the pages. Once the telescope was done, father and son found their way back together, if only for a few clear nights, standing together in the velvet-dark backyard, gazing at Jupiter's stormy eye, the golden rings of Saturn, the Moon's unchanging mountains and dusty seas. When his father's work took him away— traveling to laboratories in California, Australia, and South America, squinting at computer screens and through the long cylinders of giant telescopes, hunting for the universe's missing mass, waiting for the darkness to divulge its ancient secrets—Jonah would stand outside and gaze at the heavens alone, sketching in his notebook the lights and shadows of those faraway bodies, until one night when he turned his telescope Earthward, toward the window of a neighborhood girl whose unsuspecting body made for a far more interesting artist's model. From then on, the stars lost their hold over him.

Just six months after the accident that killed his mother, Jonah's father now lived full time in South America, someplace in the Chilean desert where he recovered from his injuries and grief by taking up with the maid who cleaned his house while he continued to search the skies for dark matter. Jonah still used the telescope, but not to look into outer space. Instead, he aimed it at the windows of the office buildings surrounding Times Square. Behind the many panes of glass, he saw neither moons nor the girl of his dreams, only an unknowable collection of strangers: sitting at desks, drinking cups of coffee, yawning in their chairs. Now he tilted the telescope to the plate-glass window next to his desk and trained it on the sleek new Condé-Nast Building across the way. He found a woman standing by her desk. She bent forward, her long hair falling in a dark cascade to her knees, and ran a hairbrush briskly through it, down and down again, sending out tiny sparks of human electricity that Jonah did not see but could imagine. He took great pleasure in watching his anonymous neighbors. In this way, he could pull them in close, press himself against the rippling white-cotton folds of their shirts, the pink whorls of their ears, the whey-like lights in the soft hairs that downed their limbs. From the distance of his cube, he felt an ineffable, warm flow of love for every one of them. He could sense the connective fibers humming and shining like strings of light between his own human body and that of every office worker who passed through his lens. High above it all, he felt magnanimous and Whitmanesque. How easy it was to love his fellow human beings when they stayed behind panes of glass. Up close, it was different.

He lowered the telescope and looked out across the immediate skyline, beginning just below, where the old Paramount Building stood like a mountain, its elegant setbacks rising to a star-encircled clock and illuminated glass globe. There, where Frank Sinatra once crooned to a theater full of screaming bobby-soxers, and Elvis Presley's first movie, *Love Me Tender*, premiered, the snarling superstars of World Wrestling Entertainment now performed their many suplexes, moonsaults, and piledrivers, strutting around the ring in their very own "twenty-first century retail-tainment complex."

"Not thinking of jumping, are you, Soloway?"

"Just looking," Jonah replied, picking up his coffee, now cool enough to drink.

"Man, have I got a story for you," Keith said as he alighted on Jonah's side of the partition. In one quick motion, he picked up the Hoberman sphere and sat on the desk, propping a sneakered foot on the corner of Jonah's chair, rocking him in the Aeron's cradle and causing Sumatra Mandheling to dribble from the sippy hole in his coffee cup. Jonah wiped his wet thumb on his pants. Keith opened and closed the Hoberman sphere, the toy universe expanding and contracting with each motion, and stage-whispered, "I met this girl, right? She's a performance studies major at NYU. Fantastic looking. Great ass. So I ask, you know, what kind of performance do you study? And she says, get a load of this, sadomasochism. Sado-fucking-masochism! She, like, works as a dominatrix, beating guys up and shit. She has her own private dungeon. This is one scary chick, right? But I'm interested, you know, so I say, show me one of your moves. She grabs me by the wrist, spins me around, and the next thing I know, she's got me cuffed, hands behind my back. It was like a total *Cops* move, like, I don't know, like something from *Charlie's Angels*, only I don't think they used handcuffs in *Charlie's Angels*. But if they did, it would be just like that."

"I'm sure it would."

"So what could I do, right?"

Keith leaned in, close enough so Jonah could see the dark flaw on the rim of his left iris (Keith's eyes were nothing special, brown and utterly common, Jonah noted with more than a hint of *schadenfreude*). "I went home with her. I mean, I had to see this dungeon, right? Some amazing-looking chick tells you she's got her own private dungeon, puts you in handcuffs, you can't say no, right?"

"Well, you can actually."

"Come on, Soloway," Keith said. "Where's your sense of adventure?"

"All right," Jonah said, "I'll bite. What happened? No, let me guess. She tied you up with silk scarves, made you call her Mommy, then chopped you into pieces. She ate most of you as a main course, then stuck the leftovers in her refrigerator."

"Come on. Don't you want to know what really happened?" Jonah waved him on, unable now to conceal his interest. He did want to know. He fought it, but he always wanted to know.

"Okay, but," Keith said, looking over the cubicle walls and scanning the aisle, "I can't really go into those details here."

Keith never went into details. He was a cliffhanger kind of guy, seducing you then leaving you hanging. Jonah fell for it every time. He figured either Keith led a truly incredible life, filled with wild sex and amazing adventures, or he lived one just as dull as his own. Jonah preferred to believe the former. It was more interesting that way.

"But let me tell you," Keith continued, leaning forward again, "it was some fucking crazy shit. Crazy shit."

"Yeah," Jonah said, "I bet. Must have been pretty crazy."

"Come on out tonight, I'll tell you all about it."

Jonah considered it for a moment, rolling his eyes toward the ceiling. "I don't know..."

"Jesus, Soloway, don't say yes. I could die from the shock."

"Where are you going? To that dive bar, the Waikiki Lounge? People get killed there."

"It's the Wakamba Lounge, and *one* guy got killed there, and that was months ago. We can go someplace else. Come on. What, have you got big Monday-night plans?"

"I like to go home after work. I like to relax."

"You say that every time. Relax? What are you, fifty? Come on," Keith pressed. "What are you going to do at home?"

Before Jonah could answer, Keith's Instant Messenger sounded its alert from the computer. He hopped back into his chair to check it. While Keith typed and chuckled to whatever girl was presumably on the other end of his IM—likely one of the high-booted Marketing Girls down the hall—Jonah turned back to his window. He sipped his coffee and looked up from the Paramount to 42nd Street where the new buildings jumped and flashed like video games. The giant, golden hand of Madame Tussaud hovered over her wax museum like a puppeteer's, pulling strings. The under-construction Westin Hotel swelled and climbed above the old Hotel Carter, whose quaint brick and chrome-embraced neon seemed to shrink beneath the multicolored checkerboard pattern of the Westin's overshadowing walls. This town, Jonah feared, was quickly turning into a city of glass. But there, still, stood the Empire State Building, broad-shouldered and solid—maybe, Jonah thought, a little proud to be, once again, the tallest building in town.

Keith chuckled again at the messages burbling on his screen. He did it, Jonah figured, to let people within earshot (Jonah) know: 1) He was a happy, upbeat guy; 2) he was a desirable guy with plenty of women beating down his electronic door; and 3) he was the kind of guy who could afford to not pay attention to his work because a job was exactly the sort of thing he could take or leave. This chafed at Jonah because it reminded him of his own inadequacies, his own longings for what Keith had—dumb, Golden Retriever-ish Keith who wanted, for reasons only he could know, to be friends with Jonah. Maybe he should go out with Keith sometime. Maybe it would lead to something, some connection with a woman. A "real, live girl," as the signs proclaimed over on Eighth Avenue. Not a ghost. But a ghost was what he had. The ghost of Rose, the girl on the sidewalk, the neighbor who never said hello. Rose of the unknown. Rose of the infinitely fillable fantasy. It seemed he had made her up in his mind. For six months he'd been holding her, giving her shape inside of him. How was that not real?

"So what do you say," Keith pressed, back again, ever energetic, sprung from one spot to another. "Wakamba Lounge. You and me. Two loose cannons out on the town. Anything could happen." He sat on Jonah's desk, picked up the Hoberman sphere again, and pulled it open, closed, open. "Come on. You've got something better to do tonight?"

Jonah thought about the work that waited for him at home, the graphic novel he called *Ephemera Automat*, a story of two friends, a retired burlesque manager and a novelties salesman. They were old men now, and didn't do much except sit by the sea at Brighton Beach and talk about the past, a world filled with voluptuous fan-dancers, comedic magicians, rubber chickens, whoopee cushions. He didn't tell anyone about *Ephemera Automat*, afraid it might disappear if he said it out loud.

"Nothing really. Same old thing," he told Keith. "You know, the usual."

"Yeah, I know. Man of mystery." Keith lazily pumped his fist, the universal symbol for masturbation.

"I have to feed my clocks and wind my cat," Jonah joked, embarrassing himself. "I have to rotate my tires. No, really, I've got my landlord coming over to fix the bathroom sink and I need to be there to let him in. The sink's been dripping for months."

It was a small lie and an acceptable one, the kind that protected him and did not hurt anyone in the process.

He added, "Do you know how many gallons a day are wasted by a slow drip? Twenty gallons. That's a lot. So I really have to be home tonight."

"You are so lying."

"I am not."

"That is totally a bullshit story. A slow drip? What are you doing tonight that's such a big secret?"

It didn't take much thought when he said it. She was already real to him. And it was, in a way, true.

"I'm going to see a girl."

"Fuck you," Keith said, punching him in the arm. "All right. That's an acceptable excuse. Is this, like, a girlfriend girl or just a thing girl?"

"I'm not sure."

"Good. You're still browsing. Next week, I'm going to a party and you're coming with me. There'll be lots of girls. And I won't take no for an answer."

Keith hopped off the desk and tossed the expanded Hoberman sphere back to Jonah. It shrank in his hands.

3

At the end of the workday, Jonah stepped out of the Mediacom Building into the neon-juiced, stutter-jumping infusion of overstimulation that was Broadway. It didn't matter that he looked at it every day, that he'd lived in New York City for several years; when he walked through Times Square, he could not help but gaze up and up, his mouth hanging open, like a tourist just arrived from the Great Plains. He buttoned his coat as he paused to read the headlines scrolling across the ABC Studios marquee. The undulating news zipper announced, "Clear skies and colder...6-month 9/11 anniversary was marked by the unveiling of a sculpture recovered from the disaster site, Mayor Bloomberg called it a tribute to 'the resiliency of the American spirit'...Doctors in Saudi Arabia performed the first human uterus transplant which produced two menstrual periods before it failed and had to be removed...Israel raided two West Bank refugee camps and fired missiles at Yasser Arafat's headquarters...Texas woman who hit a homeless man, drove home with him stuck in her windshield, and ignored his pleas as he bled to death in her garage over couple of days is not a monster, her attorney says...Clear skies and colder..."

He turned uptown, toward the 49th Street station, to avoid the rush-hour crowd at 42nd. Above, in the chaos of billboards, one piled on top of another, Revlon had arranged red, white, and blue bottles of nail polish into the shape of an American flag, telling its customers to "Be Unforgettable." Next to that, a former *Playboy* playmate and star of the most-watched TV show in world history lay naked on the toe of a giant sneaker, clutching her breasts and breathlessly declaring, "It Just Feels Bigger." A teen-pop princess, bare-bellied and blonde, reveled in the joy of Pepsi-Cola, while the Virgin Megastore announced, "United We Stand." And suspended from the lampposts above, bright banners ordered Jonah to "Do your part. Fight back NY! Go shopping!"

In the window of a jewelry store, wristwatches and necklaces glittered alongside miniature Twin Towers and crystal teddy bears with American flags hastily glued to their tiny paws. The Swarovski 9/11 tribute Brave Heart Pin was on sale for $69.95. In a souvenir shop, rolls of novelty toilet paper stacked in pyramids told tourists to "Wipe Out Terrorism" with an image of Osama Bin Laden's face printed on each single-ply sheet in non-toxic ink. The good men and women of the Midwest gathered the rolls under their arms to take back to their suburban homes, where they would dutifully facilitate the grim business of wiping out terrorism one fistful at a time. Jonah saluted them in their delirious huddle as he walked, nearly bumping into a ragged man shuffling through traffic, bent painfully under the weight of a wooden crucifix balanced on his shoulders.

At the Howard Johnson's, Jonah stopped. One of the last artifacts of old Times Square, it had endured untouched for decades while all around it buildings fell and rose anew. Like a foreign city leveled by the bombs of war, severed from its own history, Times Square was not itself anymore. So little remained of the old town. Yet, somehow, the billionaire builders had overlooked the sleepy, retrograde HoJo's,

allowing it to persevere on its square of prime real estate
with its vintage orange-and-turquoise sign that read: "It's
cocktail time at Howard Johnson's. May we suggest a decanter
of…Manhattan, Martini, or Daiquiri." In the big plate-glass
window of the restaurant, an older couple sat eating, not
talking, lifting fried clams and cheeseburgers again and again
to their silent mouths. Jonah pulled out his sketchbook and
leaned against a green newsstand to pencil the listless, sagging
faces of the man and woman. He sketched their slack mouths
opening and closing. He captured the woman's faraway look
and touched the lines that softened her face. He held the
man's shaking hands and gently traced the tired contour of his
shoulders. Finally, he enclosed the scene within a bold-faced
rectangle, the sheet of glass that stood between them.

Downtown, Jonah emerged from the subway station into
an uncluttered landscape, where the low pre-war buildings
didn't shrink him and didn't block his view of the still-blue sky.
He passed through the spawn of Starbucks that infested Astor
Place—three cafés within a block and a half of each other—
and ignored the smiling siren that called from the global
chain's logo, a fish-tailed girl in a green circle shining above
the sidewalk. Jonah was proud of his enduring resistance. He
had never once set foot inside a Starbucks, a fact that made
him feel virtuous and a little bit smug. He didn't care if his
obsessive hatred was unoriginal. From its cozy side, he would
never budge.

Sixth Street, as always, had transformed itself in Jonah's
absence. Now the metal shutters of the Indian restaurants
were flung wide open. From the windows and open doors of
Rose of India, Rose of Bombay, Bombay Dining, Raj Mahal,
Taj Mahal, and the Taj Restaurant, a billion tiny holiday lights
gleamed on tangled strings, garlands of silk flowers cascaded

from ceilings. Music flowed from turbaned musicians playing drums and stringed instruments made from animal skins and giant gourds. Jonah inhaled the smells of cooking and curry that wafted from the restaurants. He watched the golden fish swimming in the murky tanks behind the windows. Dark-skinned men in white shirts and black pants stood on the sidewalk, hawking the $6.95 early-bird specials, calling to him as he passed, "Special dinner, sir—very, very good, sir."

A few steps away, not yet in sight, Rose's face awaited him. Each day she greeted him, welcoming him home with her toothy smile, one crooked bicuspid turned shyly away. Jonah's heart lifted to think of her. He had walked this block countless times with Rose—"with" being used broadly; "alongside" might be more accurate, if not "simultaneously"—so close he could have slipped his arm in hers. Anyone looking at them, walking in step, would have assumed they were a couple. It wasn't so farfetched, was it? Now, at the thought, the unborn lie kicked inside of him, like an embryo gathering fresh cells to sprout a grabby new appendage. The possibility of what could have been buoyed Jonah and he looked up into the sky where a plane flew overhead, innocent, glinting in the sun as it gently descended into Queens. "Just a plane," he whispered, marveling at the everydayness of this event. A jet doing what jets were supposed to do. He felt good, glad to have made it this far. Six months ago, he wasn't sure that spring would come or that he'd be alive to see it. The flower stands and Indian spice shops perfumed the air with hyacinth and fennel, and Jonah breathed deep. The burning odor from that morning had completely disappeared.

At Rose Oliveri's door, he stopped short. The MISSING poster was gone. This was the right door. He checked: the empty pane of glass, the grid of chicken wire threading through it. A sliver of Scotch tape still held fast to a torn, white corner of paper. The super must have taken it down. Jonah imagined a meat-fisted man crumpling Rose's face and tossing her into the trash, saying, "That's that." Six months to the day and people were already tired of remembering. Few missing posters were left across the city. The lightposts, mailboxes, and brick walls once wallpapered with faces of lost men and women now carried flyers for "Moving Sale" and its companion, "Room for Rent," evidence of exodus from New York's less hardy residents. All that remained of Rose's doorstep memorial were a few polluted rivers of wax spilled on the sidewalk from candles that had once burned next to the anonymous bouquets of white roses that had shown up like clockwork once a week. The roses had troubled Jonah. If there were a man in Rose's life, he'd never shown his face, never stepped out the door in the morning reeking of aftershave, never walked the dog, never appeared in the evenings (as far as Jonah knew) to take Rose out to dinner or a movie or anything of the sort. Jonah had decided that another woman had left the roses, a best friend from way back, laden with memories of slumber parties and summer camp. When the roses stopped coming just after the New Year Jonah felt a guilty relief in having Rose all to himself again. He had known that the missing poster would eventually vanish, too, but still he felt the tight grip of loss, a kind of panic as he hurried into his building, rushing to get upstairs.

He checked his mail, unlocking the battered brass door marked "Soloway" with a tiny key. Two credit card offers, a request for money to help save the children, three glossy catalogs, and a past-due notice from Consolidated Edison. He slammed the mailbox shut and pushed in the second door.

"Hello there, sir!"

Zipnick, his downstairs neighbor, blocked the way. Jonah knew his neighbors only by the names printed on their mailbox doors. There was Zipnick below him and Crosby above. Next door there was ninety-year-old Podolsky, who was mostly deaf and watched television with the volume turned all the way up. There were other names, belonging to neighbors he rarely saw. Parisi and Strauss, Hotchkiss and Krakowski. One of them, he knew, played the piano on Sunday afternoons. One kept a three-speed bicycle in the downstairs hall. And all of them were men, bachelors who lived uncoupled, mostly alone. The only trace of a woman in the building consisted of the tenement smells and sounds of Zipnick's shut-in mother. Jonah had never seen old Mrs. Zipnick, but the hallway was often heavy with the cabbage-stink of her cooking and her rough-edged voice, shouting in Eastern European.

"Getting chilly out there," said Zipnick, stopping on his way out the door, the flimsy white hairs on his head standing up in the wind.

"Sure is," Jonah said, not stopping. If he stopped he would never get moving again. Zipnick would keep him here forever, trapped in an endless cycle of weather talk.

"Getting chilly, chilly, chilly. It's supposed to warm up tomorrow, they said."

"That'll be nice." Jonah began his way up the stairs. He wanted to get inside his apartment, to lock the door, to be with Rose.

"Yes sir, it's going to warm up. That's what they said on the radio. It's chilly now, though. Chilly, chilly, chilly."

In his small, dark apartment, Jonah dropped his backpack on the chrome and Formica kitchenette table. Like his workspace, the two-bedroom was orderly and uncluttered. He slept in one room and used the other as an art studio. For too long, he'd suffered through multiple roommates—

crumb-dropping, pot-smoking, NASCAR-watching, loud-talking post-adolescents who left fecal stains in the toilet bowl and smeared the bathroom sink with mint-green loops of toothpaste spit—but now he was alone. He could barely afford it, even with rent stabilization, but he needed it. Alone, everything stayed in its place. On the shelf behind the stove, the vintage John F. Kennedy saltshaker stood (deliberately askew) to the left of Jackie's pepper. A flock of ukuleles (both wooden and plastic) hung from one wall like birds in tidy formation. Framed pencil drawings from comic books covered another wall and flowed into the studio where a collection of vintage Bakelite radios (Silvertone, Transitone, Truetone Boomerang) commanded their own set of shelves over a desk piled with Jonah's painstaking sketches for *Ephemera Automat*. And over the kitchen table stood an authentic Horn & Hardart Automat, featuring five windows that once dispensed delicious dishes of cheesecake, cream cheese sandwiches, macaroni and cheese, codfish cakes, and apple pie. The prices were still readable—1 quarter and 2 nickels, 3 quarters, 2 quarters—and the knobs urged him to Turn, Turn, Turn, Turn, Turn.

He dropped the mail into a red metal bucket marked FIRE where his unpaid bills festered, unopened. He hung his jacket on the jacket peg and his hat on the hat peg behind the door and ran his hand over his skull, moist from the leather hatband, rubbing the patch of rough bristles that was once a forelock. He cracked the window to cool the steam-heated apartment. The motor of the rickety old Kelvinator clicked on and began to hum. He opened the refrigerator door and took out a bottle of beer, poured it into a glass, and sat down at the table. The light outside was growing soft, turning the color of lilacs. In his bedroom, Rose waited. He'd been in such a hurry to get upstairs, but now he took his time. It struck him, for a moment, that what he was about to do, what he'd been doing for the past six months, was all wrong. Surely it was a perversion, some as-yet-unnamed fetish practiced by isolated men across the country, in numbers too small to warrant the creation of a specialized Yahoo group. *That's what I am*, Jonah thought, *a pervert without a Yahoo group*.

He finished his beer and entered the bedroom, cleaning his glasses with a shirttail as he went. In the bottom drawer of the bureau, beneath a pile of t-shirts, lay the object of his affection. It was pathetic, really, and he knew it. Still he reached in and pulled it out. He sat on the bed and laid it across his lap, pushing away a hot ball of shame so he could open the stupid thing and just be with her again. It looked like nothing, really, just a manila file folder he'd swiped from work, the name *Rose* written in red Magic Marker on its tab. But its contents represented weeks of ardent Googling.

Rose's name had produced a sheaf of papers printed from several missing persons lists and homemade online memorials, including the WTC United Family Group's ezboard, september11victims.com, september11thmemorial. com, and 911-remember.com. She appeared on the web sites for the *New York Times*, MSNBC, and *Newsday*. She was briefly mentioned in an Associated Press article that ran on several small online news sites, including ones from Hong Kong, Namibia, Boston, Sacramento, and Athens, Georgia. The story of her life came together in bits and pieces. Born and raised in Brooklyn. A painter who enjoyed jazz and lived alone. Toiled for years in the art department of a small book publisher. Took a job in the Trade Center in 2000, hoping for something more. An only child. Survived by parents Frank and Vivian Oliveri. Not so much as a single strand of her DNA recovered from the site.

Jonah pulled out the true treasure of the collection and held it up in the light. Ripped, under cover of darkness, from a mailbox near the memorial wall at St. Vincent's Hospital, and secured in an archive-safe, clear plastic sleeve, Rose's missing poster, slightly wrinkled, crackled in his hands. She looked out at him from behind the protective polypropylene and he felt his nerves settle. He took her to the kitchen and propped her up on the table, between a pile of books and his Jackie Kennedy pepper shaker. He poured himself another glass of beer.

"You probably think I'm an idiot," he said.

She gave him her usual look.

"Remember the time you dropped your glove?"

She wasn't sure. What glove?

"The red glove. You dropped it and I—I do feel like an idiot. Talking to you. But that's what people do, right? They talk to the dead. Makes them feel better. Makes them feel— something."

A gust came in the window and she seemed to shrug, her shoulders going up and then down. What did she know about talking to dead people? What did she care? She could be difficult sometimes. Not the most chatty person.

"Walking to work together," he said, "that was my favorite time of day. Just strolling up the block with you before we went our separate ways."

He'd seen other couples do this, parting at Second Avenue with a kiss before one went north and the other went south to different subways. That's how it would have been. She'd have taken the downtown train and he'd have taken the up. He imagined a kiss at Broadway and Eighth. Rose in a Persian lamb coat. Himself in something tweed. Eternal autumn and all the trees gone gold. Memory sluiced through him, stirring the lie, making it kick, making it twirl and gather more steam.

In his tweed coat he bends to pick up her red glove, hands it to her through the bars of the subway railing as she's dashing down the stairs, one-gloved, and she cries, "Oh!" She reaches up from the steps, takes the glove through the bars, letting their fingers touch, their hands clasp until the roar of an approaching train takes her away.

"It could have happened," he told her, sipping his beer. "It could have been real."

He was a sometimes believer in alternate realities, branching roads not taken that magically continued on planes of truth he could not see, but sometimes felt. These distantly reaching decision trees, built by other choices, blossomed in one of the less accessed neuronal cul-de-sacs of his mind, feeding the lie with its lovely fruit.

"How about some music?"

He turned on the kitchen radio, a pearlized, creamsicle-colored FADA Bullet 1000 ("The radio of to-morrow to-day!"). As the tubes warmed up, the dial softly glowed and the speaker began spitting out the noise of electronic instruments, inappropriate for this radio from yesterday's tomorrow. Every time he turned on the Bullet, Jonah half-expected it to play an ancient broadcast of crooners and torch singers, but those sounds were lost, their electromagnetic waves drifting in faraway space, dead voices sent streaming into the dark. There used to be an AM station that played nothing but standards, Frank and Bing and Ella, but the Walt Disney Company had bought it out a few years before for their children's programming, and now Jonah didn't have that either. He tuned in to the news. 1010 WINS announced that the weather was cold and windy, that traffic was backed up along the Hudson River crossings, and that the Tribute in Light was about to begin.

He tugged on his coat and hat, grabbed his keys, and checked the stove. He pointed at each grease-stained knob and said the word "off" five times, rhythmically jabbing his finger at the knob with each utterance for emphasis. He felt Rose looking at him from the kitchen table.

"I have to do this," he explained. "It only takes a second or two. Off, off, off, off, off. It used to be worse. I'd leave the apartment, get two blocks away, and have to come back to do it all over again. Off, off, off, off, off. Some days, when it was really bad, I'd never get to work. But it's better now. I just have to do it once. Usually. Off, off, off, off, off."

Rose stared at him with what felt to Jonah like a look of quiet judgment.

"You're distracting me," he told her. "Did I do them all?"

He started again, pointing and repeating, five times five, until he was absolutely certain that all the knobs had been secured in their off positions and that none of the gas burners would spontaneously alight, catching the fringe of the terrycloth dishtowel that hung two feet away on an adhesive-backed plastic hook, a towel which might, by some freak combination of air movement and gradual adhesive weakness, fly from its hook and land on the flaming surface of the stovetop where it would ignite, thus causing the entire building to explode. Or something along those lines. Jonah wasn't exactly sure what could happen if the burners were left on; he only knew he had to check them thoroughly before going out the door.

It was a blustery night on the roof. Jonah buttoned his gray coat and held onto his hat. The cold wind whipped against him and spun the turbine vents into a frenzied racket. The vents reminded him of the tin-foil turbans of Jiffy Pop popcorn, and he noted the similarity between the words "turban" and "turbine," squinting at the spot where he'd last seen the towers, just to the right of the green-topped Woolworth's Building. That was where the Tribute in Light was scheduled to appear. Any minute now. He had no idea what the columns of light would look like and thought maybe they were already there, too faint to see clearly. He thought he saw a ghostly ribbon shimmering before his eyes. But that couldn't be it. Behind him the great lamp of the Empire State Building glowed in the same rocket-pop style of red, white, and blue it had worn every night for the past six months. The Con-Ed and New York Life towers mimicked in miniature with their own patriotic displays. As usual, the cool Chrysler shined silver, indifferent to holidays and memorials. Jonah shivered and looked at his watch. It was 6:45. The hole in the southern sky stayed empty.

He surveyed the nearby rooftops, expecting to see his neighbors gathered for the spectacle, but the other roofs were vacant. On 9/11, they all were here, shading their eyes and staring at the smoke. Where were they now? Life went on for them as it always had. Six months ago, people thought that 9/11 would change them in profound ways, but they were wrong. They didn't leave mediocre marriages or quit mind-numbing jobs to write the great American novel. They didn't take up skydiving or learn the piano, didn't pack up and move to Bora Bora, didn't commit to walking El Camino de Santiago on a pilgrimage for enlightenment. Most of them were still sitting in front of televisions, eating takeout Thai food and working through bottles of wine, if not scattered in various offices, enduring a long day of staring into computer screens, thinking of other places and better things. He did not know a single one of their names, yet he had the feeling of missing them. Although he loved his solitude, he was sometimes struck by an urge to be one-among-them, a desire to join in on something communal. Like baseball games, for instance. On late fall nights, when the Yankees hammered through post-season extra innings, Jonah would lie in bed and hear the excited shouts rise up from the street, heralding another home run. And though he didn't care much for baseball, he would get out of bed just the same and turn on the radio to listen to the game in the dark while the fans celebrated in the streets below. At those moments, he felt connected. He had that feeling after 9/11, too, when the whole city seemed to bind together in a friendly kind of sorrow. The baker clapped your shoulder as he handed you a warm loaf of bread, the cobbler carefully cradled your shoes against his chest, the butcher treated your meat with tenderness, and waitresses gave you sad little smiles of recognition. It was a good feeling that could not last.

A crackle of radio static broke out of the shadows. Jonah peered into the blackness, looking for its source, when a man's voice called to him, "Hello there!" It was Zipnick, transistor radio in hand.

"Hello," Jonah mumbled, tugging down the brim of his hat, his wish for human company vanquished by human reality.

"Is that them?"

"Where?" Jonah squinted hard into the darkness.

"Looks like white light down there. I think that's them."

"It's too faint."

Zipnick fiddled with the tuning dial until the live broadcast came in clear. The announcer said they were still waiting for the lights to come on.

"That's not them," Zipnick said. "Must be a trick of the eyes."

Jonah trained his vision on the dark spot of sky downtown, desperate not to miss the moment when it would fill with light. He shifted his weight from foot to foot, trying to stamp out the cold. His eyes watered from the biting wind and tears ran down his face. He wiped them away, hoping that Zipnick wouldn't think he was crying. The radio announced that a twelve-year-old girl, orphaned by the towers' collapse, was about to throw the switch.

"Here it comes," said Jonah, looking up, not daring to blink.

He and Zipnick both stood motionless, watching the sky. The radio fell silent. They waited.

"There they are!" Zipnick shouted.

The blue ghost towers seemed to unfurl up the sky, one wave-particle after another, as if the speed of light had been convinced to slow down for the solemnity of the occasion. Over the radio, an opera singer began "America the Beautiful," and Jonah listened to the familiar story of amber waves of grain, purple mountains, and fruited plains as he followed with his eyes the twin lines of light. Straight up they went, higher than the real towers had ever reached, until they curved along the inside wall of the sky's dark and starless dome. He had to tilt his head back to see where they finally stopped, at the very top of the sky where, in a brighter pool of light, they seemed to bend, disperse, then break through the atmosphere, rocketing into the vacuum of deep space, back up to speed at a constant 186,000 miles per second.

Jonah shivered in the cold.

"I guess that's that," said Zipnick.

"I guess so."

In his kitchen, Jonah opened another beer, lifting it to Rose's photo in a kind of salute. He plopped onto his sofa, turning on the television to watch the last few minutes of live news coverage from downtown. The camera, milking the moment, zeroed in on the face of the little orphaned girl as she gazed into the heavens. "They're not there," Jonah told the TV. "Because 95% of the universe is dark matter. Empty space with nothing to reflect the light. Don't bother looking." The television cut to the blue towers, showing them off from every angle, as they beamed from their eighty-eight "space cannons," each emitting 7,000 watts of electricity (Jonah did the math in his head, computing an impressive total of 616,000 watts). "They may be the brightest lights on Earth," the newscaster said, explaining that each shaft was over a mile high and visible up to twenty-five miles outside the city. "Maybe even visible from outer space."

Jonah pushed off his shoes and flipped through the television channels with his remote control. After the towers had collapsed, taking their television antennae with them, Jonah lost his reception and was forced to get cable. He felt a certain guilt about it, sometimes wondering if he should have gone televisionless, staunchly suffering this consequence of the towers' fall. Now he had more channels than he wanted and often found himself adrift in waves of mindless surfing. *Click.* A former Miss America, with her café au lait complexion and glossy lips, looked him in the eye and said, "I know you have beautiful skin under all that acne. Let AcNo-Pro reveal the real you." *Click.* Mary Jane Janicki, from Walla Walla, Washington, explained to Jonah how thrilled she was to have lost 150 pounds: "I can cross my legs now. Never in my life have I been able to cross my legs. My life has changed for sure." *Click.* A locomotive, hell-bent for tragedy, hurtled across the screen, while an anxious narrator warned, "Whether on water or on two steel tracks, whenever massive vehicles go totally out of control, the result is usually deadly disaster." *Click. Click. Click.* On the Discovery Channel, blue water filled the screen, a lobster raised her tail and, fanning her many fur-lined swimmerets, released a galaxy of eggs into the sea. Jonah settled here, mesmerized by the blizzard of tiny lobsters that danced across his screen, their new bodies as whitely vitreous as just-lost souls.

At the commercial break, the television announced that the next program would be an exploration of the ancient ruins of the mysterious city of Pompeii. When he was a boy, Jonah's mother had taken him to see the Pompeii exhibit at the Museum of Art in Philadelphia. He remembered how the people were frozen in time, encased in stone, like a game of Statues, when someone yells "Freeze," and you do. Some held their hands up over their faces, some lay sleeping in their beds, others were caught mid-stride while trying to run into the sea. There was a dog, too, and this, more than the people, pulled on Jonah's boy-sized, animal-loving heartstrings. The dog wore a collar and a chain, and was twisting back to bite at the chain, trying to break free. Jonah, as a boy, imagined the red tongue of lava oozing closer, licking the dog's paws, its tail, before engulfing it completely. He focused his X-ray vision on the stone, straining to see down to the dog's bones and teeth and black shiny fur, perfectly preserved inside. If he'd had a hammer, he would've smashed the statue open and set free the slobbering, grateful mutt he was so sure still breathed inside. His mother had held his hand and explained it to him: "They're not statues. They're real people." But she had misunderstood his questions.

It was not until an archaeology class in college that he realized he'd been mistaken about Pompeii all along. There was no lava, only suffocating ash. There were no people or dogs inside those statues, no skeletons. The bodies, encased in the cement mix of ash and rain, had decomposed long ago, leaving behind hollow molds of their final moments. When archaeologists discovered these human-shaped lacunae, they poured plaster into them, and out came the denizens of an entire city, suspended in the ephemera of their dying. His mother must have known that. He wished he could call her. "Remember the day we went to the museum and saw Pompeii?" It was a terrible thing, not to be able to pick up the phone and call your mother. Where was she now? Scattered atoms, light, and dust. A box of ashes on his bookshelf.

He got up from the sofa, staring at the cardboard box. A photo of his mother stood beside it. She was a dark-haired, dark-eyed girl in the photo, younger than Jonah, on the verge of meeting his father in the North Philly red-sauce restaurant where she served veal cacciatore and ravioli and meatballs made by her family since 1908 and served to luminaries such as Frank Sinatra, Jimmy Durante, and Dom DeLuise. Daniel Soloway was none of the above. He was a skinny astronomy student, a senior at Swarthmore College, arrogant to hide the crippling doubt he harbored—doubt about his intelligence, his goodness, his lovability. He was also Jewish and Teresa Marie Benevento was on the lookout for any man who could help her to break away from her overbearing family. She went back to campus with him that night. He took her to the observatory, showed her the hot, red ember of Mars, and created the boy who would derail his plan for winning a Nobel Prize in physics. But in the photo on Jonah's shelf, none of that had happened yet. All the fights and disappointments were still to come. The broken dishes and the hateful words, the taking of sides, the splitting apart and coming clumsily back together hadn't even been conceived. And the car wreck, of course, such a faraway, unimaginable disaster, didn't exist in any visible shape except maybe as a microscopic seedling buried in the mud of fate.

Jonah lifted the box of his mother's ashes and felt its weight. *When you're cremated,* he reminded himself, *you end up weighing about the same as a newborn—what you weighed when you came in to the world, as if all those years of growing meant nothing.*

The day of the accident, his parents were driving up the New Jersey Turnpike with a carload of dishes, silverware, a set of curtains his mother had made at Jonah's request. His last roommate had moved out and taken his kitchenware with him, and Jonah was making some home improvements. It was a beautiful September morning and they had set out early so they could spend the whole day together. It was a Tuesday, his father's day off, and Jonah had called out sick from work. Life had just been getting better. His father's team had made a tremendous discovery, the first real proof of the existence of dark matter in the universe. Finally, Professor Soloway had found a Massive Compact Halo Object, the MACHO of his dreams. With a position at the nearby University of Pennsylvania secured, his father could stop traveling, stay home again, maybe even be happy, and Jonah could stop worrying about his mother being lonely, could stop feeling guilty for leaving her for New York City. As the skyline blazed into view above the Hudson River, before their car could reach the tunnel, the first plane hit. The gleaming grill of the Sport Utility Vehicle must have looked like a monstrous set of silver teeth as it spun out of control. The driver, a nineteen-year-old girl shocked by the sight of an explosion in the building where her boyfriend worked as an intern, told the local newspaper later that she let go of the wheel to cover her eyes with both hands. The SUV rolled once then righted itself just in time to hit the Soloways head-on, crushing them from above in their vulnerable Japanese car. Teresa—who hated to wear seatbelts and never did—was thrown and killed instantly. Daniel lost consciousness, his chest a box of broken ribs. The driver of the SUV emerged shaken, weeping, but in one piece, soon relieved by a call on her cell phone telling her that everything was all right—her boyfriend had overslept—and that life would go on just as they had planned.

Jonah held the box against his chest and looked out the window. In the apartment across the way, he could see half of a table. A candle burned down, a bottle of wine sat glimmering, a glass stood half-filled with red. A woman sat at the table, talking and laughing to someone he could not see. With the candle's flame warmly illuminating her face and the flesh of her bare arms, she reached across the table, taking someone's hand. Jonah watched her gaze, for a drawn-out moment, at this other person, then smile and look away, out the window. If she saw Jonah, she must have thought him a strange sight: a man cradling a cardboard box, no bigger than a honeydew melon, in his arms. She might have wondered what precious cargo the box contained. But she made no indication of this. She looked back at her invisible dinner guest, sipped her wine, and laughed at a joke that Jonah could not hear.

He envisioned his own dinnertime scene: a table, a flickering candle, two glasses of wine casting red haloes of light on the white tablecloth. Rose Oliveri's hand in his. The two of them laughing at a little joke. If only he had been brave enough to say hello that time when she dropped her glove, everything might have been different. Maybe he could have saved her. He would have encouraged her to take a different job, to leave the World Trade Center and give up the data processor's life to pursue her true passions. She would have moved in with him. She would've picked out dishes and made curtains for the apartment, so his mother didn't have to. With one hello, Jonah could have saved them all.

A sharp memory came to him then, like a needle stick. He recalled a day on the Staten Island Ferry, just before 9/11, when he'd stood on the bow and wished the Twin Towers out of existence. Because he loved limestone and granite, aluminum and chrome-nickel steel, he dreamed of a New York City filled only with Art-Deco and space-age modernistic buildings: setbacks rising like ziggurats carved with helmeted angels, glinting eagles, and flying hubcaps, scallop-topped and tipped with mooring masts made just for the dirigible cities of tomorrow. The kind of buildings King Kong would want to climb, a wide-eyed Fay Wray wriggling in his hand. In comparison, the Twin Towers were monolithic, static monuments to commerce. They were pushy giants, bold enough to block out the sky. He didn't look at them and hear Gershwin's "Rhapsody in Blue" pounding out its jazz-age anthem the way he did with the Chrysler and Empire State. He hated the Twin Towers. So on that humid August day, when he rode the ferry to escape the heat of Manhattan, he fixed his gaze on the approaching skyline, closed one eye, and held his thumb up in the air, blotting out the towers. *Disappear*, he whispered into the salty spray. Two weeks later, they were gone.

He understood now. He alone was responsible for the disaster.

This was magical thinking, he knew, like when he used to avoid the cracks in the sidewalk, believing without a doubt that his own feet could break his mother's back. When he was angry with her, he stomped on every crack, chanting the rhyme and imagining her spine snapping in two. There was no such terrible magic, he told himself, and yet he could not deny a creeping sense of guilt.

He placed his mother's ashes on the kitchen table next to Rose's missing poster. Somewhere else, snatched from him, another life was rolling, running on some alternate track, the impossible, untaken road. He wanted that life. If he could be forgiven, he thought, maybe he could have it. That's when the lie broke from its protective sac and stretched upward, pressing from Jonah's unconscious, desperate to be born. Later, if anyone were to put the screws to him, he would always say, with total honesty, that he did not plan it. There had been no premeditation, only some strange alchemy produced by the proximity of these two artifacts on the table, these seemingly saintly relics that set his grief and hope to churning, giving life to the lie as he lifted the receiver of his chunky black Bakelite phone and dialed the number on the missing poster under the words: *If you have seen my daughter, please call.*

He was about to hang up when he heard the click of engagement, and then a woman's voice say, "Hello?"

Jonah said nothing, his finger poised on the button in the cradle, ready to disconnect. Vivian, he knew, was the woman's name. It was in his file.

"Hello," she said impatiently. "Who is this? Speak up or I'm hanging up the phone."

"Hi, uh, you don't know me," Jonah began. "My name's Jonah and I just wanted to call, to say, about your daughter, Rose?"

"You knew my daughter?"

"I did," he said.

"You're a friend of my Rose?" The woman's nicotine-scratched voice began to soften. "She didn't have many friends that we knew. How do you know my daughter?"

He thought of telling her the truth, but to say he knew Rose only from passing her each morning on the street, that they had never once spoken or even smiled at each other, that he wanted to but never had the nerve to say a simple good morning—it would sound ridiculous. Insane. Something a stalker would say. And so, in a hot swarm of panic, the lie broke from Jonah's interior, fully formed, perfect.

"We worked together. A few years ago, at Lakewood Press. In the art department? She was a wonderful artist," he said and held his breath.

Vivian sighed and went silent. Jonah worried that he had made a terrible mistake. Did he get the name of the publisher right? Had he already given himself away? He was caught. She would scold him, shame him for harassing a grieving mother. Even worse, a 9/11 mother. How could he? He would explain, say something about his own mother, about the strange things people do in the grip of mother-love, and loneliness, and grief. He had reasons. He shuffled through the Rose file, searching for the article that gave the name of the publisher where she worked. Lakewood? Or was it Wormwood? Or Lakeside? Then Vivian spoke.

"Rose could draw anything," she said. "From the time she was a little girl. She could draw anything. What did you say your name was?"

"Jonah. But I really don't want to bother you, Mrs. Oliveri. I just wanted to say that I'm—"

"She specially loved to draw horses. Never been on a horse in real life, but, boy, could she draw those horses. She loved those *Black Beauty* books and any movies about horses, so I guess that's how she learned it. But to draw a horse, like she could draw a horse, and never did she see one in real life? She could draw anything, that girl."

As Vivian Oliveri talked about her daughter, Jonah felt something new. He could not name it, but it was a feeling of real connection and it filled his throat with the taste of salt. He worried he might break into sobs.

"Tell me," Vivian said, almost whispering. "Tell me something about Rose."

Jonah began to tell her, remembering Rose as he went along. "She was always willing to help you out, whenever you needed it. Everybody liked her," he told the mother who wanted desperately to talk about her lost daughter, to gather together every last piece of Rose that she could find. "One time," he continued, "she had a lot of work to do and I had this project, this deadline project, and she dropped everything, her own work, to help me out. She was very giving."

He choked then, remembering a sweet, pretty woman who was kind to him, a Rose of his own imagination, who helped him when he needed help, who took from his own giving hand a dropped glove.

"I'm sorry," he said. "I'm so sorry."

"I know," Vivian soothed. "It's all right."

Jonah wanted to confess. He was a liar, a guilty liar. But "I'm sorry" was all he could manage to say before hanging up the phone.

He paced across the kitchen's dull linoleum floor. He found his soiled beer glass, still rimmed with a ring of dried foam, rinsed it, and turned it upside down on the dish rack to dry. Too much beer, that's what it was, and on an empty stomach. He'd forgotten to eat dinner. He ran the damp sponge over the faucet and along the edges of the sink, then followed that with a dry dishtowel, wiping away any streaks. What did it matter, really? It wasn't a terrible lie. In the greater scheme of things, he thought, it wasn't much of anything at all. And now it was over and done. He sat down at the table and listened while the refrigerator rattled and hummed. Rose and his mother sat at the table, staring at him. He couldn't tell what their silence meant.

When the phone rang, he startled. His phone never rang.

"Hello?" he answered cautiously.

"Mr. Soloway? This is Vivian Oliveri. You called me."

"How did you get my number?"

"Caller ID," she explained. "I used to get a lot of heavy breathers. Weirdos."

Jonah tried to think of something to say. Something honest.

"You miss her, don't you?" Vivian helped him.

"Yes," Jonah replied, feeling the truth of it.

"Maybe you want to come over some night, this week maybe. Do you have anything to remember her by? One of her paintings, maybe? I got too many of them. Come take one, please, to remember her by."

"I couldn't."

"What about Friday? You busy Friday?"

He wasn't busy.

"So it's settled. You'll come for supper. You're not a vegetarian, are you? When Rose was a little girl, I couldn't get her to eat vegetables. Then, in high school, she stopped eating meat. 'What's left?' I asked her. You know what she said? Cheese. Not for nothing, but that girl ate a lot of cheese."

"She did," Jonah said, remembering Rose at an office party, dipping into a platter of cheese cubes, a stoned wheat cracker in her pretty hand.

Part Two

"Who's afraid of the big, bad buildings? Everyone, because there are so many things about gigantism that we just don't know....The Trade Center towers could be the start of a new skyscraper age or the biggest tombstones in the world."
—Ada Louise Huxtable, 1966

4

It was dusk and the darkening, violet sky over Brooklyn looked low and solid, like a ceiling Jonah might jump up and brush with his fingers as he climbed the steps of the Carroll Street subway station. He pulled the slip of paper from his coat pocket for the tenth time and studied the address he'd already memorized on the train ride out. He set off down the block, hoping he was moving in the right direction. He passed a park, quiet in the falling darkness but for the menacing howls of adolescent laughter from a group of teenagers he could barely see in the shadows, their lean faces lighting up for an instant in the flare of a match. He quickened his pace until he reached Court Street, a well-lit thoroughfare trafficked by purposeful office workers making their mad dash for home; women carrying plastic grocery bags, transparent-white, heavy with cartons of milk and eggs; stooped old men shuffling toward their evening cigars at the tobacconist's shop.

The lie stirred inside of Jonah. A sly, feral thing, like a stray cat brought indoors with all the hope for domestication while, true to its nature, it nonetheless fixates on the pet parakeet. Can you blame a lie for doing what lies do? Jonah looked up to read the street signs. A billboard for a cat-and-dog funeral home informed him that "All Pets Go to Heaven." In front of a butcher shop a smiling, man-sized pig held out a platter of prepared pork products and the advertisement in the window read, "I scream, you scream, we all scream for pork." He thought about taking out his sketchpad, but there wasn't time. A gust of wind grabbed his hat and tried to yank it off his head. He pulled it down close to his ears and slouched off along Court, past lightposts tied with purple ribbons; a pizzeria that sported, in its courtyard, a life-size statue of Jesus holding an American flag; and a funeral home, this one for people, where a young man in a dark suit sat on a garden bench, sobbing audibly into his hands. Jonah noticed a bouquet of yellow flowers lying on the bench at his side. Flowers. His mother had always told him never to show up empty-handed. He stopped at a corner grocer and inspected their meager collection of ragged blooms. He picked the least sickly of the bunch, a handful of white tulips that seemed to be on their last legs.

He heard bells ringing from a nearby church as he reached Fourth Place. It was the only sound for blocks, and he stopped beneath a streetlamp to listen and to look again at the address on the scrap of paper. The brownstones and brick rowhouses had narrow, winter-worn yards rolling out before them. With Easter just weeks away, the little evergreen trees were decorated with plastic eggs, hung like ornaments from the branches and jouncing in the wind. Blue-robed Madonnas stood in floodlit, plaster grottos, casting their beneficent gazes upon every passerby. At the Oliveris' house, the brown, neglected yard overflowed with gewgaws. Beside the Blessed Virgin, a concrete donkey pulled a wagon filled with twigs and yellow weeds. A swan-shaped planter held only muddy water. In the gusting, an Uncle Sam whirligig twirled his arms, and daisy pinwheels spun like tiny turbines, making soft clicking sounds in the shadows.

Jonah looked up at the house. Over the tin cornice, the lights of Ground Zero shined. From this angle, they fused into a single beam like a fat blue laser cutting the sky. He followed the beam up with his eyes, to where it gathered in a smoky pool upon the clouds, then down again to the yellow-lit windows of the house. Decorated with rainbow and butterfly sun-catchers, the sills crowded with potted plants and figurines, every window had a light burning behind it, as if each room were filled with people, occupied with the business of daily life. Cluttered like the yard, but with a genial, lived-in feeling, the house seemed to welcome Jonah and he walked with the warmth of something resembling comfort through the gate and up the steps. A slate hung on the door, painted with a pineapple encircled by the words: WELCOME THE OLIVERIS. He stood for a moment between two heavy decorative urns, their brown geraniums and small, tattered American flags flanking the doorway. He was surprised to find the house silent. Its many lights had tricked him into expecting something different. He'd hoped to hear music coming from inside, voices shouting in a jovial, Italian way. Maybe even laughter amid the clatter of pots and pans. But the house did not make a sound.

He rang the doorbell and waited while the wind troubled the little flags in the urns, sending them into a flurry of bickering. A moment passed and then the house seemed to shift, almost imperceptibly, as if with a sudden intake of breath. He heard a faint stirring from inside. The door opened, letting out its yellow light. A woman stood peering at him from behind large, gold-rimmed glasses, running her eyes over his face. Through the glass storm door, she asked in a gravelly smoker's voice, "You Jonah?"

"Yes, I am. Mrs. Oliveri?"

"Come in, come in." She smiled then, opening the door wide. "And, please, call me Vivian. Mrs. Oliveri was my mother-in-law. God forbid you should get me confused with that one."

The woman's hair, cut short, was the color of a dirty copper penny, steel gray beneath an auburn rinse. Her pink sweater—interwoven with twinkling gold threads—gave off the smoky smell of a cigarette that had just been extinguished. She had the kind of face Jonah liked to draw, cross-hatched with lines and shadows, strong and perceptive, the sort of face that could see through you. At this thought, the lie inside him shivered and ducked, afraid to be seen. But Vivian Oliveri wasn't trying to inspect the contents of her guest. She put a warm and sturdy hand on Jonah's elbow and ushered him into a living room brimming with knickknacks and suffused with the savory aroma of cooking, garlic and rosemary, an olfactory combination that conjured his own mother and made the strange house feel at once familiar.

Jonah took it all in: pillows embroidered with BLESS THIS MESS and I BELIEVE IN ANGELS; a plaque on the wall that said, "God help me this day to keep my big mouth shut"; a mirrored curio case in the corner, populated by a menagerie of glittering crystal figurines (unicorn, Pegasus, elephant, teddy bear); an old-fashioned record-player console with built-in bar, behind which a wall of mirrors swirled with gold metallic marbling. Everything was pink and white and gold. And everywhere there were photographs of Rose. Toddler Rose in a floppy sun hat. Adolescent Rose with enormous Brooklyn hair. Graduate Rose in mortarboard cap and gown. In all the photos she was alone. No girlfriends leaning on her shoulder flashing heavy-metal hand signs and sticking out their tongues in open-mouthed teenage glee. No boyfriends gripping her from behind in oafish bear hugs. The thought of Rose being a loner like himself made Jonah love her more. He felt her presence then, a soft push against the cuff of his pant leg, as if she were emerging from the floor, rising up from the cold ground beneath the house to meet him. But it wasn't Rose. He looked down to see a yellow pug dog sniffing his shoe, wagging its corkscrew tail with mild excitement.

"You get out of here, Frankie," Vivian said, waving her hand at the dog with a gesture of defeat. "She's always underfoot, that dog. She misses Rose, poor thing."

Jonah looked down at the dog. Did it recognize him? Could it place his smell from East Sixth Street? He remembered the tattered tulips still in his hand.

"These are for you," he said with some hesitation, holding them out to Vivian, who took them in both hands, her long fingernails painted pink and gold to match her sweater—and her living room.

"Flowers? For me? You didn't have to bring nothing."

"They're not in such great shape, I'm afraid."

"They're beautiful," she said with the effusive sincerity of a mother accepting from her child a handmade gift, gummy with Elmer's glue, the glitter shaking onto the carpet. "But I better stick them in some water before they croak."

She instructed him to take off his coat and sit on the couch while she went into the kitchen. The dog stayed with him, and when she had finished sniffing his shoes, she sat down and stared up at him, waiting to be petted. Jonah put out his hand and she stood up again, wagging with joy as he rubbed the soft velvet of her black ears between his thumb and forefinger. When Vivian returned from the kitchen, the dog was seated contentedly at Jonah's feet, pressing her warm body against his leg.

"Frankie!" Vivian scolded, plopping her weight down into a La-Z-Boy chair. "She can be a real *scooch*. Is she bothering you?"

"Not at all."

"She's Rose's dog. Always getting underfoot, looking for attention. I feel sorry for the poor thing. And she drives my husband crazy. He's Frank, too. I think Rose named that dog after him just to give him *agita*. He hates dogs. The only animals he cares about are his dirty old birds."

Scooch. Agita. The language of his mother, old-world words he never heard in amnesic, ladder-climbing Manhattan.

"Your husband has birds?"

"Sure. He's up there with them right now."

Jonah looked up toward a ceiling scalloped with swirls of stucco painted pale, seashell pink.

"I told him we were having company. Let me get him down here," Vivian said as she stood with a soft grunt and trudged up the pink-carpeted stairs.

He liked Vivian. She was what he thought of as "real," which meant a lot of hyphenated adjectives like down-to-earth, matter-of-fact, straight-shooting (did straight-shooting have a hyphen?), adjectives people had used to describe his mother and which Jonah associated with being Italian American. He liked the feeling of being in Vivian's home. It had been a while since he'd been in an actual house, and the spacious coziness of it comforted him. But the lie wouldn't let him get too comfortable. It kicked him in the rib, reminding him that he was here under false pretenses. Vivian would serve him a meal and give him one of Rose's paintings, to remember her by, because he was an old friend, and that would be that. One night. It did no harm. In fact, it would be wrong to tell Vivian the truth about how he knew—or did not know—Rose. If Vivian was grieving and wanted to have a connection to her daughter, Jonah was not about to deny her. Vivian needed him. This he told himself as he petted the lie that curled in his belly, settling it down. He was making reparations, atoning for that moment when he blotted the towers with his thumb on the Staten Island Ferry. He sat back into the sofa's deep cushions and relaxed. He would tell Vivian whatever she needed to hear.

Upstairs she was calling, "Frank!" There was a pause. "Frank!" Then another pause, followed by Vivian's exasperated sigh. He heard some muffled shouting, the contents of which he could not make out, except for the words *Supper, Yes, No,* and *All right.* Then she was coming down the stairs again. Jonah looked away from the ceiling and busied himself with rubbing the dog's ears.

"He'll be down in a minute. He's up with his birds. He keeps pigeons up there. In a coop. It's all he does since he retired. And then, when we lost Rose. It's all he does."

"Marlon Brando kept pigeons. In *On the Waterfront*," Jonah offered.

"Did he? I don't remember that part. Marlon Brando. Jesus, was he a handsome bastard in his day. Before he blew up," Vivian said, inflating her cheeks to indicate corpulence. "But you can't blame the poor guy. He's had so many tragedies. You sure he had pigeons in that movie?"

"He kept them up on the roof."

"He played an Italian kid from Brooklyn, didn't he?"

"From Red Hook, I think."

"See that? It's an Italian thing. All the boys around here used to raise pigeons. I remember, when I was a girl, the sky was full of pigeons. Now it's just the old men who do it, waving their sticks in the air. But you want to know something? Those boys I used to know? They're all old men now."

"Who you calling an old man?" came a booming voice from the stairs as Frank Oliveri descended, his slippered feet soundless on the pink shag carpeting. He was not tall, yet gave the impression of being a big man. His high, round belly swelled beneath a gray T-shirt printed with an American flag and the words GOD BLESS THE UNION. His silver hair, wavy and abundant, swept back from a deep widow's peak with glistening pomade.

"Who's this guy?" he asked, his sharp eyes on Jonah, who stood up to greet him.

"That's Jonah," Vivian said. "Jonah, this is my husband, Frank."

"That hat's older than I am," Frank said, matter of fact, his hands planted on his hips.

Jonah smiled cautiously in Frank's direction, took off his hat, and extended his hand. Frank allowed the hand to hang a moment, white and slender and waiting, in the air before him. Just as Jonah began to pull it back in, Frank took it. Managing only to grab hold of Jonah's retreating fingers, he shook Jonah's hand the way some men shake a woman's, but with a firmer grip. A very firm grip, Jonah noted. Frank's hand was cold and red from being outdoors, and thick, like a porterhouse steak. Beneath the silver hairs on his forearm a blurry tattoo moved over the muscle. The bluebird of happiness, smeared now into a dark shape that looked more like a bruise than a bird, it struggled to flutter as Frank continued to squeeze Jonah's fingers.

"So," Frank began, his eyes narrowing beneath course, black brows salted with white hairs, "you knew my daughter."

"We used to work together."

"Where was that?"

"At Lakewood Press? In the art department?"

"You asking me or telling me," Frank said.

"We worked together in the art department. At Lakewood Press," Jonah said, making sure his statement sounded like a statement, and not something else. Frank let go of Jonah's fingers and folded his arms across his chest.

"We designed the book jackets. Rose did wonderful work." Jonah looked at Vivian. "She was so talented."

"So, you're some kind of artist," Frank said.

"I doodle a bit."

"You a doodler or an artist?"

"I draw portraits. Mostly. I sketch people," he turned toward Vivian again, "on the subway or the street?"

"What, like people you don't know?" Frank said.

"Right."

"They don't mind you drawing them?"

"Well, it's like—it's like anything else, really. Like a landscape."

"Like a tree or something," Vivian said, encouraging.

"Right. I mean, the tree doesn't mind if you draw its picture."

"Who's talking about trees here?" Frank said. "You draw trees or you draw people? 'Cause there's a big difference between a tree and a person. And a person might not like what you're doing."

"Well, I don't make it obvious. I mean, they don't know I'm drawing them."

"So, you do it real sneaky like."

"Oh, for God's sakes, Frank," Vivian sighed. "Leave the kid alone."

Jonah squirmed. "I try to be discreet."

"If you saw me on the train, would you draw my picture?" Frank asked.

"I guess I might."

"Why don't you draw it right now? I'll just stand right here. I won't move a muscle," Frank straightened up, sticking out his chest and raising his chin to the pink-scalloped ceiling, striking a Mussolini pose.

"All right, that's enough," Vivian said, rescuing Jonah. "We're not drawing pictures, we're sitting down to supper."

Frank chuckled. "I'm just busting them a little."

"I hope you like veal, Jonah," Vivian said.

"Sure," he chirped, embarrassed and aware that he had chirped but unable to do anything about it. "I like everything."

"Good. I couldn't make veal for Rose. Every time I made my cutlets she'd tell stories about baby cows getting electrocuted or something awful. Remember that, Frank?"

Frank walked into the dining room. Vivian watched him go.

"She was a real animal lover, my Rose," she whispered.

At the dining room table, Frank sat at one end and Jonah—Vivian insisted—at the other, while Vivian produced a heaping platter of glistening, golden-brown, deep-fried veal cutlets. She set the platter down amid overflowing bowls of salad, bread, and red sauce-covered macaroni, then she sat with a pleased sigh.

"*Mangia*. Come on, eat. Jonah, in this house, everyone helps themselves. Take as much as you want."

Jonah picked up a fork and lifted one, then another cutlet onto his plate. He took a large spoonful of macaroni and covered it with sauce and a blizzard of grated parmesan cheese. Vivian watched him, a look of satisfaction on her face, enjoying his pleasure in her food. As they ate their meal, Vivian asked Jonah about his job and his hobbies. She did not ask him about his friendship with Rose, which disappointed him. He had prepared a handful of anecdotes to share and while the idea of telling these lies made him nervous, he also hoped he would get the chance to talk about Rose, to bring her, in some way, to life. Frank sat silently at the other end of the table, reminding Jonah in some elemental way of his own father, who could go entire meals without uttering a word, calculating masses and radii, his mind adrift in the blackness of space, when he wasn't silently judging Jonah for not sharing his rigor. Frank likely wasn't thinking about baryonic dark matter, but that paternal energy, a combination of absence and potential threat, unsettled Jonah, kept him on alert. As a boy, he would spend mealtimes telling his mother about his day at school, the comic books he was reading, the drawings he made. The two of them shared certain passions—for art and adventure stories—that Daniel Soloway would not indulge, and so they created a bond that he could not penetrate. At those times, Jonah felt his father's envy, not knowing what it was, only sensing that it could reduce him to pulp if provoked. So while he told his mother about the latest issue of his homemade comic book, *Lava Man*, he kept one eye on his father, waiting for the outburst. His mother, after spending so many mealtimes in the presence of her absent, often brooding husband, casually behaved as if he were not there at all, as Vivian did now with her own husband.

"Me and Frank took one of those Alaska cruises a few years ago," she said, "and let me tell you, it was absolutely beautiful."

As Vivian talked about glaciers, humpback whales, and the splendors of the Chocoholic Buffet, Jonah watched the other end of the table. The dog sat on the floor close to Frank, following each movement of his fork, from plate to mouth and back again.

"They had a big *giambotta* pile of chocolate with an eagle—I mean this thing was huge, carved out of real chocolate—that you could eat," Vivian was explaining, when Frank finally broke his silence.

"Get out of here!" he shouted.

Jonah flinched. The dog did not move.

"Frank!" Vivian scolded.

"Jesus, Mary, and St. Joseph, if you don't take this goddamn dog out of here and lock it up—"

"Frank."

"—I'm going to boot it out of here."

"Frankie!" Vivian called to the dog, "Get out. Come on!" She cut a small piece of veal and held it out with her fingers, standing up and leading the dog into the bathroom. She locked it inside before returning to her seat at the table.

"That animal's got to go. I can't fucking take it," Frank said.

"Rose loved that dog."

"She spoiled it rotten," Frank growled. "Feeding the damn thing off the table. It wants people food."

Vivian looked at Frank then with a stare so icy, it was a physical thing, cold and cutting. Frank grumbled something about the "evil eye," stuck a forkful of food into his mouth, and slipped back into silence.

"I couldn't have a dog when I was a kid," Jonah ventured after a moment. "My father was allergic."

"You want one now?" Frank asked, shooting a look at Vivian that told her to keep her mouth shout.

"Are you serious?" Jonah asked.

"Serious as a heart attack. And if I don't get rid of that dog, I *will* take a heart attack."

Jonah looked at Vivian for approval. She shook her head and shrugged her shoulders, a mixed gesture he could not decipher.

Frank smiled then. "Jonah," he said in a tone meant not to address the man who sat across the table from him, but rather to hold the name in front of him, to weigh it and consider it, the way a man might judge a fish he held flopping on a line, before deciding whether or not to throw it back. "What do they call you, Joe?"

"No. Just Jonah."

"That's a name from the Jewish Bible, right?" Vivian asked.

"From the Old Testament."

"It's the guy that got swallowed by the whale," Frank said.

"Your people are Jews?" Vivian said.

"On my father's side. My mother's side is Italian."

"Oh," Vivian brightened, "that's quite a combination. What part of Italy they from?"

"I don't know. Calabria, I think."

"Calabrese. Same as us. That's a beautiful part of the country. Did she visit much?"

"No. She always wanted to go, but never got the chance."

"What's the difference," Frank asked, "between an Italian mother whose son won't eat her cooking and a Jewish mother whose son won't eat her cooking?"

"Frank," Vivian warned.

"The Italian mother kills her son, the Jewish mother kills herself," he said with a pleased smile.

"Don't pay him no attention, Jonah. He thinks he's some kind of comedian. Do your parents live in the city?"

"No, they—I grew up near Philadelphia. But my parents have passed away. They died in a car accident." He didn't want to explain about his father. It was easier this way.

"That's not right. So young." Vivian put down the forkful of lettuce she was lifting to her mouth. "How long ago?"

"Six months."

They sat in silence while the collective weight of the past six months settled like a heavy drape upon the table, covering each of them as if they were furnishings in a house about to be sealed for the season. Jonah regretted that his parents' accident happened on the same day that Rose was lost. He told himself that he didn't want to steal any of the grief from this place— another lie—and wished he'd said "six years" instead. He studied the half-emptied platter of veal, the long ovular dish painted with grapes and leaves, and the spent bowl of macaroni, the red sauce dried in a dark crust along its rim. Nobody mentioned Rose, but she was there. Jonah could imagine her sitting with them, seated at this same table, in the house where she grew up, telling stories about her day at school and asking to borrow the car. She must have eaten countless meals off these same plates, staring down at their faux-China pattern while she dreamed of other lives. The fork in his hand had once been in hers. It had been inside her soft, epithelial mouth, where its wearied tines had clicked musically against her teeth. He could see her there now and tried to imagine what she would say to him, sitting in her parents' house. But before Rose could open her mouth to speak, Frank put down his fork with a definitive tap against the plate and pushed back his chair.

"That's it for me," he said. "I'm stuffed."

"You're not having coffee?" Vivian looked at him.

"Nope. I'm going up," he said, standing. "Seeya 'round, Joe," and he walked out of the room, leaving his soiled plate on the table.

"He's going to those goddamn birds," Vivian said to Jonah. "It's all the man does. You want coffee?"

"That's okay."

"Stay for coffee."

"Only if you're making it."

"I'm making decaf. Can't stand the aftertaste but I'll be up all night if I drink regular. I can make you a pot, though, it's no trouble."

"No, thank you. Decaf is great."

When Vivian walked into the kitchen, the dog began whimpering behind the bathroom door. Jonah sat and listened to its disconsolate sound.

"Is it all right if I let her out?" he asked.

"Please. I hate her to cry."

When he opened the door, the little dog shivered, rubbing its grateful body against Jonah's pant legs. He crouched down to rub its ears. Vivian stood watching from the doorway.

"She likes you," she said, smiling.

"She's very sweet."

"You should take her."

"I couldn't."

"Sure you can. You'd be doing me a favor."

"Are you sure?"

"I said it, didn't I? Take the dog. Please."

"Thank you," he said, looking up at Vivian and trying to hold back his happiness, unable to stop a boyish grin from breaking across his face.

They took their cups of coffee upstairs, the dog following close behind, along with another presence that Jonah was sure he felt, imagining the soft footfalls of Rose on the carpet as they entered her girlhood bedroom. Vivian turned the light on to reveal a jumbled timeline of her daughter's life. The stuffed animals of childhood slumped together on the bed under a wall covered with teenage posters of punk rock bands. Her young adulthood spilled from cartons brought back from the city. The open cardboard boxes, flaps hanging down with a look of tired resignation, revealed an ample record collection, and a wardrobe of skirts, blouses, and sweaters someday bound for the Salvation Army, but not today. On the bureau sat a TV, a VCR, and an iBook laptop in tangerine, their unplugged cords dangling limp at their sides. An empty fishbowl held a hairbrush, make-up, styling products. Her hat, the one she wore so often, perched atop a lamp. There was a paint-spattered easel and a stack of paintings, a few of them hung right over the posters, making it clear that Vivian could not bear to change a thing. On top of a pomaded singer's black-clad body there hung a painted scene from East Sixth Street. Jonah recognized it right away—the bright bouquets of the flower stand, the red awning of the Indian spice shop, the peeling gray paint of his own apartment building. She must have been standing on the opposite corner, over by the launderette, when she painted it. It looked like a late afternoon in summertime, with the sunlight creamy on the bricks and sparking off the fire escapes, turning them to copper, transforming the grimy windows of Jonah's own bedroom into panes of shimmering gold. He imagined Rose standing outside his apartment, looking up at his windows. Was he there that day? He leaned in for a closer look, searching for some trace of his past self moving behind the sun-splashed glass, inside the frothy layers of paint.

"That one's of her street," Vivian said, noticing Jonah's interest, "on the Lower East Side. She lived there ten years. Ever since college."

"I recognize it," Jonah said, then caught himself. "I used to visit her there."

"You were good pals?"

"Sure." He scrambled to recall one of the anecdotes he'd prepared, but they were all office-related, scenes of coffee breaks and water-cooler jokes. He hadn't planned to tell friendship stories. "We went out for drinks now and then. And she threw terrific parties. She had good music, plenty of food and beverages. She was very generous with her friends."

Beverages. When did he ever say *beverages?* Still, as he told this tale, he felt Rose's presence expand in the room, a pink and fleshy glow beginning to illuminate the dark corner where her closet door gaped. She was like a lamp that came on dimly at first, its bulb delayed, as if its current wasn't running on full steam.

"Rose always had trouble making friends," Vivian said. "She was shy and we spoiled her rotten. She was an only child so I guess that's our fault. My fault. I couldn't have more children. But that's neither here nor there. I worried about her being alone in the city, but you couldn't tell that girl nothing. You said she had a lot of friends? Maybe she was growing out of it. I wish we got the chance to meet her friends. We didn't have a memorial service. A lot of families did, but we just couldn't bring ourselves. Anyways."

"She was a wonderful girl," Jonah said, watching the glow of Rose to see if he could encourage it to grow. "I used to visit her on that same street. Whenever she had one of her parties. You know, she loved jazz and she had an incredible record collection. We could spend all night just listening to those records."

Vivian touched his arm and said, "Take the painting."

Jonah hesitated. He looked to the Rose light where it pulsed and hummed, gathering more light, coming into form. It seemed to Jonah that his lies were giving her shape.

"You're giving me too much."

"What am I going to do with all these things? Put them in boxes? Throw them in the garbage? Better it goes to a friend than some stranger from the Salvation Army. It makes me sick to think of it," she said, picking up a book from its stack and putting it down. "Is that the painting you like best?"

Jonah hadn't considered the other paintings. They all were fine, pictures of other East Village buildings, fruit stands, flower stands, Tompkins Square Park green in summer and gray in winter, and they were all laced with that brilliant late afternoon light. In her corner, the Rose shape-shifted, became an almost-girl, telepathically projecting the words *Take it.* At least, that's what Jonah thought she might say, if she could say anything. She might have just as easily been saying *Take me.* But that would have been too much, even for Jonah's imagination.

5

It wasn't until he got to work and looked at the calendar that Jonah realized it was the first day of spring. The cold morning rain had picked up and was streaming down the big office windows, blurring the view and ruining it for spying through his telescope. The whole city was gray. Even the neon signs below seemed drained of color, like a black-and-white photograph of an older Times Square. The sparse crowds on the sidewalks moved hidden beneath black umbrellas. From the forty-second floor they were dark disks rushing east and west independent of people to propel them, like the shadowy saucers of deep-sea stingrays gliding by. The Empire State Building was gone in fog. Completely invisible, it had been erased by a great, gray drop cloth. *This is what it would look like if things had gone differently that day*, he thought, *if the planes had taken a different target.* He remembered his thumb blotting out the towers and turned away from the window.

Something strange had happened earlier and left him with an edgy feeling. He had woken up and walked the dog, as he'd been doing now for the past few days. In the mean little rain, the walk was quick and when they were done, Frankie stopped at the door of Rose's building. She had been doing this each morning since Jonah had taken her home, standing with her front paws on the little concrete step and looking at Jonah, her wet eyes filled with expectation. The first few times, he tried to coax and drag her away, but this morning he just scooped her up under his arm. He held her, damp and trembling, and peered through the window into Rose's hallway, a dark and empty corridor distorted by the blurry lens of rain on the glass. A human shape moved in the darkness. Jonah narrowed his eyes. It looked like Rose coming toward him, her face shrouded inside a silvery hood, lifting his hope that she had followed him from Brooklyn back to East Sixth Street. She opened the door and faced him, looking into his eyes.

"Can I help you?" she asked.

Whatever apparition he had imagined in Rose's abandoned Brooklyn bedroom, this was not it. The middle-aged woman worked her hands beneath her chin, tightening the ties on a plastic rain bonnet.

"I'm just," Jonah said, "waiting for someone."

"Wait inside," she said gruffly, after assessing him for threat, "out of this rain."

She held the door open and Jonah stepped inside. He didn't know which apartment number had belonged to Rose. On the mailboxes and the doorbell panel, the name Oliveri had been removed and replaced. He looked up the stairs, imagining Rose walking up and down them over the years. Sometimes she was tired, carrying bags of groceries. Sometimes she was light, hurrying down in clacking heels, running out to work. Other times she was distracted, reading the mail as she went up. Hefting down a bag of garbage, a sack of laundry. Lugging her easel to the park. Taking the dog out for a walk.

Jonah put Frankie on the cracked tile floor and crouched before the antique stairs. The hallway was silent, smelling warmly of brewed coffee and burnt toast. He reached out and slid his hand across the worn spot on one slab of faded stone.

This is where her foot had landed thousands of times. At least four times a day, he calculated, three hundred and sixty-five days a year, for ten years. Almost fifteen thousand times, Rose's foot had landed in this spot. He pressed his hand to it, willing her to materialize. She did not.

"Come on, Frankie," he said, unhooking the dog's leash to let her lead him up the stairs. She would know the way. They reached the landing and rounded the corner. At the end of the hallway, in front of apartment #3, Frankie stopped and aimed her face at the jamb, waiting to go inside. Jonah cocked his ear toward the door, listening for the stirrings of inhabitants. A television grumbled. He reached out, watching the warped reflection of his own hand growing on the gleaming faux-brass surface of the doorknob. He touched the knob gently with his fingers and held it. Frankie began to whine. Jonah pressed his cheek and then the length of his body against the cool metal-reinforced door, as if it were a woman that might open to him. He closed his eyes and felt the closeness of Rose, pressing herself toward him from the other side.

Now, at the office, he shook away the reverie. On his computer screen an article on "springtime family getaways" waited to be line-edited. He wondered if he was losing his mind. The more he thought about Rose with her water-cooler jokes and wonderful parties, the more real she became. Vivian said she was a loner. He wished more than ever that he'd had the courage to speak to her. If he had, where would he be now? Not sitting here editing this article. He'd be with Rose, enjoying these same springtime getaways: flying kites along the blue expanse of the Great Lakes, camping in the giant sequoia cathedrals of Northern California, canoodling on the dune-swept beaches of Cape Cod where he could hear the sibilance of the compass grass bending in the wind, twirling to trace perfect circles in the sand. The sad fact of the matter was that he was thirty years old and had never had a real girlfriend.

He yawned. Louder than he meant to. He'd been having trouble sleeping, his mind busy creating memories of Rose.

"Tired, old man?" came Keith's voice over the partition.

"Exhausted. I think I have chronic fatigue syndrome."

"Well, I have a hangover, so cry me a river. Speaking of getting trashed, tonight's that party I told you about. For the spring equinox. There's going to be a lot of foxy chicks just sitting around trying to balance eggs and shit. You're coming."

"It's a Wednesday night."

"You're coming."

"I have a dog to walk," Jonah said, looking at the empty blue and khaki beach on his computer screen.

"I'm not taking no for an answer this time."

"That balancing egg thing is a misconception. Just because the Earth's axis becomes perpendicular to the Sun, it doesn't make any difference. You can stand an egg on its end any time of the year."

"Jesus, Soloway, who gives a rat's ass about balancing eggs?" Keith got up and glared over the partition. "Did you hear what I said about the foxy chicks?"

Jonah thought about that and considered 1) He couldn't remember the last time he'd had a conversation with a girl, never mind kissed one; 2) the sort of girls who would attend a spring equinox party, complete with egg-balancing parlor games, were probably unintimidating hippies or squinty graduate students; and 3) he had spent his morning embracing the door of a dead woman's apartment.

"What kind of girls are going to be there?" he asked.

"The best kind," Keith said. "Available."

The party was in a spacious loft apartment on a crummy street in Chelsea, just around the corner of Seventh Avenue. The neighborhood had been getting popular and the loft was exactly the kind of place that strikes apartment envy in the heart of most New Yorkers: glistening amber wood floors, windows on three sides, and ample room for bookshelves—although this apartment had none, a fact that troubled Jonah. On one exposed-brick wall hung a giant, vintage Mobil sign, the neon tubes of Pegasus flickering with red gas-station light. The kitchen sat smugly in its armor of brushed steel. Not a single magnet marred the pristine, matte-finished expanse of the substantial refrigerator. The industrial sink offered a mountain of ice and bottles of beer nestled among a bevy of trendy new "malternative" beverages: Smirnoff Ice, Bacardi Silver, Skyy Blue—sweet mixtures of sugar and malt liquor. He felt a pang of longing for Vivian's pink-and-gold living room with its glass menagerie and embroidered pillows. As soon as he'd walked in the door, he knew this was not his kind of party, whatever that might be. The girls here were neither hippies nor earnest, studious Ph.D. candidates. It seemed that every single one of them wore knee-high leather boots under a black slit skirt, a new kind of city-girl uniform in which they all were smiling, tilting silvery glinting bottles of malternative beverage to their shimmering lips. He imagined that, underneath their tops, they all were sporting the Victoria's Secret Click Miracle Bra (now with gel-filled pads), ratcheted up tight for maximum cleavage. Jonah couldn't imagine a single one of them even attempting to balance an egg on its end.

Before he could flee, Keith grabbed him by the elbow and ushered him deeper inside, where the air was scented with warm bodies, perfume, and the Votivo red-currant candles Keith said everyone was burning these days. Loud music that Jonah did not recognize poured out of the tremendous black speakers that a dreadlocked DJ presided over, along with a massive turntable cluttered with wires and complicated switches. The polished wood floor pulsed with the deep sound and a few young women, with eyes closed, were dancing—their skinny bodies languorous, their pumiced feet bared as they tossed their boots carelessly to the side. Jonah disliked them, dismissed them, and hungered for them all at once. What would be required to take one home with him tonight? The impossibility of the answer sunk him where he stood. At least he'd have Keith—good-looking, amiable, socially confident Keith—to buoy him along, smooth the waves, maybe even introduce him to a shy, sweet girl, some wallflower who had also been dragged to this soirée by her own more vivacious friend-from-work. But, within minutes, Jonah's pod-mate, spotting his evening's prey on the other side of the room, excused himself and disappeared into the throng of dancers, chatters, and flirters, leaving Jonah with nothing but the flimsy cover of his porkpie hat to protect him from the pressure to produce long, meaningless streams of small talk while trying to look bored but not boring.

"Look at that hat," some sleek-haired guy said to his buddy. "My grandfather used to wear one just like it. I think we buried him in it." Laughter. Back-slapping. Jonah looked around for a drink, something to hold in his hand, like a shield or a weapon. He spotted the bar set up in one corner, where a girl in a white shirt and black bow tie stood mixing mojitos and caipirinhas, the cocktails of the moment. Jonah grabbed a bottle of beer from the ice-filled sink and found an empty wall to slouch against, which wasn't hard to do. The fact that there wasn't a single bookcase in the place continued to upset him. Across the loft, not only were there no bookshelves, there were no books. Not even a lone cookbook standing like a sentinel atop the towering Sub-Zero fridge. What kind of people didn't have books? They had to be there, somewhere. In the bedroom, or a study. In the bathroom, even. He set off to investigate.

He moved from room to room, pretending to be admiring the décor, a perfectly natural disguise. In the bathroom a few chunky modern design magazines were neatly displayed in a brushed-steel rack, but there were no books. In the bedroom, where the partygoers' damp coats were piled in a uniformly black lump on the bed, he found only *Sheer Bliss: The Art of the Orgasm*, which was right then enjoying its number-four slot on the *New York Times* bestseller list. *Did it qualify as a Book, with a capital B?* Jonah wondered as he slid it from its place atop the blonde wood chifforobe and leafed through its colorful pages. He put down his beer to inspect one of its more clinical illustrations. A giggling couple stumbled into the room, tipsy from what must have been their third or fourth malternative beverage. *Sheer Bliss* fell out of Jonah's grasp, landing with a wet-sounding splat—all too appropriate for its lubricious content—on the glossy wood floor and, to Jonah's warmly blushing dismay, face up.

The couple, already on their way to being undressed—the young man's belt was unloosed and his partner's black skirt hitched up in the back to reveal a fleshly curve of thong-bared ass, no doubt built by Pilates and sculpted on the Atkins Diet—froze where they stood and stared down at the filmy cover of the self-help manual. They erupted with laughter, the woman squealing, threatening to pee herself, until Jonah, after clumsily replacing the manual, slipped past them, escaping back into the anonymity of the crowd.

He'd left his beer behind and, without slowing down, reached into the sink full of ice and grabbed another bottle, then headed straight for the opposite end of the loft, as far away from the bedroom as he could get. Stopping to catch his breath, he came upon another door. Inside, he found a smaller room that appeared to be a study—it had a desk with a chair and a lamp—but what was being studied there, Jonah could not imagine. Like the kitchen refrigerator, the desk was a boundless expanse of uninhabited space, made of brushed steel and cool to the touch. The room in which it sat, like all the others, was empty of books. It was also, thankfully, empty of people.

Jonah closed the door on the pulsatile beat that thrummed through the cavern of the loft. He sat down on the ample window ledge, opened his bottle, and took a long swallow. The taste was shockingly sweet and citrusy—not beer at all, but an icy, silver-blue malternative tang. Begrudgingly, he sipped the cold drink and began to relax, looking out at the view. Seventh Avenue stretched below him, a canyon among canyons, cutting its mercury vapor-lit swath of asphalt all the way down to West Houston, where it metamorphosed into Varick, narrowing to a slender reed as it brushed past Chinatown, then molted once more, changing its name to West Broadway and plunging, inexorably, straight down into that inconsolable sixteen-acre hole in the ground.

The sky above was dark. The twin beams of the Tribute in Light should have been shining, but the cloudy conditions prohibited it. FAA regulations. On a dreary night like this, airline pilots could lose themselves in the diffusion of light, like migratory birds distracted from their springtime path along the Atlantic flyway. They could spend the entire night swirling around the big blue beams in a spiral of utter confusion, then crash to the sidewalk below. The birds, not the planes. But maybe it made no difference. The idea was to eliminate disaster, to keep a few more poor creatures safe and sound, for a little while longer. With the lights out and the towers gone, the birds swept north, undisturbed on silent wings, bound for Arctic breeding grounds. The airline passengers made their way unscathed through the fog, tray tables jostling beneath ice-filled drinks in plastic cups, happy to be coming or going. Just the same, Jonah missed seeing the towers of light. They helped fill that hole down there. They made the eyes go up. They were something to look at again.

The noise of the party suddenly spilled into Jonah's sanctuary. A plank of light fell upon the floor as a shadow slipped inside bearing the smell of cigarette smoke and a faint perfume that might have been cucumber. The door closed and the shadow let out a deep, dramatic exhale of relief. She hovered there, this apparition, her back pressed to the door, while Jonah watched, careful not to make a sound. He didn't want to scare Rose away. He could just discern the general shape of her, the dark hair brushing her narrow shoulders, the white skin of her legs glowing beneath the shadow of a skirt—she was not wearing knee-high boots and he could see the tender curve of her bare ankles illuminated in the blue streetlight. With another theatrical sigh—this one less relieved than the first, more like a sound of surrender—the shade lifted an unlit cigarette to her lips and, searching through her purse for a match, stepped, head down, toward the window ledge where Jonah sat unseen, the watery phosphorescence of Seventh Avenue absorbed by his dull black shoes and thrift-store suit.

In the sudden ignition of her Zippo lighter, the shadow turned into flesh, her face blushing in the tangerine firelight, the little rhinestones on the cat-eye corners of her eyeglasses sparking into embers. It wasn't Rose.

"Jesus!" she cried. "I didn't see you there."

"Sorry."

"Why didn't you say something?"

"I didn't think you could see me," he said.

"Well, I couldn't. Didn't I just say that? I didn't see you. You scared the pants off me."

"Sorry."

"I was just coming in for a cig." She held out her pack and squinted at Jonah. "Smoke?"

He'd smoked in college and then in art school, when smoking was required to successfully master the image of a brooding and anemic loner who hung out at the campus café chain-drinking black coffees and sketching the faces around him so fervently in his notebook that no one dared interrupt such a passionate creative process. Jonah had mastered the image a bit too successfully. No one dared interrupt, although he wished they would. He'd filled dozens of sketchbooks with portraits, his life inversely empty of people. He had since quit smoking.

"No, thanks," he told the woman.

"Nice hat," she said, smiling, the city light painting her teeth blue.

Jonah braced for another joke.

"I love men in old-fashioned hats," she said. "I wish they'd come back into style. And those glasses. Very Woody Allen. Is that insulting? His movies lately have been awful. *Curse of the Jade Scorpion*? Maybe you're going for the Buddy Holly look. So what are you doing in here anyway?"

"Hiding, I guess," he said.

"Mind if I hide with you? Or does that ruin it? You're not exactly hidden, once you've been found." She took a long drag from her cigarette while Jonah considered her questions.

"I don't think it ruins it. I'm still hidden from *them*," he said, pointing his chin toward the door.

"Isn't this a nightmare?" she said, sitting down on the other side of the ledge. "All these people talk about is real estate, their jobs at such-and-such magazine and so-and-so web site, and their summer plans in the Hamptons. It makes me feel all sticky and dirty, know what I'm saying? Jeez Louise. You don't work at some web site, do you?"

"I'm an artist," Jonah said, not really lying.

"Do you live in the city?"

"East Village."

"Me too. Well, 14th Street, if that counts."

She had a funny way of holding her cigarette out in front of her, then moving her mouth toward it, and taking a drag.

"You're not inhaling," he noted.

"I'm trying to quit. It's really an oral fixation for me. Very pre-Oedipal. I just like to have something in my mouth. Get a load of this." She opened her purse, reached in, and pulled out a handful of lollipops. "I'm supposed to just suck on these all day. Like a pacifier. It's pathetic, really, when you think about it. I mean, how needy can you get, right? My mother had tubular hypoplastic breasts. You know what that means."

Jonah did not know.

"No breastfeeding for me. Now I'm addicted to nicotine and Blow-Pops. Want one?"

"Sure."

"What flavor? I've got them all."

"I bet you don't have green apple."

With a triumphant grin, she handed him a green apple lollipop, then opened a cherry one for herself and stuck it in her mouth, the candy clicking against her teeth, making a wet, lingual sound. Something inside Jonah began to stir. He looked at her dark hair, cut straight across her forehead in a Louise Brooks kind of silent-movie-star style, and the beauty mark on her cheek which, he felt certain, was drawn on with a pencil, and he thought about leaving the room. But he didn't. He watched as the woman took one more hungry drag of the cigarette, licked her fingers, then (with a hiss) pinched out the snipe and slipped it back into the pack before dropping it into her purse.

"You know what else I have in here?" She reached into her bag again, and pulled out a hardboiled egg. "Want to try it?"

Jonah opened his mouth to tell her that the whole thing about balancing eggs on the spring equinox was a popular misconception, but stopped himself. He shrugged an okay, the fabric of his jacket sighing against his bony shoulders.

"Come on," the woman said. "Let's give it a whirl."

She sat forward, Indian-style, and attempted to stand the egg in the narrow space between her body and Jonah's. The perfume underneath her smoky smell was definitely cucumber, mixed now with a sticky-sweet, artificial cherryness that mingled in Jonah's nose with his own sugary green apple smell as the lollipop clicked and rolled around inside his mouth. The egg fell over again and again.

"Maybe it won't work," she said, crestfallen. "Maybe it's just a stupid myth."

"No. It'll work," he lied. "Tonight, night and day are equal in length. The Earth's axis is perpendicular to the Sun. I am sure we can balance this egg."

Jonah steadied the egg between his fingers, fitting it into an invisible groove in the wood grain of the ledge. "You just have to get it—get it—in tune. With the obliquity of the ecliptic. And the gyroscopic force of the Earth. In conjunction with the Sun's immense gravity," he said, looking at the woman to see if she was impressed. "It will stop. This egg. From falling. Over."

He took his hand away and the egg stood on its own, balanced in the palm of the irregular wood beneath it. Indifferent to the tilt of the Earth's axis, oblivious to the machinations of the Solar System, it stood, glowing creamily in the blue-white light spilling in from the avenue, like a precious orb, container of secrets, the opalescent, chicken-preceding egg of life.

"You did it!" the woman cried, clapping her hands and leaning forward to plant a cherry-sweet kiss on Jonah's cheek. He looked at her then, seeing a limpid reflection of himself in her lenses, and slid the lollipop out of his green-stained mouth. Her name. His mouth hung open, getting ready. He would ask her name. But before he could do that simple thing—that obvious, normal-human-being, everyday thing—the clamor of the party burst into the room, as the door opened wide and a dark shape strode toward him.

"I've been looking all over for you," it said, irritated. "What are you *doing* in here?" The shape seemed not to notice Jonah, who closed his green and open mouth again around the lollipop.

The young woman unfolded her legs and swung them off the ledge, knocking the egg to the floor, where it landed with a soft crack.

"We *were* balancing an egg," she explained. "It really worked."

The shape screwed up its face, ran a hand through its slick, black hair, and said, "Whatever," looking at and not looking at Jonah, who felt small, ridiculous for having a lollipop in his mouth. He took it out again and tried to hold it casually, manfully, in his fingers.

"Come on. Get your coat," the shape said to the young woman, whose name Jonah still did not know. She stood up without protest, pulling her skirt down and smoothing it along her thighs.

"Thanks for the cool trick," she said to Jonah, before following the cologne-riffled wake of the shape as it wafted out the door.

"Thanks for the treat," he said, waving his lollipop in the air, watching her as she disappeared.

In the dark room, Jonah waited for some time to pass, enough for the nameless girl and her date to get their coats, say their goodbyes, and go. He didn't want to run into them on his way out. He didn't want to see them together, arm in arm, hailing a cab on the street. They were all wrong for each other. She was intelligent. She said "pre-Oedipal" and "Jeez Louise." And she had interesting glasses. She was not a Marketing Girl. But her boyfriend was an ape. He was one of those guys. There seemed to be more and more of them in the city every day. The ones with closets bursting with identical blue shirts, magazine racks filled with mail-order catalogs, stainless-steel bathroom shelves from Pottery Barn loaded down with hair products. Jonah couldn't remember the last time he had the gooey pleasure of using a hair product. Underneath her interesting exterior, Jonah thought, the girl must have been a nincompoop.

When enough time had passed, he unfolded his legs—a bit painfully—and put his feet on the floor. Holding onto the smooth wooden lip of the window ledge, he looked down at his shoes and wiggled his big toe behind the hole it had worn in the leather. Next to his wiggling toe, the broken hardboiled egg sat, dim now without the glow of the streetlamps to make it luminous. He bent down and picked it up, and let it drop gently into his jacket pocket.

Out on the street, the rain had stopped. Violet clouds washed across the sky, revealing a darker firmament, a few bright stars, and Jupiter radiating high overhead. Somewhere to the right of Mars, the comet Ikeya-Zhang streamed by unseen, wagging its bluish ion tail through the Solar System for the first time since 1661. With his telescope, he could have seen the moons of Jupiter, but not the comet—the lights of the city were too bright. Still, he knew it was there. He could not delete the information, and the curiosity, his father had put into him about the stuff of science and space. He thought of satellite pictures of New York, in which the unwieldy city is a glittering explosion of photons, a splash of spilled milk dammed by the black Atlantic to the east, overflowing westward into a web of white light riddled with shadow, fading finally into the unlit expanse of the country's heart, where the city lights never reach. Here and there, the map was pinpricked with a few shining towns, but mostly the heart of America was drenched in night, its houses marked only by soft, moth-yellow porch lights, too faint to be seen by the satellite's eye, too weak to staunch the darkling flow. Here was where the real brutalities flourished. What were his lies compared to that? Out there, under cover of the gloaming, psychopaths roamed the back roads, their headlights dimmed. Hooded men gripped pitchforks in the shadows, waiting for the right moment to strike. In gloomy forests, the shock of gunfire was a common, comforting sound. And mothers, tucking their children into bed, told stories of a vengeful God, how the world was divided simply into the righteous and the purely evil. In those blue-black deserts and plains, the evening sky was littered with the stuff of the universe. Stars burned and planets whirled. Meteors rained down from the heavens. It was a region of believers, human beings still clinging to portents and signs, bracing for battle as they watched themselves hurtling helplessly through the blackness of space.

But in brilliant, insomniac, godless Manhattan, this fact was easy to forget. There was no Earth spinning below, no universe above. Even midnight wasn't black, but a pale shimmering blue, smudged with city light. Here, the darkness had been banished by a billion kilowatts. Still it filtered in, slicing through everyone, at every moment, gliding through rooftops, skulls, and spines, out through feet, floorboards, basements, down through the core of the Earth and out again, in reverse, through the feet, spines, skulls, rooftops of men and women on the other side of the planet. That theoretical hole you might dig to China had already been excavated by infinitesimal tunnelers, dark fragments of the Big Bang, the black holes, the supernovae. Right then, at that very second, trillions of cosmic neutrinos were passing through Jonah's body, undeterred by meat and bone, existing in the vast empty spaces that made him, deftly dodging every subatomic particle in their path. Like sunlight sifting through a windowpane. But not sunlight—more like sundark. Who could think of it? All the time, this dark darkness, like water, rushing to fill every empty space—nose and mouth, the wet, throbbing lacunae of the lungs. You could drown in all that blackness.

The sky over Manhattan had cleared of clouds and now, as Jonah rounded the corner onto the avenue, there shone before him the twin beams of the Tribute in Light, like a pair of blue comet tails themselves—plunging to Earth or rocketing away?—free again to illuminate the skyline. It was good to see them. The city had direction again. There was south.

He knew which way to go and turned toward the lights, his shoes slipping along the wet sidewalk. "Don't step on the cracks or you'll break your mother's back." A girl had kissed him tonight. Not a big kiss. Just a peck on the cheek. But she was cherry-sweet and seemed to like him. Why? He was no square-jawed, slick-haired, smiling brute. No pretty charmer. He was no Keith Starling (who had probably found his way into another girl's bed for the night). Still, she seemed to find him appealing. For a moment, anyway. She was probably drunk. Bored. A natural flirt. She probably flirted with every guy she met, handing out those lollipops like calling cards— come up and see me sometime. It meant nothing. He stuck his fists into his pockets and looked up at the lights.

With a low growl, the shadow of a 767 glided into view, its anti-collision blinkers winking red and green, its nose heading straight for the towers. Jonah stopped to watch. Scalpel-smooth, the plane slipped inside the first beam and blazed silver-white. It hung there a moment, illuminated, just a second longer than a lightning flash, and then passed right through, a shadow blending again into the dark on the other side. It sailed out over the harbor, its four hundred passengers wondering about that sudden brightness that had, for just an instant, so enlightened them.

Inside his pocket, he opened his fist and found the egg, a white moon eclipsed within his black jacket. He held it, still looking up at the towers of light where they stood unwavering and unbroken. It seemed a miracle. What had been upset? A few photons, air particles—like a regiment of bees buzzing in formation, undisturbed by a ripple of breeze. The airliner motored on across the sea. The towers of light stood. In this way, they were a vast improvement over those monoliths of glass and steel. If only we could live in light, suspend our desks and telephones and keyboards upon beams and boards of light. Make a honeycomb within those buzzing towers of imperturbable, indestructible light.

They were up there still; he could see them now as he walked toward the towers. The thousands of office workers levitating at their luminous desks, holding the lanterns of telephones to their lambent mouths—not filled with light, but made of light. Secretaries tossing the sparks of their hair. Window-washers swinging bucketfuls of liquid phosphorescence at their sides. Executives in moon-white shirts, their shoes shined to burnished alabaster. All of them, up there, bustling in their twin hives of light, held aloft on girders more powerful than steel, cradled on rafters more mighty than wooden boughs. These towers could not break. These bodies would not fall. Even an airplane crashing through them was like a ghost gliding through a solid wall, a speck of cosmic dust whistling through a human heart. Not a single beam, not a bolt, not a bone would be disturbed.

Jonah felt the egg with his fingers, investigating the dimpled crack sustained in its recent fall. He pressed his thumb into this soft fontanel and began to peel the shell. Working it away from the slippery white with his thumbnail, he let the shell fall to the bottom of his gritty pocket and lifted the egg to his lips as he walked. He took one bite, then another, keeping his eyes on the towers of light, gazing through the invisible windows at their luminous inhabitants. He scanned up and up, searching the length of the first tower for its eighty-ninth floor, where he could see Rose seated at her floating desk, drinking a silvery cup of mist, crossing and uncrossing her milky legs. If he'd had his telescope with him, he could have gotten closer, seen her as she turned to look at the view down Seventh Avenue. Could she see him, too? Single him out from all the other specks hurrying along the sidewalk, hands in pockets, crossing against the red lights?

Compared to Rose, what was some girl with a lollipop? Compared to Rose, ascending now from her desk in the photon tower, a woman not falling but flying, made of light, the lollipop girl was nothing. He watched Rose drift down to him, the wind fluttering her skirt. He opened his arms to catch her. But before she could touch the concrete with her toes, the eighty-eight space cannons shut off for the night, and their beams evaporated, taking all of their apparitions with them until the next dusk.

Jonah checked his watch. Eleven o'clock. Right on time. Maybe he was wrong about the towers' strength. How strong was light without a source? You couldn't really depend on something that, no matter what, would always be racing away at 186,000 miles per second, so eager to leave you behind.

6

On Friday nights, the East Village swelled with bridge-and-tunnelers, out-of-towners, and young Upper East Siders bored by their necktie lives. They came in troops like a marauding army to pillage the streets, moving from bar to bar in boozy platoons, the men breaking out into fistfights, the women breaking out into song, screaming the lyrics to 1970s television themes, "That's the way we all became the Brady Bunch!" On Friday nights, Jonah stayed inside and remembered the peace of the post-9/11 restrictions when only residents were permitted south of 14th Street. You had to show identification to get into the East Village. With only the neighborhood people to walk them, the streets were silent. He had stood on the avenue then and heard crickets. He'd never known there were crickets fiddling right outside his door. But the restrictions had long been lifted and the cricket song was smothered again in the savage, invading din.

Jonah tried to drown it out. He put on a Roy Smeck record. The tunes of "Limehouse Blues" began to play, a tinny vaudeville sound. He picked up *Ephemera Automat* where he had last left off. Stan (the burlesque manager) and Giggy (the novelties salesman) were sitting on the boardwalk at Brighton Beach. Throwbacks to a more formal era, they dressed in threadbare suits and ties, though it was summer in their world.

They held their hats on their laps and let the warm wind blow their flimsy hair while they told tall tales to each other. A girl walked by in a bikini. Giggy held up a pair of X-Ray Specs and said, "If only the promise were true!" The next panel was a white blank. Jonah added some ink to the shadows in the folds of Stan's trousers. He whited out a stray cloud that didn't look right. But he could not imagine what to do in the next panel. He'd been staring at that white square since September, once in a while trying a little something—a cloud, a seagull, a passing hot dog cart—just to take it out again. Now the paper in that square was furred with erasures and moonscaped with dried blobs of Wite-Out.

He put down his pen and turned to a box of old magazines and comic books. These were not special, collector's comic books. They were scrap for source material. He kept boxes and boxes of such paper ephemera throughout his apartment: vintage girlie magazines, *Life* and *Popular Mechanics*, a 1956 edition of the Manhattan Yellow Pages. As the boxes filled up, he took the time to organize—a form of procrastination that felt productive, but bordered more closely on obsessive. He cut out the items he liked and arranged them into files according to category: men, women, automobiles, food, televisions, kitchen appliances. When he needed to place an authentic Big Ben Westclox alarm clock beside the sleeping head of one of his characters, he simply took out the file marked Clocks and found the perfect example.

He took the box out to the kitchen, where he placed the comic books in a neat stack next to a pile of file folders. He paused to admire the symmetry of the two stacks sitting perfectly parallel to each other, then sat down and selected a July 1979 *Superman*. On the cover, the Man of Steel posed athletically in the air over Metropolis, movement lines like white ribbons streaming from his muscled arm as he hurled the needle of the Empire State Building like a javelin at an incoming ball of fire.

"That huge meteor is loaded with deadly Kryptonite," said Superman. "If I don't hit it dead center, Metropolis will be just one big crater!"

Jonah wondered if Rose liked comic books and decided that she did. He opened the comic to the first page of small-print advertisements. When he was a kid, even more than the stories of superheroes and the supernatural, he loved to read the ads. He could get completely lost in a page-long catalog from the Johnson Smith Company, of Mt. Clemens, Mich., the Fun Factory of Palisades Park, or the Abracadabra Magic Shop of Rahway, NJ, with their offerings of amazing finger-choppers, whoopee cushions, hot pepper gum, atomic joy buzzers, snowstorm tablets, Hypno-Coins, secret spy scopes ("Bring distant objects closer—great for spying, sports, girl watching"), and, most intoxicating of all, X-Ray Specs—"See bones thru skin! See thru clothing! Fantastic illusion! Astound and embarrass your friends with X-ray vision!"

Jonah used to beg his mother to send away for these amazing novelties. At the dinner table, on Saturday nights, it was the Soloways' custom to read while they ate takeout pizza and drank a liter of orange soda. Daniel Soloway read scientific journals, wishing his competitors tough luck. Teresa Soloway buried herself in romance novels, most of them set in Italy, the homeland she longed to visit but never did. Jonah poured through his comic books. He favored the supernatural, like *House of Secrets* and *The Unexpected*, comics filled with ghost stories and "true" tales of terror. It was on such a night that Jonah, enraptured by an advertisement in between the pages of a horror story about a woman who turned into a giant spider on her wedding night and sucked the life out of her new husband, read aloud, "Make anyone do anything you mentally command—with your mind alone! Silently command, control, dominate anyone. Say nothing— watch even perfect strangers do what you wish willingly and cheerfully. Absolutely uncanny!"

"Read silently, Jonah," his father said. "Please."

"Can I send away for this?" Jonah turned to his mother. "It's only a dollar."

"Sure you can."

"No, he can't," his father interrupted. "Those things are junk. They're hoaxes. Lies. You can't control people with your mind."

Jonah was past the age when he had an imaginary friend, but he could still remember Arthur, a very clever dog, who did everything that Jonah commanded him to do. He fetched slippers and stood on his head. He told funny jokes and helped Jonah with his homework. So Jonah knew that it was possible to control people—or dogs who were like people—with your mind, but that some people, especially large people, were difficult to control and the task required special help of the sort offered by the Johnson Smith Company, of Mt. Clemens, Mich., et al. His father, out of all the large people in his life, was the most difficult to control.

Jonah turned his request to X-Ray Specs. "What about these? You can see through skin and everything."

"More bullshit," his father said. He lowered his journal and looked at his son. "They put those ads in there to prey upon the susceptible minds of boys like you. Boys who read comic books instead of playing sports. I know, because I used to be a boy like you."

Jonah pouted. He didn't want to have anything in common with his father.

"You want to control the minds of your parents, outmuscle the boys on the playground, see through the skirts of girls."

"I do not," Jonah said, feeling exposed. He looked down at the pizza crust on his plate, the crescent shape of his teeth marks in the red sauce-stained dough. He thought about Dawn Paulauskas, the girl who sat in front of him in Social Studies, and felt his face get hot. His father could read his mind. Maybe he had sent away for that course: "Mindreading: Learn the secrets and amaze your friends—complete course $5.00 + $1.00 postage—JoJo Deutch, Box 508, Glenwood Landing, NY."

"Advertising is all lies," his father continued, "snake oil. They'll tell you anything just to get your dollar bills. Don't believe everything you read. Have a little healthy skepticism. There are plenty of suckers in the world already."

"Don't be such a bully," Jonah's mother said.

A member of the Skeptics Society, Daniel Soloway believed in the power of disbelief. A dedicated disprover, he routinely demystified the mysteries that fired Jonah's imagination. The Bermuda Triangle? A hoax. The Loch Ness Monster? Bullshit. Bigfoot? That was the worst.

Jonah loved Bigfoot. In his boyhood bedroom he had a special sasquatch wall on which he tacked a still photo from the famous 1967 Patterson-Gimlin film, showing a tall and hairy humanoid hustling through the National Forest; a U.S. map marked with stars to indicate sightings of the cryptid; a page from *Popular Mechanics* showing a plaster cast of Bigfoot's seventeen-inch footprint; and an advertisement from the back of *Boys' Life* in which Beamer Expeditions of Conoga Park, California, promised to take intrepid hikers, backpackers, and snowshoers on one of their "Unforgettable 22-day wilderness expeditions" in the Pacific Northwest, where "scientists, naturalists and trackers" would help you to search for the real Bigfoot. Jonah sent in $3.00 and received their detailed catalog. He made an impassioned plea, claiming that such a trip would be a great way to spend some father-son time, but his father still said no. So he was surprised when his father agreed to sponsor their own Bigfoot expedition, taking him up to the Delaware State Forest for a night of camping along the Thunder Swamp Trail. After hours of staring at the obscenely pink brick of Spam they'd hung from a tree limb as bait, Jonah fell asleep. Near sunrise, his father woke him. The Spam was gone. Two giant footprints stood in the moist earth beneath the dangling, Spamless length of twine. They measured exactly seventeen inches long. Before Jonah could frantically unpack his track casting kit, his father grabbed him, pointing into the brush where something was rustling. Jonah froze. He could sense the sasquatch's presence, large and powerful in the purple dark of dawn, not a man and not an animal, but a potent combination of both. It was everything he could ever want. Bigfoot was real. He knew it and now his father knew it, too. A delicious stream of terror and joy ran through him. But when the hairy ape-man came lumbering out into view and could not contain its strangely familiar, nasal-honking laughter, revealing itself to be Daniel Soloway's teaching assistant and protégé, the beloved Carl Wallace, the dirty truth of his father's scheme came to blazing light. Jonah lost it. He attacked Carl, leaping up to rip off his gorilla mask and punching him in the belly and kidneys until his father pulled him off. He could have killed his father in that moment. No matter how many times during that bruised summer, and over the years, Daniel Soloway insisted "I did it to inspire the skeptic in you," Jonah felt only humiliation and hate, along with a renewed fervor to believe.

Alone now in his own kitchen, he read an advertisement for the U-Control 7-Foot Life-Size Ghost—"acts lifelike"—and his thoughts wandered back to Rose. From the window, open to allow cool air to counteract the force of the radiator still pumping out its steam heat, came the high-pitched bark of female laughter. With the laughter came a ribbon of perfume from (he imagined) the same laughing girl, the speed of smell lagging behind the speed of sound. This mixture of sensations (scent of musky apples and flowers, throaty *ha-ha* diminishing to giggles), combined with his memories, made him aware of his loneliness with a purple throb in his chest. He went into the dark living room where Rose's painting hung on the wall. He looked forward to the morning when he would be going back to Brooklyn. Vivian had asked him to help out with some yard work and he'd gladly said yes. He was going to tell Vivian about the time he and Rose skipped out of work to see a movie.

The office is empty, all of the bosses out of town at a sales meeting, and he and Rose take a long lunch break. He'd done a Google search earlier on the Academy Award-winning movies of 1999 and decided they would have gone to see *American Beauty*, a movie that he had actually seen, just in case Vivian asked him about the plot. *They see* American Beauty *and share a jumbo bucket of popcorn, their fingers meeting for greasy interludes in the dark.*

"Remember that?" he asked the empty apartment.

No one answered.

He looked out the window. On the street below, the throngs staggered their way up and down the street. Young men and women, their faces glowing red from the festive lights in the windows of Indian restaurants, jokingly pushed and shoved against each other, slamming their bodies into passing strangers and roaring. Three blonde girls, dressed identically in knee-high leather boots and belted camel coats, raised their arms to hail a cab, screaming obscenities at every driver who passed them by, taxis already filled with other blondes in other boots. One of them fell to the street, squealing drunk. Her friends, also drunk, tried sloppily to lift her by tugging at her coat until it slipped off and her blouse hiked up, showing her bare breasts for a split second in the blushing light. Jonah backed away from the window, forgetting he could not be seen in the unlit room.

He made a mental list of the bare breasts he had seen in real life. Most recently, there was a woman sitting in a parked car on West 10th Street. She pulled her sweater up over her head, lifting her blouse for a moment and revealing no brassiere underneath. Then she tugged the blouse down, and the breasts were gone. It was only a second that it happened, yet it stayed with him, a luminous, twinkling moment. That was the most recent time. There were a few topless dancers in there. And a few fumbling encounters with unhappy art-school students, breasts mostly forgettable. There was Nikki Wilson, in junior high, a rough-edged girl who would reveal anything for the right price. A dollar for breasts, two if you wanted her to lift her skirt. She had a grudge against undergarments and never wore them. When his turn came, Jonah only had a dollar. Nikki lifted her Def Leppard t-shirt, counted to ten, and told him to "get lost." Before Nikki, there was lonely Mrs. Biskind, who had a hare-lipped son everyone called "The Biscuit." Jonah and The Biscuit were friends for the duration of sixth grade, until The Biscuit caught Jonah spying on his mother one afternoon while she was changing out of her work uniform and into her housedress. The Biscuit's mother was a tired, joyless woman, but her breasts, Jonah was surprised to find from behind her bedroom door, were buoyant, youthful things, pink and fresh as just-scrubbed cheeks. He tried to explain this to his friend, but The Biscuit did not understand.

Before that, there was only one: the first breast, the maternal prototype. He could not call up a mental image of his mother's breasts, and that was just fine with him. As an infant, Jonah's mother had told him years later, only the breast could soothe him. She would try everything to calm his cries, which were painful to her, piercing and red, turning his whole body into a boiled lobster of unsatisfied need. She would hold him and croon his name, sing to him, insert a pinkie finger into his screaming mouth, but none of it would quiet him. "Only the breast," she told him, embarrassing him. "I used to stick your little head under my shirt and you'd shut right up, just to be near it."

What were Rose's breasts like? He felt ashamed to even think it, but there was the thought anyway, with no one around to punish him for it. Did he dare to imagine the body of a dead woman? It felt like the saddest thought in the world, to imagine breasts turned to dust, two sorry puffs of smoke. But how good it would feel to be held close to the real flesh, before fire rendered them into something regrettably forgettable. Who could blame him? Look at his miserable list of failed and awkward connections. *I am a man to pity*, Jonah thought, as the record stopped on its turntable and he heard mice skittering overhead in the hollow spaces of the ceiling, their claws scraping through tunnels of wire and fiberglass fluff. Something vital was taken from him that morning, years ago, on the Thunder Swamp Trail. In his father's fraudulent conjuring of the beast that held, in its big hands, a piece of Jonah's urgent boyhood, something was stolen. He never trusted his father again. But he continued to believe in Bigfoot, the way he believed now that the sound of mice was not entirely the sound of mice, but the arrival of a woman through his window.

She hunkered there, by the radiator where his mother's curtains moved, sort of slumped in the shadows. She was bent over like she had a stomach cramp. Maybe she was tired from the long climb down from the sky, or up from the mud, wherever ghosts came from. Or maybe it was just that she wasn't yet fully formed. So far, she'd only been a glow. The sasquatch came to mind again, that vague shadow in the brush, barely realized before it became unreal. Jonah knew, from his days with an imaginary friend, that the way to make such things real, and to keep them real, was to talk to them.

"You followed me," he said to the shape.

It managed a shrug.

"From Brooklyn, I mean. I saw you there. Or felt you there. In your room."

The shape huffed a heavy sigh that might have been exasperation and might have been more of whatever kept it bent over in that uncomfortable-looking position.

"Are you in pain?"

No answer.

"That was a stupid question," he said. "Who wouldn't be in pain after all of that? After what happened to you. What did happen to you?"

The shape had nothing to say. Most likely, Jonah thought, she didn't have the capacity to speak. Not yet. She was like a newborn. It would take time. She might not even know what had happened to her. She might have blocked it out, like a traumatic memory. He didn't want to upset her.

"That can wait," he said, "for another time." And he went back to his work, cutting out images from the lost world of the past, leaving the ghost shape alone to do what it needed to do.

7

On Sunday morning, under the Oliveris' magnolia tree, heavy with buds, Jonah and Vivian chatted while they worked in the yard for the second day in a row. Already they had cleaned out the front yard, pulling weeds from planters and picking up scraps of trash, and there was plenty more to keep them busy in the back. Autumn and winter had trampled the ground, littering it with leaves and brittle twigs, detritus blown in from the street—paper cups, candy bar wrappers, lost receipts, the refuse of neglected time.

"On Friday," Vivian explained, "he'll be crucified and next Sunday he'll rise from the dead, after three days in the grave." It was the beginning of Easter Week and she had spent the morning in church, coming home with a handful of fresh, young palm fronds.

"He died on Friday and rose on Sunday? That's only two days in the grave," Jonah said, moving a rust-colored rake across the patchy grass.

"He died and went into the ground on Friday. 'On the third day he rose again, in fulfillment of the Scriptures.' That's what they say in the Mass. Three days." Vivian paused to take a drag from her cigarette and consider these calculations. "All right, maybe not three *whole* days, but you can't be picky about these things. The point is, he died, he was buried, and he rose from the dead."

Vivian dropped a handful of twigs into the plastic garbage bag at her feet.

"My father doesn't believe in life after death," said Jonah. "He didn't, I mean."

"I do that, too. Talk like she's still here."

She is, he wanted to say, sensing Rose's foggy presence at the margin of the yard, watching.

Instead, he said, "My father was a scientist. Ashes to ashes and dust to dust. That was his motto."

"What about your mother?" Vivian asked. "She was a Catholic, wasn't she?"

She held open the garbage bag while Jonah filled it with crunchy, half-rotten leaves. The earthy smell of mud and decay returned him to his own backyard years ago, how it felt to lie in the cool grass and watch the autumn stars. He was comfortable here with Vivian. After just a short time, they had fallen into a way of relating that felt familiar. She told him to brush the leaf litter from his trousers and he did, slapping his knees as he explained, "My mother believed in everything. Ghosts. UFOs. Past lives. She loved magic shows, too. Especially the escape artists. You know those guys who tie themselves up with chains and hang upside down in tanks of water?"

"Sure I do. I used to see them out at Coney Island, in the summertime. Coney Island was wonderful in those days."

"What she loved about them, about the escape artists, was the thrill of seeing them submerged, barely struggling, in the seconds before their escape. She didn't want that moment to end. When they finally broke free, she'd be disappointed. Not that she wanted them to drown or anything. It wasn't that. She just, I don't know, she liked that underwater part. I can understand that. Before the guy gets in the water there's all this preparation. They make a big show of it. The straitjacket. The chains going around and around. Then, at the end, it's the big ta-da, he comes splashing out, gasping for air. But in the middle, everything is quiet. It looks like nothing is happening, but everything is happening. That's where the magic really is."

Vivian dipped the end of a green garden hose into her birdbath and filled it with clean, fresh water, flushing out the brown scum that had gathered there over the cold seasons.

"My mother had a psychic, too," Jonah continued, stopping his rake to watch the water fill the brown-stained bowl. "She believed in everything."

"I went to one. After 9/11," Vivian said. "An Italian lady out in Bay Ridge. I just showed her a picture of Rose and the lady said, 'You lost her in the World Trade Center, didn't you?' Just like that. How did she know? And then Rose's spirit came in the room. I couldn't see her or nothing, but she was talking and this lady could hear her. The lady said she was okay—I guess they always say that. But she said her spirit stayed around to help the other people down there. Ground Zero's loaded with lost souls, she says, people who can't let go. They just wander around down there in that hole, not knowing what to do with themselves. But Rose's spirit was strong and she stayed to help."

"That sounds like her," Jonah said. He had already told Vivian the story about skipping work to go to the movies, though he left out the part about their fingers mingling in the bucket of popcorn. "She was always helping other people. We worked with an older woman—Betty Lamb was her name—and one day Betty didn't come in to work. A week went by and no Betty. Rose asked about her and it turned out she wasn't a missing person. She'd had a stroke and couldn't work anymore. She didn't have close family, so Rose made a point to go to Betty's apartment and bring her groceries and magazines. Stuff like that. She sat with Betty and read to her. And then Betty died. But Rose was very good to her. She was just that way."

This was not entirely untruthful. There really was a Betty Lamb, a photo editor at *Boxboard Today*, who really did have a stroke and stopped working at the magazine. And Jonah did have a coworker who kept Betty company until her hastened death—but it wasn't Rose, it was another woman he had a crush on, a mousy proofreader named Debbie Moody with whom Jonah might have had a chance had he ever bothered to make conversation.

"I love to hear these stories," Vivian said. "It's like I'm getting to know another Rose, the girl I always knew was in there, but I never saw her. Not never. It's just—Rose was a very private girl. She didn't tell us much about her life. We never had the chance to be pals. I always thought, once she got older and matured, we'd have that chance. Now she's gone. She just left, too. She didn't even come back to haunt me. She just took off."

Jonah considered telling Vivian that her daughter was standing just yards away, slouching against the chain-link fence, but he didn't want to take the risk. He might just embarrass himself. And he wasn't sure if the presence that trailed him was the real Rose or his own created Rose, or something else altogether.

"Do you ever watch that show on the Sci-Fi Channel?" he asked. "The one where the guy talks to people who've passed over?"

"I love that show, but Frank hates it. He thinks it's all bullshit. He don't believe in nothing. He don't even believe he has a soul. Once you're gone, that's it, he says. It's depressing. You have to believe in something."

The birdbath was full of clean water now, overflowing onto the grass. Vivian pulled out the hose and let it run onto the threadbare lawn.

"Turn off the faucet, willya?"

Jonah walked back toward the house, carrying the bag full of leaves and twigs with him. He dropped the bag into a Rubbermaid barrel and turned off the spigot. It was cold and leaking, and he rubbed his gritty palms together to rinse them.

"It's back-breaking work, but I like cleaning up the yard in spring. Don't you?" Vivian said.

"I haven't had a yard in years."

"But I bet you helped your mother when you did."

"My father wasn't much for yard work."

"It's tough, doing it alone. Frank's useless. Useless. I can't fault the poor bastard, though. His back's no good, after working construction all his life. Did you know he built the towers? Well, he did. He was an ironworker and strong as an ox. He loved those buildings. Anyways. It feels good to clean it up."

Vivian reached into the pocket of her jacket, the teal and pink nylon top of a jogging suit, and pulled out a pack of cigarettes. She put one in her mouth and lit it, took a drag, and surveyed her modest property. A few spindly trees, a chain-link fence, the birdbath, and a small garden struggling to come back to life. Jonah tried to imagine a younger, more agile Frank climbing the towers when they were still skeletal, nothing but I-beams. He thought of a famous black-and-white photo of Depression-era ironworkers lunching on a girder, lined up like birds on a telephone wire. Recently, an enterprising artist had turned the photo into a life-size sculpture and started carting it all over town on a red, white, and blue-painted flat-bed truck.

"After that day," Vivian said, "this whole yard was full of dust. It was all white. Like snow. I couldn't even come out here. Couldn't stand to leave the house. Frank cleaned it up, with this hose. I didn't want him to, neither. It's stupid, but I thought, maybe, a little bit of Rose was in there. In the ashes, you know? Now isn't that ridiculous? Ach." She waved her hand in the air. "Frank just washed it all away."

The hose gurgled at her feet as the water stopped running and she bent to pick it up. She shook it, throwing silver droplets into the air.

"He saved the papers, though. This place was loaded with papers. They came down out of the sky like confetti at a ticker-tape parade. All kinds of papers. Business cards. Letters. Nothing important. Just office junk. But Frank, he saved it all. Said it might be important to the FBI. Please. What does the FBI want with someone's business cards? He took a bunch of it down to the precinct. I don't think it helped any investigation. But, hey, if it makes him feel useful, who am I to say? I thought maybe I'd save some of the ashes. Scoop them up in a little medicine bottle or something. Is that morbid? Anyways, I didn't do it. Now they're giving all us families some ashes from the site. In an urn and the whole nine yards. It was the mayor's idea. I don't want it. She's not in there. I mean, not for nothing, but what's the chance? Three thousand people, plus all that other junk from the buildings. The urn I get? Probably it's gonna be filled with ashes from some other mother's kid. And then she'll get my Rose. It's all mixed up. Everybody's gonna be confused. They should just leave it alone. Let it be."

"I have my mother's ashes," Jonah said.

"You're lucky. You know where she is."

"You really don't want the urn?"

"Let the mayor keep it. Frank says he don't want it either, but he's full of shit—he kept most of the papers that fell in this yard. He's still got them hidden away somewhere. Up in his bird cages, I bet. He pretends like he's not sentimental, but you'd be surprised. He can be a real pack rat when he wants to be."

Vivian looked down at the garden hose still in her hand, its dark mouth dribbling water. She doused her cigarette in the spout, then tossed the butt behind her. "Come on, help me get this hose away."

Jonah took the hose from Vivian and wound it around the length of his forearm, looping it over his elbow and the crook of his thumb, while Vivian walked to the house, wiping her wet hands on the back of her slacks, leaving dark prints on the shiny, synthetic material.

"When you're done, come in and clean up, and we'll drive out to Costco's," she called to him before disappearing through the kitchen door.

The Rose shape by the fence had vanished. Jonah looked up at the blue sky and saw a few dark silhouettes overhead, clapping their fast, flickering wings before coming to rest on the Oliveris' roof. He wondered if they were Frank's birds or just anonymous neighborhood pigeons, unnamed and unloved, intruding on the domesticated brood above. He thought, for a moment, that he saw Frank looking back down at him, but in the glare of the sun, he couldn't be sure.

He picked up the rake and shovel and put them away, grabbed the box of three-ply garbage bags, and went inside to wash his hands. In the kitchen he saw Frank for the first time all weekend, standing in front of the refrigerator, hypnotized by something on the door. From the hallway, Jonah watched him silently, again trying to imagine him, big-bellied in his sweatpants and slippers, tiptoeing across a steel girder one hundred stories above the city. What was it like, he wondered, knowing your daughter died in something you built?

As if he could feel Jonah's thoughts intruding on his own, Frank looked up and startled.

"What you want, to give a guy a heart attack?"

"I was just washing my hands," said Jonah, moving to the sink.

"So wash 'em already. Nobody likes a spy," Frank said, lumbering away with a bottle of beer in his hand. As Jonah dried his hands on a dishtowel, he looked at the refrigerator door. Under a magnet in the shape of a watermelon slice hung a photograph of Rose. It was from an Instamatic camera and had a thick white border. In the blank space at the bottom, written in silver Magic Marker, it read, "Me: 12th birthday." Her hair pulled back in a ponytail, she was wearing faded blue jeans and an athletic jersey with the number twelve printed on the chest. Her expression was impatient, but playful. A silly hurry-up-and-take-the-picture-so-we-can-go kind of look, her eyes wide, her mouth just about to break into smile. Under her arm, a football waited to be tossed into the hands of the man behind the camera.

The parking lot of the Costco warehouse club in Sunset Park was filled with cars—big, thirsty American cars with names that yearned for a world beyond the urban, for the Rocky Mountains and Serengeti plains, for the endlessness of uncharted territories: Navigator and Range Rover, Pathfinder and Explorer, Outback and Avalanche. Now and then, they dispensed with metaphor and just shouted the dream out loud: Escape. This must have been what each driver wanted from the vehicle, to escape the world of pavements and sidewalks, streetlights and stop signs. To go native. To go wild. Mountaineer, Trailblazer, Yukon. In the television commercials, Jonah had seen these same vehicles fording whitewater rivers, driving herds of cattle across the open ranges, climbing the vertical slopes of Mount Kilimanjaro. The vehicles in Costco's parking lot seemed to shout that the people who drove them resented city life. They were lovers of nature, and bought these tons of metal and plastic and rubber to make them feel connected to the lost, unspoiled world outside the city. Was that what the woman on the Jersey Turnpike had wanted just before the explosion, before the rollover and the crash, before everything burst? Was she a lover of nature? Jonah felt relieved to be riding in a Lincoln Town Car. A conveyance for the city, uptown and down, it made no pretense about being a creature of the natural world. It knew where it belonged.

Vivian circled and circled, weaving through the lot, looking for a spot close to the entrance. She didn't like to walk. Nobody liked to walk. All the nearby spots were filled.

"I saw a bunch of empty spaces toward the back," Jonah offered.

"I want to get close."

"I read in a magazine that, if you just parked further away from the entrance when you went to the store, and walked the rest of the way, you could burn about a thousand extra calories a week," Jonah said, recalling his latest Mediacom men's room reading.

"What are you saying, I need to burn calories now?" Vivian asked as she sidled up to a black Cadillac Escalade with its back hatch wide open, a man and a woman stuffing the cavernous cargo hold full of family-sized products: a 16-roll case of Softique toilet paper, a 200-ounce jug of Tide Clean Breeze laundry detergent, a gallon of Windex, three 28-packs of Duracell AA alkaline batteries, 66 pounds of Fresh Step clumping kitty litter, 72 cans of Friskies Buffet (in the variety pack), one Michelin steel-belted radial tire, and a 100% wool imitation Persian-design rug.

"Wouldn't it save time if you just parked back there and walked? Instead of lurking around the lot?" Jonah instantly wished he had not used the word "lurking."

"Who's lurking? I'm waiting. I wish these people would hurry the hell up."

A new Volkswagen Beetle in candy-apple red approached from the opposite direction and slowed down.

"Don't even think about it, sweetheart, this is my spot," Vivian said, eyeing the driver. When the Beetle came to a stop, Vivian pointed to the Escalade, then to herself, mouthing the word "mine" so the other driver would understand. The man and woman closed their hatch and got into the SUV. Jonah watched their taillights turn red, then white as the man put the vehicle into reverse. Vivian gripped the steering wheel and readied herself, her sneaker hovering over the gas pedal.

The Escalade eased out of the parking space, backing up, then breaking, backing up, then breaking. The passenger looked out her window and Vivian gestured to her, pointing at their spot. The woman smiled and turned to her husband, filling the window with a cloud of yellow hair. A moment later, she turned back with a serious look and gave Vivian the "okay" sign. The fix was in. The Escalade pulled out to the left, forcing the driver of the Beetle to back up, then the Escalade stopped and idled, blocking the Beetle and giving Vivian the time she needed to maneuver her ample Town Car into the space.

"How do you like that?" Vivian said as she stopped just short of the yellow cement parking block. She stuck her hand out of the open window and waved a thank you to the couple in the Escalade, who honked their horn and roared away with their load of booty.

"Thank God there's still some Americans left in America," she said.

Jonah turned to look at the Beetle. Inside was a gaggle of teenage girls, dressed in tank tops and blowing pink bubbles of Bubblicious gum. They looked angry and they weren't leaving.

"That car is still back there," he said.

Vivian glanced up into the rearview mirror. "I'm not afraid of them." She pressed the button to close the automatic windows, turned off the car, and grabbed her turquoise faux-crocodile purse.

"Come on," she said. "*Andiamo.*"

Jonah didn't move.

"What are you, afraid of a bunch of girls? Teenagers are like dogs, they can smell fear. Let's go."

They got out of the car and closed the doors. The driver of the Beetle, a skinny girl with her dark hair pulled back into a tight ponytail, called out, "Hey, bitch!" She hung her arm out of the open window, dangling her middle finger toward the asphalt. "Didn't you hear me? Or do you need me to turn it up?" She rotated her hand so the middle finger was now pointing toward the sky. An eruption of laughter spilled from the car and the music they were playing, a thundering percussive rhythm, got louder as they peeled away, toward the available spaces at the back of the lot.

"They're young," Vivian said. "They can walk it."

They stepped into the cool air of Costco, where Vivian flashed her member card to the greeter inside the door. The woman looked almost military in her official red smock covered with patriotic buttons adorned with the slogans: "These Colors Don't Run," "United We Stand," "God Bless

America," and one with a photo of Osama Bin Laden wielding an automatic weapon and encircled by the words "9/11/01 Never Forget, Never Forgive." The greeter also had a hole in her throat where her trachea used to be. As Jonah and Vivian passed, she pressed an electrolarynx speech aid under her chin and said, in a robotic voice, "Welcome to Costco." Then she waved the electrolarynx like a wand, with a royal flourish, as if she were salaaming her guests into the Taj Mahal.

Inside, Jonah immediately lost his sense of place. He wasn't sure where he was. It didn't feel like New York. It didn't feel like Brooklyn. It could have been anywhere else in America. Everything was too big to be New York. The shopping carts had room enough to carry a small refrigerator, a twenty-pound tank of propane, a metal rooster lawn ornament ("This cock of the walk has a lot to crow about"), and a dozen packages of Fruit of the Loom underwear. Indeed, this was the exact combination of items Jonah saw rolling past him as he walked in. The shoppers, too, were super-sized, hefting their bulk down aisles as wide as Jonah's street, stopping at every intersection to taste a free sample of Peter Piper's Pumpkin Potstickers, Pizza-Bagel Buddies, Delimex Beef Taquitos, Polish kielbasa, and 100% bison meat Buffaloes-in-a-Blanket.

"Costco buys and sells fifty percent of the world's supply of cashews," Jonah offered.

"Did you read that in a magazine, too?"

"The only product they have that outsells cashews is toilet paper."

"I love cashews," Vivian said, hefting a two-and-a-half-pound plastic jug of Kirkland Signature nuts from its laden palette. She dropped the jug into an empty, abandoned shopping cart. "I eat them like they're going out of business. Drive, willya?"

Jonah took the cart in hand. In this Brobdingnagian world, he felt like a cipher, slipping behind Vivian as her dusky shadow. She moved through the warehouse like she owned it. This was her territory and she tasted everything, even helping herself to a few green grapes in the produce aisle that were not offered as free samples. Jonah glanced around to see if anyone was watching, but no store detective descended.

"Let me buy you some new clothes," Vivian said, eyeing Jonah's dark thrift-store trousers. "Something with a little color maybe."

"I don't know."

"For helping me out with the yard work. Come on. You worked hard all weekend."

"You've done enough. Inviting me into your home, feeding me. It's too much. Really."

"You're a friend of Rosie's. Come on, let's take a look." Vivian took Jonah by the arm, in the tender spot just above the elbow, and steered him—and the cart—with the forceful skill of a mother who had spent years not taking no for an answer.

In the men's section, the shirts on display were resplendent, flower-splashed sails billowing high up on the metal-rack shelving, enough fabric to carry a schooner around the world and back again. The pants, too, were built for suburban Paul Bunyans, their axes retired, their fists swinging long-handled barbecue forks and spatulas through the chemical-green backyards of their final days. Jonah blanched at the sight. Not a single scrap of fabric was in a color or pattern he would ever dream of wearing. A favorite line from an old Smiths song came into his head, swimming back to him from adolescence: "I wear black on the outside 'cause black is how I feel on the inside."

"Dockers look so nice on men," Vivian said, holding up to Jonah's waist a robin's-egg-blue pair with a double-pleated front.

"They're a little colorful."

"All you got is old pants with the cuffs falling down. You look like a *mamaluc*. You don't like these? They're nice pants."

"Sure I like them," Jonah lied. "They're very nice pants."

"Good. They're yours," Vivian said, dropping the Dockers into the cart. "See anything else? How about some socks? And don't give me an argument."

"I could use some socks. Maybe the ones with the reinforced toes."

Vivian dropped three packages of black socks into the cart, making Jonah aware of a sudden satisfaction, and though he was unable to identify it as the feeling of being taken care of, he felt it just the same.

"Now. Remind me," Vivian said. "What did we come here for again?"

"The Backyard Entertainment Pit," Jonah said. Vivian had shown him a picture of it in her Costco catalog. The pit was a filigreed copper urn, on curled iron legs, that you filled with "Entertainment Logs" and "Fashionable Lava Rocks" to create an "Authentic Roman-style Outdoor Fireplace Experience." Jonah wasn't sure what that meant. As well as viaducts and sewers, did the Romans invent outdoor fireplaces? Maybe the copywriter intended to say "outdoor campfire," instead of "fireplace," in which case the word "outdoor" would be unnecessary. And were the Romans known for their fashionable and entertaining campfires? He didn't think so.

They located the pit in the yard section of the warehouse, which was well stocked, considering the relative yardlessness of New Yorkers. Even in Brooklyn, where many people had small backyards, it didn't seem possible that there would be much demand for "Titantic-style" teak reclining deck chairs and picnic tables topped with enormous, fringed umbrellas. But demand must have been high, because there was only one authentic Roman-style Backyard Entertainment Pit left on the wooden palette.

"Jesus," Vivian said, "this looks like the last one. Hurry, before somebody grabs it."

The box it came in had a full-color photo on it, featuring a happy family seated around the pit on Titanic-style deck chairs, lifting their nuclear-fruit-colored drinks in the air and saying, "Bring the warmth of inside—out!" Jonah wrapped his arms around the box and lifted it, careful to bend at the knees, and secured it in the cart.

Their work done for the day, they sat down to a Costco feast. At the food court, surrounded by the cacophony of electronic cash registers beeping and children screaming in rattling shopping carts, they drank berry smoothies and ate steaming-hot Chicken Bakes—Costco's copyrighted mixture of chicken, bacon, melted cheese, and Caesar salad dressing, wrapped in a foot-long cocoon of dough. The plastic picnic table they sat at was protected by a broad red umbrella advertising Hebrew National kosher franks ("We answer to a higher authority"). The umbrella was superfluous, Jonah thought. They were indoors, where neither sun nor rain could assail them. The umbrella only shielded them from the ultraviolet rays floating down from the fluorescent lights above. He listened to their somnolent hum and took a bite out of his Chicken Bake.

"Didn't I tell you this Chicken Bake was something else?"

Jonah took a long, silent sip of his ice-cold smoothie to soothe his burning tongue.

"Sometimes I come here just for the Chicken Bake," Vivian said. "I don't even shop. I just come straight into the food court and order a Chicken Bake. To go. But, once in a while, I'll sit and eat. Rose never came with me. She said she wouldn't be caught dead in this place."

Jonah put down his smoothie, furrowed his brow, and pinched the bridge of his nose with his thumb and finger. "Brain freeze."

"Don't drink so fast. You drink too fast. Slow down."

"It's going away now."

"I don't mind eating alone," Vivian said. "Sometimes I see people I know. Old friends. They stop and say hello, then they keep right on walking. You wouldn't believe how many friends I lost. You think, when you lose a child, your close friends are going to come even closer. But after a while, they get tired of hearing about it. They don't want to come too close. Like death is catchy. People are stupid. They ask how I'm doing but they don't want to know. I tell them I'm fine. That's all. Forget about it."

Jonah nodded, wiping his mouth with a paper napkin.

"But how can I forget," Vivian continued. "Six months and I should forget already? You lost your parents, and that's a terrible, terrible thing, don't get me wrong, but a child is another story. I still have nightmares. Terrible nightmares about falling buildings and my Rose falling into fire, like Hell. I reach out, but she slips away. And then everything comes crashing down. It's like I'm right there. The floor just drops, right out from under my feet. I jump in my sleep. In the bed, I jump. Wake up with my heart going like crazy—ba-da-boom, ba-da-boom, ba-da-boom. It's like Frank used to do, after Korea. He'd wake up shouting about going over some hill. Then he'd try to jump out the friggin' window. Only with me, it's like I'm falling a million stories, and I can't stop. It's awful. But I'm all right. It still hurts like a sonovabitch, don't misunderstand me, but I'm all right."

The cash registers, all twenty-five of them, beeped and blipped in their electronic language. The crank on a gumball machine gnashed its teeth and spat out a tiny toy handgun, hermetically sealed in a plastic globe. A jumbo Coca-Cola fell to the floor of the food court in a clatter of ice cubes and fizzing dark syrup.

"I still see her everywhere I go," Vivian said. "You see that girl over there, by the jewelry? She's not as pretty as Rose, but she looks like her, a little bit. Out of the corner of my eye, when I look at her, I see Rose. It's not a terrible feeling, seeing someone who looks like her, just for a second. It's like having her here. Just for a second."

Jonah looked over to the jewelry counter to see a Rose standing there, resting her palms on the edge of the case, tapping her fingernails on the glass. He watched her, the gold anklet that looped around her slender ankle, the way she jiggled it, one foot in the air, while she browsed among the necklaces and earrings. He missed Rose, too. He knew it wasn't the same for him, not like it was for the woman who sat across from him, sipping her berry smoothie and watching, too, this woman neither of them knew, but who conjured, for them both, memories of another. For Vivian, the memories were substantial. A lifetime of memories, of birthday cakes and temper tantrums, prom dresses and picnics, and everyday little scenes in front of the television or sunbathing in the backyard. For Jonah, there wasn't much. Passing moments on the street. A single instant of near-touching, her red glove in his hand, her voice on the air: "I've got it." That's all. It wasn't much. No—it was less than that. It was nothing. He wanted more.

"It is like seeing Rose, standing there," he said.

"But not as pretty."

"No," Jonah agreed, "not as pretty."

There was something in his eyes, a struggling look that betrayed him.

"You loved her," Vivian said.

He nodded.

She took his hand. "Poor Jonah."

"There was one time. At the office," he said, watching the Costco employee mopping spilled Coke from the food court floor. "I dropped—I fell. I slipped on some ice cubes in the kitchen. She gave me her hand. She helped me up. And I had cut my finger on, I don't know, on the file folders I was carrying. A really bad paper cut. She took my hand, put my finger under the running water, and pressed a clean napkin to it. To stop the blood. She was so gentle. That was the moment. I fell in love with her."

Vivian shook her head, her eyes watering.

"I'm amazed," she said. "I never knew she could be like that. Maybe as a little girl, sometimes, but once she hit high school? She was—I don't know how to put it, but gentle's not the word. You don't know how much it means to me, having you here and telling me these things."

Jonah looked down at his lunch. No longer hot from the microwave, the cheese had stiffened geographically against the paper plate to form a wavering coastline, with isthmuses and spits where his teeth had torn the landscape. He hated himself for telling lies to this woman, this heartbroken mother who trusted him. He was greedy and selfish and ought to be punished.

"I'll never forget her," he said.

"No. You can't," Vivian patted his hand. "But it'll get better. Every day, it'll get a little better. Won't it?"

"I think so."

"Now eat your Chicken Bake," Vivian said. "It's getting cold."

8

"BIG APPLE ON ORANGE ALERT: Area synagogues under heightened security for Passover holiday." Jonah stopped to read the front pages at the Al-Habib newsstand while Frankie wound herself around his legs, tangling her leash. At the bridges and tunnels, squads of Hazmat officers were spot-checking trucks and vans, searching for hazardous materials. "Hazmat" had a certain ring to it. It sounded like the name of a Hebrew prophet. He pronounced the word out loud, with a phlegmy H and two long A's: "Chahzmaht." To Rose's ghost beside him he said, "And Jehoshaphat begat Nebat and Nebat begat Hazor and Hazor begat Hazmat, and so began the Book of Hazmat." She smiled obligingly. She was coming into being, her foggy edges more focused.

The bearded newsvendor watched him with suspicion from inside the cluttered shop. NO READING read a handwritten sign taped inside the bulletproof window between advertisements for a special sale on duct tape and No-Rad radiation pills. Jonah untangled Frankie from his legs and walked on. Duct tape and radiation pills. They were selling out fast all over town. People wanted to be ready for a "chemical release event." Jonah didn't bother. If a dirty bomb did explode, he explained to Rose, it would release radioactive materials like cesium 137 and strontium 90, not iodine, and those little pills would be useless. As for sealing up the windows on his apartment, he doubted if duct tape and plastic sheeting could produce a truly airtight chamber; and if it did, what would happen once his supply of oxygen ran out? His only survivalist move was to keep in his backpack one transistor radio, four fresh AA batteries, and two small bags of almonds. Almonds, he figured, were full of protein and would keep him alive for a while if he was trapped in an air pocket under a collapsed building. *Is that how it was for you*, he asked Rose, but she didn't like to remember that day. And she still wasn't talking.

In the window of Moishe's Kosher Bake Shop the silver trays were empty of pastries, the hamentaschen and rugalach evacuated to secure shelters somewhere in the back. Paper doilies sprinkled with crumbs lay naked and bereft under a hand-lettered sign: CLOSED FOR PASSOVER. Jonah didn't know much about the holiday. He had experienced a seder only a few times, early in life, when his father's mother was still alive. He remembered salt water and boiled eggs, and being frightened by a ghost who came through the door in a cold gust to sit down to supper beside him. Still it was nice to get out of work early, to have some hours of daylight to himself. Being half Jewish had its perks. There was time yet before the Angel of Death would come swooping down, searching for firstborn sons to liquidate. Instead, a big seagull, strayed from the harbor, glided over Second Avenue. Startling in its size and whiteness, it cruised the air predator-style, eyeing a mangled slice of pizza that lay like roadkill on the asphalt.

"Did you hear? Al Qaeda is planning another hijacking," said an elderly man hobbling past.

"Where'd you hear that?" asked his companion.

"Don't you watch the news?"

"What's the use? It's all the same. Any minute, we could all go up in flames."

A fire truck turned the corner and wailed down the avenue, flashing its red lights and sending the seagull into the air, winging its way back toward the salty harbor.

"See that?" asked the second man, smacking a pack of cigarettes against his palm.

"See what?"

"It's already happening."

Jonah and the dog continued down East Sixth Street, Rose's ghost following behind, dragging her feet. It seemed to Jonah that she didn't really want to be there, as if she had better things to do, but had no choice, like a girl brought along on parental errands when she'd rather be home watching television. They passed the open back door of a Chinese restaurant kitchen, the aroma of fried pork salting the air, and then the Community Synagogue, a red brick building that had once been a Lutheran Church whose congregation perished with the steamboat *General Slocum* in 1904, the worst disaster in New York's history until 9/11. The Synagogue was quiet, but Jonah hurried past, as he hurried past all synagogues these days, imagining he could hear the ticking of a terrorist bomb. He passed his building and moved on to Avenue A, where he tied Frankie's leash to a parking meter and stepped inside San Loco. Rose stayed with the dog while he ordered two Guaco Loco tacos from the girl behind the counter, a sort of punk-rock Latina who mixed black leather and spikes with spit curls and gold hoop earrings that announced her name to the world in swirling script, "Blanca." While he waited, a young woman with WASP-blonde hair and low-slung jeans walked in carrying a tiny, tremulous Chihuahua against her breast. He watched as Blanca asked her to please take the dog outside.

"What are you talking about," said the woman, letting her mouth go slack with contempt. "You're saying I can't bring my dog in here?"

Blanca pointed to the prominent sign on the door and told her about the health code that enforced the law.

"Okay, but this is a *teacup* dog? That means she's super small? So I have the right to take her wherever I want," said the woman. "I'll have one burrito with chipotle chicken and black beans, no rice—too many carbs—with guac and tofu sour cream *on the side*. Last time, you didn't put it on the side and I had to throw the whole thing in the trash."

"We don't have tofu sour cream," said Blanca, "and you gotta take that dog out."

"I thought we settled that," said the woman. "I spend a lot of money in here."

The two of them exchanged stares, each daring the other to make a move. The Chihuahua trembled with Parkinsonian fervor. The glitter dust on the woman's skin sparked in the overhead light, making her face metallic. Blanca's wrist chains chimed as she opened and closed her fist over a bowl of Saran-wrapped Rice Krispie treats. The woman's cell phone screamed in her back pocket, making her jump. She slid it out and flicked it open with her free hand.

"Perfect timing," she said to the caller. "Listen to this. I'm trying to get a burrito and this beyotch is telling me I can't take Paris in here. I'm getting *takeout* for Chrissake. I have a right to bring Paris with me wherever I go. She's *small*. She's a *teacup*. That's *allowed*. I am going to write a letter to the management. Oh yeah. She'll be out on her ass by next week."

"You want to throw my ass out right now?" Blanca countered, shaking her finger in the air. "Come on, bitch, let's go. Let's go."

"I don't need this harassment," the woman shouted into her phone before Blanca could climb over the counter. "I know the rules! She's a fucking *teacup!* Forget it. The food in here is all contaminated anyway, like with mad cow disease."

Jonah considered sticking out his foot to trip her as she headed to the door, but did not give in to the impulse, as delicious as it would have been to see her go toppling headfirst onto the sidewalk. His Guaco Locos were ready. He put an extra dollar in Blanca's tip jar while the woman stood on the sidewalk, still screaming, "Mad cow disease! They have mad cow disease!"

Deep inside Tompkins Square Park, the light was still blue and the trees had a greenish aura about them, a trembling, urgent idea of green that soon would solidify into leaf. Under black elms, homeless men and women squabbled over cigarettes. They were dressed surprisingly well. Wearing the tossed-away clothing of the newest East Villagers, two long-haired men sported New York Sports Club t-shirts, a junkie nodded out in Ralph Lauren, and a teetering crack whore carried a Prada handbag that had seen better days.

Jonah released Frankie from her leash inside the gates of the dog run. As she went sprinting off into a melee of fur and happy slobber, he sat down on a bench with Rose at his side and watched the dogs at play. There was an odd abundance of French bulldogs, the newest dog-of-the-moment. He saw them all over the East Village now. He explained to Rose that some telepathic message must have gone out to the people who cared about things like dogs-of-the-moment, and they each ran out and bought one. Maybe there had been a hit movie recently that starred this dog. Maybe the animal was featured in a prominent advertising campaign for $200 designer jeans. Maybe a hot celebrity was seen walking one of them on the up-and-coming Bowery, stepping over the bums. Whatever it was, the tipping point had tipped and the French bulldog was in. That meant that the beagle, in particular, was out. Just a year before, the beagle was the "it" dog and the neighborhood was filled with young beagles, happily flapping their floppy ears, unaware that their day in the sun would be all too short. Jonah muttered out loud, "Where have all the beagles gone?" He imagined the new East Villagers bringing their passé beagles back to the pet stores, hauling them into the ASPCA, abandoning them on street corners like they did with everything else they had grown tired of. Like the countless dumpster babies of America, the beagles of New York City were cast away, set to drift among the reeds or "put to sleep" in the back rooms of veterinarian offices. "We just can't handle him anymore," the owners opined, "we just bought white carpets," all the while secretly planning their purchase of a $2,000 French bulldog, the perfect accessory to go with those new shoes. But even now, Jonah could see, the fickle trend was shifting again. The future was coming in fast and the French bulldog was on its way out of favor. More and more, creeping in at the very margins of coolness, Jonah was seeing Chihuahuas—perched shivering in the muscled arms of gay men, peeking out from the thousand-dollar handbags of emaciated women, creating havoc in taco joints. *Mark my words*, he said to Rose, *by this time next year, the cramped cages at Petco's rescue center will be filled to capacity with out-of-style French bulldogs.* Rose appeared unimpressed by his prognostication.

A woman standing nearby had been watching him with interest. He could see her only peripherally. He wasn't sure what of his dog diatribe he had kept inside his head and what he had said out loud. He had also been making hand gestures.

Now he straightened his posture, feeling the woman's curious gaze on him. Rose's ghost fidgeted on the bench.

Go, she said.

Her first word.

Go.

Jonah couldn't gauge her tone. Was she jealous? Or did she want to get rid of him, unload him on another woman like those people did with their dogs?

Is that what you did, he silently asked Rose, *when pugs were all the rage?*

All the rage. Rose wrinkled her nose. She didn't like that expression.

Were they fighting? He didn't understand how a figment of his own imagination, with such a limited vocabulary, could be so disagreeable. It was his fault. He was being judgmental. Before he could take back his comment, the woman who'd been watching him walked over and stood in front of him.

"I know you," she said.

He recognized her now as the girl from the loft party. The lollipop girl. Had he just said that out loud?

"You could call me that, I guess, but my name's Jane."

She sat down on the bench beside him. He worried she would sit on top of Rose, but the ghost was gone. He looked across the dog run and didn't see her anywhere. Her sudden leaving felt like a rebuke, but he hadn't done anything. He hadn't invited Jane to sit. Jane with her rhinestoned cat-eye glasses and the Louise Brooksian wedge of bangs that glistened on her forehead like a black silk cap. The beauty mark, he could see now, was real.

"So. Which one's yours?" she asked, looking out at the circus of dogs, kicking up the pungent dust.

"The pug. The yellow one right there. Her name's Frankie."

"Cute. Mine's that big oaf sniffing around the French bulldog over there."

"Which French bulldog?"

"I know, right? They're like an infestation. Siggy! Siggy!"

She put two fingers in the corners of her mouth and emitted an impressive ear-piercing whistle. A golden-brown Bullmastiff came loping over to nuzzle his black muzzle against her bare knees. Jane lifted her skirt to keep Siggy from slavering all over it, revealing to Jonah the lacy hem of a black satin slip. He hoped Rose, wherever she was, didn't notice.

"This is Sigmund Freud. But you can call him Siggy."

Jonah put out his hand and Siggy slobbered on it before galloping away to join a daisy chain of sniffing already in progress. Jonah held up his hand, a viscous string of slobber cats-cradled between his fingers. Jane clucked her tongue softly in her mouth and pulled a tissue out of her purse, a clear Lucite box through which Jonah could see lipsticks, pens, cigarettes, folded-up scraps of paper, and lollipops.

"New dog? I haven't seen you here before."

"Yeah," Jonah said, uneasily permitting Jane to take his wrist with one hand and, with the other, wipe his fingers clean. "Thanks. I just got her. Never had one before."

"Well, they're a little piece of Heaven, now ain't they?" she said, in a joking hillbilly accent that made Jonah feel embarrassed. There was a Spanish expression for that feeling. Embarrassment on behalf of another. But he couldn't remember it.

"Yeah," was all he said.

They sat a while without talking, just watching the dogs. It was a pleasure, this dog watching. To enjoy the sight of them in unashamed dogginess, snuffling and sniffing, jumping and humping. Jonah could not stop being aware of Jane's bare legs.

He ventured a question. "Why Sigmund Freud? Your dog, I mean."

"I'm in training to be a psychoanalyst," Jane said. "I know, it's kind of a cliché."

"What is?"

"An analyst naming her dog Sigmund. It's so predictable."

Jonah tried to think of a clever response or a good follow-up question. "Tell me more about your psychological training," he said.

"Psychoanalytic, not psychological. It's very different. I love it. It's something I should've done years ago, but I wasted so much time."

"Doing what?"

"It's a long story. Are you sure you want to hear it?"

"Sure," Jonah said.

With a deep breath, like she was about to launch into an aria, Jane began, telling Jonah how she'd completed her master's degree in social work and now she was "going on with it," training at one of the psychoanalytic institutes on the Upper West Side.

"I changed careers midstream," she explained. "I bounced around in book publishing for a while, eventually taking a job as the assistant to a very powerful literary agent. Marcia. She had an enormous apartment, an eight-room, three-bathroom floor-through overlooking the Hudson River, largely subsidized by the runaway sales of how-to books on living the Buddhist way. I thought I'd be reading manuscripts, writing critiques, taking authors to lunch and all that. But I was starting from the bottom all over again. I was not only Marcia's office assistant, I was her *personal* assistant. Her 'gal Friday,' she liked to say. Jeez Louise, right? She had me pick up her dry cleaning. Sent me shopping for pantyhose. Had me buy psyllium husks for her constipated bowels. She was so anally fixated. I wouldn't be surprised if she was a total coprophiliac. She loved to talk about bowels—her bowels, my bowels, the dogs' bowels. After I walked her dogs, a pair of Afghan Hounds, Basil and Bashira—she called them her 'children' because she didn't have any children of her own— after I walked these hounds each day, picking up their shit in little baggies, Marcia would grill me on the texture. 'Was it soft,' she'd ask me, 'like soft-serve ice cream? Or more like rocky road?' That is a direct quote."

Jane paused for effect before plunging on. "She also had cats. Three cats. Of course, her palatial home was big enough for all these animals. They had their own bathroom, all to themselves. One of the cats, Minxie, was suffering from PTSD. Post-traumatic stress disorder? She kept peeing on the sofa, so Marcia had me find a feline psychiatrist. I never imagined that such a person even existed, but there's actually more than one in Manhattan. So I called this feline psychiatrist and made an appointment for Minxie. 'Dr. Dave.' He was a veterinarian with a Ph.D. in psychology. After one session, Dr. Dave prescribed a daily psychotropic cocktail of catnip and Valium and recommended that Minxie be kept in a locked room, away from the other animals. He also made an audiotape of his session with the cat. The tape was for the cat, so Minxie could listen to it during the day when she was feeling anxious in her locked room. I had to go out and buy a special tape player that ran on continuous loop. Every morning, I went into that locked room to set up this tape and give Minxie her Valium. Have you ever tried to give a cat Valium? I'd go in there and have to listen to the feline psychiatrist's voice, on the tape player, saying Minxie's name over and over again, cooing in falsetto, 'Minxie, Minxie, Minxie, Minxie, Minxie...

what a nice kitty you are. What a beautiful kitty,' as if the cat was suffering from low self-esteem and could understand the meaning of words like 'nice' and 'beautiful.' Anyway. So, to get the Valium into this cat, I had to stick my fingers in the corners of her mouth, kind of wedge it open, then throw the pill down her throat. She'd spit it up, and I'd have to do it all over again. Again and again, until finally she swallowed the thing. This went on, I don't know, for months. But the cat wasn't getting better. She was getting worse. Totally decompensating. She started peeing on the carpets, too."

"Then one morning, there's no Minxie. 'Where's Minxie?' I ask. Marcia is silent. Tight-lipped. 'What happened to Minxie?' And Marcia says, without a tear in her eye, 'I had to have her put to sleep.' Can you imagine? She says it broke her heart and everything, but she just couldn't take it anymore, I mean, what about her bazillion-dollar carpets?"

Jonah said, "People are always getting rid of pets to save their carpets."

"Right? Like you were saying earlier, about the French bulldogs? It's so true."

He felt himself blush to know he had been talking out loud, but Jane didn't notice.

"It's a real problem," she continued. "So, anyway, I quit. Right on the spot. I just walked out. What a great feeling. Then I moped around for a while, trying to figure out what to do next. I went into a deep depression. You know, medication, suicidal ideation, the whole works. I decompensated. Then I decided to go for my social work degree and become a shrink myself—for people, not cats. I did my internship working with Holocaust survivors. I'll tell you, that's the way to get your priorities in order. Talk about perspective. Some old lady's sitting across from you, telling you how she was gang-raped by Nazis, and suddenly, all your stupid problems and your whining about bigger apartments and better furniture just fly out the window. I never felt better in my life."

Jane stopped and looked at Jonah. He felt her waiting for him to say something, but he couldn't think of anything. He was dazzled by the amount of talking she was able to sustain.

"I know it's a cliché," Jane said, "but it makes me feel purposeful. Fulfilled. You could say I did it for Minxie. Well, the human equivalents of Minxie. The poor, the marginalized, you know—the yearning to breathe free."

They fell silent again. Jonah didn't know how to respond. Jane apologized, explaining, "I tend to talk a lot when I'm nervous. Like around men."

Men. Did she mean him? He mustered a response, saying, "I guess you love animals. You've been coming to the dog run for a while?"

"Since Siggy was a pup."

"What can you tell me about that femur?" he asked, pointing to the large wooden carving of a bone that stood upright in the muddy center of the dog run.

"Used to be a tree. Oak, I think. Maybe elm. It was a wonderful shade tree, then it died. I'm not sure how. Dutch elm blight. Soil compaction, maybe, from all the little feet running circles around it for so long."

Jonah heard himself say, "Might it have been the doing of the Asian Longhorned Beetle?"

Just the day before, he had found a yellow flyer stuck to his front door from APHIS, the Animal and Plant Health Inspection Service, warning residents about the annual springtime appearance of the Asian Longhorned Beetle, a.k.a. the starry sky beetle, Latin name: *Anoplophora glabripennis*. On the flyer, there was a picture of a shiny black creature with white spots and long antennae striped like tiger tails, along with a description of the Longhorned's history and behavior, and the following request: "If you see a beetle that resembles the Asian Longhorned, please call right away. SAVE TREES! KNOW THE SIGNS OF ALB!"

"The only beetles I know anything about are John, Paul, George, and Ringo," said Jane in a Cockney accent that reflushed Jonah with the heat of alien embarrassment. What was that Spanish term?

He said, "The Asian Longhorned is a new invasive species."

"Instead of the British invasion, it's the Asian invasion." Jane laughed at her own joke.

"They're totally alien to U.S. soil," Jonah continued, feeling his stride, afraid to break it. He wasn't used to talking to attractive women—at least not living ones. "They were introduced to this country from China, stowed away in hardwood packing crates on ships. They bore holes in trees to lay their eggs. But it's the larvae that do all the damage, devouring the tree from the inside out."

"I like that term. Invasive species."

"They also call them alien species. There are thousands of alien species in the U.S. Everything from those Ailanthus trees over there—"

"Those big ones? I always called them Trees of Heaven."

"They're called that, too. Everything from Trees of Heaven to the Africanized honeybee, the West Nile virus, and the European starling."

"I like starlings, how they move in formation by the bazillions," Jane said. "There's a poem about that. I can't remember. It was on my AP English exam, years ago. Oh, God, there was this great image of the starlings all sitting on, like, a golf course or something, and then they all lift up into the sky at once 'like a black scarf,' the poet said. Something like that. Isn't that wonderful?"

"Starlings, unfortunately, can be a real menace," Jonah informed her. "They force out many native species, destroy farmers' crops, carry horrible diseases, and even cause aircraft disasters." He was aware of sounding preachy, but could not stop himself. "A flock of starlings hitting an airplane in mid-flight can completely destroy the plane's engines and send it crashing to the ground. Hundreds of people have died because of starlings."

"You could also say that hundreds of starlings have died because of people," Jane said. "Probably more than hundreds, because the starlings are so small."

"Well, that may be true," Jonah said, unable to find the connection between the starlings' diminutive size and their rate of destruction by humans, "but the point is, invasive species can really do a lot of damage to the native environment. And things are getting worse. The more global the world becomes, the more we destroy ourselves. And, much of the time, we do it for beauty. There's a species of rose, the Multiflora, that has been called a plague. It is so aggressive, it takes over the land, stealing it from other plants. The weaker plants can't compete and they disappear. Then the insects that depend on those plants disappear. The fish that depend on those insects disappear. And on it goes."

"A rose is a rose is a rose is a rose," said Jane.

He couldn't feel Rose's presence at all now. He noticed that he hadn't even been thinking of her, and a sickly flutter of guilt throbbed in his gut.

"There are some good things about the Multiflora rose," he said. "Its thickets are so tough, they're used on highways, as crash barriers. A soft place to land."

He imagined his parents' Subaru wagon alighting, unharmed but for a few thorn scratches, on a bramble of pink and white roses. His mother. He never saw her ghost after she was gone. He remembered what Vivian had said. Maybe his mother couldn't wait to get away from him.

"Do you know who said that?" Jane asked.

"What?"

"A rose is a rose is a rose is a rose."

He wished she would stop saying *rose*.

"Gertrude Stein," she said.

He wished he had not brought up the subject of roses at all.

"What about that dog of yours," she said. "Is she a native species? No. She's originally from China. Just like that beetle. And what about you? Where is your family from?"

"I don't think it's the same thing." Jonah found himself caught off guard by her challenge. She did it with a half-smile on her face. Maybe this was flirting. He was never sure when a woman was flirting versus when she was taunting him.

"It's not the same thing at all," he reiterated.

"Sure it is. It's called microevolution or something like that. People and animals move from continent to continent. Butterflies swarm in from Mexico. Dandelion tufts float across the ocean. Ancestral Africans walk out of Africa and eventually become Caucasians who eventually become members of the Ku Klux Klan. Because it's in the world's nature to change and then forget its own past."

Jane turned back to where the dogs were playing and slapped her hands on her knees. "Come here, Siggy, come on!" The Bullmastiff, an alien species himself, native to England's great estates, came bounding over to cover Jane's bare legs in his clinging slobber.

"Forgetting is an important, useful tool," Jane continued,

hugging the dog to her and slapping his side, making a hollow thud against his ribcage. "It's a defense. On the individual level, we need defenses to protect our egos from traumatic events in our past. Believe me, you don't want to remember everything. And what if things never changed? You know what we'd have? We wouldn't have dogs and trees, I'll tell you that. The whole world would be like, I don't know, like the moon. Look at it. It's dead up there."

Above them, in the violet-turning sky, the moon hung pale and tentative in the ether.

"The moon changes. It has its phases," Jonah said. He was grasping. He knew the moon didn't change. It was only the human perspective on it that shifted from day to day, throughout the lunar cycle. The moon was constant. No tectonic plates to shift. No atmosphere. No erosion. Even the footprints of astronauts stayed the same on the moon, unmoved by winds and weather, undisturbed by creeping plants or animals. A million years from now, if you built a telescope powerful enough, you could see them, the ridged boot soles of Armstrong and Aldrin stepping across the Sea of Tranquility, that "magnificent desolation," a quarter of a million miles away.

"You know what I mean," Jane said, rubbing Siggy behind the ears.

Jonah looked for Frankie. She was on the other side of the dusty run, wrestling with another pug, a fellow leftover from the breed's late-twentieth-century heyday. He called to her and she came, sat at his feet, and pressed herself into his leg, breathing hard and fast. He leaned down and rubbed her ears.

Siggy sniffed Frankie and Frankie sniffed Siggy. Their tails wagged.

"I think they like each other," said Jane. "We should make a play date for them."

A date. She'd said "date." Of course. For the dogs. But a double entendre maybe. He said okay.

"I like talking to you. You're smart," she said. "It's a rarity. Someone smart."

"That guy you were with at the party? He didn't seem very bright."

"He has his moments. And, I must warn you, that guy's my boyfriend, so watch your tongue. He's no MacArthur genius, I admit, but once in a while he comes up with some good ideas. He works in television. You're not one of those kill-your-television people, are you?"

"I watch TV."

"Thank you. I hate those people. Okay, so, you know that reality show, *Phobia Phactory*, where celebrity has-beens are tortured with spiders and tight places and stuff?"

"I don't watch that kind of TV," Jonah fibbed, knowing exactly which reality show Jane was talking about. He had just watched it a few nights ago, enjoying the moment when a dethroned pop-music princess choked on a sheep's eyeball she was attempting to swallow whole, washing it down with a maggot milkshake, and the show's beefy, brainless host (a former American Gladiator) had to give her the Heimlich maneuver, fracturing one of the princess's ribs in the process.

"Mark helped develop that show for the FOX network. I must confess, I gave him a little inspiration on the original concept, but he saw it through. The main thing is, we have a lot of fun together and he's totally unafraid of life. Most people, men especially, no offense, are scared shitless. But not Mark. Mark's just Mark. He also reminds me of my father. I admit, it's an Oedipal thing. I make no pretenses about that. Anyway, when I want to have an intellectual conversation, I just call up one of my friends. Or meet them at the dog run.

What do you say? Play date. Next weekend. Same bat time, same bat channel?"

"Okay," Jonah said, but as he said it, he wasn't certain he would show. Being with Jane had stirred a turbulence inside of him, as if a dusty moth, trapped and still behind the bars of his ribcage, had decided to beat its tired wings and make one last dash for the light at the end of the tunnel. Back in his apartment he chewed a couple of Tums, hoping to settle it, but it would not quiet. For the rest of the evening, the moth struggled upward until it got stuck behind the suprasternal notch of Jonah's throat, where it stilled its wings, but kept its feathery antennae alert, leaving him with a tickle of anxiety that had nothing to do with the recent elevation of Homeland Security's Threat Advisory. Rose stayed away all night.

9

"You can help us create a more secure environment:

- Be alert. Please report any unusual activity, suspicious packages, or substances to Transit personnel.
- Avoid bringing food on trains so that crumbs, powder, or spills are not mistaken for something else.
- Please take your packages when you leave. The inspection of unattended packages may cause delays.

Here at MTA NYC Transit, your anxiety and comfort matter most to us."

Jonah looked at that last line again. The word was not "anxiety," but "safety." Your *safety* matters most to us. He had read it wrong, but it seemed right. It was like they were trying to make him anxious. As if being trapped in an underground tunnel wasn't scary enough. The subway car was packed too tight. He breathed deep and fixed his gaze on an unmoving spot, the left ear of a woman who pressed against him. He focused on the fleshy whorls of the woman's auricular organ, its pink and lightly fuzzed atrium, the meaty lobe and pinna. The train lurched and the woman fell against him, not taking her eyes from the magazine article she was reading: "How to Forget Him and Get On with Your Life in Just Three Minutes a Day."

He wanted to forget about Jane. She was not Rose. And she was unavailable. But wasn't Rose also unavailable? That was different, Jonah told the sarcastic voice inside of him, the part of him that thought the whole endeavor with Rose and Vivian was ridiculous. A farce, or worse, a crime. Rose was different. Still, he kept imagining Jane's bare legs glazed with dog slobber. He looked deeper into his neighbor's ear, down into its dark auditory canal, past the tympanic membrane—a leaf of tissue paper vibrating—to penetrate the vivid-red sluice of her Eustachian tube. Below his waist, behind the puffy pleats of the baby-blue Dockers he'd put on this morning—for Vivian's sake, because today was Good Friday and he'd be spending the evening in Brooklyn where Vivian would certainly (he hoped) be pleased to see him in the pants she'd picked out especially for him—in the ample folds of 100% stain-resistant, DuPont-treated cotton twill, Jonah felt an erection swell. He imagined a spyglass extending, segment by segment, and tried to think of other things. He turned away from the woman and sniffed the air for toxins. Cyanide smelled like burnt almonds. Sarin gas smelled like Juicy Fruit gum. Or was it the other way around? The woman's hair smelled like mint shampoo. He should buy a gas mask but the news reported that every Army/Navy store in the city was sold out. He pulled his backpack around and slipped it low on his arm to cover the front of him, the way he used to clutch textbooks to his trousers in junior high.

The train jostled, its cabin lights flickering. For a moment, they were in darkness, watching the tunnel walls hurtling past outside the window. They could have been in an airplane, 30,000 feet above, jerking over speed bumps of air. But they were deep below. Jonah felt a pressing down, the ceiling of the underworld with its many tangled layers, one hundred feet of steel beams and concrete, sewer pipes, gas pipes, and water mains, storm drains and telecommunications cables, electrical vaults and steam vaults, all of it chugging and buzzing and gurgling above him, closing in, like the long, constricting stomach of a snake. Like the mucosal traceries of a body's recesses, the city's gut was a ganglial web of arteries and chambers, ducts and lobes, filaments and veins. A swampy, squiggling network of warm, wet intestine. And Jonah was smothering in it. He wanted this woman to move away but she only relaxed into him, as if he were a pole to lean against.

He closed his eyes and breathed as the train slid into Times Square Station. If anything terrible were to happen down here, he'd never see the sky again. He deserved it, too. For lying to Vivian. And for other things, but mostly that. He was such a dirty liar. Liar, liar, pants on fire. Did he turn off the stove this morning? He couldn't remember. If he couldn't remember, he reasoned, then it was possible that he had left the stove on. The burners were going. He could see their blue flames undulating, rising, grabbing at a nearby dishtowel, eager to burn down the entire building. He fought against the intrusive thought, against the urge to get off the train and take the next one back downtown, to check the stove again. He must have been under stress. His stove anxiety increased when he was under stress. He breathed deep, picturing himself on a faraway beach watching the waves roll in and out, in and out. If his apartment were in flames, he thought, so be it. He was late, again, for work.

On Broadway he rushed past a trio of Emergency Police officers in black Darth Vader helmets and bulletproof vests, M16s in their hands, a German Shepherd lounging at their boots. Two men dressed in Imperial Stormtrooper costumes wandered by, holding blaster guns and looking at a map. *Star Wars* conventioneers, Jonah reasoned, as he waited for the

WALK signal on the island between Broadway and Seventh. He used the time to read a few lines of news zipper: "A suicide bomber blew himself up in a hotel lobby in Israel for the Passover holiday, killing 15. * Scientists report Antarctic ice shelf is melting at an alarming rate. * Plenty of sunshine, high around 65." Global warming was making the March day unseasonably temperate and enabling entrepreneurs to harvest the Antarctic. According to an advertisement he'd seen, they bottled its melting ice and sold the 15,000-year-old product for $10 a pop as the purest, most immaculate water on the planet. Even the worst disaster could be a blessing, Jonah thought, to those who knew how to exploit vulnerability. Ambulance chasers, carpetbaggers, war profiteers, real-estate speculators. At the Army recruiting station, National Guardsmen in green camouflage and peaked berets stood like statues, holding rifles half the length of their bodies, greased banana clips absorbing sunlight. Jonah wondered what would happen if he held his backpack up in the air and yelled "Bomb!" These statues would come to life, their rifles releasing streams of bullets like dotted lines, a chain of lead connecting them to him. Blood on his new blue pants. He wouldn't have to go to Brooklyn tonight. He could stop lying to Vivian. The signs changed, telling him to WALK.

Forty-two stories above the streets, excited conversation buzzed around Jonah at his desk, easily penetrating the flimsy partitions of Plexiglas and pine. Mediacom was one of the few family-owned multinational corporations in America, still operated by the McQuades, a clan of devout Irish-Catholics who closed their business at three o'clock on Good Friday, just as church bells would be tolling Christ's official time of death across the city. Like kids giddy on a half-day at school, Jonah's coworkers were good for nothing today but chatting and playing games. Two guys from the marketing department tossed a Nerf football back and forth overhead while Keith went back and forth to the next work-pod to flirt with their female marketing cohorts. It took Jonah all morning to get through the article on his computer screen, a how-to guide for throwing your child a Hawaiian luau party with a cake that looked "just like" the Pacific Ocean, complete with a killer tsunami. He was trying to make up for lost time, to be extra productive to compensate for his lateness, but it was difficult when, in the pod behind him, the Marketing Girls were talking loudly about designer jeans. Sometimes, to cope with such auditory intrusions, he scribbled their dialogue on a piece of yellow legal paper. One day, he thought, it might make it into a scene in some as-yet-unwritten graphic novel.

> Marketing Girl 1: Why is she so obsessed with the Sevens? Does she even *fit* in the Sevens? I don't think so.
> Marketing Girl 2: God, no.
> Marketing Girl 1: I don't fit in the Sevens. I mean they fit, but they do nothing for my ass. They make my ass look flat.
> Marketing Girl 2: Could you, like—
> Marketing Girl 1: Stop talking, for once, about my ass? No, I don't think I can. Let me tell you, I got a pair of corduroys from Bloomingdale's for $175 and they were *not* the Sevens. The Sevens cost, like, $250. So she just got screwed. And the corduroys I got are made of stretchy material, so they fit over my fat ass.

Jonah smiled to himself, comforted by the stupidity that flowed over his cubicle wall. He could be late every single day and still never be as stupid and unproductive as the people who surrounded him. His job was safe. One of the marketing guys winged the football into a hanging television, changing the channel from PinwheelKids' broadcast of their popular show *Num-Num Town* to CNN's coverage of a dusty town square littered with human body parts. Outside Jonah's window, above the river, a U.S. Army helicopter beat its way down the island's coast, hunting for evildoers.

> Marketing Girl 1: Some words of wisdom. You can always go out and get a new outfit and haircut, but your ass is a totally different story.
> Marketing Girl 2: That's true. I guess, at some point, you're going to have to tooth-and-nail it back to what it once was. I mean, my yoga's not going to help that.
> Marketing Girl 1: I have one word for you. Pilates.

At lunchtime, Jonah went out to search for subject matter. He carried his sketchbook to Eighth Avenue, where Disney's juggernaut of mallification had yet to demolish everything left over from the twentieth century. A few video peepshows (NO LIVE GIRLS) operated out of dilapidated theatres from the days of burlesque and McHale's bar and restaurant still stood, its bulky neon signage shining in the light of day, advertising liquors, steaks, and air conditioning. He took a seat at the bar under autographed pictures of Mickey Mantle and a racehorse named Always Good Thanx, ordered one of McHale's signature giant hamburgers and a beer, and opened the sketchbook. He chose the office girl who sat alone, leaning her bright elbows on the amber wood of the bar (wood originally salvaged from the 1939 World's Fair and since worried smooth from decades of countless other elbows). Like all the women Jonah liked, she had a Pre-Code Hollywood look, her heart-shaped face pallid and her large eyes made larger in gray shadows of makeup. She lowered her eyes and lifted her sepia drink in the pumpkin glow of the globe lamps overhead, their chains furred with half a century of dust, while Jonah's pen moved across the paper and the moth in his throat flicked its sensitive feelers. He thought of Jane but it was Rose who took a seat on the stool next to him.

You came back, he said silently.

Do I have a choice, she said, reaching for a French fry on his plate, before changing her mind and letting her cool hand drop back to her lap.

He wasn't sure why she was angry.

I'm going to your mother's tonight, he said. *I'm wearing the pants she gave me.*

She smirked and said, *Baby blue?*

Not exactly my style.

No, but that's my mother. She was always trying to get me into dresses and things I didn't like. She never understood me.

You're talking in full sentences now.

Rose shrugged like it was no big deal.

She said you were distant, your mother.

I had to be. She drove me crazy.

Do you mind, he asked, *my spending time with her?*

Rose shrugged again. *You don't have a mother of your own, so.*

Do you think, what I'm doing, telling her about you, do you think that's okay?

Rose looked at the French fries longingly. *This is the worst part about being dead*, she said. *You feel hungry, but you can't eat.*

Together, they walked in silence along Eighth Avenue, past the video-only peepshows and a joke shop selling "unusual books" with titles like *The Cheap Date Handbook*, *Sell Yourself to Science*, *Weapons Caching 101*, and *Your Revenge Is in the Mail: How to Get Revenge on Anyone from the Comfort of Your Own Home*. He stopped to admire the window display of novelties, a collection of itching and sneezing powders, exploding pens and whoopee cushions, ice cubes with flies suspended in their centers, explaining to Rose how much he'd loved these things as a boy when he saw them advertised in his comic books. He pointed to a pair of X-Ray Specs, leaning down to inspect them closely. They'd always been a mystery to him and he wondered how they worked their magic—just a pair of round horn rims with cardboard lenses decorated with bull's-eye circles shrinking down to a black hole for peering out. The advertised purpose of the specs was to see through clothes, to see breasts, but they looked like a pair of breasts themselves. The thought brought to mind a Magritte painting he'd seen long ago in one of his mother's art books, a woman's face made of a woman's body, with breasts for eyes and a pubic mouth.

"My father wouldn't let me have them," he said out loud.

Breasts, Rose asked, *or the glasses?*

No fair. You were reading my thoughts.

I am your thoughts, she said.

He considered this, knowing it was true, but still baffled by the way a thought could think of itself as a thought. Maybe that's what was meant by self-consciousness. The self-conscious thought. Before he could respond, a man sidled up and hissed in his direction.

"Hey, chief. Yeah, I'm talking to you. You looking for real live girls? I got a private place with lovely, lovely ladies. I can take you there. Check it out."

The man held out a slip of paper, the promise of something dark and wild. Jonah shook his head, but the man persisted. "Come on now, chief. You're a man and a man's got needs." He pressed Jonah, shrinking his personal space until he was trapped between the offer and the window full of X-Ray Specs and plastic vomit. Rose had abandoned him. He felt a flutter of panic, a commotion of mothy wings at his throat. He pushed past the pimp and hustled back toward the office. In the crush of Seventh Avenue, dodging and weaving, he miscalculated his way around a scrum of standing tourists and bumped hard into an elderly man, knocking the heavy wooden cross from his shoulders.

"I'm sorry," Jonah said, stooping to lift the cross.

"Leave it now," said the man. "That's too heavy for you."

Jonah had seen the Cross Man many times over the years. He'd seen him in Times Square mostly, but also near Grand Central and in Central Park, in Greenwich Village and down by the South Street Seaport. The Cross Man got around. But Jonah had never seen him up close. He was as thin as a blade of dry grass and bent into the shape of burden. His face was the color and texture of cured tobacco leaves, and his eyes were milky blue, like blind golf balls. In one hand he held a wash bucket filled with squeegees and with the other he reached down and easily lifted the seven-foot cross back onto his bony shoulder as if it were made of Styrofoam and not two thick planks of weathered wood.

"I'm so sorry," Jonah said again. "I wasn't looking."

"Damn bottle's gone and popped its top for good," said the Cross Man, gazing up toward the sky.

Jonah turned to see the airspace over Broadway cluttered with its usual signs, but the cap on the world's largest Coca-Cola bottle was missing. Standing forty-two feet high in its sexy contour, the bottle usually performed a mechanical burlesque-style routine over the crossroads of the world: it lifted its cap, an enormous drinking straw floated out, the cola color drained away as the bottle magically emptied, and then it flashed its neon lights, telling everyone that this was The Real Thing. But now there was no cap. Jonah felt a ripple of upset traveling through him, a continuation of the upset he'd felt at being pinned by the pimp. He hated things to be out of place and this was his favorite Times Square sign, a three-dimensional classic in a sea of giant TV screens.

"Maybe it's being fixed," he said to the Cross Man.

"No such thing as fixed. Once broke, always broke."

Jonah wasn't listening. He thought the man was alluding to money. He held out a dollar bill.

"I don't need that," said the man. "I got windows to wash."

Jonah held his offering out a moment longer, wishing the Cross Man would just take it, as if some crime could be undone by the simple donation of a dollar bill, but the Cross Man wasn't interested. Jonah watched him walk away, reading the hand-scrawled words on the back of his shirt: "If any man will come after me, let him deny himself, and take up his cross daily, and follow me. Luke 9:23, King James version."

Keith found him moments later, still looking up at the topless bottle. He slapped Jonah on the back and told him to wake up, the day was done. But it was only 2:00.

"You seriously want to go back to work for just an hour? Come on. No one cares if we're gone. And you look like you need a drink. What do you say? You and me. The Wakamba Lounge. I won't take no for an answer."

Jonah let Keith steer him back down Eighth Avenue, past shoeshine stands, a few holdout prostitutes, and men pushing bolts of fabric on rolling carts. Keith crossed each street oblivious to the DON'T WALK signs, not caring if cars were speeding toward him. He lived in a world where bad things didn't happen to people like him. Jonah was extra careful when it came to crossing the street. He stopped, looked right, left, then right again, always in that order. If a car had the green light, and was less than half a block away, Jonah would not cross in front of it.

"Come on," Keith called from the middle of the road, throwing his hands in the air.

"I'll wait here."

"Let's go!"

"I'm fine here," Jonah said, waiting for the way to be clear.

When they met up on the other side Keith said, "Jesus, Soloway, what are you so afraid of?"

"I just don't feel like getting hit by a car. Do you know how many pedestrians are hit by cars in this city every year? Thirteen thousand. Thirteen thousand people."

As they walked, he thought about all the people he'd seen just after they'd been hit. There was the copy boy smashed on Fifth Avenue while carting a hand truck loaded with boxes of Xeroxed documents, an explosion of paper littering the street, spattered red. There was the man dragged by a bus for half a block on West 41st, heading into Port Authority, a trail of blood, white sheet under wheels. But he mostly remembered the woman on Second Avenue who lay in the street twitching, her skirt hiked up around her hips while the lady driver of the car paced in mad circles, muttering, "I'm a murderer, I'm a murder, I'm a murderer."

When they reached the bar, Jonah said, "This is where that guy was shot and killed. He bled to death, right on this sidewalk. Right where we're standing."

Over the bar's red faux-stone façade, a red awning was painted with the words, "The Distinguished Wakamba

Lounge," one of the arms in the W decorated to look like a palm tree.

"He was a drug dealer or something," said Keith, taking Jonah by the shoulder and pushing him inside. "And we're not drug dealers. So don't worry about it. One beer, that's all I ask."

Behind black-curtained windows, the bar was dark and cool, a cozy grotto dimly lit by flickering red lanterns. Strings of Christmas lights and glittering, five-and-dime garlands draped the ceiling. Salsa music played from the jukebox. Behind the bar, two Puerto Rican girls in black short-shorts and tube tops, their long hair pulled back in ponytails, lazily smoked cigarettes and poured the occasional drink. One girl was small and cute, with painted lips that curled into a glossy smirk, while the other was heavy in her limbs, too tall to be cute, a natural-born thrower of the shot put.

Keith didn't discriminate. A girl was a girl. He ordered a round of beers and spoke Spanish to the girls, making them laugh and toss their hair. Jonah was curious to know what Keith was saying, but it didn't matter. Keith could recite the Periodic Table of Elements and girls would laugh and toss their hair.

Jonah hated Keith. Just for a second. Then he shook the feeling away. He needed the company. Rose was nowhere in sight.

Keith asked, "So what's up with all this worry about being killed?"

"What do you mean?"

"You won't cross the street. You're afraid to come to a bar where some drug dealer was shot. You have the statistics in your head about how many people are run over by cars. What's up with that?"

"I had a girlfriend who was hit by a car," he lied, easily.

"Shit. She died?"

"Yeah. She did."

"When?"

"I don't know. About six months ago."

"How long were you together?"

"Like a year."

"Shit, that's a long time. I'm sorry, man."

Jonah nodded and sipped his beer. Keith ordered two shots of Jameson's and made Jonah drink.

"Her name was Rose," Jonah said. "She was from Brooklyn. Italian girl. I thought maybe we'd get married."

"Damn. That's harsh. But I read somewhere that it takes half the time you were together to get over someone. To grieve and whatever. Six months is half of a year. So, I mean. I'm just saying that it seems like you've been grieving pretty hard for a while. Maybe it's time to move on. Find another girl."

"She *died*," said Jonah, insulted. "She didn't dump me. She didn't move away to, I don't know, Chicago or someplace to go to grad school. She *died*. Do you understand how hard that is? It's traumatic."

Keith nodded and kept his mouth closed. He ordered another round of beers. Jonah couldn't believe what Keith was saying. Get over Rose after just six months? As if grief had an expiration date. No, he would not be hurried. The poor woman died on the Jersey Turnpike and no one cared.

But that wasn't right. Rose died in the World Trade Center. His mother died on the Jersey Turnpike. What difference did it make? Six months was not long enough. He would savor his grief, hold it close, milk it for all it was worth.

"Did you know I used to be a Harpo?" Keith said cryptically.

Jonah thought of the Marx Brothers and tried to picture Keith in a curly wig and hobo's hat, his mouth gone mute. It was hard to imagine.

"Do you know what a Harpo is?" Keith pressed.

"Please," said Jonah, "enlighten me."

"You know Oprah Winfrey's company, Harpo Productions? It's her name spelled backwards. I used to work there. In Chicago. You reminded me of it when you said Chicago. Anyway, I was in Viewer Communications, which means I dealt with the fan mail, basically. People sent in all kinds of crazy shit. Plaster busts of Oprah, wooden carvings of Oprah, velvet paintings of Oprah, quilts with Oprah's face sewn right in the middle. I mean they worshipped Oprah. They sent perishables, too: cakes, cookies, fruit. As if Oprah fucking Winfrey herself was going to take home a plate of cookies from some fan and serve them to her guests at tea. Yeah, right. We threw out all the perishables. You never know what some nut job is capable of. But I did eat a brownie once. I was hungry. Whatever. It hasn't killed me yet."

"That was your whole job, opening the mail?"

"It wasn't like a mail-room job, if that's what you're implying. I was the first line of defense. I sent out form letters, 'Thank you for the gift, etc., etc.,' and collated information for the market researchers. It was a fun job, but kind of claustrophobic. It took over your entire life. Nobody had any friends on the outside. It was just us Harpos."

Keith emptied his bottle of beer and said, "I gotta break the seal," before heading off to the men's room.

Jonah ordered another round. He had plenty of time before he had to board the subway to Brooklyn. He wasn't thinking about Rose, or his mother, or Vivian, or Jane either. He wasn't thinking about anything except the present moment. It was a rare and airy feeling. At the urging of Keith and the girls behind the bar, he switched from beers to margaritas. He took off his jacket and rolled up his shirtsleeves. Business was slow and the girls hung around, making small talk and flirting. The bigger one of the two, the shot putter, leaned over the bar and told Jonah she liked his hat and asked to try it on. Before he could answer, the girl grabbed it and put it on her head.

"Very nice," said Jonah, smiling, feeling like a stranger to himself. If he never made it to Brooklyn tonight that would be just fine. "Bonita!" he shouted over the salsa music.

"Vamos a bailar," said Keith, getting to his feet.

"What?"

"Let's dance!" said the girl in Jonah's hat. She and her partner came out from behind the bar, showing off their long legs. Jonah stood up, unsteadily, realizing how intoxicated he was, and took a few wobbly steps toward the dance floor. He wished he wasn't wearing baby-blue pants. His pelvis looked bloated, filled with gas. He mashed it with his hands, trying to force the air out of the balloon, but the double-pleated Dockers refused to deflate. The big girl in the hat took his hand in hers.

"You know how?" she asked. He shook his head. "Follow me."

The strings of light flashed above as they moved across the floor, one-two-three, forward and back, side to side. The girl put her hands on Jonah's hips. An old man sitting at the bar clapped his hands in time to the music, watching them dance, smiling with no front teeth. One-two-three, forward and back. Jonah felt the lights above him turn to liquid and the music pounding under his heels. He was shorter than the girl and felt ridiculous looking up at her, like a boy dancing with his mother. He looked down instead at her squinty belly button swaying in the soft, brown expanse of her bared midriff.

"Look at me," she said, lifting his chin in her hand. "Look here."

She pointed to her eyes. Jonah obeyed. This part harder than the dancing. Her face looked strange in the lights. Her open mouth had too much water in it and her nose was a waxy protuberance. He let his eyes roam over her shoulder toward the jukebox, then let them fall to her breasts, to the deep, dark line where they pressed against each other.

"Here," she insisted, "look here." She lifted his chin again and locked him with her gaze. "Good, good," she said, laughing and showing the wetness of her tongue.

He felt something click into place, a part of him loosed by the liquor, and he gripped the girl tighter, one hand on her hip, pushing her pelvis back and forth, lifting her hand to make her spin in a circle, her ponytail slapping his face as she turned, laughing, her teeth shining red in the lights. Here was the thing he'd held in check, the thing he'd jerked back from Rose's fallen glove that morning long ago in the snow. It surged now from the base of his spine up to his skull, thrumming a blood-wet rhythm against his teeth. With it, a sour bubble of nausea burned the back of his throat. He swallowed it and kept dancing. If he stopped now, he knew, he would lose it.

They went on dancing as the fast music ended and a slow song took over, a sultry, updated version of "Besame Mucho." The girl fell against Jonah and smashed him into her breasts, smearing his glasses. He put one arm around her and squeezed, feeling her breath beneath her tube top. He wanted to hold her for a long time. She put her hands onto his bald and sweating head, pulled it to her, and kissed it with mushy lips. They moved together as the girl urged against him, making soft sounds with her mouth. She held him tighter, wrapping her arms around his back and locking them together, pressing the air from his pleated puff of cotton twill. He felt a stirring in his pants. The sour taste rose again into his throat. He couldn't stop it now. He pushed the girl off him and rushed into the men's room where he got down on his knees and vomited into the toilet, trying not to touch the filthy rim of the bowl with his hands.

While he knelt on the cold tiles, waiting for the next wave to overtake him, he recalled the first time he had had too much to drink. He was at Marla Pipkin's sweet sixteen birthday party. Marla Pipkin was known around school as something of a spaz. She wore peasant blouses, kept honeybees in her backyard, and played the hammered dulcimer. The other important thing about Marla Pipkin was that she was somewhat oversexed, and very aggressive about it. This was the main reason Jonah sat with her on the school bus every day. It made no difference to Marla Pipkin that Jonah was strapped into a Milwaukee brace. Maybe she even liked it, having him captive beside her. Maybe, with all his metalwork, he reminded her of the dulcimer she loved to hammer. She grabbed his hand, shoved it up her peasant skirt, and let him feel her all the way to school. She never touched him back, however, leaving him uncomfortably unsatisfied, filled with a chafing frustration for the rest of the school day. He went to her sweet sixteen party in the hopes that the opportunity for reciprocity would finally arise. It didn't. Even when he pillaged Dr. Pipkin's liquor cabinet, thinking that a few cocktails would change him into someone suave and more desirable, he only walked home drunk, alone and untouched, to vomit on his front lawn—which wasn't easy to do in a Milwaukee brace—with his father standing over him saying, "Every action has an equal and opposite reaction. This is a valuable lesson you are learning. Action, reaction. Action, reaction." It was his mother who finally brought him into the house, unshackled him from his iron maiden, cleaned him up, and put him to bed where he lay, still longing and ashamed.

Jonah heard his father's voice now as he knelt on the men's room floor of the Distinguished Wakamba Lounge. He hung his head over the bowl and mumbled, "Action, reaction. Action, reaction," waiting for his penance to be over.

10

Later that evening in Carroll Gardens, Jonah walked, still a bit woozy, past wooden crucifixes on front lawns, their crossbeams draped with purple shrouds reflecting the violet sky. The lamplight illuminated the magnolia trees, their flowers just beginning to open, bright fists unfurling in the dusk. In the empty street teenage boys played a game of stickball, swinging the stick hard, connecting with a rubbery pop, and calling out to high fly balls, "To the moon, Alice!" They quoted Jackie Gleason as if they were not the boys of today, but ghosts left behind by men now grown, husks cast off in their flight toward the future. Like last year's dry leaves scuttling down the street, the ghost boys gave the night a Halloween feeling, though the houses and yards were bright with Easter decorations. On the lawns, giant inflatable eggs glowed like alien pods and man-sized rabbits clutched bioengineered super-carrots like weapons. Jonah didn't feel up to this.

When he saw Vivian waiting on the steps of St. Stephen's and Sacred Hearts Church, he considered turning back. But then she spotted him. She waved, her gold bracelets jingling, calling his name. He felt an adolescent recoil, as if she were his own mother and the strangers on the street were school friends in front of whom he'd be embarrassed by the spectacle of maternal love. Maybe that was just the lingering alcohol talking. When she kissed him hello he turned away but not before she caught a whiff of whiskey, beer, and tequila under the spearmint gum in his mouth.

"You smell like a distillery," she said. "You been drinking?"

"We got out early today. I had a drink with a friend. Just one, though. I'm okay. Look. I'm wearing the pants you like."

"They look good. So much better than those rags you wear. Come on."

She ushered him inside, where she dipped a finger into holy water and made the sign of the cross. Jonah didn't want to dip his finger, but he did. God was watching from the blue vaulted ceiling. The bearded Father, like something out of Blake, reached down from the streaming heavens as if to take Jonah by the throat and throttle him. So he dipped and made the sign of the cross. Obediently, he followed Vivian around the church, past life-sized plaster statues of saints she introduced as they made their way toward the altar. "This is St. Angelo, St. Michael, St. Lucy. Here's St. Anne, with little Mary (Anne was the Blessed Virgin's mother). Here's St. Rita, St. Francis of Assisi (I always loved him the best)." She put her fingers to her lips and then to the toes of St. Francis, worn smooth from decades of kisses. Everybody loved St. Francis the best. They walked past St. Bartholomew, who held a meat cleaver in his hand ("Patron saint of butchers"), St. Theresa the little flower, Our Lady of Carmel draped in glittering scapulas, the Infant Jesus of Prague, and St. Rosalia, holding a human skull in one hand. Finally, at the altar, inside an illuminated glass box, Christ's languid body lay for the viewing. With his head resting on a golden pillow, he looked like he was sleeping and might awaken at any moment.

Jonah peered into the basket of money next to the glass coffin. His hands, with minds of their own, ached to grab fistfuls of cash. He was a liar, he thought—maybe he could also be a thief. But the only thing he'd ever stolen, in his entire life, was a pack of naked lady playing cards from a shabby boardwalk gift shop on a family trip to Atlantic City. Guilt gripped him later and he never even opened the pack before tossing it from the car window as they sped home over the Walt Whitman Bridge. The cards were probably still at the bottom of the sluggish Delaware River, loosed from their cardboard packaging, the naked ladies scattered and swollen in the dark. He didn't have the stomach for thievery. Still, he leaned over the basket to look at the swirl of tens and twenties, just to feel the tingle of potential crime. A dark figure shocked him, making him jump back like a boy caught in the act of a bad idea.

Above him, tall and shuddersome, stood the Sorrowful Mother. Not the beneficent blue-robed Mary, her girlish cheeks still innocent; this was a changed woman, a mother who knows suffering, her worst nightmare come true. Her face was a wreck of misery. Silver tears speckled the lace hankie she held in her hand. And through her black robes, a knife stabbed her heart as she wept, inconsolably, over her lost child.

The Congregation of the Madonna Addolorata wound its way from the church, a slow processional of flag bearers, funeral drummers, altar boys in white robes waving censers in the air. Christ in his coffin was lifted high on the shoulders of men dressed in black suits. A group of women mourners came next, carrying battery-operated candles and singing an Italian funeral song. Finally, the Sorrowful Mother floated into view, standing high above the procession, her litter supported on the shoulders of four large men. She swayed back and forth, a slow metronome, her robes fluttering in the wind, her stricken face a ghostly moon in the dark sky. Behind her, a small brass band crept through a heavy dirge.

Jonah felt the last ounces of alcohol drain from his neurocircuitry as he and Vivian walked amongst the silent crowd, past families gathered on front stoops and solitary men smoking cigars in beach chairs unfolded on the sidewalks. Old men and women crossed themselves and kissed their fingers when the coal-black silhouette of the Madonna came swaying past the telephone wires and blossoming trees. Teenage girls showed themselves off in tight jeans and perfumed hair, eating hot Italian bread out of paper bags and exclaiming, "Oh, I could eat the whole loaf!" From an upstairs window, a woman leaned out and shouted to the world, "She had a boy!" Babies were born, people were dying, bread was broken and eaten, as all the while, for a long while, the procession snaked its way down one block and up another. What city was this, Jonah wondered. What time? It felt like a distant Brooklyn decades ago, or like his mother's Philadelphia, the one she used to tell stories about, a place of stickball players and sidewalk sitters and people shouting from windows, a place before television kept everyone captive. The full moon ascended over the malodorous Gowanus Canal, rising above the rooftops, making children turn around to shout, "Look at the moon!" The altar boys, in the fog of their censers, turned to look. The Chinese men standing outside Ling-Ling Young-Young takeout turned to look. Jonah and Vivian looked into the sky, too, where the Towers of Light shined blue beside the full moon as the Sorrowful Mother and the body of her child passed below. He felt Rose nearby, a watching presence in the dark, but she would not come close.

"I've had enough," Vivian announced at last. "My feet are killing me. Let's go back to the church and wait."

He thought he saw tears in her eyes as she slipped her arm through his and they broke off from the parade. There was a chill in the air and she held on tight, hugging his arm to her soft body.

"You're a good boy," she said, "to stay with me for the whole thing. Frank would never do it. 'I got a backache,' he says. His excuse for everything. I don't even ask no more. Why bother? You're a good boy."

He bristled and ached to pull away, again that adolescent tug, but her sadness held him tight. It reminded him of when his mother began to treat him like a man, after his voice started to change, calling him her date for dinners out, for movies and museum trips, events that his father refused. What would Jane the psychoanalyst have to say about that?

Before he could free himself from Vivian's fleshy grip, they came upon a frenzy of women, a crowd surrounding a little mustached man selling buttons and magnets out of a plastic bag, dollar souvenirs with pictures of saints on them. The women struggled against each other, diving for the bag in the little man's hands.

"You got St. Francis?" one of the women asked. "I need a St. Francis."

"Oh," said the little man, "I have so many St. Francis at home, I said who's gonna buy St. Francis?"

"Well, I woulda bought it," said the woman. "You got St. Peter?"

"How 'bout St. Francis?" another woman asked.

"I got no St. Francis!" said the little man.

"How 'bout St. Joseph?"

"Forget it, St. Joseph is *my* saint," said a third woman, lunging for the bag and knocking the man's felt hat into the street.

"I'm gonna give you five dollars, just for a magnet of St. Michael," said another woman. "*Uno magnetico*. For my car."

"No, no. One dollar," said the man. "It's a sin to take extra money. I don't wanna steal your money."

"If you find a St. Francis while you're going through," said the first woman to the one searching the bag for St. Joseph, "my daughter wants to trade for it."

Vivian said, "Watch this." She pushed her way into the melee, waving a dollar bill in her hand. When she emerged from the throng, she was triumphant, holding in her hand a magnet with a picture of St. Francis on it, a tiny bird perched on his shoulder. She pressed it into Jonah's hand as a gift. He thought of the saint's shiny pink toe, back at the church, covered in saliva.

"I can't," he said.

"*I can't*," she repeated. "That's what you always say. Just take it, for God's sakes. Put it on your fridge."

He pictured the magnet on his pistachio-green 1953 Kelvinator. What would his father say? A Catholic saint in his kitchen. But his father would never see it. He took the magnet and slipped it into his pants pocket. He felt guilty for his earlier feelings, for pulling away from Vivian, and now he wanted to make amends, to give her something in return. But he had nothing to offer. He tried to think of a new Rose story he could tell.

As they sat to rest on the steps of St. Stephen's Church, a small crowd formed, waiting for the procession to return. Old Italian ladies kissed each other and bid, "*Buona pasqua.*" A few people stopped to say hello to Vivian, telling her, "God never gives anyone more than they can handle" and "When He closes a door, He opens a window." Vivian thanked them, making a bitter face to Jonah when they'd gone. "Stupid people," she muttered.

A step behind them, two middle-aged women were talking just above a whisper.

"Valerie's pregnant," said the first one.

"What? That's wonderful! I didn't know that," said the second.

"You never know nothing. You're so *stunata*. Did you hear? The Genduso baby died."

"What? Oh, that's terrible."

"But it's for the best. 'Marie,' I said, 'when you have a baby like that, it's for the best.' He was only a *pound*."

"Poor thing."

"She had a hard time with the first one, too."

"She's a beautiful little girl now."

"She is. But she has so many problems. They have to take her to the doctor all the time for her eyes. She has trouble breathing."

"So sad. I feel so bad for them."

"Everything happens for the best, though, that's what I always say."

"That's right. Everything happens for the best."

Jonah looked to Vivian to see if she had heard, but she was paying attention to a young couple a few steps below. They held each other in the chill, and the boy covered the girl's shoulders with his school jacket.

"I hope Rose got the chance to know love," Vivian said. "Just once. She could be so hard, that girl, so cold sometimes. And the boys she picked. One *schmuck* after the other. Always honking their horns from the street. They couldn't come to the door? There were some nice guys, but she never let them get close. I can't understand why she was that way. Maybe I didn't teach her how to be loved. By a man, I mean. Maybe, seeing how things were between me and Frank, she never figured it out for herself. It kills me to think she died with no one to love."

Jonah sat silently, thinking to say something but not allowing himself to say it. It was too much.

Vivian prodded, "Did she have any boyfriends that you knew? Someone special?"

He felt as though she were inviting him to say the thing on his mind, encouraging him to write the next chapter of his evolving lie.

He said, "She had me."

"I know," she patted his hand. "Poor Jonah. You loved her."

He could not meet her eyes and looked up the street instead, where the flags of the procession appeared over the rising asphalt. The reverberation of funeral drums grew louder. Why did she assume that his love for Rose was unrequited?

"She loved me, too," he said, a bit defensively, pushing his glasses up the bridge of his nose.

"You were a good friend."

"No. I mean we were in love."

Vivian gave him a wary look.

"I guess that's hard to believe," he said. "I know. I'm not her type."

"She liked *schmucks*, and you're not a *schmuck*."

She looked at him closely then. He could feel her probing for the truth, for the source of this so obviously implausible story. He felt his whole house of cards shudder and threaten to collapse. He had gone too far. No mother would believe that her daughter could love a man like him, a stoop-shouldered, bald-headed, nearsighted cretin. *That's exactly the word for me*, he thought. *Cretin*. He might have blown the whistle on himself, there and then, but something in him felt protective of his own fragile self. Was he really so awful? Was it so unbelievable that a woman like Rose could love a man like him? Didn't he dance tonight with a hot Latina bartender?

"Like you've said yourself," he blurted out, "maybe you didn't know her so well."

"Don't push it," she said, pointing her finger at him. "I know my Rose. How'd she pick a guy like you? Help me understand this."

"Well, you've talked a lot about how the two of you had grown apart. I didn't know her before, from the time you talk about. I only got to know her after all that. Maybe she was a different person. Maybe she matured."

"Maybe."

"People change."

"That's true."

"That'd be good, right?"

"Of course. I wanted that. I just wanted her to be happy. To be content with her life. Not running around looking for the wrong things. No, I wanted that for Rose. Maybe she did change. So the two of you were going together. Why didn't you tell me before?"

"I told you before. At Costco."

"At Costco's? When?"

"At lunch. With the Chicken Bakes. I told you I loved her."

Vivian looked at him, trying to remember exactly what he'd said and didn't say, and what could have been implied. He held his breath until he felt her relaxing into it, accepting it as truth.

"You did say something that time," she said. "I guess I misunderstood. You're right. I didn't know her, how she'd changed. I wish I did. I wish I knew the Rose you knew."

Jonah felt it all made right again, the house of cards solid now, steady. Vivian took his hand and patted it.

"I'm glad it was you," she said. "A good boy. Only half Italian but that's better than none at all."

Relieved and emboldened, Jonah pushed further. "Rose was the good one. She kept me centered. She kept me grounded. I never thought I'd meet someone like her, so generous and kind. I trusted her completely. And, it wasn't anything official, but we talked about getting married someday."

Vivian's eyes glistened in the lamplight. She put her arms around him and pressed her lips to his cheek. The procession with its drums and trumpets came to rest at the foot of the church steps. Vivian pulled away and wiped her eyes. She looked happy and Jonah was glad for that.

"That's what I wanted to hear," she said. "What I always hoped for."

The men in black carried the Sorrowful Mother toward the naked, slumbering body of her son. She towered over him, a black apparition, the knife shining in her breast. Vivian squeezed Jonah's hand. The Mother seemed about to collapse on top of her son in ecstatic grief, lurching forward as the pallbearers knocked their two litters together, like hitting stones to make a spark. They knocked three times and the church bells sounded out a threnody of three desolate notes.

"Why three times I always wondered," said one of the whispering women from behind.

"It's something about how they met three times," said the other, "on the road before he died. There's supposed to be a lot of threes in the Bible. He was in the grave for three days. And there's the father, son, and holy spirit."

"I ask because my kid asks me these questions. 'You go to church,' he says. Hey. Just because I go to church, does that make me a theologian?"

"Three's a lucky number."

"Not so lucky for Mary Galasso. Did you hear? First her husband with the stroke, then she's got the cataracts, and now her son's into drugs. She's got the horrors."

Back at the house, Vivian set out an Entenmann's pound cake and poured the decaf. She sat down heavily at the dining room table and let out a long, weary sigh. Frank was up on the roof, leaving them alone, which Jonah preferred. Frank made him nervous.

Vivian said, "Let me tell you, it ain't easy doing that, walking the procession. That was something me and Rose always did together when she was small. I want to hear more about you and Rose. You must have spent a lot of time together. What things did she like to do?"

"Lots of things," Jonah told her. "We went out to Coney Island and she used to say, 'The beach is divine,' which was a joke because, you know, the beach there is pretty disgusting. We went to baseball games and the bleachers were fine with her, she didn't mind at all. She loved rowing on Central Park Lake." He hoped Vivian would not notice he was paraphrasing lyrics from Rodgers and Hart's "The Lady Is a Tramp."

"Rowing on the lake. I always wanted to do that. It looks so romantic. Maybe you'll take me sometime? Frank never will," she said, picking up the knife. "My son-in-law. You're the only one I can count on. I sure as hell can't count on *him*." She pointed the knife toward the ceiling and the roof beyond, where Frank sat with his pigeons. "He's useless," she said, slicing the pound cake. "Useless."

She lifted a thick, yellow chunk of cake and placed it on Jonah's plate.

"Do you know he cares more about those towers than he does his own child? Where do you think he was, the day Rose was born? I'm in the hospital, having a baby, and where do you think he is? I'll tell you where. He's up on those goddamn towers. *They* were his babies. That's what he called them, too— 'My babies.' And, boy, was he proud of *them*. So proud of what he built, with his own two hands. Why'd they have to build them so tall? I'll tell you why. This is how men think they get to Heaven. Like in the Bible, with that tower of Babel. Stupid.

And God knocked it right over. When the towers came down, did he cry for Rose? For those *buildings*, he cried. For a pile of metal. Do you want to see what's left of *my* baby?"

Vivian ran her fingers along the knife's edge and popped the gathered crumbs of sticky cake into her mouth. She heaved herself up from the table and went to the sideboard to retrieve a blue velvet bag that Jonah thought was a covered bottle of Crown Royal, the kind his mother liked. But instead of a bottle of whiskey, Vivian pulled from the bag a mahogany urn engraved with the date: 09-11-01. She set it on the table and told Jonah to open it. She seemed angry. Jonah wondered if he had done something to upset her, if he had gone too far with his lie. She pulled a cigarette from her metal mesh case and told him again, like a dare, "Go on, open it."

He took the urn in both hands. The smooth, polished wood was the color of a ruddy chestnut. He was afraid of what he might find inside, imagining the horrible—body parts, a finger or a toe, like the shriveled relics of saints. What was the word? Reliquary. He didn't want to open it, but did as he was told. Inside he found only a small plastic bag tied with a red bow. A packet of gray dust, like a sample brought back from the moon. When the astronauts returned from space, they said the lunar dust smelled like gunpowder. Jonah wondered if these ashes smelled like that, or like the burning odor he had breathed all autumn long.

"She's not in there," Vivian said. "There's probably nobody in there. They can't even test it for the DNA. I asked the guy. He said the DNA dies in fire that hot. He said this was just *symbolic*. A spoonful of dirt. What kind of symbol is that? Take it. I don't want it."

"It isn't mine."

"As her husband, you should have it."

"We weren't married."

"As her fiancé then. For once, please, don't argue with me. Just take it. I don't want it in my house. It only upsets me."

Jonah agreed to take the urn.

"Coffee's ready," Vivian said. "Go up and get him down here, will you? I'm not in the mood to yell tonight."

Near the edge of the roof, Frank stood with a pair of binoculars, looking out across the rooftops while a radio softly played. Jonah was certain that Frank did not like him. He tried to imagine how it would be now if Frank had become his father-in-law. Jonah would have to make an effort. He would have to assert himself. A man like Frank would respect that. Jonah stepped across the black tar surface. The skyline of Manhattan rose like a shadowy palisade, a glittering mountain range across the river. The blue towers shined together like a searchlight's single beam, a bar of light that seemed to hum, vibrating with the particles of swirling life.

"Vivian asked me to come get you."

Frank grunted, keeping the binoculars up to his face. Jonah looked around. On the table was a nearly empty bottle of amaretto and a juice glass with a finger of amber liqueur at the bottom.

"The pound cake and coffee's ready," he tried, making his voice sound authoritative on the subject.

"Tell me something," Frank said, lowering the binoculars and turning around. "Why does a young guy like you want to hang around with an old broad like her? Don't you have a girlfriend somewhere? It's Friday night, for Chrissakes. Friday nights are for getting drunk and getting laid, not eating pound cake with old ladies."

Jonah didn't know how to answer this. He tried pretending he was someone else, someone with a name like Rocco, who knew what to say and how to say it to a guy like Frank. He said, "Getting drunk and getting laid. Good idea. Mind if I have a drink?" It didn't come out right.

"Help yourself. But don't ask me to fuck you," Frank turned back to whatever he was looking at. "There's an extra glass back there."

Jonah found the glass in a sagging wooden cabinet built next to the loft and poured himself a finger of the almond liquer. It burned a little, but tasted sweet.

"Nice view."

"Used to be a helluva lot nicer," Frank said. He was drunk, Jonah realized.

"Those towers were my favorite buildings," Jonah lied. "It's just not the same without them. They were works of art. Must've been something, building them. What job did you do?"

"I was a connector in the raising gang. You know what that means? Of course you don't know. I connected steel on the North Tower. That was my tower."

"Rose's, too."

"It was the first one those sons of bitches hit, and the last one to fall. I built it right. A lot of people got out of there."

"What was it like? Working up there."

"I loved it," Frank said, taking down the binoculars and letting them rest against his belly. "Most exciting time of my life. Second to Korea. Korea was the most exciting time. But erecting that tower, that was a close second."

Frank sat in a folding beach chair, the plastic slats sighing under his weight, and took a crumpled pack of 555 cigarettes from his shirt pocket.

"In the spring and summertime, it got real nice up there. We had an unbelievable view. On foggy days it was what I call ghostly, 'cause you'd boom out over the side with the crane, drop the load block down ninety, ninety-five floors to the street, and you didn't see nothing but the cable going down into the fog. The engines are whining and you know this load of steel is coming up from the street, but all you see is the cable moving in the fog. Then, all of a sudden, foom! This load of steel would break out of the fog. It was ghostly." He stopped to put a cigarette between his lips, then continued, "One winter we had an ice storm. It was like something out of Disneyland. The four cranes with their booms up, like so," he raised his thick arms into the air to demonstrate, "boomed up, as you call it, with the ice built up overnight. Everything was nothing but glistening ice, all along those towers. They were like trees in a forest, just frozen in time."

He offered the pack of cigarettes to Jonah, who took one, feeling like he was finally getting through to Frank. He didn't know the man was capable of such poetry and he didn't want to break the spell. Frank lit the cigarettes and leaned back in his chair. It had been years since Jonah's last cigarette and with one drag the fresh blast of nicotine sent his neurotransmitters into giddy spins. His brain fizzed.

"The best day was when we passed the height of the Empire State. I mean, here we are, just a bunch of young guys, you know, I was pretty young then, and we're bypassing the Empire State. In my family, you'd talk about buildings and the Empire State, *ma'donn*. My father built the Chrysler. He was still working with hot rivets back then. The Chrysler was his baby and he fucking hated the Empire State. 'Cause it topped the Chrysler, see? Empire State's got 102 floors, so when we went for the 103rd floor steel on the North Tower it was a great feeling. You felt like King fucking Kong. I set things straight. And my father was proud. Thank God he didn't live to see this. Fucking Empire State."

Frank swallowed the rest of his drink and looked out toward the distant Statue of Liberty, a small, green figurine illuminated in the harbor. The pigeons purred in their loft.

"I heard on the news," Jonah said, wanting to sound like someone who knew something about it, "it was the trusses that gave way and that's why the towers collapsed."

"The towers collapsed because who in their right mind designs a building to stand up against a jet dumping 20,000 gallons of fuel in it? Nobody," Frank snapped. "Everyone's trying to figure out why they fell. It's like Monday-morning quarterbacking. But when you start to think. I don't know. The floor system that was in there, I mean—look, I'm not an engineer but I've been around a lot of structures—it was impossible for it to stand up."

"You think it was the trusses?"

"They call them trusses in the newspapers. We don't call them trusses, we call them bar joists. It's a truss, I suppose. Like you have in a shopping center. It's lightweight crap. Tinfoil. They told us to connect them and we connected them. I wasn't the fucking engineer. I didn't write up the plans. If it was up to me, I mean, a bar joist ain't a lot of support for a building. I think—and this is only my opinion, which probably don't mean shit—but I think if it was column and beam, it would have stayed up a lot longer and maybe a lot more people would have gotten out of there. A lot more."

Frank took a last drag on his cigarette and dropped the butt into a Chock Full O'Nuts can at his feet. He pinched the bridge of his nose and closed his eyes while the radio sang about harbor lights. He stayed this way, like he had a bad headache and didn't want to move. Jonah didn't know what to say. He walked around the pigeon loft and looked in at Frank's birds, huddled in feather-strewn nests made from orange crates filled with straw. He watched them bobbing their heads like actors in early motion pictures, stuttering and monochromatic. *It might be nice*, he thought, *to be a pigeon.* He had started back for the stairs when Frank hoisted himself up with a groan and said, "You wanna see something? Look at this here."

He opened the cabinet on the loft and reached inside, past a jar of mixed nuts, a deck of playing cards, and a fresh bottle of amaretto, to pull out a dark chunk of metal the size of a brick. He put it in Jonah's hands. It was much heavier than it looked.

"Don't fucking drop it," Frank warned him. "That's steel. It's a piece of a column I connected. From the Trade Center. Read the numbers."

Jonah angled the steel to catch the light and read the etchings: 11 TON, 803B, 18 21, 552 EAST.

Frank said, "This belonged to a column. See? It's 11-ton going from the eighteenth to the twenty-first floor. That's the wall of a column from the northeast corner of the building. That corner was the last section standing. You probably saw pictures of it in the papers. That's the steel I erected. I did it right."

He took the artifact out of Jonah's hands, hefted it once to feel its impressive weight, and placed it back in the cabinet. He shut the door and closed the latch.

"We should've put in column and beam," Frank said. "But I wasn't the engineer. I just followed orders."

11

The next morning, Jonah awoke with a headache and the vapor of a dream lingering in the sheets. As he came to consciousness, the details began to fade. He grasped for them, managing to hold only a scrap, the memory of being encased in a glass box. The glass might have been red, like the painted windows in a church. He was definitely naked. Outside the box, dark silhouettes moved back and forth, looking in. A cloaked shadow hovered above. Jonah reached for more, trying to slip back past the liminal doorway of sleep, but the more he tried, the less successful he was. Beside him, sensing his wakefulness, Frankie got to her feet, walked to the pillow, and breathed into his face. By the time Jonah had dressed, quickly checked the stove, and hurried out the door, he had forgotten the dream completely.

The day was sunny and warm, and as he walked with Frankie toward the dog run, where Jane would be waiting to greet them for their play date, he tried not to think about whether or not the stove was off and the apartment was filling with gas, ready to explode. He shouldn't have been in such a rush when he checked the knobs, he thought. He considered going back upstairs to check again, but he didn't want to be late. He passed a hot-pink flyer taped to a light pole. "Are your thoughts killing you?" it read. "Get out of your head and into your self. Feel your aliveness with body psychotherapy." Jonah considered tearing off one of the tabs that had the phone number on it, but decided not to. Body psychotherapy would probably involve getting into a fetal position and having some stranger touch him in uncomfortably intimate ways, all the while whispering in his ear, "It's okay to let go. It's okay to be angry. It's okay to cry." He couldn't handle that. Maybe he could talk to Jane. She was a therapist. She might have some good advice about why he felt compelled to check the stove so often.

At the dog run, he let Frankie off the leash and watched her go tearing across the dirt. There was Jane with a lollipop in her mouth, already seated on their bench.

Our bench, he thought.

That's chummy, said Rose, making her appearance. *And to think you and I were engaged not long ago.*

You can't be jealous, he told her.

That was awfully bold of you, telling my mother that. You're really pushing your luck. And why can't I be jealous?

Because you're a figment of my imagination. And besides, I'm not your type. Your mother said so.

What does my mother know?

Jane looked up and waved, and Jonah noticed that she looked good, dressed in weathered blue jeans and a cowboy shirt.

She has a boyfriend, he told Rose, *so there's nothing to worry about.*

There's plenty to worry about, said Rose, following him across the dog run to Jane.

"You beat me," Jonah said to Jane.

"I like to be early," she said, taking the lollipop out of her mouth. "I hate to be late."

"I'm not late, am I?" he asked, even though he knew for a fact that he was two minutes early.

"You're right on time. I appreciate that. I hate people who are late. There is nothing more inconsiderate, I think, than tardiness. Especially since I'm always early. But you know what shrinks say: 'Early anxious, angry late.'"

"Do shrinks say that?"

"It's like an inside thing," she said, lifting a plastic cup of iced coffee and taking the straw between her lips. The cup in her hand was branded with an all-too-familiar green circle. Jonah stared hard at the corporate logo, at the woman in the circle. She wore a smug little smile, long hair demurely covering her breasts, flanked by a pair of curving fish tails.

"Is that a mermaid," Jonah asked, trying to disguise his contempt, "or is it a siren, luring men to their doom?"

"This is actually quite interesting," said Jane, looking at the cup. "The original Starbucks logo was much more explicit. It was a totally bare-breasted woman holding a fish tail in each hand, kind of like she is here? But in the original you can see that her lower half is split into two tails and she's spreading them like legs. These double-tailed mermaids are sirens, and they're related to Sheela-Na-Gig, the ancient Celtic figure who terrifies and seduces men by spreading her legs to show them her powerful vagina. The womb and the tomb. I didn't make this up. I read it on the Internet. A guy named Fenkl wrote all about it. It's not bullshit—he's a mythic scholar and an interstitial novelist." Jane sucked her lollipop and continued, "Interstitial. Between the spaces. Anyway. One could also argue that the Starbucks siren is actually Echidna, the half-woman, half-serpent of Greek mythology who spawned an army of terrible monsters. She was the sister of Medusa, that classical castrator, and the daughter of Ceto, the sea monster, from whose name we get *cetacean*, for whale. There's a weird connection here to *Moby Dick*. You know they named Starbucks after a guy in *Moby Dick*."

"I never read it."

"You're kidding. You'd think with the name Jonah you'd want to read all the whale stories you could."

"I couldn't get through it in high school. It went on for too long."

Kind of like this woman, Rose interrupted, lingering by the shrubbery along the fence. She thought Jane was monologuing.

"Well, Starbuck is the first mate," said Jane, "I think. He symbolizes the faithful, God-fearing Christian type, you know, the one who refuses to face the reality of evil and darkness. His unwillingness to see the truth gets him swallowed up in the end. That's my Cliff's Notes version. I can't believe you never read *Moby Dick*."

Jane sucked on the straw until the coffee was gone. She rattled the ice and set the cup down on the bench, putting the lollipop back into her mouth. Jonah looked over at Rose. She was plucking the new leaves from a lilac bush. She didn't look happy.

"I want a cigarette," Jane said, "and I'm going to have one." She opened her clear Lucite purse and took out a pack of Camels. She removed the lollipop from her mouth and replaced it with a cigarette. She lit the end and took a deep drag, pulling the smoke down into her lungs, then exhaled a blue plume into the air.

"You're inhaling," Jonah said.

"Yeah. Fuck it," she said. "I have no impulse control. Especially since I moved up to four days a week on the couch. I'm all about letting my instincts run free. Freud said the ego is like a rider on a horse, controlling the much stronger animal—that's the id—who only wants to run wild. It's exhausting work. So I'm taking a break. Let's just say, the rider is off the horse."

Jonah looked back to the lilac bush. Rose was gone. He felt around inside his consciousness but couldn't find her. He watched Jane as she took another deep and gratifying drag. He noticed how real she looked, how alive, unlike Rose's ghost, who never failed to have a not-all-there fogginess about her. Jane took the cigarette out of her mouth and put the lollipop back in. She continued to make this exchange—lollipop, cigarette, lollipop, cigarette—until the Camel had burned down to its end. Then she took a violent bite out of what remained of the lollipop, crunching through the hard candy to get to the bubblegum inside. Jonah watched while a large, sparkling pink bubble swelled from between her lips. He thought about that thing that teenagers do in movies, something he never got to do when he was a teenager, when you kiss a girl and her bubblegum ends up in your mouth.

"I am haunted by real estate," Jane said, out of nowhere. "My nightmares used to be about Nazis, about men with guns breaking down my door. Now they're all about real estate. About a world in which there is nothing left to buy."

Jonah nodded, trying to think of a way to work in his question about checking the stove, but before he could open his mouth, Jane jumped to another subject, saying, "I've been thinking about going back to the German language. I took it in high school, but I forget most of it. And if I'm going to be a psychoanalyst, it just makes sense. How many German words can you think of?"

"I never took German."

"Everybody knows some. You must know *schadenfreude*. Delight in the misery of others? That's one for me. Now it's your turn."

Jonah offered, "*Weltschmerz*?"

"Good one. *Flintenweibe*. It means gun-woman or something like huntress, but it has this whole castrating phallic mother component to it. *Weib* is not a nice word for a woman. It's like 'bitch.' So she's the bitch with a gun-slash-penis."

"Sounds like a bunch of *Sturm und Drang* to me," Jonah said, feeling clever.

"Very nice. It's also rather *unheimlich*. Freud's word for 'uncanny.' He used it to mean the sensation that comes over you when the familiar becomes strange. He said we have this experience most often when it comes to death, dead bodies, ghosts, and the return of the dead. And when inanimate objects, like dolls, come to life. Do you remember that *Twilight Zone* episode where the doll comes to life and terrorizes the nice suburban family?"

"Talking Tina. That doll was totally freaky."

"Totally *unheimlich*," Jane corrected.

"All right. I've got a good one for you. This one's going to knock your socks off. Are you ready?"

"Shoot."

"*Gleichmacherei*."

Jane screwed up her face. "What is that? Same-maker?"

"It means something like, 'That which makes everything the same.' Starbucks would be a good example of a *Gleichmacherei*, homogenizing everything in its path. Did you know that, within a five-mile radius of where we're sitting right now, there are 156 Starbucks? That's about thirty-one Starbucks for every square mile. With twenty street blocks per mile in Manhattan, that's at least one Starbucks for every block. They're like a plague of locusts. I can't believe you would drink their coffee."

"Contempt for Starbucks," said Jane, patting his thigh condescendingly, "is such a cliché."

"You're the second person to tell me that."

"You know what I was thinking about the other day? The Angles, Saxons, and Jutes."

"What about them," Jonah grumbled, irritated by Jane jumping topics, but excited by her hand on his thigh.

"Well, the Angles and Saxons are still around, right? All the WASPs of the world. But whatever happened to the Jutes? You never hear a peep out of those Jutes."

"Did they come from Germany?" Jonah asked.

"No, Denmark I think."

"What do they have to do with German?"

"Nothing. It's totally unrelated to the German conversation. Just something I've been thinking about. That's how my mind works, Jonah: I free associate. Sometimes, I can be overly associative. It's like logorrhea of the mind. I know—it's annoying. Most guys can't stand it when I get talking."

Jane took her hand back to light another cigarette and they lapsed into silence. They looked out across the dog run. Jonah had no idea how to steer her around to his question about the stove-checking ritual. A fragment of that morning's dream returned to him, bobbing up out of the depths. The glass box. It probably didn't mean anything. It was just a remnant of the night before at the church. Christ in his glass coffin. Churches were filled with boxes. The little golden box where they kept the communion wafers. The confessional box. But that was more like a booth. A small, dark cubicle. The window with its shade going up, and Jonah peering through to see the mystery on the other side. "Forgive me, Father, for I have sinned. I talked back to my mother, took the Lord's name in vain. I had impure thoughts," he would whisper, so quietly the priest had to ask him to speak up. On the other side of the velvet curtain, his mother sat in the pews, waiting for him to finish. She could hear him, Jonah was sure. She was out there, with her ear cocked, listening to his darkest secrets. She used to sneak him into church just for confession. There were fights about it with his father.

"Technically," his mother would argue, "he's not Jewish. Only your mother can make you Jewish."

"Is that right, Jonah?" his father would say. "Are you Catholic? Do you believe in the magic of Jesus Christ?"

Jonah would sit silently between his two parents, refusing to answer his father's impossible question, waiting for his mother to intervene on his behalf.

"Don't put him in the middle," she'd say. "Jonah, you don't have to answer that." And she would set him free, telling him to go play in his room. On the way down the hall, he could hear his father saying, "Let the boy have opinions, Terri. He's not a baby. Let him fight his own battles."

When they weren't fighting about it, his father made jokes. In the morning, with orange juice and bagels, he would drape the dishtowel like a purificator over the glass of juice, lift it up sparkling in the risen light, and say, "This is my blood." Then the bagel, the same way, held aloft: "This is my body." He sliced the bread through its middle, plastered it with Philadelphia-brand cream cheese, and raised it to his mouth.

"You're not supposed to chew it," Jonah said. "It hurts Him when you chew it."

"It's just bread—yeast, flour, sugar, eggs. No magic there." His father bit down hard and made a show of his chewing so Jonah could see that no bolt of lightning came to strike them dead. But Jonah saw something else entirely. Sin was something you collected over time. That bolt of lightning waited for you, dangling overhead like the sword of Damocles. You could never be sure when it would drop, only that it eventually would. But if you were heartily sorry and you confessed, you just might stay ahead of it. And so Jonah looked forward to his secret confessions, when he could wash the sins away and get out from under that sword, at least for a little while. He liked best the part of the confession ritual when it was all over, when the priest gave him his penance and he knelt on the scratchy red carpet before the altar to recite his five Hail Marys, his ten Our Fathers, and be cleansed. He felt at those times a just-scrubbed joy. He was a blank slate and could start over.

He knew now that what he really wanted was not to talk about checking the stove, but to confess, and who better to hear a confession than a shrink? It felt dangerous to say it out loud, as if Vivian, all the way in Brooklyn, might hear. But Jonah could not keep it to himself any longer.

"Can I tell you something?"

"Anything," Jane said, turning toward him.

"I realize you're probably tired of people spilling their guts all the time, but I have this thing—"

"Just dump it out."

He checked for Rose by the lilac bush, but she wasn't there and wouldn't hear—except that she heard everything. It didn't matter, he reminded himself. She wasn't the one he'd been lying to.

"I had this neighbor, named Rose," he began. "She died in the World Trade Center. I never really knew her. I mean, only in passing. On the street. And now I have her dog."

"Are you telling me you stole a dead woman's dog?"

"No. Her mother gave the dog to me. I didn't steal anything. I'm not a thief."

"Why did her mother give you the dog if you didn't know this woman?"

"The dog's not important," Jonah said. "The dog is not the story I'm trying to tell. Let me start from the beginning. Just before 9/11, I was on the Staten Island Ferry and I blotted out the Twin Towers with my thumb. You know how you can do that, by closing one eye?" He demonstrated and continued, "Well, that's what I did. Two weeks later, the towers were gone."

"Powerful thumb."

"Right? So that's why I called Rose's mother. Vivian. I only meant to apologize, but then all these words came out of my mouth." As he confessed, he felt an electricity jab through him, like a hot pinball bouncing around his insides.

"You meant to apologize for destroying the World Trade Center," Jane said. "With your thumb."

"Right."

"From the Staten Island Ferry."

"I know it sounds crazy, but that's not the crazy part. The crazy part is that now I'm engaged to be married to the woman, to Rose," he said, the pinball caroming between the bumpers of his lungs.

"Your dead neighbor."

"Right. Because of all these lies I've been telling to her mother. About how we worked together and we were *together* together, a couple. And last night I went too far. I told her we were getting married." He felt the pinball zoom through his heart, lighting it up like a cheap plastic toy. "And it doesn't make any sense, because I've never been much of a liar. When I was a kid, my mother would ask me did I eat a candy bar before dinner or did I wash my hands, or whatever, and I couldn't lie. I just couldn't do it."

"You were a regular George Washington."

"She saw right through me. My mother, I mean. The times I did try to lie, she knew. I couldn't fool her. But Vivian? She believes everything I say. And it's like I can't stop myself."

"I'm not sure I'm understanding this," said Jane. "Can you start over, and go slowly? Fill in all the blanks."

Jonah told Jane the whole story, with all the details, from Rose dropping her glove to the moment he called Vivian, right up to the night before when he took the memorial urn of non-Rose ashes off Vivian's hands and carried them home, where they were now sitting next to his own mother's actual ashes. Finally, he told her about being haunted by Rose and how he talked to her ghost.

"What do you think?" he asked when he was done. "Am I crazy? Am I terrible?"

"If you're so troubled by it, you could just tell this woman the truth. Or don't. Either way, it's no crime. And she seems to be getting something out of it."

The pinball dropped with a leaden thud somewhere in the vicinity of Jonah's lower intestine and went straight down the drain. He was disappointed. Jane didn't look shocked in the least. He had expected her to gasp, to scream, to slap his face. He wanted penance. But she only sat and stared at him, her eyes serene behind their rhinestone glasses.

"Is that all?" he asked. "Don't you want to tell me I'm scum, I'm a horrible person? Tell me I have to confess my lies?"

"Is that what you want me to tell you?"

It was the old head-shrinker trick, turning everything back around. But he did want her to say those things. He wanted to feel clean, to undo his crime. He could sense that sword swinging above him, heavy and pendulous, straining to drop. He had one more sin to confess.

"When I'm with you," he said, "Rose goes away. It's like she just wanders off."

"Do you always fall for unobtainable women?" Jane asked quietly.

Jonah thought he saw a blush spread across her cheek like a blossoming lichen.

"I haven't fallen for anybody," he said.

"What about Vivian? You've spent time with her the past three weekends and you're going back tomorrow."

"It's Easter Sunday," Jonah explained. "And get your mind out of the gutter. Vivian is old enough to be my mother."

"Eureka," Jane said. "This is why I am going to be a brilliant analyst."

"Because you got me to say the word 'mother'? Big deal."

"Interesting how you rhymed 'gutter' with 'mother.'"

"Those words don't rhyme."

"It's a slant rhyme. And look what happens when you translate 'mother' into German. You get a visual rhyme: gutter and *Mutter*. What do you think it means?"

"I think it means you have a tendency to read too deeply into things, to see things that just aren't there."

Jane smiled and picked up her Starbucks cup. She rattled the ice, showing Jonah the siren with her spread tail, like a symbol he was meant to interpret. The ice had melted enough to make water and Jane sucked it out until the straw made an obscene noise.

"I read between the lines," she said. "That's where the truth lies."

12

Jonah stood at his ironing board waving a can of Niagara spray starch over a clean, white shirt, spritzing as he went along, carefully removing the wrinkles with a hot iron. His mother had taught him how to do this. The box of her ashes—holding all her knowledge about ironing shirts and which cleaning products to use for which types of messes (Fantastic worked wonders on stovetops but Scrubbing Bubbles was better for bathrooms), along with facts about Renaissance art and the history of the Roman Empire—sat next to Rose's urn on the shelf. The box looked flimsy and cheap in comparison. Maybe it was time to buy his mother a proper container.

From a corner of the room, Rose's ghost watched him. He could feel here there, like a cat that drifts in without a sound. Frankie lifted her head from the couch and whined once before going back to sleep.

You spend more time with my mother than you do with me, Rose said. *Not to mention Jane.*

"You could come with me," he said out loud to the empty room.

Easter Sunday with my parents? No, thanks. I left Brooklyn for a reason.

"Suit yourself," he said as he finished the shirt. He unplugged the iron and placed it on the middle rack inside the oven, just in case it should burst into flames. He figured that inside the oven was the safest place for a hot iron to be, since the oven was always a little hot anyway, due to the burning presence of the pilot lights. He checked the knobs on the stove, pointing and repeating "Off, off, off, off, off," then put on his best suit, an olive-green sharkskin that he had bought in a second-hand store off Canal Street. His beat-up wingtips were looking shabbier than ever, the left sole working itself loose. Making a mental note to buy some Shoe Goo, he propped one shoe at a time on the toilet lid, spat on the toes, and rubbed his fizzing saliva into the leather with a dirty sock. He left Rose sitting on the couch, looking out the window with a pout.

On Court Street, he stopped at an Italian bakery and picked up a loaf of Easter bread—a braided ring woven around pink and blue eggs—to bring to Vivian. His own mother had always loved this bread at Easter, and he thought Vivian would appreciate the gesture. He rang the Oliveris' doorbell and stood waiting on the front steps in between the plaster urns with their miniature American flags unmoving in the still air. The yard that had been in disarray when he first arrived was now raked clean and well organized. In the muddy plots and decorative pots that had once held only weeds, crocuses and snowdrops now stood in bunches, bright dabs of color in the dark soil. No one answered the door. He checked his watch and rang the bell again. He was early. It was a warm day, with clouds that only looked like rain, and the inside door was wide open, letting in the spring air. Jonah cupped his hands around his eyes to peer through the screen. The television was on. He saw it shimmer across the room and heard it say, "Take a gander at this eight-millimeter imitation diamond solitaire ring—it's all about that monster rock."

He tucked the Easter bread under his arm and put his hand on the latch, pushing the worn button with his thumb. The screen door clicked and popped open. *Brooklyn*, he thought as he stepped inside, *the land of unlocked doors.*

"Hello?"

"This ring is all about the rock," the television answered. "The fire, the brilliance, the spectacular—the finest cubic zirconia in the world."

The kitchen smelled sweetly of rosemary and roasting leg of lamb. Jonah set the bread down on the table and looked out the window over the sink, into the backyard. It was empty. He walked up the pink-carpeted stairs, following a trail of radio music, and stopped in front of Rose's room.

"Hello?"

The room was dark, the shades pulled down against the late-morning light. The air smelled of scented candles and unwashed clothes, a tangy mix of vanilla and faint body odor. He ran his fingertips along the polished top of the pink dresser. A pink hand mirror lay face down, its matching hairbrush beside it, bristles woven with long, dark strands of Rose's hair from before she bleached it blonde in places and streaked it with Manic Panic. He touched the brush and considered slipping it into his jacket pocket. From one of the many cardboard boxes, Rose's dirty laundry—her last load— spilled forth an abundance of blouses and t-shirts, jeans and skirts, socks and white cotton briefs. A sudden noise, like knuckles knocking on wood, stopped his breath. He froze, sure that Frank stood behind him, and braced himself for a blow. But no one was there, only the dark hallway behind him, a tremor of light coming from the master bedroom where a window shade clapped.

Vivian's bed was neatly made with a floral spread and heaped with pink pillows like whipped frosting on a girlish confection. He could not imagine Frank sleeping in this feminine place where delicate, long-lashed China dolls lined the shelves, their skirts a riot of frills; crocheted antimacassars laced the backs and arms of sitting chairs; and the mirrored bureau shouldered an entire city of perfume bottles, a smoky skyline veiled in a smog of flowery scents that made Jonah's nasal passages itch. There was nothing masculine here, the only sign of Frank an ashtray on the far bedside table crammed with 555 butts. On what was, presumably, Vivian's table, a half-squeezed tube of BenGay and a crossword puzzle book reminded him of his mother, her aching neck and insatiable need to solve the riddles of the *Times*, bending dull Sunday mornings under the sway of her tooth-ravaged pencil. No television, no radio, no rowdy board games were allowed. Everything stopped until the code was broken, the morning silent but for their back-and-forth calls and responses. What's a seven-letter word for "electrical units," an eight-letter word for "universal," a nine-letter word for "soft-toned flutes"? Jonah would lean against her shoulder and offer his best, boyish answers, counting out the letters on his fingers and shouting any word that came to mind: Voltage! Cosmos! Woodwinds! His father shushed them from behind his own dull section of the newspaper with its gray faces and war reports. "You two are quite a *team*," he'd say in a way that made the good word sound like something bad.

Jonah slipped the pencil from the pages of Vivian's puzzle book, holding her place with his thumb. Her teeth had eroded the blue foil stamping, but he could still make out PAPERMATE, a pair of hearts printed between PAPER and MATE, followed by the word AMERICAN and the number 2. He could easily steal the pencil and Vivian would never know. She would assume it had rolled out of the book on its own power and disappeared in the vast shadows beneath the bed, where she would not bother to search because it would trouble her knees. But then he would lose Vivian's place. To dog-ear the page or turn the book over so it opened where she had left off would be to call attention to the theft of the pencil. He could not steal it. Instead, he took the pencil between his teeth and gently bit down, feeling the tender wood yield, tasting the flaked yellow paint and searching with his tongue for the splintered divots of Vivian's previous bites. What he wanted from this act he could not explain, even to himself—it was an *impulse*, he thought—and as he stood in the flickering sunlight of the room, pushing the pencil back to his molars until it fit like a bit in a horse's mouth, he wondered what Jane would have made of it. Something filthy, no doubt.

The sound of radio music filtered down the hallway and Jonah replaced the pencil, just glazed with saliva, into the book. The music came from the roof but when Jonah got there Frank was nowhere in sight. His beach chair sat empty. On the metal folding tray beside it, a dark cigar smoldered in a ceramic ashtray rimmed with gold plating. The radio sang, "It was a very good year," as the pigeons prattled to each other in their loft. He walked once around the coop, looking in at the birds, and stopped in front of Frank's cabinet. The door hung open. He regarded the binoculars, the deck of playing cards, the steel brick from the North Tower. But it was a shoebox that held his attention. He wondered if this was where Frank kept those papers Vivian had mentioned, the Trade Center confetti he had watched swirling in the smoky sky like snow. He checked once behind him and lifted the shoebox's lid. A cloying perfume of sweet, organic decay escaped from the box. It was filled to the brim with roses. No singed interoffice memos or ashy corporate stationery, just dozens of white roses that had turned sepia and dry. No stems, just the heads.

"She's not back from mass."

Jonah turned with a jolt to see Frank standing behind him.

"No one answered the door," he explained, feeling his face warm. Where had Frank been all this time? He wondered if he'd been watching, seen him hovering over Rose's underwear and tasting Vivian's pencil in his teeth. It looked bad.

"Probably bullshitting with that *mulignon* priest over there," Frank said, reaching past Jonah to grab the bottle of amaretto and a glass from the cabinet.

"What kind of priest?" Jonah asked, attempting a casual tone.

"The Indian. He's not a real Indian, like in the movies. He's from India. Can't understand a friggin' word he says," Frank said, sitting down in the chair and pouring two fingers of liqueur into the glass. He swallowed it, then picked up the cigar, stuck it in his mouth, and stoked it until the end glowed an irritated red.

"So," Frank said, pointing to the opened shoebox, "you found out my secret."

"I was just looking for a cigarette."

Frank reached into his shirt pocket and pulled out a soft pack of 555s. He tossed one and Jonah put it between his lips. He didn't have a light and Frank didn't offer one.

"Secrets," Frank said cryptically, exhaling a pungent ribbon of cigar smoke. "Those roses look familiar?"

"I don't know."

"Sure you do. Think about it."

Jonah remembered the white roses that had appeared, week after week, on Rose's doorstep.

"Vivian thinks you didn't care," Jonah said, "but you must've visited her door a lot."

Frank looked away, over the rooftops, and said, "My wife says Rose wanted to marry you."

Jonah wished he could light the cigarette that hung stupidly from his mouth. "We just talked about it."

"See, that doesn't make sense to me," Frank said, staring hard now at Jonah. "Rosie wanting to marry you? No offense, Joe, but you're not her type."

"Vivian said the same thing."

"You don't know Rose."

Jonah froze, feeling that pinball of panic setting itself up in his gut, ready to launch.

"Not like I knew her," Frank continued. "She could be a real little bitch when she wanted to. And the guys she went for? *Minchia.* Freaks with tattoos and stupid hairdos. Guitar players. Barfighters. She picked some real winners, all right. She did it just to piss us off. It drove her mother crazy. When she was in high school, I can't tell you how many punks I chased away with a baseball bat. That bat right there, in fact. Hand it to me, willya?"

Jonah picked up the wooden bat where it leaned against the pigeon coop. He thought better of it, but gave it over to Frank anyway. This was it. He could feel it. The sword was about to drop. Frank used the bat like a cane, pressing the fat end against the roof to push himself up from the chair. Jonah looked to the door, hoping to see Vivian climbing the stairs, coming to rescue him the way his own mother used to rescue him from his father's angry tirades. Frank stepped toward him, took the cigar from his mouth, and aimed the hot end at Jonah's face. Jonah flinched.

"Light?"

Jonah pressed his unlit cigarette into the cigar's cherry. Frank stayed close.

"How come, with all your stories about you and Rose, you never once mentioned that you lived right next door? You were neighbors. Funny how you never mentioned that part."

Jonah started to speak, but Frank stopped him.

"Don't bother lying about it. I saw you going in the building next door. I was there yesterday. I thought you looked familiar, in that ratty old hat, the first time you walked in this house." Frank raised the baseball bat to touch Jonah's chest with the barrel, where the words LOUISVILLE SLUGGER were burned into the faded gray wood. "You never had me fooled for a minute. My wife, on the other hand, is what you call gullible. You really pushed your luck with that getting married thing. But Vivian trusts you. She needs to trust you. I don't."

The hot pinball inside of Jonah rocketed through his rib cage, slamming from side to side. He'd made this happen by stupidly confessing his lie to Jane. He was sure of it. He never should've said the words out loud. Words had a way of making things happen. He saw how it worked, how his confession had flown up from the East Village, over the river, to Brooklyn, to this rooftop, to Frank, where it settled like a message fastened to a pigeon. He felt stupid and ashamed for all of it, wishing he could crawl into a hole and never come out. He deserved a beating, he thought.

"I'll tell her the truth," he said. "I swear."

Frank pushed the barrel of the bat under Jonah's chin. "What's your angle?"

"Angle? I'm not a con artist or anything."

"No shit. You don't have the balls to pull that off. But everybody's got an angle."

"I just wanted to get to know her. Rose, I mean. And Vivian, too. She's been so good to me."

Frank grinned, going for the gut as he said, "Your mother's dead, right? Is that what this is all about? You thought you'd get yourself another mother?"

"I didn't plan on lying, at first, and then it just came out. It didn't seem so bad. But I'll stop. I promise. I'll tell her everything."

"No, you won't," Frank said, taking the bat away and letting it swing down in his fist. "I've been thinking this over and you're not going to tell her shit. Sit down."

Jonah sat awkwardly on a rusted gallon can of paint and rubbed his throat while Frank stood over him and explained, "Since you've been coming around, my wife's been off my ass. She gets out of the house. She's not crying all the time. For some reason, and don't ask me why, she loves you like a son. Me, I don't trust you as far as I can throw you, but the way I see it, you're harmless. A bug. Now, here's the deal. When my wife gets in from mass, she's going to serve the Easter dinner. You're going to eat it with a smile on your face like nothing's any different. You're not ever going to mention this conversation and you're not going to tell any truth. You're going to let her keep believing what she wants to believe. That her little girl was a perfect fucking angel and not a royal pain in the ass. You're going to keep coming around, have tea and cookies, take her shopping, the whole nine yards. But heed my words. I've got my eye on you. One false move, and you will feel my wrath. Have I made myself clear?"

"Yes, sir."

"Crystal?"

"Crystal."

"Good. Now let's have a drink, *son-in-law*." Frank sat in his chair with the baseball bat between his knees and poured a second glass of amaretto. He handed it to Jonah, lifted his in the air, and said, "Salut." They drank. The liqueur was sweet and hot, and it burned its way down Jonah's throat.

At the dinner table, they ate gnocchi and roast leg of lamb. Roasted potatoes and stuffed artichokes. Vivian was bubbly, heaping the men's plates. Jonah ate as fast as she could serve. She watched him, praising his healthy appetite and enjoying his pleasure in her food. During dessert, Frank asked him to tell a story about Rose—"something nice," about their favorite restaurant. Jonah's mind went blank. He felt forced, gripped by a kind of stage fright.

"I can't think of anything right now," he said, looking at Vivian as she waited for him to divulge.

"Come on," Frank pushed. "You kids didn't have a favorite restaurant? Every couple's got a favorite restaurant."

Jonah didn't like this. The lies were his to tell, at his own pace, in his own way. He said, "We liked a lot of restaurants. Rose loved Italian, of course. She always said she loved the food that tasted like home. Ravioli was her favorite. Like her mother made."

"You hear that, Viv? She loved your ravioli."

Vivian smiled and shook her head, remembering the difficult teenager who once rejected everything about her, marveling now at her daughter's heretofore unknown capacity to mature and evolve.

"Could I please have another piece of ricotta pie?" Jonah asked, careful to be extra gracious in Frank's watchful presence.

"Did he just ask for another piece of pie? I'll slap his face," Vivian said.

"Sorry."

"Come on. I'm teasing. Don't be so polite. You're family. You don't have to ask, just help yourself. Did she really eat Italian food?"

"She did," he said, pressing his fork into the slice of pie Vivian put on his plate. "And not the fancy kind, either. She liked spaghetti, meatballs, manicotti. All the good stuff. Like you make."

"Meatballs? She stopped being vegetarian?"

"For meatballs like yours, she said, she could make an exception."

"Amazing," said Frank. "Who would have thought? Meatballs."

When the meal was over, Vivian presented Jonah with a basket filled with chocolate eggs, jellybeans, and a big white-chocolate rabbit nestled in a bed of green cellophane grass. He couldn't remember the last time he'd gotten an Easter basket. Frank grunted and lumbered off to the bathroom.

"Next weekend," Vivian said, "I want to drive out to Costco's again. They have this Waterfall in a Box—it comes with or without a pond—and I need your help with it."

"I meant to tell you," Jonah started.

"Look in the basket," Vivian whispered. "There's a little something extra in there."

"About next weekend, I have to work," he lied. "It's a busy time. Deadlines. Actually, the next couple of weekends—"

"Look in the egg," Vivian interrupted. She reached through an opening in the cellophane wrapper and pulled out a frothy panorama Easter egg.

Jonah held the egg up to peer through the peephole but a roll of bills blocked his view. He pulled it out, unfolding a crisp pair of fifties. Before he could protest, the guttural plumbing sounds of Frank finishing in the bathroom stopped him. Vivian grabbed the bills and stuffed them deep in his pants pocket.

"I got it," Jonah said, standing up fast.

Vivian took his hand and squeezed.

"Thanks again for everything," he said, feeling like an adulterer, as Frank walked back into the dining room adjusting his belt. "It was a wonderful meal."

"You're not leaving," Vivian said, standing up to grip his arms.

"I should."

"Stay and watch a little television," Frank insisted.

"I really should go."

"You need to digest," said Frank.

"It's getting late," Jonah said to Vivian, waiting for her to let him off the hook.

But she didn't. She said, "Stay for just an hour."

"I don't want to wear out my welcome."

"You'll stay," said Frank, clapping him on the shoulder with his meaty hand. "No arguments."

In front of the television, they munched licorice-tasting fennel stalks—*finochio*, Vivian called it, another word he hadn't heard since his mother was alive—"for good digestion."

"If kids are shooting guns in class," the television said, "shouldn't the teachers be allowed to return fire?" *Click*. "I like a sense of humor and real, natural beauty in a female." *Click*. "Her death had been quick and painless, unlike that of her victims." *Click*. "Sue underwent eight plastic surgeries in pursuit of the perfect face. But today, Sue still feels ugly." *Click*.

"Frank, that's enough," Vivian said. "You make me crazy with all this clicking."

The television said, "Police feared they had stumbled upon a killer's makeshift cemetery." *Click*. "Check your blood sugar as often as you should." *Click*. "The shooter is on the loose right now and police want to find him." *Click*. "Get a medium one-topping pizza free." *Click*. "Operation Anaconda." *Click*. "The world's deadliest predator is closer than you think."

"Frank, for Chrissakes, pick something."

Frank muttered and pressed the button again. On *60 Minutes* the reporter said, "That's when the mysterious woman picked up the telephone and called Tammy's parents to tell them that she was their little girl, missing since the age of ten, now grown up."

Frank put down the remote control.

"Did he finally pick something?" Vivian asked in Jonah's direction.

"I picked something," Frank said, using his toes to push off his shoes and pulling the lever on the side of the couch to activate the Lounger. With a metallic twang, a footrest sprang out from under him, lifting his legs into a relaxed position. He sighed and folded his hands over his belly while the television showed townspeople beating a grassy field with sticks, hound dogs sniffing through the brush, a brown-shirted sheriff taking off his cowboy hat and looking toward the sky. The reporter explained how Tammy's mother and father were suspicious at first, but the mysterious woman knew many details about their missing girl, including her favorite flavor of ice cream (chocolate) and her favorite color (pink). The parents put aside their doubts and threw a "Welcome Home" party, complete with Tammy's favorite meal: fried chicken, corn on the cob, and homemade biscuits. It was a happy reunion that lasted just one week. Local police recommended that Tammy's parents pursue a DNA test, just to be sure. When the woman refused to go through with the test, the investigators discovered a history of petty crime. She was a writer of bad checks. She had multiple personality disorder. She was running away from a sexually abusive satanic cult. She was not Tammy.

Jonah looked at Frank. Had he picked this show as a message to him? Frank just stared at the screen as the television camera, from the window of a moving car, panned across a row of crooked wooden houses, dogs barking in dusty yards, barefoot children pedaling Big Wheels. "She has always been flaky and high maintenance," said the woman's sunburned landlord, wiping the sweat off his neck with a red bandana, "but there was nothing to give you the impression that she would do something like this."

"She just likes the attention," said a former acquaintance, holding a dirty-faced baby on her hip. "She creates chaos because she thrives on the attention." Neighbors said that she was a quiet woman who "just sat on her porch in a plastic lawn chair, talking on a cell phone and smoking cigarettes." Sure enough, when police searched the woman's home, they found a thirty-gallon trash can filled to the top with Marlboro Ultra-Light cigarette butts.

Jonah tried to imagine what people would say about him in the *60 Minutes* exposé on his own Tammy-like drama, a story that would end in someone's murder, he was sure of it, now that there was no way out. Keith Starling would tell Morley Safer, "He was a real loner. Never wanted to come out after work, no matter how many times I invited him," and "He had trouble holding his liquor." His boss, Michelle, would say that he was often late for work, that she had considered letting him go many times, but that he was "too pathetic to fire." She felt sorry for him. Maybe the *60 Minutes* people would even track down his father, traveling to the Chilean desert to stick a microphone in Professor Soloway's face so he could tell them about his son's embarrassing lack of experience with women and his unhealthy attachment to his mother. Jane would make an appearance, too, putting forth her psychological analysis of what she'd call "a classic Oedipal triangle," and plugging her true crime book based on Jonah's story. She would title it *Liar, Liar, Pants on Fire*. In prison, or in the grave, whichever way it went, Jonah would be far away, where he couldn't do any more damage.

On the television, the hoodwinked father of the missing girl, sitting at a table in his trailer home, told the camera that he believed the real Tammy was still out there somewhere, and that she would come home to him someday. A wet and strangled sound came out of him, like dishwater making its way down a half-clogged drain. He put his hands over his face and shook with sobbing. The camera stayed on him, unblinking, until the man got up and walked into his bedroom, closing the door behind him. The reporter came onscreen to wonder aloud about the real mystery behind the woman caller and her cruel hoax. "She never made any request for money," the reporter said. "Perhaps she is nothing more than a lonely and troubled young woman, looking for love in a place where there is plenty to go around."

The *60 Minutes* stopwatch appeared on the screen, ticking down the seconds, and then the television shouted, "The new super-charged Sport Utility Vehicle from GMC. It's not more than you need. Just more than you're used to."

"People today," said Frank. "The world's full of kooks. This woman ought to be locked up for the rest of her life."

"She don't need prison," Vivian said.

"Throw away the key."

"She needs help."

"She needs a boot in the ass, that's what she needs."

"She was trying to get away from one of them satanic cults."

"That's an excuse?"

"Bumper-to-bumper warranty," said the television.

"They brainwash you in them cults," said Vivian.

"That's what you call an excuse?"

"Her real parents abused her."

"She probably deserved it."

"Your hairbrush may be killing you," said the television.

"Physically *and* sexually."

"That's no excuse."

"She needs to be deprogrammed. That's what they call it, when they take you out of a cult and get rid of the brainwashing. They call it deprogramming. Isn't that right, Jonah?"

"What's that?"

"Deprogramming," said Vivian, "when they take you out of a cult, to get rid of the brainwashing."

"That's right," said Jonah. "It's called deprogramming."

"See? I was right. Jonah agrees with me."

"I still say she ought to pay for her crime," said Frank. "What do you think, Joe?"

Jonah shrugged. He wasn't taking sides.

"Come on, you must have an opinion," Frank badgered him. "Speak up."

Jonah looked to Vivian, but she only waited for him to agree with her.

"Don't look at her, she's not going to save you," said Frank. "What's your answer?"

Jonah turned to the television. On the screen, helicopters swarmed like wasps in the dark sky over the Brooklyn Bridge while helmeted police officers searched the contents of an unmarked white van. It was time to leave. He would do as Frank told him and not tell Vivian the truth, but he wouldn't lie anymore, either. He would just stop coming around. He would simply slip away.

"No opinion," Frank chuckled. "We've got the gutless wonder over here."

On the television, the *60 Minutes* stopwatch was ticking like a bomb.

13

"I've been giving some thought to what you said last weekend," Jane said, "about that woman who died in the Trade Center. The one you're in love with? I found this note on the Memorial Wall in Grand Central the other day. It was tacked up high, next to the missing poster for a Japanese businessman. Check it out."

"I'm done with that," Jonah wanted to say as Jane held out the note. "I'm done with Rose and Vivian, too, and ready for you." He wanted it to be true. Instead he took the piece of cream-colored stationery, monogrammed with the letter S in curling script at the top, and read it. In neat penmanship, a woman had written:

> "My dear new friend, Mr. Kobayashi,
> Every day your face is the first one I see. Is it because of my substantial height, or is it some destiny? Is it that I come from Connecticut and go to the Lexington Ave. train that causes me to always pass by your face—and keep you in my heart? Or is it the sparkle in your eyes? The gentleness in your face, that drew me to you? I don't know. I only know that I will pray for you for the rest of my life. Bless you my silent friend. I look forward to meeting you one day.
> Susan R."

It was the saddest, most pathetic letter Jonah had ever read. He felt ashamed for himself and for Susan R., for their sentimental fantasies about the dead, the incinerated, the turned-to-smoke. *Someone should slap Susan R.*, he thought. *Someone should tell her to snap out of it.*

"You stole this from the Memorial Wall," he said.

"The MTA is cracking down on renegade notes like this one. All they want up there are the missing posters and pictures of the victims, but people can't help themselves. The notes keep multiplying. If I hadn't taken this, it would be in the trash by now. Anyway. That's not the point. What do you think of the letter?"

"I think it's very personal."

"Except that the writer chose to post it in a very public place."

Jonah handed the letter back to Jane. He didn't feel like talking about this anymore. He was over it. Frank had taken it away from him. The stories he told Vivian had been his own, something he created just for her, and now they weren't. He couldn't force them, couldn't produce them at gunpoint, or at the business end of a baseball bat. That's where Frank was wrong. It had been nearly a week now since Easter, since he'd last spoken to Vivian. She'd called twice in the past two nights about going to Costco that day, to pick out a Waterfall in a Box. He didn't return her calls. He told himself that he would call her tomorrow. He just needed some space. He needed to figure things out.

He stretched his legs out in front of him and gazed across the dog run where sprays of lilacs were coming into bloom over the fence. Rose wasn't there, in her usual place. In fact, she hadn't visited him once in the past week. He thought of the lilac tree that used to grow in his backyard, how his mother would go out every spring, in the dewy mornings, with her shears in hand and cut an armload of the heavy-drooping clusters. How the house smelled royally of lilac. He wanted to press his face into that inviting inflorescence and return, return, return. Maybe Frank was right when he said "this" was "all about" his mother.

Jane reached into her Strand Books tote bag and pulled out a small, yellow square of paper. "Here's another. A kind of haiku. The handwriting is different, but the sentiment is the same."

Jonah read again:
"Every morning
I see you
smiling.
I miss you.
We never met."

There was no signature. He handed the Post-it note back to Jane and shrugged.

"Don't you see," she said. "You're not the only one. People all over the city have fallen in love with these dead strangers. Isn't it fascinating? I mean, the lonely, tall Susan R. from Connecticut, hurrying to the 6 train every morning—'is it because of my substantial height,' she says! Can't you just imagine her?"

Jonah could imagine her. One of those gawky girls who slumped at her desk in school, afraid to be seen, wishing she were shorter, never getting the guy. Of course he could imagine her. He *was* Susan R., mooning over the photograph of a ghost.

"It's pathetic," he said.

"You're projecting," Jane told him. "People have this fascinating need to lay claim to these victims. Susan R. picked

Mr. Kobayashi, the haiku writer picked someone else, and you picked your neighbor. What was her name?"

"Rose."

"A rose is a rose is a rose is a rose," Jane said.

"It's not the same."

"I find it fascinating," Jane went on, "because it's something I don't relate to—this citywide, nationwide—I won't say global—emotional outpouring for the victims of 9/11. I engage the world primarily through my cortex—my frontal lobe, to be exact—and I did not have this emotional reaction after 9/11. Maybe that makes me a freak. I don't know. But, to me, those deaths are no more important or significant than the deaths of the thousands who perish in a cyclone in Bangladesh or get killed by American troops in Afghanistan. Not to get political. I am totally apolitical, that's not my point. My point is, I just think there is something phony about mourning the deaths of *these* strangers but not *those* strangers."

"She was my neighbor," Jonah said.

"Right, so there was some sense of familiarity there, which I guess is the whole thing. You hear about a random death on the turnpike and it means nothing. You put a face and a name to it, and wham, you're in mourning. And we spent months surrounded by their faces and their names, plastered up all over town. They became identified in the public imagination, not just anonymous, statistical victims. I remember walking past one particular face, over and over again—his name was Marcello—and it got to the point where I felt like I knew him, on some level. And I'd say, 'Hello, Marcello,' whenever I passed his missing poster. But I would be a complete hypocrite to mourn the death of Marcello and not the death of some Afghani kid who got blown to bits today in a horrible explosion. And since I can't possibly mourn every stranger's death, I choose not to mourn any of them. I can make that choice, engaging the world as I do through my cortex."

"Your frontal lobe."

"That's right. Look at me."

He looked at her. He looked at her forehead, using his X-ray vision to see her frontal lobe pulsing behind the curtain of dark hair, those sharp black bangs that reminded him of pin-up girls. Of Bettie Page in patent leather and leopard skin. He looked away.

"So you're saying that because I mourn for Rose I'm a phony and a hypocrite, is that right?"

"I'm saying that you're part of the clan mentality," she said. "I read this article in the *Times* about how humans evolved in small groups and so they mourn those closest to them. You *think* you're close to all these strangers because you saw their faces on television and on missing posters for months. They became like celebrities, and people have this delusion of closeness when it comes to celebrities, too. So I understand this response. It's totally natural. I just don't relate to it. Personally, I reject it wholesale."

She was right, to a point. It was delusional, all his chasing after a ghost, a woman who wouldn't give him the time of day when she was alive. He wasn't a guitar player or a bar fighter or a tattooed schmuck of any sort. He worked now to conjure her, to pull her up from the depths of his mind, imagining her taking shape by the lilac bush, her face the face of the girl in the Soyer painting. With some effort, she materialized, lingering by the lilacs, plucking at the leaves like a petulant little girl.

Where've you been, he asked.

You don't call me anymore, she said. *Not that I mind, really. And why are you ignoring my mother?*

I need space.

That's what they all say. I know what it's about.

What?

Jane. You think more about Jane than you do about me.

That isn't true, he said.

She didn't like it when he talked to Jane. Cool, analytic Jane who stripped him bare, right here in the dog run, in the middle of all that humping and sniffing, the stink of piss and other secretions, spit and mud, the new leaves unfolding above, green and raw and ready for action. Jane went on talking about death as Rose sat down in the narrow space between them on the bench, like a pushy subway rider squeezing herself into a tight spot.

She's so pretentious, Rose said. *Listen to her.*

She's smart, he said.

She's full of shit. What does she know about death? Ask me about death, I'll tell you. She intellectualizes something that's beyond the intellect. Her frontal lobe! Her precious cortex!

Your father said you could be a pain in the ass, he said.

I know you're thinking about fucking her.

I wish you'd stay out of my head.

I am your head.

It was true and Jonah knew it. He had no response.

Rose said, *I don't hold it against you, wanting to fuck her. She's real. She's alive. How many real girls have you even kissed?*

Jonah recited a list of girls he might have kissed but didn't. Marla Pipkin, of course, on the school bus with his hand between her legs. Emily Ross, a girl in high school who wore wool skirts with lace slips hanging down from the hem and whom he once dreamed of kissing in a summer house with the green grass sloping outside the window like a cool sheet, her mouth tasting of sweet plums, a taste he tasted for weeks after dreaming it, as if it had really happened. Katie Reynolds in college one rainy night behind the Student Center; she took his hand but he didn't take the hint. Debbie Moody, the mousy proofreader at *Boxboard Today* who dropped notes on his desk like it was seventh grade, her i's dotted with hollow bubbles, a detail that made him think "dumb" and served to convince him that he didn't want to kiss her anyway.

You, he added. *If I'd had the courage, if I'd grabbed your glove that day like I wanted to.*

That glove, she said. *You're obsessed with that glove. Like a fetish object. What does it mean? What does it symbolize?*

She was talking like Jane now and not like Rose. This was something that happened to fantasies if you didn't control them. They began to change on their own.

"You see it all the time when it comes to the deaths of celebrities," Jane continued, "especially the *untimely* deaths of celebrities. Think of the heaps of flowers that flowed onto the coffin of Princess Diana, onto the street in front of JFK Jr.'s apartment building. Remember that?"

"I remember," Jonah said, watching Rose while she waited for his answer. Why *was* the glove so important?

He looked at Rose and imagined kissing her. But, in looking at Rose, transparent as she was, he inevitably looked through her, so it was Jane who received his gooey gaze. He saw her see it, the look not meant for her. Or was it? Her eyes and mouth went soft. He hazarded a moment of physical contact, reaching out to touch her shoulder, specifically, to squeeze the muscle between her shoulder and neck. *Trapezius*. Like trapeze. Girls in tights swinging through the air. Kicking their legs.

Who are you touching, Rose asked. *Me or her?*

Jane closed her eyes, then leaned away. She said something about the warmth of the sun, doing her awkward imitation of

Scarlett O'Hara, and unbuttoned her denim shirt, revealing a white t-shirt underneath that said, "Bryn Mawr College: 108 Years of Castrating Bitches." Jonah wasn't sure how to interpret the signs. Had Rose somehow blended into Jane to create this moment of tensile stress? Jane would have used the word *frisson*.

Of course she would, Rose sniffed.

"Mark's working on a new reality show," Jane said. "I helped him with the original concept. It's fascinating. Do you want to hear about it?"

Jonah didn't want to hear about Mark but he shrugged his assent.

"It's called *Celebrity Death Wish*," Jane said, relishing the title. "Regular people come on the show to experience first-hand the deaths of their favorite dead celebrities. First, they get a complete makeover. Hair, clothes, everything. Even plastic surgery. They literally become the celebrity. Then, at the climax of each episode, they play the starring role in the recreated death scene. The network already has a number of episodes lined up. An ersatz Princess Diana crashes through a tunnel in Paris. A John Lennon fan gets shot in front of the Dakota building. A former nun and devotee of Joan of Arc is burned at the stake. There's one guy who wants to be crucified, but the network is afraid of the Christian-right backlash. And I almost forgot—a father and son do a double JFK: Dad gets his head blown off in Dallas and Junior plunges into the Atlantic off Martha's Vineyard."

I loathe this woman, said Rose, who never used the word *loathe*.

"These people actually die on camera?" Jonah asked. "That can't be legal."

"No, of course not. Nobody really dies. I mean, they sign a waiver, just in case. But the death scenes are elaborate stunts.

The players are trained by professional stuntmen. They're outfitted in bulletproof vests, protective headgear, asbestos suits, whatever is necessary for their chosen death. The rest is all special effects. Exploding blood bags under their clothing, blood capsules between the teeth, pyrotechnic machines, and a lot of editing, to make it look more realistic."

"Someone could really get hurt," Jonah said.

"That's the whole appeal of a show like this. The potential for actual death. The audience tunes in because they are secretly hoping that somebody will die. It's a Roman Colosseum thing. Like bullfights and circuses. Like watching tightrope walkers perform without a net. People will watch *Celebrity Death Wish* for the same thrill. It's Thanatos. The death instinct. But the show also caters to the audience's erotic instincts."

Jane was excited now. She got excited when she talked, like talking was sex. She clutched Jonah's thigh for emphasis. He was wearing wool trousers, a bad choice on such a warm day.

"You the viewer will enter the body of the celebrity, the object of public lust. You will *penetrate* Princess Diana or Jayne Mansfield, James Dean or whoever, via numerous sensors that will be monitoring your heart rate, blood pressure, brain waves, everything. You have to face it—death is erotic."

"I've never felt that way," Jonah said, feeling the heat of Jane's hand on his leg and an uninvited erection beginning to unfurl in his pants.

I knew it, said Rose, enjoying his discomfort. *I knew you wanted to fuck her. And you are getting off on it. Death. You're a regular necrophiliac.*

"I've never gotten off on death," he said out loud.

"Sure you have," Jane insisted. "Unconsciously. In infancy we aim for erotic mastery over the object of the breast, and in so doing, we aim to destroy the breast. Later on, this all comes out as sadomasochistic wishes and acts during sex. All sex is sadomasochistic, on some level. We all want to annihilate or be annihilated, at one point or another. In French, the words for *love* and *death* are closely related. *Amour* and *mourir*. They call orgasm *le petit mort*, the little death."

She gave Jonah's thigh a playful slap and took her hand back to feed a cigarette into her mouth. He felt the warm spot on his leg where her hand had been and wondered if they were fighting or flirting. Maybe, for Jane, it was the same thing.

"I know what you're thinking," said Jane.

No, said Rose, *I know what he's thinking. I know everything he's thinking.*

"You're thinking that someone as intelligent as I am shouldn't be fucking around with these dopey reality TV shows."

That's not what he was thinking, said Rose, laughing as Jonah crossed his legs uncomfortably.

"But they're more than just dumb entertainment," Jane went on. "They can be a kind of therapy for people. Call it theratainment. For instance, by watching *Phobia Phactory*, you can learn how to problem-solve and overcome your greatest fears. Especially now, since 9/11, people are terrified. They need this kind of, you know, triumphing over terror."

Rose rolled her eyes. She had no patience for Jane and her theories. She probably wanted to be out with some tattooed schmuck, drinking beer while he hammered on his electric guitar, doing whatever possible to make Vivian miserable. Was that who Rose really was? Frank had called her a bitch. Jonah wasn't sure anymore. There were so many Roses she might have been.

If you don't like it, Jonah said to Rose, *you can go.*

Are you kidding? Ask her about the glove. Come on. I want to hear what she comes up with. How much you want to bet she says it's a vaginal symbol?

Jonah didn't want to ask about the glove. He wanted to ask about the stove.

"I've been meaning to ask your advice on something," he said to Jane. "A problem I'm having. A sort of irrational fear, I guess, though I wouldn't call it terror."

"Shoot. I need the practice," Jane said, exhaling a mouthful of blue smoke. "Tell me about your muzza," she added in what she must have thought was a mock-Viennese accent, but sounded more like Bela Lugosi's Count Dracula. *Vergüenza ajena*, he remembered—that was the Spanish expression for when you felt embarrassed on behalf of another.

"She's not my problem," he said.

"If that were true, you'd be the first. Kidding. Really, tell me what's troubling you."

"I have this thing. I can't leave the house without checking the stove. To make sure it's off. I have to check each knob, like, five times. Five knobs, five times each. Is that crazy?"

"The oven's a very interesting metaphor. It both feeds and devours. Like the good and bad mother. This is primitive stuff. Very Kleinian. Think of the cannibalistic witch in Hansel and Gretel with her horrible, devouring, vaginal oven."

Bingo, said Rose. *I knew she'd say something about vaginas. Now ask about the glove.*

"That's a bit much," Jonah said, ignoring Rose.

"What are you afraid would happen if you didn't check the stove?"

"I might leave it burning."

"And then?"

"The apartment would blow up."

"And then?"

"I don't know. Everything would be destroyed. I'd have nothing."

"Maybe you *want* your apartment to blow up."

"Come on."

"Really. Maybe you have a secret, unacceptable wish that your apartment would just blow up. People who have these kinds of unconscious wishes, it's like you're wishing that, if everything just exploded, you wouldn't have to be responsible anymore. Then you can go home to Mommy and she'll take care of you."

"That's not going to happen," Jonah said.

"It could."

"No, it can't."

Tell her, Rose said. *You know you want to. Play the dead mother card. Go on.*

It's not a card, he told Rose. *It's just reality.*

Tell her, said Rose.

"My mother's dead," he said to Jane. He watched her face shift. It was not his intention to make her feel shitty, but he did enjoy it. "Car accident," he explained. "It was a long time ago. Anyway, the thing is, my problem has nothing to do with that."

Jane was quiet for a moment, then said, gently, "Will you tell me about the accident?"

"Not much to tell. My parents were driving on the Jersey Turnpike. An SUV rolled over and totaled their car. One of those unnoticed deaths you were talking about. It happened on 9/11, too. The driver got distracted by the first explosion and lost control."

The first explosion, said Rose, *was my explosion. Maybe I died at the exact same moment your mother did. Maybe that's why you're obsessed with me. In your mind we're intertwined. Have you ever thought of that?*

Jonah said, "My father survived and my mother didn't."

"Where were they driving to?"

"Does it matter?"

"Maybe."

"They were bringing me some kitchen junk. Some old things they had down in the basement. I needed the dishes."

"You needed the dishes," Jane repeated meaningfully. "For your food."

Jonah nodded. "And curtains."

"They're in the apartment you're still living in?"

"Yes."

"The one you don't want to blow up?"

"I guess."

"Did you ask them to bring you the dishes and the curtains?"

Rose said, *She's really digging deep now. Shrinking your head. Ask about the glove already.*

"Shut up," Jonah said out loud, to Rose.

"Did I touch a nerve?"

"No. But. What are you trying to say? I know it's not my fault. It was the SUV."

Jonah scanned the dog run for Frankie's yellow body. He found her wrestling with a dachshund under the lilac bushes.

"Look. I just thought you could help me with the stove-checking thing," he said. "Give me some advice, like I should put a rubber band around my wrist and every time I check the stove, I should snap the rubber band. Something easy like that."

"That sounds painful, like a form of punishment," Jane said.

"A little negative reinforcement never hurt anybody."

"You want to be punished."

Yes, said Rose, *he does.*

"Stop it," he said, out loud again, to Rose, then to Jane, "You know what? Never mind. Forget I asked about this. Okay?"

"You asked."

"I know I did. But just forget about it. Let's change the subject." Jonah called to Frankie. Rolling frantically on her back, she was half lost in a cloud of dust. He called to her again and she came running, her tongue curling out of her mouth. He picked her up and held her panting on his lap.

"Where's your father now?" Jane asked.

"South America. He moved right after the accident. Sold our house and everything in it. He's an astrophysicist. Works at an observatory down there, looking for dark matter, the missing mass of the universe. The big nothing. Black holes and shit."

"Sounds like you're angry at him."

"I'm not angry. I used to be, but I got over it. He sends a postcard now and then. It's always the same picture. He must have bought a hundred postcards of the same Incan ruins. We were never close to begin with."

"Are you angry that he lived and your mother died?"

I take it back, said Rose. *She is very intelligent. I think you should fuck her. In fact, I give you permission to fuck her.*

"I don't want to play the therapy game right now, okay? I just wanted to ask about the stove thing, that's all."

"The stove thing is what we call 'signal anxiety.' It's like a flag waving on the surface, telling us about a deeper problem. Like, for instance, your feelings about your mother and father. Do you blame him for your mother's death? He was driving the car, wasn't he?"

"Let's not talk about this here, okay?"

"Do you blame yourself? What happened to your parents was like a reversal of the Oedipal wish. You wanted to kill your father, but instead—"

"I have to go now." Jonah snapped on Frankie's leash and stood up, brushing the dusty paw prints from his pants.

"What do you think?" Jane asked, looking up at him, pushing her glasses up the slope of her nose. He felt like slapping them right off her face.

Do it, Rose egged him on. *Slap her. She'll probably like it.*

"I'm not one of your schmucks," he told Rose.

"My schmucks?" said Jane. "You mean Mark."

"You know what I think? I think your boyfriend's idea for that TV show stinks. Worse than that. I think it's sickening."

"You're angry."

"It pisses me off to hear about somebody turning other people's tragedies into profit and entertainment. It's morally reprehensible."

"Mark doesn't think of it purely as entertainment. He sees it as a kind of art. A hybrid of the two. 'Artertainment,' he calls it."

"That's asinine. Do you know that? Artertainment. Theratainment. Christ. I hate these made-up fucking words. These—what do you call them—mixed-up new words."

Frankie tugged on the leash and Jonah jerked her back.

"Neologisms," said Jane.

"Like *malternative* beverage. And *cremains*. That's what they called my mother's ashes. Fucking cremains. What the hell kind of word is that? It sounds like some creamy meal-replacement diet shake. Just mix with yogurt and milk. Fuck!"

Atta boy, said Rose. *Come on, you can do it.*

He felt the tension in his limbs vibrating like rubber belts in an engine. A sickening sensation rose up inside of him and stuck in his throat.

"Your boyfriend is a schmuck," he spat. "Just like all the other fucking schmucks in this city. How can you be with someone like that? You're too smart for that asshole."

"I like you when you're angry," said Jane. "And I agree. Mark is a schmuck. And an asshole. Actually, I think we might be breaking up."

Frankie pulled on the leash to go but Jonah did not move. He wasn't expecting agreement.

I didn't see that coming, said Rose.

"Do you feel like walking?" Jane asked. "I feel walking."

Go ahead, Rose told him. *You want to be alone with her? I'll go.*

And she went.

At his kitchen sink, Jonah filled two bowls with cold water and set them down on the floor. Sigmund Freud gulped and splashed, while Frankie lapped cautiously, one eye on the mastiff.

"This is a great place," Jane gushed, looking around. "You have two bedrooms all to yourself? How much is your rent? I'm sorry—I forget people get uncomfortable with that question. You have your own Automat? And all these radios. Jeez Louise. Are these your drawings? They're wonderful. Oh, God, this is like one of those 'come up and see my etchings' kinds of things, isn't it? Well, oh well. Can I see more?"

"Sure." Jonah was happy to show off his work. He went into his studio and selected a portfolio of stand-alone drawings, passing up the unfinished *Ephemera Automat* where Stan and Giggy still sat watching the girls go by on Brighton Beach.

"This is an amazing vintage collection," Jane called from the living room. "Obviously, you're suffering from chronic nostalgia. Great word. From the Greek. *Nostos* means 'return home,' and the rest means pain. Or sickness. Homesickness. That's what you are. Homesick. I'm probably the opposite of nostalgic. I have wanderlust. I guess that makes me *apodemialgic*? Sorry. I minored in Latin."

Jonah came out to the living room with a brown leatherette portfolio. He sat on the couch, portfolio on his lap, and watched Jane admire his possessions, moving around the living room like a museumgoer with her hands behind her back. She had her denim shirt tied around her waist and he could see she wasn't wearing a bra.

"What's that t-shirt all about?" he asked, pretending to scrutinize the slogan.

"You know Bryn Mawr?"

"I grew up in Philadelphia. It's a good girls' school."

"Excellent women's college," Jane corrected, pointing at Jonah with her lollipop.

"So you're a castrating bitch?"

"Of course. Haven't you figured that out yet?"

She stuck the lollipop back in her mouth and bit down with gusto, crunching through the hard candy spheroid with her teeth, making a real production out of it. He figured this was for his benefit, an illustration of just what a castrating bitch Jane could be. She crunched and crunched and, when she was done, she pulled the neutered stick out of her mouth and held it up so he could see it. Bits of red candy clung to the end. She opened her mouth in a ghoulish grimace so he could see her red-stained teeth.

"Scary?"

"Terrifying," he said.

"I've been reading about the *vagina dentata*," she said, pulling a paperback from her tote bag and showing him the cover. An image of a woman's disembodied, lipsticked mouth floated on its side, resembling the folds of a labial opening. Between the parted lips, a set of teeth glistened. *The Monstrous-Feminine: Film, Feminism, Psychoanalysis*, by Barbara Creed. Jane went on, "Freud never talked about the *vagina dentata*, but it was right up his alley. This author talks about how, for Freud, the mother's genitals appear to be castrated, and that's what's so scary about them, for the little boy who takes a peek. But what is really *terrorizing* about Mommy's genitals, is not that they are castrated, but that they are *castrating*."

"I wish you wouldn't say things like 'Mommy's genitals.'"

"This idea of being nostalgic, or homesick, is connected to the *vagina dentata*. Can I read you something from this book? The author here is quoting Freud. She says, 'It often happens that neurotic men declare that they feel there is something uncanny about the female genital organs. This *unheimlich* place, however, is the entrance to the former *Heim*'—which means home in German—'of all human beings, to the place where each one of us lived once upon a time and in the beginning.' Amazing, right? And look at this, Freud says, 'There is a joking saying that Love is home-sickness.' See that? It's all connected."

It was warm in the apartment with the windows closed. Jonah didn't want to hear more about the *vagina dentata*. He took the heavy portfolio from his lap and put it on the coffee table. He spread his knees far apart and thought about taking off his wool pants. On the linoleum floor, the dogs sprawled, their muzzles still wet from drinking water.

"What kinds of books are you into," Jane said, investigating the spines on Jonah's bookshelves. "Hemingway, Hemingway, Salinger, Fitzgerald. I could have predicted this. Not a thing by a woman and nothing published after the JFK assassination. What's in here?"

She tapped her finger against the plain cardboard box that stood between T.S. Eliot's *The Wasteland* and the 1939 *WPA Guide to New York City*.

"That," Jonah told her, "is my mother."

"You keep her ashes in a cardboard box? Why not get an urn, I mean, if you're going to keep them."

"I wasn't supposed to keep them. She wanted them scattered. I've been meaning to get around to that."

Jane tapped the mahogany urn marked 9-11-01. "And this must be Rose."

"She's not in there," Jonah said, hearing the echo of Vivian's own words.

Jane bit her lip and turned toward the window. *I should open that*, Jonah thought, wanting to take off his hat, his shoes and socks, to strip down to his boxer shorts. But it wasn't *that* warm. Still, he was sweating.

"How about a beer," he said. "I could use a cold beer."

From the fridge he grabbed two bottles of beer by the necks in one hand. He closed the door and ran his other hand over the smooth, rounded edges of the pistachio-green 1953 Kelvinator. He loved this fridge. Funny, how you could love a fridge. He remembered a day years before, when a pair of delivery men came into his house to bring his mother a new refrigerator—and to take the old one away. Jonah had hid under the dining room table, where he could watch from a safe distance as the men loaded the old fridge onto a metal hand truck and carted it off. "What in God's name are you crying about," his mother had asked. "It's just a refrigerator. And a crappy one. This new one is so much prettier. Look at it." The new refrigerator was silver, metallic, a stainless-steel spacecraft. Hulking and square, with sharp corners. Jonah hated it. He kicked it with his sneaker. "Stop crying or I'll give you something to cry about," his mother told him. Jonah cried harder. For days he was inconsolable, mourning the old refrigerator like it was a lost dog.

"This is brilliant stuff," Jane called from the couch, browsing through the pages of his portfolio. She had opened the window and the breeze moved the short bangs across her forehead. He handed her a bottle and sat down beside her. Together they looked at the faces of anonymous New Yorkers. A girl lifting a fork to her mouth. A young couple on the subway, not touching. A tired woman standing next to a washing machine, waiting for her laundry to finish spinning. An old couple eating burgers and fried clams at the Howard Johnson's window in Times Square.

With the portfolio spread out across both their laps, Jane turned the pages, reaching across Jonah each time to take hold of the next one, brushing her arm against his body. The Bakelite bracelets on her wrist made the soft, hollow sound of bamboo chiming together. She was close enough for him to smell the layers of scent in her hair: grapefruit-essence shampoo, basil-flavored styling crème, the musky oils secreted by her sebaceous glands, and that hint of cucumber. She kept turning pages until she came to the nudes, sketches of half-naked women drawn from vintage girlie magazines, posing with improbable items like typewriters and chess sets, tie racks and pipe stands.

"They were so sexy back then," Jane said. "All hips and ass. Curves. Whatever happened to curves?"

"You've got curves," he said.

Jane smiled and ran her finger across the plastic protective sheet, tracing the outline of a girl seated on a rose-patterned couch, tasseled pasties hanging from her nipples. Jonah watched as her finger circled each breast and ran down the curve of the girl's back, along her hips, buttocks, down her leg and then off the page, where it paused for just a second, as if considering what to do next, before following the inseam of Jonah's pants, up to the very end, where it could go no further.

He looked at her hand in his lap and shifted his hips a bit, from side to side, spreading his knees apart. Jane opened her hand and clutched him, making him hard. Without a word, she closed the portfolio and placed it next to her beer bottle on the coffee table. She unzipped his pants, maneuvered on top of him, and guided him into her. It happened fast, before he was ready for the soft shock of texture and temperature, and he couldn't stop wondering what had happened to her underwear. Had she not been wearing it, that whole time, at the dog run? Or had she removed it, quietly, while he was in the other room? He considered asking her, but thankfully the obsessive thought stopped when she put her tongue in his mouth and kissed him, tasting of cherry candy and smoke and beer. She took off his glasses and placed them on the end table, but she kept hers on. She grabbed the back of the couch for balance and began to rock, the words on her t-shirt going in and out of focus as she oscillated toward and away from him: castrating bitches, castrating bitches, castrating bitches. Jonah wasn't sure what to do. It had been a very long time since he'd had sex with someone other than himself. What was that Woody Allen joke? "Don't knock masturbation. It's sex with someone I love." But what about self-loathing? Jonah tried to stay focused. Should he move his hips or keep them still? Should he do something with his mouth? He kept his hands at his sides, his left balled into a fist and his right gripping the cold beer bottle, afraid to touch this woman lest she prove not to be real. But she was no ghost made of air and smoke. He could feel her pubococcygeal muscle grasping and releasing in a virtuoso rhythm, and he wondered if she had learned this special technique while at Bryn Mawr.

"I do my Kegel exercises religiously," she said, reading his mind. "I used to know this woman, a competitive bodybuilder, who believed in strengthening every single muscle in her body. Her cunt was like a vise. She could hold a guy so tight, he couldn't pull himself out. It never ceased to amuse her. Don't worry, though, I'm not that strong. No *vagina dentata* here."

She stopped rocking and began rotating her pelvis in lazy circles. She said, "I like to talk while I fuck. It relaxes me. Do you mind?"

Jonah croaked.

"I'll take that as a no. Okay. I have a new German word for you," she said. "*Zwischenraum*. It means 'the space between things.' That's a good one, right?"

She spelled the word out loud for him, Z-W-I-S, and began pumping faster. C-H-E-N. Beer sloshed out of the bottle, onto his hand and onto the couch cushion. R-A-U-M.

"It refers to the silences. Between musical notes. White spaces. Between words on a page. Subatomic voids. Between electrons and neutrons. Pauses in thought."

Sweat condensed on her throat. Dark locks of hair stuck to her skin in humid curls.

"Empty spaces in the body. Tunnels and chambers. The dark sky between the stars."

She gripped his sweat-slick head and held it to her breasts with one hand while she reached down between her legs with the other. She stopped talking then, burbling into his ear in a pre-verbal mammalian language, ululating vertebrate that she was, slippery porpoise, hump-backed and snorting. He answered back with an echolalic prattle of his own as he felt her body shudder and open wide, pulling him in deeper. He allowed himself to be swallowed whole, a white mouse pulled down the long tunnel of a viper's throat. The salty tang of her body's insides gave him a metallic chill, like biting into tin foil. He felt her bite, a frantic clench, and she cried out, loud enough for the neighbors to hear, before her whole body shuddered and stuttered to a halt.

She rolled off and collapsed to the couch, her skirt hiked up, showing him where he'd been. *Sheela-na-gig*, he thought, thinking of the Starbucks logo and trying not to look. Then he looked. An old rhyme came back to taunt him: "Made you look, you dirty crook, you stole your mother's pocketbook," then something about sauerkraut he could not remember, a feeling of shame on the playground, being caught doing something he was not supposed to be doing. He reached for Jane but she only petted his hand, saying "Now, now," like some old movie actress. *Yes, now*, he thought. She stood up and fixed her skirt, turning it around her waist until the zipper was in the back. She pushed her hair from her face, bracelets chiming. The April breeze from the open window cooled his sweaty limbs, but not his longing. What were all those embarrassing terms in his mother's bodice-rippers? "Turgid member" came to mind.

She noticed him at last. "You didn't finish."

"I was waiting for you."

"Most guys finish first."

"I wasn't sure if," he started, silenced by the boiled-red crustacean of shame that crawled through his belly. Most guys.

"Such a gentleman," she said, sitting down again.

She took hold of him and began to stroke while talking about her plans for the evening, which included Mark and seemed to take her far away.

"It's complicated," she said and finally stopped talking.

He turned his face away, toward the corner of the room, to see Rose standing there.

I knew you were going to fuck her, she said. *You didn't ask about the glove, did you?*

He shook his head.

Just one thing I asked you to do and you couldn't do it?

Fine, he said. He looked into Jane's eyes and said, "Glove," but it came out in a hoarse whisper so that it sounded like "Love."

Jane smiled at the word and said, "There, there. There, there," as she lifted her t-shirt and offered him a breast.

14

A yellow Post-It note stuck to his computer screen, scribbled with Keith's handwriting, informed Jonah that he had completely forgotten about the early morning staff meeting. He was fifteen minutes late, arriving at the Pool Area to find the only seat left available was the unpopular Philippe Starck gnome stool. Everyone else was comfortably ensconced in the Adirondack chairs and swings, notepads on their laps, pens poised in hands. Jonah hated sitting on the Starck stool. It was low to the ground, so his knees bent to his chest, and when he looked down between his legs, the evil gnome grinned back up at him.

"Good of you to join us," said Michelle, the senior producer, from her position of power on the high lifeguard's chair. Michelle was rarely in the office. She'd been out on maternity leave so she could bond with the baby she'd just brought back from China. Now that she was fully bonded and the baby was in the care of a nanny, Michelle was back, ready to "play catch up" and "get up to speed." Jonah liked the office better without Michelle in it.

"We were just going over the new Golden Questions," she said, pausing to guzzle from her twenty-four-ounce bottle of Poland Spring water—motherhood was dehydrating, she often remarked, and she needed to keep herself well moistened. She passed a goldenrod-yellow sheet of paper to Keith, and Keith handed it to Jonah, giving him a nudge with his elbow that Jonah knew meant "Did you get lucky last night" and which Jonah ignored. He looked down at the paper. In the playful "Kidprint" font, bold-faced and 48-point, the following three questions asked:

- Will it make their lives easier?
- Will it make them happy?
- Will it make them a better person?

These questions, Michelle explained, had to be considered in the writing and editing of every article for the online magazine. PinwheelKids did not want to extol the virtues of any product, recipe, expert advice, or activity that could not answer a resounding "yes" to each of the three Golden Questions.

As the group discussed and debated the implications and merits of this new editorial tool, Jonah considered the more personal questions that had been pinballing through his own mind, though they weren't in any way golden.

- Should I chase after Jane?
- Should I call Vivian and tell her the truth?
- Should I give up on humanity completely?

Nearly a week had gone by since his strange and mind-altering sexual encounter with Jane. He could still conjure the smell of her hair, that mix of citrus and oils, and the faint, vegetal sheen of her skin, as if she'd rubbed the slopes of her neck with warm cucumber slices. He had called her a few times, but she'd only left one cryptic message on his answering machine, saying that "things with Mark" were "complicated." He could easily find her at the dog run, he thought, and follow her home, peek up at her windows to see just how complicated things really were with the maestro of "artertainment." It didn't seem fair that Jane had awakened a longing in him then left him hungry and hanging open, like a pathetic mouth. In his chest, he felt a nest full of baby birds, all of them straining, open-beaked and ugly-necked, waiting to be fed. Of course, he was guilty of a similar crime. Nearly two weeks had passed since Easter and he still hadn't spoken a word to Vivian. Another weekend was approaching. She had called again the night before about going out to Costco for the Waterfall in a Box. Again Jonah did not answer. He felt ashamed of himself, then ashamed of his shame, so the feeling spiraled into a self-replicating loop out of which he could not extricate himself. As for giving up on humanity completely, that option did have a certain appeal.

He doodled on the Golden Questions in his lap, sketching the scene outside the window, across the empty canyon above the street, behind the glass of a hotel's celebrated revolving restaurant. In that close but distant dining room a waitress dressed in a white blouse pushed her silverware cart from table to table, carefully laying out forks, knives, and spoons. Watching her, far away in her little movie-screen frame, comforted Jonah. There was just the right amount of space between them. Before the brunch rush, in the quiet, empty restaurant, sunlight gleamed on the rims of stemmed water glasses. Soon people would come clamoring to consume Eggs Benedict and Huevos Rancheros while the restaurant turned on its axis like a sluggish carousel. They would leave the forks and knives and spoons feculent with food bits and smeared in saliva, the dishes splotched and smudged, the water glasses smacked with greasy lip prints. But in this moment, the table settings were still unsullied, the napkins neatly folded, and the waitress's uniform was a pristine sheet of white, fresh from the Cascade laundry truck. Somebody's mother, somebody's daughter, somebody's wife, and maybe all three at once, the waitress became an everywoman in Jonah's imagination. She held a glass up to the sunlight like a precious gem. He thought of all the women he'd be giving up should he opt to part ways with the human race.

After work, he decided to walk home. It was a long way from Times Square to the East Village, but walking and wandering helped Jonah sort out his thoughts. Weather-wise, it was the kind of day he had come to think of as a 9/11 day: cloudless, warm, and blue. A million daffodils bloomed all over Manhattan thanks to Dutch bulb tycoon Hans van Waardenburg, the city of Rotterdam, and the thousands of volunteers who planted the bulbs last fall in the hopes that spring would come again. The daffodils buttered the streets, crowding every planter and muddy plot, a riot of flower reflecting the sun. It was the kind of day that made Jonah feel good at first, then nervous. How long, he wondered, would days like these be tarnished?

He headed over to Eighth Avenue to avoid the crowds, and ran through the questions again in his head. If he failed to find Jane at the dog run, he'd be sunk. He could not find her address because he didn't know her last name. So how was he going to stalk her? He tried to imagine himself ducking in the shadows, sliding along the city's walls, trailing Jane, pulled along by the draft of her cucumber wake. It was a dumb idea.

He stopped to look in the windows of Arnold Hatters. Two large displays flanked the shop's recessed entrance so that Jonah stood inside a deep and abundant corridor of hats. Surrounded, he felt the calming, enveloping presence of fedoras and derbies and homburgs, boaters and cowboys and pith helmets, all seeming to float in midair, levitating on imperceptible hooks, revolving on mechanical glass platforms, each with a neatly hand-lettered sign proclaiming its name: El Dorado, Centerdent, Lindy, Astor, Summit, Big Apple, Belmont, Galaxy Velour, Silk Finish Eleganza, The Untouchable, The Godfather, Pacer, Senator, Topper, Red Rider, Stingy Brim Porkpie Stinger.

Go on, Rose said, appearing by his side. *Go in.*

Where've you been? It's been days.

I had things to do, she said. *You wouldn't believe how hectic being dead can be. Besides, how much, really, have you been thinking of me?*

Jonah ignored her question and pushed through the heavy glass door, stepping into the shop. All along the walls hung pictures autographed by famous and almost-famous hatted men: character actors Fyvush Finkel and Mike "Butch the Hat" Aquilino, bally-stage performers like the Human Pincushion and a midget wrestler called The Haiti Kid, and a circus ringmaster in a black satin top hat covered with live parakeets. A dark-skinned man dressed in a white linen suit, with white alligator shoes on his feet and a white Panama hat on his head, helped Jonah find his size in the Stingy Brim Porkpie Stinger. The symbolism of The Untouchable was not lost on him—untouchability being what a hat could provide, some armor from the world—but in the triple-folded mirror he liked the Stinger best. If Jane had been there, she'd have ventured a clichéd interpretation of "stinger," always the phallic on her mind.

She's with that big-jawed brute, Rose said, *and don't think for a minute she's going to leave him for some schlub like you.*

Brute? Schlub? Since when do you say schlub?

I say a lot of things, Rose said, running her misty hands over the soft brims of hats nestled in their stacks.

"That hat you came in with looks pretty beat," said the salesman.

"I wear it a lot."

"Time for a change."

The guy's right, said Rose. *You never change anything. It's just a hat.*

"Maybe," said Jonah. "It's a good old hat, though."

"Sure, it's a good old hat," said the salesman. "But it's no good for summertime. This here's a good summertime hat. It's made from real coconut leaves."

"I'll take it," Jonah said, tilting the Stinger's brim down to his eyebrows, imagining himself as a stalker moving through the dark. No, he couldn't do that. Maybe he could leave town, find his father, move permanently to South America. A hat made of coconut leaves would be just right for the sunny climes of Chile where an outdoor café in Santiago called to him. What would it be like, he wondered, to leave everyone without saying goodbye?

Should I call her? he asked Rose, taking out his wallet to pay the man.

Like I said, don't get your hopes up. One fuck, that's all you got.

I meant your mother. I'm thinking I should call Vivian and tell her the truth. About you and me.

What is the truth about you and me, Jonah? Are you going to tell her I'm a ghost, that you're haunted, obsessed? That'll go over well.

With the Stinger still on his head, Jonah put his old hat in the box the salesman gave him and looked once more in the mirror.

I don't want to freak her out, he said to Rose as they walked back out to the warm late afternoon, into the crowds of after-work people hustling up and down. At a raggedy collection of wooden stools and broken chairs on the sidewalk, shoeshine men sang, "Shine 'em up, shine 'em up, shoeshine!" One of the men, missing both legs and sitting with his empty pants folded beneath him, looked at Jonah's worn-out shoes and bellowed, "It's not too late!"

Jonah felt the sole of his shoe flapping against his foot.

I can't believe you walk around like this, said Rose, trailing him.

"You're hoping for a miracle now!" the shoeshine man called, his ample belly shaking with laughter above the stumps of his legs. "Shine's not gonna cure you, but it can't make things worse."

If you're not going to fix the shoe, said Rose, *you might as well get them shined. You should take a little pride in your appearance.*

You sound like my mother.

"You're hoping for a miracle, I can see that." The shineman grinned as Jonah took a seat on the stool and placed one shoe on the wooden footrest. The legless man wrapped his fingers with a smutty rag and rubbed them in a tin of polish, tracing smooth circles in the black cream. With his sketchpad propped on the hatbox in his lap, Jonah made a quick drawing. A few steps away, a barker stood outside the Playground XXX peep show and called, "Beautiful nude ladies. They're here, they're live, and they will leave nothing to your imagination." A girl made out of neon kicked her legs on a glowing trapeze behind the glass. As the shineman buffed his shoes, Jonah sketched the neon girl. The barker caught him looking and urged him to check out the beautiful nude ladies and fifty-percent-off DVDs.

I know what you're thinking, Rose said. *You're thinking maybe you should give up sex, give up women, and dedicate yourself to a life of masturbation. The art of autoeroticism.*

Stop reading my mind. And stop talking like Jane. Rose would never say autoeroticism.

You don't know what I would say.

Well, Jonah said, still sketching, *it's not your worst idea.*

So do it. Buy yourself some dirty movies. Peep at the naked ladies.

What are you now, the devil on my shoulder, telling me what to do?

You wish, she said. *Then you wouldn't have to take responsibility for your decisions. You could just be passive-dependant. Blame me for everything. Is that right?*

You really do sound like Jane.

First I sound like your mother. Now I sound like Jane.

I don't know who you sound like, but you're not the Rose I remember.

What you remember of me isn't even real, she said, exasperated.

When his shoeshine was done, Jonah stepped inside the porn shop and walked down the aisles marked with hanging signs—Gang Bang, Asian, Best of Anal. He tried to imagine a sexless life. It wasn't difficult. Most of his life had already been sexless. But to deliberately dedicate himself to celibacy, that would be a different kind of life goal. He tried the Golden Questions on it: Would it make my life easier? Would it make me happy? Would it make me a better person? It was impossible to know. A sign for Classics lured him toward the back where, hoping for mid-century stag films, he found nothing but uncelebrated sequels to 1970s hardcore hits, shrink-wrapped copies of *Deep Throat 3* and *Debbie Does Dallas 4*, sextravaganzas sure to disappoint. A second room opened up behind the Classics rack and in the shadows he saw female shapes, girls sitting on stools, kicking their legs with the boredom of their work. They called to him, "Come here baby, come on." He pretended to browse a rack of dusty kung fu videos. "Seven minutes in Heaven," one of the girls called, sweeping her hand down the front of her private booth and opening the door like a game show model flaunting a prize refrigerator. Temperature-controlled meat pan! Extra deep spill-proof crisper bin! Easy-Stream liquid dispenser puts refreshment at your fingertips!

Together, Jonah and Rose walked through the Garment District, heading east across town, past shops filled with tiaras, buttons, appliques, faux furs, bridal headpieces and veils. He considered again returning the calls from Vivian that he'd been avoiding. He could just pick up where they had left off. Not tell her the truth. He could do what Frank had instructed him to do—keep telling stories. A trip to Costco this coming weekend could be just what he needed. He could tell Vivian a new story, something about wedding plans, how Rose had read every bridal magazine she could get her hands on, how she tried on a dozen dresses, how she looked so beautiful in her white gown and veil.

She'll never believe it, said Rose. *I was never the Modern Bride type.*

Rose was right, he knew. The idea had less substance than the glittering cascades of beaded and brocaded fabric that swept across the windows with names like "Metallic Sparkle Slinky-Knit Shantung," "Embroidered Chantilly Illusion," and "Iridescent Fish-Scale Sequined Silk Chiffon."

He felt undone. That was the word that came to mind. He wasn't sure what had done the undoing. Vivian's growing need for him and his lies, he realized, had begun to feel like a pressure to perform. Frank's command for him to keep lying had spoiled the fabrication's fizz, revealed it as untruth, leaving it flat, like seltzer without its spark. Rose's ghost wasn't behaving the way he'd expected; a product of his mind, she somehow had a mind of her own. And Jane—he didn't want to admit it, preferring to think of himself as hermetically sealed, but sex with Jane had opened some part of him. He felt penetrated. If he'd always been behind a sheet of glass, now he was reachable, get-at-able. He'd been infiltrated. Touched. By all of them.

A faded sign above a shoe repair shop promised to provide its customers with "Soles in 15 minutes." He smiled at the pun and imagined a line of soulless New Yorkers, waiting to be vitalized in just a quarter of an hour. He could use a new one himself, feeling his own sole flapping open, threatening to break loose as he passed hot-roasted nuts stirring fragrantly in a burnt copper bowl, a boy muscling his whole weight against a rolling rack full of fluttering fabric on bolts as thick as tree trunks, a girl wearing Jane's cat-eye glasses. He thought of Frank and his baseball bat, and his thoughts ricocheted away again, away from admitting the truth to Vivian and back to Santiago, that outdoor café, a stray dog dozing in the sun, and some kind of Hemingway-esque drink in his hand. Pernod, milky green and tasting of licorice.

"Absinthe makes the heart grow fonder," he said out loud.

Rose rolled her eyes, unamused. She had no patience for puns.

On the brilliant green blanket of Bryant Park, a crowd had gathered, every face looking up. Standing atop a tapered, one-hundred-foot pillar, a world-famous stunt magician performed deep-knee bends, stretching his weary legs. He had been standing for 31 hours, 38 minutes, and 7 seconds—according to the big digital timer inside the restricted media circle—without benefit of food, water, or bathroom breaks. He had another 3 hours and 20 minutes to go. Later that night, he planned to leap from the top and land in a pile of cardboard boxes. He was a young, handsome magician who could often be found posing shirtless in stylish magazines, showing off his well-muscled chest. Down below, a group of earthbound girls called up to him, shouting in unison, "We love you!" as they waved their bare arms in the air to catch the magician's attention. A lone woman sitting on a red bicycle held up a sign that read, WOW.

"Just what does that fool think he's doing up there?" asked a man in the crowd.

"Pretending to be the goddamn Statue of Liberty," his companion responded.

"You ever seen him levitate?"

"Sure I have."

"How's he do it?"

"Invisible strings."

"No, sir. I'll tell you how—he's the devil. That man done sold his soul."

Jonah opened his sketchpad and began to draw the scene—the open-mouthed crowd, the pillar, the magician standing still and stiff, small in the distance, like the decorative pommel at the end of a sword's hilt. A breeze riffled the magician's gauzy tunic and the sunlight etched a golden outline around his head and shoulders, making a kind of nimbus, an almost holy aura. A publicity poster taped to the metal police barricade explained how the magician had found inspiration in the hermit saint Simeon the Stylite who, disgusted by the decadence of his time, spent 37 years standing on a pillar, far away from other human beings and closer to the divine. Said the magician, "I love the image of a man on a pillar alone in the world." Jonah added these words to his sketch. He had trouble relating to the celebrity magician, but he did feel an instant kinship with St. Simeon the Stylite.

That's another option, Rose said, interrupting Jonah's thoughts. *You could become a monk. Find yourself a pole and sit on it.*

Jonah considered this solution to his dilemma. He would not have to face Vivian or Frank. He could forget about Jane, committing himself to a higher calling. He tried to imagine what it would be like to live like the hermit saint Simeon, far above at the top of a mast, a man alone in a crow's nest. *Would it make my life easier,* he asked himself. *Would it make me happy? Would it make me a better person?*

Downtown, at Astor Place, Jonah took his usual shortcut through the Park-Rite parking lot, under the giant clock of Carl Fischer Music Publishers (since 1872), and stopped at the makeshift adult-magazine stand on the sidewalk. Rose had left him somewhere in the east 20s and, alone, he had made his decision. He would not call Vivian and he would not tell her the truth. He would not stalk Jane, nor would he give her another thought. He would become a monk, isolated in his walk-up apartment, perched on his own metaphorical pillar, dedicating himself to solitude and art. Let Jane call it *autoeroticism* if she wanted to. It seemed a noble pursuit, he thought, as he sifted carefully through milk crates full of magazines, handling each volume by the edges only, searching for errant vintage girlies like *Flirt* and *Eyeful* ("Glorifying the American Girl"), *Whisper* and *Wink* (promising "Gals, Gags, and Gayety"). All that came up were modern-day hardcore mags, gynecological and soiled.

"You've lost weight," said the porn peddler to one of his regulars. The peddler was a heavy-set man with a red face blazing behind a robust gray beard and Elvis Presley sunglasses, a sovereign of smut, enthroned upon his beach chair day after day, presiding over his indecorous inventory of *Lactating Lesbos* and *Fat Ass Gals*, *Hometown Nymphos* and *Nasty Debutantes*, *Cherry Boys* and *Tender Chickens*.

"I've been on a diet," said the customer, a Wall Street type in pinstriped trousers and a crisp blue button-down shirt. "I get so bloated over the winter. As soon as the weather gets nice, I go on a crash diet. To lose the bloat. Nothing but lean chicken and vegetables. I go totally low carb."

Jonah watched while the Wall Streeter picked out every copy of *Barely Legal*, *Anal Schoolgirls*, and *Cherry Pie* he could find. Teenage twins get it on. Wet and wild high school girls. Young and shaved.

"You're a stronger man than I," said the peddler, smacking his belly. "I couldn't go a day without red meat and grease. I've got my own deep fryer at home. You'd be amazed by the things you can deep fry."

Jonah pictured himself at the top of a pillar, above the noise and press of people, above desire and loss, above Wall Street and winter bloat.

"You can deep fry just about anything," the peddler said. "Hot dogs, bagels, candy bars. Ever try deep-fried Oreo cookies?"

In between *Black and Stacked* and a well-thumbed *Beaver Hunt*, Jonah unearthed a pristine 1953 copy of *Whisper* (with the keyhole cover) that promised to reveal the true stories of "Ferocious Fightin' Femmes, Curvy Corseted Cuties, The Half Woman-Half Lion," and "What 8,000 Girls Confessed to Dr. Kinsey." This would be his nourishment atop the pillar. He handed the peddler five bucks and hurried home, where he opened the magazine and a bottle of beer at the kitchen table. In his sketchpad, in a blank space between the shoeshine amputee and the Playground barker, at the foot of the magician's long pillar, he drew a pair of female legs, crosshatched in fishnet stockings, side by side in a kind of V shape. The telephone rang. *A Stylite shouldn't have a phone*, he thought. If it was Jane, he wasn't going to pick it up. He had made his decision. Even if she asked him for a date. Even if she told him she had left Mark.

But it wasn't Jane. It was Vivian. Fighting the guilt that tried to swamp him, he let the machine take it.

"Jonah? Are you there? Are you screening? It's me. Vivian. Remember me? I'm still alive, in case you were wondering. Pick up if you're there. I'm worried about you. All right. I guess you're not there. Call me, will you?"

He put the sketchbook aside and turned to *Ephemera Automat*. Stan and Giggy were still sitting on the boardwalk at Brighton Beach where nothing ever changed. The girl walked by in her bikini, the breeze lifted Stan's thinning hair, and Giggy held up his X-Ray Specs, wishing their magic were real. Jonah put back the stray cloud he had whited out a few weeks before and moved on to the next panel, that oceanic blank that had been haunting him for months. He penciled the line of seashore, the bench, the men viewed from behind. The girl was gone now. The men stared out to sea. He framed the next panel. The men stared out to sea, the clouds slightly shifted, a gull dipped across the sky. He loved the exquisite quiet of a silent panel with its Zen-like pause. Life was really like this. A lot of waiting, a lot of watching, not much happening. Being a monk could be all right. He could take up meditation. He could fast and perform cleanses on his colon, swallowing a fabric rope until it worked its way out his other end. He continued the silence into the next panel as the nose of a prop plane nudged the upper right-hand margin of the frame. And then the whole plane came into view, its tail tied with ropes and the beginning of an aerial banner wrinkling on the wind. Stan and Giggy looked up. An important message was coming. The phone rang again. Jonah closed his eyes, exercising his newfound monk-like willpower.

"You have been selected to receive a four-night, three-day vacation in Orlando, Florida," chirped a cheerful female voice, "including Universal Studios passes, plus your choice of four days in Fort Lauderdale, Daytona, or Cancun, Mexico— all for only $99 per person (kids under eighteen stay for free). Plus, for acting today, you will receive an additional stay in Colonial Williamsburg, Virginia, and a $100 cash bonus. Congratulations! As President Bush said, 'Fly and enjoy America's great destination spots. Get down to Disney World in Florida. Take your families and enjoy life, the way we want it to be enjoyed.' Don't let the terrorists win. For more information and to speak to a representative, please press the 9 key."

He returned to *Ephemera Automat* but the momentum was gone. He turned on the television, where CNN reported on the forces and weapons of the War on Terror. He stood listening to the words Hellfire, Daisy Cutter, Tomahawk. Stinger, Hornet, Hawkeye. Sentry, Prowler, Stratofortress. On the screen, against khaki-colored landscapes, helmeted men in goggles jogged and ducked, clutching their rifles while the sky filled with dust. Special ops. Airborne. Nightstalker. Linebacker. Bunker-buster. Mirage 2000.

It was a fair springtime night and the box fan in the window blew a cool breeze against his skin, bringing with it all the smells from the street below. Perfume and cigarette smoke, Indian spices, rotting garbage, the sweetness of fresh watermelons sliced by South Americans at the corner fruit stand. New York's special mix. The effluvium of strangers. A pork chop frying in a neighbor's pan. A cigar in the mouth of a passing man.

The television said: Massive Ordnance Air Blast bomb. Thermobaric bomb. Laser-guided bomb. Precision bomb. Fifteen-thousand-pound bomb.

Monks probably don't watch television, he thought. He decided to go up to the roof, where the towers of light reminded him of the legs of the girl in his sketch, or else the legs of a tremendous water bird, slightly trembling, waiting to take off. What if he could climb them? What if they, fused at the top into a single beam, could be his pillar? He tried to imagine himself scaling the shimmery blue timbers—they were like parallel bars turned vertical, or like a ladder without its rungs—gripping and inching his way to the sky's pearl-lit dome where he made his perch. But no matter how much he might try, he could not be alone in that place. The airspace was crowded with ghosts. They'd be gone soon, those towers. After another night or two the eighty-eight space cannons would be packed away until the next 9/11. And then where would he be? Maybe his own roof was high enough.

He listened to the convulsive egg-beater of swarming newscopters. Somewhere, a building was on fire. He could smell it. The sky spread black directly above, filled with dark matter. What was Jane's word? *Zwischenraum*. It was a good word. Especially on such a clear, black night—unusually clear for New York City—when he could actually see stars. He tried to count them. Of all the billions and billions, he could only see about 15. Where his father was, away from city lights, you could see a couple thousand. In the southern hemisphere, it would be winter now, and maybe there was snow, although he wasn't sure it ever snowed in South America. It would be cold, anyway. Someday, the whole universe would be cold. Once everything accelerates to such a degree where it all blew apart and there was no heat left in anything, there would be a frozen universe, planets blue and hung with icicles. The Sun a crackling ball of ice. "Dark matter is in a fight with dark energy," his father liked to say, "and dark matter is losing."

When Jonah was a boy, his father took him once or twice to the university observatory and let him push the button that opened the great dome. There was a dazzling sliver of black sky, salted with stars, but light did not attract his father. It was the dark spaces in between that he got excited about. "Look," he'd say, "in the dark, there are things we cannot see, but they are there. Great big chunks of matter just rolling around. Bigger than the Earth. Bigger than the Sun. Big enough to swallow us all." To his father, the stars were only tools, luminous lenses he used to see the invisible, devouring stuff of the dark. "Finding that darkness," he told Jonah, "will be the ultimate Copernican revolution, because not only does the universe not revolve around you, you're not even made of the same things. Yes, we are stardust, as the song goes, but stars are the minority component in the universe. We are just the foam on the ocean."

As Jonah looked up at the city's few stars, he tried to picture them as they really were, not twinkling pinpoints of gentle light, but massive roiling furnaces. How hot was the Sun? He quizzed himself, digging back into his grade-school memory banks for the answer: 10,000 degrees Fahrenheit at the surface, hot enough to turn you to dust in just a flash. Here on Earth, the cremation of a body took longer. About an hour and a half at 1,800 degrees Fahrenheit. The fire that burned in the towers was just as hot as a cremation chamber.

At that temperature, muscles and skin contract, forcing the body to curl into what is called a "pugilistic attitude."

Jonah stepped to the rooftop's edge. He looked at his watch. It was just about time for the stunt magician to make his leap. Jonah dangled a foot out and over the rusted tin cornice. *This is my pillar*, he told himself, trying to feel the sensation of falling.

15

A record-breaking heat wave rolled in from the subtropics on a Bermuda High, scorching the spring flowers. It was only mid-April. The million donated daffodils never knew what hit them. The ruffled edges of their trumpets burned brown. Their perianth segments shriveled. Their green stems bent and broke under the weight of the weather. In Albany county, the Center for Disease Control would soon confirm one death due to West Nile Virus: a blue-black crow found stiff and buzzing with flies under a boxwood bush where children played hide and seek. There was talk already of spraying. In the torpor, mosquitoes multiplied in still pools all over the Mid-Atlantic. In tepid birdbaths and rain-filled tire swings, their eggs hatched into wriggling larvae. The city filled its fogger tanks with Scourge and Anvil and Malathion, primed for the kill.

Jonah woke to the sound of his radio alarm clock informing him, "The Baked Apple soars to 97 degrees today." He hit the snooze button and kicked off the sweaty covers. Two words stuck in his mind, repeating themselves over and over: Tardive dyskinesia. He didn't know what these words meant, or where they had come from, but he couldn't stop hearing them. This happened. He sometimes woke with a word he did not know, a bit of flotsam from an unused portion of his brain, bumping around inside his skull. *Lugubrious* came to him years ago and haunted him for a week. *Adipose*, he remembered, and *ex cathedra*. Now he had "Tardive dyskinesia." It sounded like a medical term. A disease of some kind. Maybe something the radio had uttered in between snoozes. He broke the words down into parts. Kinesis, like in *telekinesis*, he knew meant "motion." And "dys" was bad, difficult, disagreeable in some way. Bad motion. The "tardive" part was troubling. Maybe it was somebody's name. The name of the discoverer of the disease. Dr. Tardive. His thoughts jumped to Fran Tarkenton, ex-football player and co-host of the early 1980s reality TV show *That's Incredible*. People used to go on the show and catch bullets in their teeth, jump motorcycles through hoops of fire, and play baseball with only one arm. *It must have been tough*, Jonah thought, *making your way in football with a girlish name like Fran.*

The weekend had passed without a call from Jane, but Jonah was over that, or so he told himself. Vivian called just once, did not mention Costco or the Waterfall in a Box, asking only if he planned to show up for Rose's birthday cake next Saturday. He hadn't forgotten—how could he forget with Rose there to remind him? She haunted him all weekend while he worked unsuccessfully on *Ephemera Automat*, talking about her "un-thirty-first birthday" and the sad futility of a cake.

Is she going to have a cake for me every year, Rose had said while he was trying to watch the Nightly News, *to celebrate my un-thirty-second and my un-thirty-third, or will it just be the milestones from here on out? Un-forty, un-fifty. I'll never get old. Never sag or lose my wits. Never have to take those pills. I guess only old people watch the Nightly News. So many pill commercials. I feel sorry for the living. Celebrex for your arthritis! Vesicare for your overactive bladder! That's what you have to look forward to. Doan's for your bad back! Fixodent for your dentures!*

"Enough," Jonah had said out loud to the room and its ghost. Frankie, at his side, looked up. He petted her and said to Rose, "I get it. You'll never get old."

That's right.

"And you'll never stop haunting me."

Do you want me to?

"There you go sounding like Jane again."

On the news, the reporter announced that a man in New York City had been arrested for riding his bicycle past nearly a hundred SUVs and squirting them with red paint from a ketchup bottle. The man was a volunteer at Ground Zero. "The red paint," said the reporter, "apparently was meant to symbolize blood."

Are you going to my birthday party? Rose asked.

"Are you?"

No, thanks. If I know my mother, she'll get a cake covered in roses. She thinks I'm still a little girl. You should call her, though. You owe her.

Rose was right, he knew. He thought about that now as he boarded the sweaty subway to Times Square. "Tardive dyskinesia, Fran Tarkenton," said his brain. "Tardive dyskinesia, Fran Tarkenton." Over the heads of sleepy commuters, an advertisement issued an Important Drug Warning:

"If you've been injured by taking PPA, Rezulin, Propulsid, Fen-Phen, Pondimin, Ephedra, Lamisil, or Sporanox you may be able to recover lost wages, medical expenses, and a money award. Call 1-800-LAW FIRM. (Injuries include hemorrhagic strokes, severe liver damage, heart attacks, Sudden Infant Death Syndrome, heart valve damage, Primary Pulmonary Hypertension, congestive heart failure.)"

He felt his own heart congest and clutched his throat with his hand. He could not remember if he had checked the stove before he left. His head began to sweat inside his Stingy Prim Porkpie Stinger. For the fourteen underground blocks between 14th and 28th Streets, he debated whether or not it was a good idea to get off the train and go back to make sure the stove was off, off, off, off, off. If he did, he would be very late for work. But if he didn't, his apartment would burn. His artwork would be destroyed. Frankie would perish. Everything would be gone. His collection of radios and ukuleles, his Rose file with her missing poster, and his mother's ashes—freed from their cardboard box, they would be lost, mixed with the anonymous pile of ash his home would become. He tried deep breathing. He tried picturing himself on a faraway beach, watching the gentle waves roll in and out, in and out, but it was no use. When the train stopped at 28th Street, he got out, crossed over to the downtown side, and headed home again, where he was surprised to find no fire trucks jamming the block, no smell of smoke, no bright flames waving from his apartment's busted windows. Upstairs, the stove sat still and guiltless, just as he'd left it, a white box of innocence. As he pointed, counted, and recited his "off"s, Jonah had to admit, he couldn't remember the last time he'd even turned the stove on, dimly recalling a pair of fried eggs, a pot of ramen noodles, from months, or maybe years, ago. Mice, he was almost certain, had claimed the greasy interior of the oven for their nests.

Over an hour after he had originally set out for work, he slid his ID card into the insert reader at the glass security door on the forty-second floor of the Mediacom Building. Scanning the flux reversals on the card's magnetic stripe, the reader approved his access, turned its tiny red light to green, and unlocked the door to let him in, quietly noting the exact time of his late arrival.

He spent the morning working hard to make up for being late and read through a batch of Parenting Expert articles that had been waiting in his electronic inbox. In one about easing children's fears in a time of terror, the expert talked about how, due to recent elevations of the Terror Alert from yellow to orange, the television was flooding the airwaves with replayed images of the Twin Towers exploding and collapsing. The expert advised parents that small children who watched the replay footage over and over might believe that 9/11 was happening again. "It is best," said the expert, "to limit your child's exposure to the media during this time. Don't let them sit in front of CNN for hours. Put in a DVD of their favorite movie. Distract them with games. When all is clear once more, let your child go back to their regular television schedule." The expert then advised parents to make up a fun game during times of crisis: "To prepare for a parking lot sniper attack, for instance, have your kids play a running game to see how fast they can get from the car to the mall entrance and back again. Kids will be so caught up in the fun, they won't have time to worry about getting shot."

Jonah hit the backspace button on his keyboard and erased the words "getting shot," then replaced them with the less vivid "potential dangers." He looked at the yellow piece of paper tacked to his corkboard and considered the three Golden Questions. Such a running game might make the parents' lives easier, getting the kids in and out of the mall quickly and efficiently. It might also make their kids happy—kids did like to run. But would it make the parents better people? This was the toughest of the three Golden Questions to answer. Jonah wasn't sure what constituted a better person. Did hurrying across the parking lot of Wal-Mart, ducking your head while keeping an eye out for snipers, make you a better or worse human being?

He leaned back in his chair and stretched his arms over his head, focusing his eyes on an object at least twelve feet in the distance, as he'd been advised to do by a *Men's Health* magazine article on how to avoid eyestrain while sitting at the computer. He stared at a red fire extinguisher mounted on the wall and counted to thirty, as recommended, while he listened to the telephone voice of the intern seated in the cubicle behind his.

"Hi. I'm Susie from PinwheelKids online? We're doing a story on fashionable baby clothes and accessories," she said, extra perky, "and since supermodel Kate Moss is like the biggest trendsetter in the world? She's like Miss Trendsetter? And since she's pregnant, I was wondering if she's been shopping in your store and what she's bought?"

The thirty seconds up, Jonah turned back to his computer screen with rested eyes and opened another article. This one gave advice on how to cope with "beige eaters." Beige eaters, it explained, were children who insisted on only eating foods that were the color beige, such as French fries, cookies, and bread. Such pickiness caused major problems for parents these days.

The internal IM box popped up on his screen. It was a note from Michelle asking him to please "eyeball" the new poll on the Family Guide to New York City that was going live that afternoon. Jonah went to the Travel section to look at the poll. It asked, "Which tourist attraction do you most want to visit in the Big Apple?" There was a list of attractions with radio buttons beside them that users could click to indicate their top choice. Ground Zero held the number-one spot with 44% of the votes, leaving in its dust the classic heavy hitters: Empire State Building, Statue of Liberty, Times Square.

He wrote back to Michelle, *There is something unsavory about calling Ground Zero a tourist attraction.*

Thats what it is, Michelle's IM shot back.

It's kind of tasteless. They're still pulling out human remains.

Doesnt matter. It's a top atraction. Toursits want to go there.

Jonah didn't have time to write back when another IM from Michelle bounced onto his screen. *Anythig else? poll good to go???*

I really think we should take out Ground Zero, Jonah typed.

GROUND ZERO STAYS IN. ;-)

That was so like Michelle, to mix the aggression of all caps with one of those annoying emoticons, as if a wink and a smile could undercut the brute force of capital letters. He called to Keith over the partition. Keith pulled his headphones down around his shoulders, the music spilling out in jagged sound waves.

"Would you consider Ground Zero to be a tourist attraction?"

"Tourists are attracted to it," Keith replied. "Like ants at a picnic."

"But do you think we should call it a tourist attraction? On the site? Don't you think that's rather ghoulish?"

"Give the people what they want. Hey." Keith took off his earphones and hopped over to Jonah's desk. "Check out ProphetExchange.com. Go ahead. Type it in."

Jonah did as Keith instructed and the web site for ProphetExchange.com materialized on his screen. It was an online bookie, or a kind of stock market, with a twist. Not only could you bet on sporting events, you could also lay your money down on the imminent deaths of aging celebrities, assassination attempts, the second coming of Christ, even the date and time of the impending nuclear holocaust.

"Go to Current Events," Keith said.

"I really have a lot of work to do," Jonah complained. "I am so behind. Now that Michelle's back from her quote-unquote maternity leave."

"Go to Current Events."

When Jonah clicked on the link, the screen informed him that he could bid on the following claims: Death of Osama Bin Laden, Nuclear Suicide Attack on NYC, U.S. Invades Iraq.

"The cool thing about these electronic prediction markets is that they're incredibly accurate," Keith said. "Check out U.S. Invades Iraq."

Jonah clicked and a graph with a jagged green line appeared on the screen. The line was rising steadily, showing high odds that the U.S. would invade Iraq by the end of 2003. Shares were selling at $85.

"That means there's an 85% chance we'll invade," Keith explained.

"That's not a good bet. Why invade Iraq? They weren't involved in 9/11."

"I'm telling you, these prediction markets are more accurate than national polls or political experts. The U.S. Defense Department is developing their own, something called FutureMAP, so that ordinary people all over the world can help predict the next terrorist attack."

"And if they predict it correctly?"

"They make a shitload. I've got my money on a dirty bomb going off in Times Square by the end of summer."

"You work in Times Square," Jonah pointed out. "How are you going to collect when you're dead?"

"I'm predicting it happens on the weekend."

"Why not just bomb Times Square yourself? I mean, an actual terrorist could put all his money on a bomb going off on a particular date, at a particular time. Then he could plant a bomb, just like he predicted, and when it goes off, not only does he score one for Allah, he also wins a million dollars. Right?"

"You got it," said Keith. "And it's sponsored by the U.S. government."

"It's a sign of the apocalypse."

"You can bet on that, too. See? There's a whole section on Armageddon. So you've got a lot more to worry about than whether or not to call Ground Zero a tourist attraction. It already is a tourist attraction and it always will be. Nothing you can do about that."

"It's a smoldering mass grave," said Jonah, turning back to the story on beige eaters.

From the other side of the cubicle wall a voice repeated, "Supermodel Kate Moss is like the biggest trendsetter in the world? She's like Miss Trendsetter? And since she's pregnant, I was wondering—"

Jonah stepped out for lunch. The heat wrapped him in its wet wool blanket and burned blindingly on the metal bodies of passing cars. He hurried to air-conditioned Howard Johnson's, where the radio played Perry Como crooning, "Mama loves mambo. Papa loves mambo," and Jonah felt the chaos of life drain away. The music reminded him of Vivian's house. He missed the comfort he felt with her there, away from dirty bombs and Internet terrorism casinos, away from people who crackled along the surface of life like scavengers in their plastic exoskeletons, hungry for stimulation's next crumb. A line of high school poetry came to mind: "The world is too much with us." He could not remember the poet, but the line felt true—true out there, but not in Howard Johnson's. Snug in an orange Naugahyde booth by the big plate-glass window, he doodled on the paper placemat, roughing out a sketch of the last panel he'd done in *Ephemera Automat*—Stan and Giggy on their bench, the prop plane pulling an aerial banner across the sky—but he couldn't decide what the sign should say. It should be something important, something prophetic, a warning to the wayward world. Before he could add another line, the waitress, a tired-looking blonde with an Eastern European accent, covered the placemat with his order—cheeseburger, fries, and a Coke. He watched her shuffle away, to the back of the restaurant, where she hoisted herself onto a swivel stool and lit a long, slender cigarette. There wasn't much else for her to do. Jonah was one of only a few people in the place. At the ice cream counter, an elderly woman sat alone, turning the pages of a magazine. The soda jerk, a large, slow-moving Middle Easterner, stood with arms crossed over his apron and heaved a sigh beneath the list of once-popular flavors: maple walnut, butter pecan, rum raisin. At the register, the cashier hit the keys on his old machine, making the internal mechanism grind and the metallic bell sound its archaic ring in the empty restaurant. Decades ago, Howard Johnson's was hopping. The milkshakes and clam strips overflowed in the arms of busy waitresses and the cocktail lounge rocked with theater-crowd revelers getting crocked on drinks no one knew how to order (or mix) anymore—Golden Cadillacs, Pink Ladies, Singapore Slings.

At his post behind the register, the cashier stood sipping coffee beneath shelves filled with dusty boxes of saltwater taffy. Jonah followed his gaze as the man squinted out at the street. Directly across the teeming square, tourists and office workers flowed in through the doors beneath neon-lit Golden Arches, ravenous for the fast and familiar. The cashier may have been longing for those crowds, but Jonah was happy to have Howard Johnson's just as it was—an oasis of calm, a brown wood-paneled portal into a muted past, around which the multicolored pixels of Times Square jostled and honked. Outside, the throng surged up and down Broadway, a stupendous effort of human motion matched only by the motor traffic. Hundreds of hurried bodies, their arms swinging, climbed and clawed their way through the deep canyon of billboards and wattage, focused only on moving forward, paying no attention to one another, forgetting the places they'd left behind. But then the rhythm stuttered and broke apart. The traffic stalled. The desultory energy shifted inside Howard Johnson's, almost imperceptibly, the way a group of people waiting for a train will subtly shift, feeling the breathy rush of a subway coming from blocks away. A crowd accumulated at the corner.

"She's not moving," said the cashier, hurrying to the window.

"I saw her fingers move," said the waitress.

"That's just the electricity leaving her body. She's gone."

Jonah took the last bite of his burger, gulped his Coke, and slid out of the booth to join the onlookers at the window. At the curb, a woman's body lay face down on the asphalt. She looked deflated, almost flattened. Her right arm was flung out to the side, white and bare, bent at the elbow and ringed with bracelets. Her feet were turned at uncomfortable-looking angles. One of her sandals had come off and Jonah could see the sole of her left foot, the pink heel ridged with callus, the tender arch rippled and pale. From under her head, a trickle of blood ran red and brilliant against the white reflective paint of the crosswalk stripe on which she lay. A trio of EMS workers arrived and stood dumbly around the body, their hands in blue rubber gloves hanging idle at their sides.

"If she had a chance, they'd be rushing her out of here," said the cashier, waving his hand dismissively. "She's gone."

Jonah weaved through the crowd on the sidewalk to get closer. Men craned their necks. Women covered their mouths with their hands. A few sightseers dialed numbers into their cell phones and narrated the spectacle. "I tried to swerve," said the driver. "She walked right out in front of me." Jonah stepped forward into the barricade of a blue arm, a police officer ordering him to get back. This was what she must have looked like. Her body emptied of life, a deflated raft, a someone turned into a nothing. She might have been talking or staring out the window. She might have been looking at her fingernails.

Do you mean me, Rose said, *or your mother?*

It unnerved him when she popped up out of nowhere like that.

He asked her, *Is that what it was like?*

I wish, she said. *A thud and then out like a light. That would have been easy.*

At the curb, a tube of lipstick, cast from the woman's spilled pocketbook, foundered in the dark river of blood. A young paramedic snapped his rubber glove impatiently. The ambulance backed through the crowd. The workers placed a board beside the woman's body and gently rolled her over onto it, her crumpled face turned toward the sky. Her body was compliant, heavy with oblivion, like a sleeping child that must be carried into the house after a long night's drive. Like his mother's body must have been when they carried her away. Like Rose's body could never be. The ambulance doors closed. No sirens, no lights, no hurry. She was gone.

It's over, Rose said. *Nothing more to see.*

Tell me what happens, he said, *after death.*

How should I know? I only know what you know. Don't be stupid.

"Tardive dyskinesia, Fran Tarkenton," he said out loud, standing dizzy in the heat under Howard Johnson's blue and orange neon sign, waiting for something more to happen. Two police officers built a fence of traffic cones and yellow tape around the scene. A pair of state troopers used a small wheel mounted on the end of a stick to measure the distance from the blood to the curb. They stood around with the police officers, arms crossed, and joked about things Jonah could not hear. How quickly everything went back to normal. Most passersby paid no attention. A few glanced over and looked away. A couple of portly tourists approached. While the wife stared at the red stain, trying to decide if it was blood or just a melted cherry slush, the husband shouted into his cell phone, "We went to Ground Zero this morning and spent about two hours there. Yeah. Came back and had lunch. Yeah. Now we're in Times Square. Well, we were gonna go out to Fresh Kill, to see the wreckage and stuff, but it's only for official personnel. Yeah. Too bad. I heard they have parts of the planes out there. But we're having a great time. Going to St. Patrick's Cathedral next."

"I'm going to snap," Jonah said.

You wish, said Rose. *What a relief. To snap. Who alive doesn't want to snap?*

What was the name of that shooter, the one in the Texas clock tower? Jonah thought, *I could climb to the top of the pyramidal Paramount Building and stand under the clock face, just like—what was his name?*

Charles Whitman, Rose said.

I thought you only knew what I know.

I know things you forgot you knew, she said.

Like what?

Like you don't have a gun and even if you did, you couldn't do it.

She was right. Still, he thought he understood what made shooters like Whitman do such things. People on the television news were always saying, "How could this happen?" It was a stupid question. How could it *not* happen? His bones jangled and a pressure rose up in his throat like a stony pill that would not go down. He had to keep swallowing, running his fingers over his Adam's apple. According to the Paramount clock, the lunch hour was over, but he wasn't ready to go back to the office. He decided to walk a few blocks and loop back around, to clear his head. The heat intensified in the midday traffic, in the choking fumes of exhaust, the sticky too-closeness of so many bodies. He could die for a cold drink.

That's when he saw her: the twin-tailed siren in her green ring, calling to him through the waves of humidity. She spread her lower limbs and smirked. He could hear the mermaid singing. *Do I dare?* he asked himself. *Do I dare to drink a Starbucks?* Plunked down on the median in the middle of Broadway, before a glittering backdrop of jumbled JumboTron images and the U.S. Armed Forces Recruiting Station's giant television selling the War on Terror, stood a Starbucks coffee bar built entirely from blocks of ice. Billed as "the world's coldest Starbucks," the glacial café steamed and melted musically in the globally warmed springtime heat, streams of water gurgling to the gutters. Office workers in sweat-stained shirts, tourists shielded under 9/11 souvenir baseball caps, Buddhist monks wearing saffron robes with Nike sneakers—they all stopped to taste free samples of Starbucks' latest product, iced coffee in a can, pre-creamed and pre-sugared, ready to drink.

Do it, Rose said. *Someday you'll be dead, like me. All these people will be dead, too. The tourists, the office workers, the Buddhist monks. We all end up in a heap. We become the dark matter.*

Jonah felt a chunk inside of him break off and slip away, like the thawing end of a tidewater glacier calving into the sea. Why fight it? Rose was right. The world was ending. Signs of the apocalypse were everywhere. He couldn't beat them and so he joined them, grabbing a mini cup from the tray offered to him by a smiling, green-smocked barista. He swallowed the contents in one shot. It was good. He strode to the bar, pressed his hands to the slippery arctic surface, and did the unthinkable. "Iced coffee," he ordered, uttering the heretofore blasphemous copyrighted size, "Venti."

Sipping from the extra tall, green straw of his twenty-ounce Starbucks beverage, he had to admit to feeling refreshed. As he drank, he walked on down Broadway past the Naked Cowboy playing guitar in his underwear, a tattoo of Jesus Christ on his arm and his white western boots filled with dollar bills. He passed a doomsday prophet carrying a sign on a stick that warned, THE WINDS OF THE END TIME ARE BLOWING, and an enterprising young man holding up a placard that offered "101 Sexual Positions: $1." Jonah felt the extra-caffeinated twenty ounces jolt through his bloodstream, making his teeth ache and his spinal cord crackle. The Cross Man shuffled by, bent under the burden of his crucifix, wash bucket swinging in his fist, the back of his t-shirt scrawled with the words, "If any man will come after me, let him deny himself, and take up his cross daily, and follow me." Jonah turned to watch him go, tempted to follow, but a new spectacle stole his attention.

At the window of the Paramount Building, where World Wrestling Entertainment had its headquarters, a small crowd gathered in front of a "living window display." Behind the glass, in front of a faux suburban house with a white front porch, a red behemoth of a Sport Utility Vehicle parked its monster tires on a sheet of plastic lawn. Above, the glossy latex sky beamed with fluffy cotton-ball clouds, and from the SUV's rolled-down windows, a handsome family of three smiled and waved at the crowd like minor celebrities in the Macy's Day Parade. On the sidewalk, two excited young men wearing hats sprouting golden ram's horns and t-shirts bearing the slogan "Grab Life by the Horns" waved people over to the window. Jonah asked what the stunt was all about.

"These folks are grabbing life by the horns," said the ram guy, grinning. "If they can survive for five days in this brand-new Dodge Durango 4x4 SUV, they get to drive it home. Plus, for every day they spend in the Durango, DaimlerChrysler will donate $5,000 toward ending homelessness, because no one should have to live in a car if they don't want to. Would you like to say some words of encouragement to the folks inside?"

Ram Guy pushed a walkie-talkie in Jonah's face and Jonah stepped back from it. A young woman leaned in to it and asked the people how they ate.

"We've got a super celebrity chef bringing us all our meals," said the mom into her own walkie-talkie, "and they are delicious."

Another onlooker asked if they felt uncomfortable being watched all the time. Mom said, "We're performers, so we're used to being on display. I was a professional cheerleader in the NFL and my husband is a singer at Disney World. He played Ken in the Ken and Barbie Show. So we're used to it. And this SUV is loaded with things to keep us distracted."

"This new Durango is HEMI powered," said Dad, flashing his bright teeth. "And, boy, is it big. It's seven inches longer, three inches taller, and three inches wider than last year's model."

"Give me your number," shouted the son, a baseball-capped teenager, as he waved his cell phone at a blonde girl outside the glass.

The crowd chuckled. Jonah wanted to scream. He considered hurling his cup of gritty Starbucks ice cubes against the window.

Do it, said Rose. *Find a brick. Smash the window.*

He told her, *The people who design SUVs make them big to trick drivers into feeling safe when they're not. The excessive number of cup holders inside SUVs is another false comfort, lulling these idiots into an unconscious memory of ample breastfeeding.*

She shook her head and said, *Now who sounds like Jane?*

He continued, *SUVs clog the air with poisonous carbon monoxide and hydrocarbons. This Durango isn't going to protect anyone. Not from dirty nukes or from chemical release events. It won't deflect a crashing Boeing 767 or stop a falling skyscraper. Statistics show that SUVs cause more accidents and kill more people than smaller cars. They are not safe.*

You're being too intellectual, said Rose. *You want to snap, so snap. Throw the cup. Better yet, find a brick. Smash the window.*

What are you anyway, he asked her, *my id?*

Did Jane teach you that? There's no such thing as id. I'm all the voices in your head. Obviously. Now do something. Go!

Jonah walked up to Ram Guy and grabbed the walkie-talkie.

"They're raising money for the homeless," said Ram Guy, all white teeth. "Would you like to give them some words of encouragement?"

Jonah leaned in to the speaker. He felt the twenty-ounce Venti exploding his synapses, turbo-charging his rage. He growled in his throat.

Tell them they are all going to die, said Rose, pushing him. *Tell them, no matter what, they end up on the heap. Ashes and dust. Tell them to go fuck themselves!*

He ached to say these things and more, but when he opened his mouth to speak, courage abandoned him (he could never have been a successful clock-tower sniper, not even drugged on a gallon of Starbucks). Feeling his bladder swell, he asked just one pitiful question: "Where do you go to the bathroom?"

The family smiled in unison behind the glass.

"We get asked that all the time," said the mom. "We've got some real spiffy facilities back here, behind the little house? It's real comfortable. We can even take hot showers."

The family waved to Jonah, frantically shaking their tanned and muscled arms from the windows of the SUV as if they were cruising along a country road instead of standing still on a plastic lawn behind a plate-glass window. Jonah waved back. It was hard not to wave when someone waved to you first, and he didn't want anyone to think he was some kind of a jerk.

I'm done, said Rose. *You're on your own.*

When Jonah turned to look at her, she had vanished into smoke. It was the last time he would see her, but he didn't know that yet.

I need to spak with you. In my office. please. Right away, read the Instant Message from Michelle. This time she hadn't bothered to include a smiley-face emoticon.

"Hot out there, isn't it," she said, sucking on the plastic nipple of her twenty-four-ounce Poland Spring sport bottle with pop-top. The label said: "Win Prizes" and "Thirst for Adventure."

"Brutal," said Jonah, sucking on the green straw of his second twenty-ounce Venti.

"Do you like working here?"

He considered the question, looking away from Michelle, up at her shelf of bobble-head dolls. There was a bobble-head Jesus Christ and a bobble-head Satan. There was Mickey Mouse, Elvis Presley, and the Virgin Mary. On the desk she kept her favorites: a bobble-head George W. Bush and a bobble-head Osama Bin Laden. Jonah's caffeinated skull bobbled, too.

"Jonah." She smacked her hand on the desk and the grinning heads of George W. and Osama bobbled in agreement. "Are you even awake?"

"Tardive dyskinesia, Fran Tarkenton," he said out loud.

"What did you say?"

"I'm not sure."

"I asked you a question. Do you like working here?"

"I'm not sure."

"Because you don't really seem engaged. You don't make an effort to be part of the team. You just don't seem...excited to be here."

"I didn't realize that expressing excitement was part of the job description."

"Jonah, this is a really fun place to work, but you don't have any fun. You come in late. You take long lunches. You're not with the program. All right. Let me cut to the chase. I'm not the royal bitch everyone thinks I am. You are being given a warning. I'm being very generous with you. Do you understand? If you're late one more time, that's it. And don't give me a hard time about Ground Zero, okay? It's a tourist attraction. Let's keep sentimentality out of it."

"No," he said.

"Sorry?"

"Tardive dyskinesia, Fran Tarkenton," he said.

"I don't know what language you're speaking. Is that Russian?"

"Tardive dyskinesia, Fran Tarkenton."

"Is that Arabic? Are you threatening me in Arabic? Are you trying to make me think you're some kind of sleeper cell?"

"I quit," he said.

Michelle didn't put up a fight. She called Security and had a guard escort Jonah to his desk. The guard hovered, hands on his belt, ready to subdue Jonah should he need to be subdued. But Jonah wasn't going to go postal and he wasn't going to blow up the Mediacom building. He collapsed his telescope and dropped the Hoberman sphere on Keith's desk. There was nothing else he wanted here. Keith was over in Marketing, tossing a Nerf football with the girls. Jonah didn't bother to write a note. They were never friends.

Back outside, in the brackish heat, he slogged through the crowds, telescope tucked under his arm, swimming up humid Broadway. He returned to The World's Coldest Starbucks, still melting like a glacier in the broiling April sun, and ordered his third Venti iced coffee. A fresh 400-milligram dose of caffeine cascaded down into his stomach and coasted into his bloodstream, joining the 800 milligrams already sizzling Jonah's nervous system. With the equivalent of six No-Doz Maximum Strength tablets fueling him, he jittered his way back to Eighth Avenue with live, nude girls on his mind. The Playground had just been shuttered to make room for a new skyscraper. Show World had already become a legitimate off-off-off-Broadway theatre specializing in Chekhov plays. Peepland had replaced its live girls with video screens. The Hungry Eye sold only souvenir t-shirts, snow globes, and kung fu movies. In the windows of all the shops hung crude, hand-lettered signs that said, "No Live Girls. Beware of con artists."

He turned to go when he heard a slithery voice aimed in his direction. "Psst, psst, hey chief. Big chief. Yeah, you. You looking for live girls? Lovely ladies. Right here, chief. Check it out."

The man stuck a slip of paper into Jonah's hand. There was an address printed on it and the word ADMIT.

"Check it out, chief. Lovely, lovely ladies. One-dollar dancing girls. You won't be disappointed."

The entrance was a blighted passageway in the bowels of Hell's Kitchen, a kind of alley beneath a building consumed by generations of neglect. Shaking from the Starbucks, Jonah gripped the rotted handrail as he made his way down the steps, careful to avoid the fresh stains of human effluents. As he descended, the sunlight dwindled. Before him, weak bulbs protected in wire cages led the way down a long underpass where water dripped from above, collecting into fetid puddles at his feet. He felt like he was passing into a separate space, an alternate reality. The stink of urine was strong and he was glad to emerge at last into a junk-filled courtyard where the ailanthus trees grew from the wreckage of baby carriages and yellowed mattresses and where the sun slanted in at an odd angle, shining on a door graffitied and unmarked except for a taped-on sheet of paper that read, CLAM BOX.

Jonah brushed away his second thoughts and opened the door. Before him loomed a large, dark-skinned man with a thick cigar tucked into his capacious cheek.

"Show me the ticket."

Jonah held up the slip of paper he'd received on the street. ADMIT.

"Welcome to the Clam Box, chief," the man said, grabbing the ticket and stepping aside to let Jonah through.

The basement room was a grotto decorated in an underwater theme with blue neon lights and fishermen's nets hanging from the low ceilings, stuffed with plastic simulacra of aquatic life: lobsters, crabs, starfish, and various mollusks. It smelled of standing water and mold, the shoreline soup of seaweeds and rot. He headed for the token booth in the center of the room. Salvaged from the ruins of old 42nd Street, the booth was a leftover from Times Square's more glorious days, sporting a rounded glass window with tarnished brass details along its margins. The sign said: TOKENS $1. He stepped up and slipped a ten-dollar bill through the semicircular opening in the window. The person behind the glass, who may have been a man and may have been a woman, pushed ten tokens toward him. They were brassy and light and felt good in Jonah's hand, like old subway tokens, faded and well-handled. On one side was stamped the image of a naked female torso; on the other was a horseshoe and the word LUCKY. He dropped the tokens into his pocket, enjoying the jingly sound they made, and stepped toward the entrance.

Under the scrolling blue neon "Clam Box" stood a pair of swinging double doors painted with the image of a giant bivalve. The monstrous, vulval clam stood on its end, so that each door held half a shell, and where the doors met, the pink meat of the clam's mantle glistened in sprayed-on glitter. Jonah thought of Jane's *vagina dentata*. He steadied himself, hefted the telescope further up under his arm, and pushed his way inside.

Girls stood everywhere in the blue shadows, cat-calling and coaxing to him. "Come here, come here," they cried, waving their feathers in his direction. There were all kinds of girls. Girls of different colors and sizes, ages and abilities. There were eager young women dressed as schoolgirls and nurses. There were wrinkled old women smoking long cigarettes, too bored to call out to him. A female dwarf dressed in a frilly Shirley Temple frock, lollipop in hand, tugged on his pant leg and called him Daddy. Seated on a ratty divan, an enormous woman with arms like ham hocks pulled Jonah onto her lap and pinched his cheeks, slapping his thigh and laughing uproariously. Jonah felt his teeth chatter and he couldn't tell if it was from fear or a dangerous caffeine overdose. Next to the fat lady sat a skinny girl with no legs. She was laughing, too, dressed in a bikini bottom and nothing else. He pitied the girl and all of them, these castaways from old Times Square, stranded on their island of misfit strippers.

"What do you want for Christmas, little boy," bellowed the big woman, holding Jonah tight on her warm and massive lap. He looked down at the rolls of flesh on her body, like volcanic mounds of oozing lava, her beluga-white skin turned red in the shifting bordello light.

"I was just looking," he said through chattering teeth, "for the dancing girls."

"A peeping tom," purred the giantess, running her swollen red fingers up the length of the telescope. "Is that right? You like to look at girls with this?"

"You like to watch the girls and jerk off," the skinny amputee hissed. "Didn't your mother ever tell you little boys go blind when they jerk off too much?"

His sympathy for this girl withered.

"Why don't you let us take care of that for you," the big woman said, her hand crawling up his leg, finger by finger, like a fat red tarantula. "A little boy like you could get lost in a gal like me."

"The man said there were dancing girls. For a dollar."

"Cheapskate," the woman growled, her whole body convulsing. "Another cheapskate peeping tom."

The amputee rolled her eyes and sucked her teeth in disgust, looking away from Jonah as if he were just too awful to behold. The big woman slapped him again on the thigh, laughing with her open mouth, and tossed him from her lap. The telescope slipped from his hands, fumbling, and he caught it, hugging it to him before it could fall to the floor.

"Thataway," she said, indicating the direction with her thumb. "The way of all flesh."

He followed a neon sign that said CLAM BUFFET $1 to a row of narrow doors. He picked one at random and locked himself inside, his heart drumming in his throat. The booth was as dark and tight as a steamer trunk. It smelled of organic things—of brine and algae, musk and root vegetables gritty with mud. The only light came from the money slot, a red digital glow that said INSERT. He took out the tokens and nearly dropped them, his hands trembling, before he slipped all of them, one at a time, into the slot. Part of the wall glided up to reveal a window of Plexiglas, reminding Jonah of his childhood visits to the church confessional, the screen through which he expelled all of his sins in exchange for total absolution.

Through the Plexiglas, fogged with lip marks and greasy handprints, he could see a real, live girl seated in a dimly lit faux-wood paneled cubicle. She was a broad and strong-looking girl, dressed only in a pair of knee-high black vinyl boots. She had black hair and paper-white skin, her eyes rimmed in black, lips painted a bloody red. She wore yellow cat-eye contact lenses like the Gothic punk-rock kids he saw hanging out on St. Mark's Place. Around her right bicep wound a tattoo of Uroboros, the snake with its tail in its mouth.

The piece of paper taped to the wall behind her held her stage name: Virginia Dentata. Jonah felt his brain throbbing in his skull. Was it possible, he wondered, to hallucinate on three Starbucks Ventis? Could he die here, from caffeine poisoning?

"Want a dance?" the live girl asked, her mouth close to the daisywheel of perforations drilled in the window. "You have to tip," she said, waggling her tongue, the end of it surgically cleft to resemble a snake's.

"Is this enough?" Jonah asked, holding up a $20 bill. He didn't want to be called a cheapskate again.

The girl nodded and grinned, showing him an impressive pair of sharpened canines. "Twenty gets you the whole show."

He pushed the bill through a slit carved in the Plexiglas and watched as the girl tucked it into the top of one boot. She stood up, slowly unfolding, revealing her long body. Her torso filled the whole window until she was framed from her collarbones to the middle of her thighs. Jonah could not see her face, and he was relieved at this. It wasn't just that her face was unnerving and vampiric; he didn't want to be seen while he stared hungrily, as he did now, at her doughy white breasts, the blue veins running through them, her nipples and glitter-dusted areolas the size of saucers. Just above the dark and untrimmed thatch of her pubic hair, there shimmied a tattoo of an atomic mushroom cloud. A fire-orange inferno exploded from her pubis as if a nuclear warhead had just penetrated the region.

The mushroom cloud waved and danced in front of Jonah's face. He watched and his whole body jerked, one big muscle-fiber twitch. The idea of jerking off to the sight of a gyrating multi-megaton explosion was too much. All those cancerous gamma rays and X-rays, churned up with dirt and debris. The blinding flash. Besides, he could not control his hands. They danced and flapped in the air with a Parkinsonian jazz riff.

"Tardive dyskinesia," Jonah said.

The girl's hands squeezed her breasts and worked their way down to part the snarled patch of hair. He thought with distaste of the term "meat curtains." He had heard Keith use this term from time to time, as in "I parted her meat curtains." It made him think of the thick plastic curtains in meat-packing warehouses, the cold of meat freezers, and men in blood-spattered coats. He thought of blood. Of the woman dead on Broadway with her tender head broken open. He thought of his mother. He shook these thoughts as the girl pressed herself against the Plexiglas, sliding open to show pink flesh smearing a viscous, pelagic substance. He was hard now, and managed, twitchingly, to unzip.

The girl's torso looked like a giant face, the nipples staring at him, wide-eyed, the mushroom cloud like a terrible nose, the genital tongue in its tangled beard twirling against the window. He got the sensation of deja vu, of something furry and moist rising up from deep inside of him, some familiar, ineffable shape. Dark blob of memory, it swelled and slithered beyond his mental grasp, sliding into the shadows. He tried to follow it, watching the body-mouth whirl, twirling the lacteous smear into artful spirals, like a hypnotist's spinning disk. His eyes lost focus and he saw his own face reflected in the Plexiglas, his own ghost hovering before him in the darkness, his own eyes looking back at him. His face transposed over the rheumy glaze, over the bubblegummy flesh that kept on spinning, seemed strangely unfamiliar and yet. If he could just name it. There were so many layers. His face, his ghost, the window, the smear, the flesh. The womb, the tomb. The bomb, the flash.

A salty, milky taste rose up in the back of his throat and, all at once, Jonah knew the body dancing before him. Knew it in an untellable way. The knowledge was blurry yet comforting. He felt himself floating in a familiar, cushiony place. He had been here before. Maybe he had never left. White pillows surrounding him. A bull's eye hovering near, a target at which he aimed all of his yearning. It was good, so good. Like nothing else in this world. Like all the vanilla ice cream you could eat. Like snow plows pushing through the morning streets. Like warm in bed, all bunny-cuddly between white sheets. And the bull's eye swelling toward him, red and urging. He was getting there. Salted milk. A deep interior tug of letting go. And then an indecorous splat.

It was done and all he wanted was to leave, but the digital timer said he still had minutes to go. A slender icicle of something like fear slipped up his spine, needle smooth. The bull's eye blubbery mass was coming to devour him. His throat closed. The room shrank. He hadn't noticed before how tight it was. How warm. He was sweating and dizzy. It had to be the caffeine, he reasoned. Everything was spinning, as if the box that held him had begun to pitch and dive, a moving thing with its own volition. The snug chamber seemed to heave up from the bolts that held it down. It rocked and leaped in a balletic flip and then began to plummet, sounding for the abyssal depths. Jonah held onto the black walls for balance, but they were sticky with rancid secretions, viscid glandular jellies that lived and died on those hot partitions, never to see the light of day. He gulped for air, his mouth briny with the tang of salt, as deeper the box plunged. And still the vulval mouth swam toward him, gulping in its frenzied hula dance, singing in its mermaid tongue.

There was a rush of pressure in his ears, a feeling of rising all at once. Express to the top. The walls pressed and heaved, pushing him against the door, where he found the latch and stumbled out of the booth. To his right, the women called to him, Here kitty, kitty. He turned left, fleeing down a dark corridor toward a glowing light, the warm ember of an EXIT sign. His shoes slipped in something wet that leaked through his tattered sole and soaked his sock. He kept on going. "Emergency Only," said the door. He flung himself against it and burst out into the white-hot afternoon of a peaceful side street. He didn't know where he was. He had the bewildering, transformative feeling of emerging from a matinee, a horror movie, and then blinking in the sun and everything being okay again. The sidewalks bloomed with cherry trees and pear trees. On the corner, a hot dog vendor knelt beside his cart, forehead pressed to the rug beneath him, murmuring his afternoon prayers in the direction of Mecca.

Jonah took a deep breath and looked down at his hands. The telescope, his father's gift to him, was gone. He wheeled around, but the closed door had no knob. He scrambled for the edges, but the seal was tight and the only way to get back inside was to start from the beginning. The very idea exhausted him. He pulled a handkerchief from his trouser pocket, removed his Stingy Brim Porkpie Stinger, and mopped the sweat from his shining head. He was aware then of an extreme hunger in his belly. He walked to the hot dog cart and waited while the vendor finished his prayers, rolled up the rug, and stowed it through a small door in the side of the cart.

"What can I do for you, my friend?" the vendor asked, picking up his silver tongs. The hot dogs floated like carp in their steamy bath and the cans of soda glistened like jewels.

"Make me one with everything," Jonah said, delivering the punch line of an old joke.

16

The message, when it came to him at last, was simple. It was nothing revelatory or apocalyptic. It was exactly the kind of unimportant, depressing message you would see flying overhead on a day at the beach. Jonah inked the letters over his penciled outlines, making them ripple a bit in the wind behind the propeller plane that flew over the heads of Stan and Giggy. "GET BACK TO," it said, slowly revealing itself from the right-hand frame, giving the men (and the reader) time to wonder what the aerial banner wanted them to get back to. Get back to nature, maybe, or get back to reality. Get back to work and get back to business. Get back to basics, get back to normal, get back to sleep. But the banner didn't say any of those things. Its message was utterly of the moment: GET BACK TO MISCHIEF WITH VIAGRA.

This is what people wanted. Instant erections. Instant fun. Male multiple orgasms with 500% more sperm. Penis enlargement in a pill. Whiter teeth in one week. Spray-on suntans. A beach-ready body in just ten minutes a day. Instant messages. Anytime minutes. Hi-speed access. Mega-malls and megapixels. Dual-zone climate control. HEMI power. Who was he kidding? No one was going to read a graphic novel about a retired burlesque manager and a novelties salesman, two old geezers who did nothing but sit and talk, or else not talk at all, just sit. Jonah put down his pen and picked up the remote control. He'd been unemployed for three days but it felt like weeks. He hadn't spoken to another human being, hadn't gone outside except to let Frankie relieve herself on the sidewalk, and he still hadn't returned Vivian's calls. He was now a master of monkhood. But tomorrow was Rose's birthday. There would be cake. Vivian was expecting him. How could he miss it? He pushed a button and the television sprang to life. Jane's boyfriend's reality show *Phobia Phactory* was on. Perfect. He settled in to watch as the host explained to one of the contestants the stunt he was expected to perform in record time.

"You will have to lie in this glass coffin and be covered with hundreds of pounds of cow intestine," the host spelled out, relishing each word. "Then you have to bite into the cow intestine and suck out the intestinal fluid, then spit the fluid into this glass. Then, when the glass is full, you will have to drink all of the fluid out of the glass."

The contestant pumped his fists in the air and climbed into the glass coffin. Muscular assistants dumped bucketfuls of slippery cow intestine on top of the contestant. The digital timer appeared in the corner of the television screen and the race was on. *This must be what it's like to be dead*, Jonah thought, *and go to Hell.*

"Puke! Puke! Puke!" the opponents chanted from the sidelines as the contestant chewed through the bowel casings to suck out mouthfuls of oily brown swill. The contestant was performing very well. When he had finished sucking and spitting out the bile, he picked up the filled sixteen-ounce glass without hesitation and chugged the gastric fluid as if it were a mug of cold, frothy lager.

"Swallow it," the host insisted. "And show me."

The contestant opened his mouth for the camera, showing the world that he had swallowed all the fluid.

"Awesome, bro! You did it," the host slapped the contestant on the back. "Two minutes and thirty-four seconds. You just won $50,000. What do you say?"

The contestant winked into the camera, his face smeared with chunky intestinal broth, and said, "All the ladies are gonna give it up to me—now they've seen what I can eat!"

Jonah turned off the television.

At the dog run, he scanned the crowd, looking for her. Groups of young men and women gathered at the picnic benches, smoking cigarettes, laughing, flirting, and slapping each other on the arms. They dressed in cut-off shorts and t-shirts, sandals and sunglasses, straw cowboy hats and trucker caps bearing the iron-on patches of rugged brands like STP motor oil and Philips 66, brand names foreign in a city that relied on public transportation. *When did everyone in the neighborhood get so young*, he wondered as he browsed through the women. Uniformly thin and slouched, wearing their practiced looks of utter boredom in the shade of their hats, none of them were Jane.

He found an empty bench while Frankie plopped under her picnic table, panting in the shade. New leaves and pink cherry blossoms languished in the heat. Even the wooden slats of the bench felt moist with the melt of global warming. Dogs loped across the dusty wood chips, too hot to run. The dog days of summer they called it, but it was only the first month of spring. A slobber-mouthed boxer leapt upon Jonah, pinning him to the back of the bench.

"Maximus!" shouted the boxer's owner to her dog, who was now painting the front of Jonah's shirt with his foamy saliva. "Maximus, be nice! I'm sorry." She was a young woman with a silver hoop pierced through her lower lip and a wide strip of electric blue painted into her hair. She looked a little like Rose, but a crusty version of her, in tattered shorts and stubbled legs. He missed Rose.

"He can be rambunctious at times. That's how he shows his love."

Jonah looked down at the dog, half seated in his lap, and noted that the animal was sporting a pink and dewy erection.

"It's okay," Jonah said, even though it wasn't really. This was the part of the dog run he hated. You were supposed to be okay with being pounced on, humped, and licked. You were supposed to laugh and rub the offending animal behind its ears, ignoring its unsheathed and ready genitals, and say something affable, like, "Oh, you silly doggie, you!" All in good fun. He grimaced, wiping the saliva from his neck, as the woman dragged her dog off by the collar.

"Mind if I cop a squat?"

He shrugged and tried a smile, even though he hated the expression "cop a squat," which reminded him of shitting in the woods. He forced an unnatural grin onto his face and kept his eyes on the gate, hoping Jane would walk through and rescue him. The woman plunked down beside him with a grunt, a little too close. There were too many people at the dog run today and none of them were Jane. On his other side sat a not-so-young but youthfully dressed mother, wearing a straw cowboy hat, pink-tinted sunglasses, and a pair of sheepskin galoshes called Uggs, which must have stood for "ugly," though they were all the rage. Parked at her feet sat the double-wide Urban Ironman Sport Utility Stroller. Jonah knew it from editing an article on Best Gear for Baby. With its hundred-pound capacity, shock-absorbent rugged-rubber tires, and handlebar console with enough cup holders to carry three twenty-ounce beverages, the $700 Urban Ironman was hailed as the "SUV of strollers." In one of the deep bucket seats sat a boy of at least eight years old. With legs grown too long even for the ample Urban Ironman, his knees pressed against his chest, folding him like an adult squeezed into a child-sized vehicle, one of those clowns who ride around in tiny go-karts at parades. Jonah worried about what would happen to this generation of push-cart children, imagining future epidemics of obesity, laziness, a weird longing to roll through life in electric wheelchairs. This boy was perfectly comfortable in his cramped and stunted position, hypnotized by the fighting action on his Gameboy screen, which Jonah eyed over the kid's shoulder.

"See that guy over there, with the black dog," the woman with the blue hair said. "With the Akita?"

Jonah looked up. "I see the dog."

"See the guy in the trucker hat?"

"I see about six guys in trucker hats."

"His dog is always trying to hump my dog, and that guy is like a total close talker. Every time I come in here, he's always trying to talk up in my face, and it's just like *he's* trying to hump *me*. Get it? Like *his* dog trying to hump *my* dog. It's amazing how people resemble their dogs."

The boy in the stroller announced to his mother, without looking up from the Gameboy, that he was in desperate, immediate need of a snack.

"My dog is just like me," Blue Hair continued. "He doesn't make friends easily. He's friendly at first, says hello, then he sticks to the margins. He likes his space. And he doesn't want to be presumptuous."

Without a note of singsong the mother said to her child, "Is my hungry man ready for his snackety-snack-snack," as if she were speaking to an adult, in a grown-up voice but with baby words. She leaned down and dug through the bags she had stored in the stroller's spare seat, giving Jonah a good look at the neon-green thong that stood out from the waist of her low-rise denim skirt, and pulled out a quart-sized Ziploc baggie full of trail mix. She unzipped the Easy Zipper and held the bag out for the boy to reach his hand into, keeping his eyes on the Gameboy screen, where his character was ardently sawing the head off another character with a meat cleaver. Animated blood spurted across the screen in bright red pixels.

"Like maybe one day I'll come in here and have a really good conversation with some guy," said Blue Hair. "We get along well. But the next time, when I come in, I won't go right over and say hello. Even if we make eye contact. And maybe then he thinks I don't like him. But that's not it. I just think people come here for some privacy and I want to respect that. See? I don't want to be presumptuous. Exactly like Maximus. And that's just one way my dog and I are so alike."

In the middle of the dog run, the unassuming Maximus was trying to rape an uptight Shiba Inu. The owner of the Shiba Inu, a willowy Asian girl, was all aflutter, waving her hands in the air. "Don't hump my doggie," she said in a cute and friendly voice, smiling so as not to offend the rules of dog-run society, "please don't hump my doggie." Blue Hair watched from the bench and smiled. Jonah's head hurt. He tried to give in, to be easygoing and not hate the world, but all he wanted was to go home.

He dragged Frankie up St. Mark's Place, past the giant hot dog that said EAT ME and the buzzing tattoo parlor/ cappuccino bar, past the missing posters that had ceased searching for lost people and now sought only lost dogs and parakeets, mislaid necklaces and wristwatches, mysteriously absent backpacks and notebooks. Frankie fought the leash and lay down on the sidewalk, refusing to budge. Jonah jerked her chain but she wouldn't give an inch, too hot to take another step. He let her rest while he read the flyers taped to the light pole. "Missing Cat," read one. "If you have seen her, or if you saw her fall from the window, or especially if you see her hurt, please let me know, as she is very much missed." Another flyer read, "LOST: Framed photo of my father in a field of daffodils. It is my only photo of him. If found please call." He remembered the time his father first told him that the dark matter of deep space accounted for more mass in the universe than all of the stars, planets, and moons combined. "It's all the stuff you can't see, the stuff we can't even find," his father had said, "that fills up the universe." The inequity in this fact staggered Jonah, the way he felt when he calculated that the dead of the world vastly outnumbered the living. The universe was cluttered with lost objects, the people and things that were no longer here, the stuff that somehow, without warning, had slipped away without a trace. He scooped Frankie into his arms and carried her home.

Walking down First Avenue, he thought he heard someone calling his name. He imagined Rose, up ahead on Sixth Street, waving to him over the confetti blooms of the corner market, flowers and fruits like a magic carpet cloud of color at her feet. Rose is a rose is a rose is a rose. She hadn't visited him lately. Tomorrow, had she lived, she would have turned thirty-one—a year ahead of him. He was Pisces and she was Taurus, two neighboring configurations of stars, the pair of bound fish limping at the back of the caravan along the circular conveyer belt of the sky's ecliptic. While Jonah's father had shown him the faint stars of Pisces, disappointingly dim in the black, his mother had told the thrilling story of how Aphrodite and her son jumped into the Euphrates River and turned themselves into fishes to escape a terrible monster, and how they stayed forever intertwined in the heavens. To Jonah, Pisces was the fish out of water, always lagging behind, the clammy piscatorial tail end of the zodiac. And here he was chasing after Rose, or at least her shimmering mirage that vanished when he reached the flower stand, lost again. He had lost them all. He'd tried to hold on, but there was only so much holding you could do.

Jonah punched his key into the door. He heard his name again. But it was only the trick of sound, a certain pitch in the engine noise of passing trucks combined with music from an open window, mixed with swirling voices. Across the street, a man on a stoop had canaries in a cage and they were singing bright yellow songs. Jonah stepped into the vestibule, putting Frankie down on the cracked tile floor, and checked his mail. The narrow box was overstuffed with catalogs. Pottery Barn. Hammacher-Schlemmer. Sharper Image. J. Crew. Ann Taylor Loft. He grabbed the wad of catalogs and yanked, but the old mailbox was narrow and they resisted.

"Come on, come on," he growled, pulling until the first catalog ripped in half and the rest came cascading onto the small vestibule floor, slick and glistening like wet fish. Frankie tiptoed out of the way, hiding behind him as he squatted to pick up the mess. It was too hot for this.

"Jonah, hey!"

He looked up through the gated door. It was Jane.

"Jeez Louise, didn't you hear me calling? I've been trying to catch up to you."

Her summer skirt glowed with summery light—pistachio green, cool as ice cream. Jane.

"Are you going to let me in?"

Without standing, balancing catalogs on his lap, he reached for the doorknob and she pushed open the gate, letting Sigmund Freud knock him against the wall. The two dogs, happy to see each other again, wrestled and slipped on the floor of spilled catalogs, shredding the slick pages.

"You got a lot of catalogs there," she said, stepping behind him inside the crowded vestibule. "You must do a lot of shopping to get all those catalogs."

"Actually, I don't," he said, balancing himself and pushing the dogs apart so he could pick up the litter of mass mailings. He was angry at the catalogs for interfering with the gladness he should have been feeling, seeing Jane again. But maybe he shouldn't be glad. She had probably come to give him the bad news that she would leave him longing forever while she stayed with Mark. She stood close enough for him to smell the scent of sunscreen and sweat caramelizing in the heat on her skin. He could see just her bare ankles and her seashell-pink-painted toes where they poked out of open shoes, pistachio green slip-on things. Delicate lilac veins marbled her ankles. On her shins, a constellation of irritated follicles glowed red from a recent shaving. Her knees (if he raised his eyes without turning his head too much he could just glimpse them) hovered in the shadows of her skirt, darker skinned and plumped at the tops where her thighs began. He stifled the urge to kiss her knees, to bury his face in the cotton drapery of her skirt like a boy clinging to his mother before she goes out for the evening, perfumed and made-up and never to return.

Jane reached down and grabbed a catalog from Ann Taylor Loft, looking at the back cover where a svelte young woman stepped onto the bow of a motorboat against a backdrop of turquoise Italian water.

"Why do you get stuff for women? And who is Ms. Joan Soloway? I didn't know you were married."

"That's me. I had a sex change. Used to be a woman. Could you hold your dog, please?"

Jane took Sigmund Freud's leash and pulled him to her side.

"Too much computer cross-pollination," he said, sorry that he'd snapped at her. "I get junk mail for Joan Soloway, Joseph Soloway, Jano Soloway. Occasionally something for a Jonah Solomon. And sometimes Jane Soloway."

"Jane Soloway," she said, trying it out. "That's better than my name. Lipshitz. Isn't it awful? I swear I used to get so tormented in school. Boys didn't want to kiss me because of my so-called lip shits."

The thought of Jane going unkissed throughout her tormented adolescence pained Jonah. He was tired of deprivation in all its forms. If Jane had come to take one more thing away from him, then there was something he had to get from her first. With all of the catalogs gathered in his arms, he stood up and dizzily, artlessly kissed her on the mouth. Their eyeglasses crashed together. He could tell right away that it was not a good kiss. It was too dry and his tongue timidly stayed turtled in his mouth. He was an amateur. This was a mistake, he decided, pulling away—but then she kissed him back, her glossed lips smearing his, her tongue coaxing his out of hiding. The catalogs, crushed between them, crumpled and complained. He considered dropping them in a cinematic gesture when the gate opened and they quickly parted, like kids caught at something they ought not to be doing. It was Zipnick.

"Just coming back from the market," he said, averting his eyes. "Don't mind me, folks. Boy. It's hot out there. It's Florida in April. They say we broke some records."

Jonah and Jane stepped aside, pressing themselves against the mailboxes to let Zipnick go by.

"Does he bite?"

"No," said Jane. "He's a good dog."

Zipnick stopped to pet Sigmund Freud's wrinkled head.

"What kind of dog is this?"

"He's a Bullmastiff."

"That's a big dog. Oh boy! Look at all that junk mail. Let me get the door. That's a lot of junk mail you got there. I don't know how they get ahold of your name, those junk mail people, but there ought to be a law, don't you think?"

"Yes, I do," said Jane, following Jonah up the stairs with the dogs in the middle and Zipnick trailing behind.

"People have a right to privacy in this country," the old man continued. "But that's how they getcha. That's how they getcha. Boy oh boy. They getcha coming and going. Coming and going. I was hit by a car a few years back."

Jonah had heard this story a million times. He knew not to turn around, just keep walking.

"That's terrible," Jane said sincerely.

"It was terrible, dear, just terrible. I still have this pain in my hip when it rains and did I get any money? Not a dime. Not a dime. It was a hit and run. My insurance wouldn't even pay the hospital because the doctor wasn't in their whatdoyacallit? Their network. That was before I got my Social Security. Now every time it rains I get the pain and boy does it burn me up. But that's how they getcha."

Jonah heard Zipnick open his apartment door. The old man kept talking, moving back to the subject of record-breaking heat. Jane would be there forever, frozen on the stairs listening to the weather reports. Jonah didn't stop until he reached his own door and got it open, the catalogs slipping in his hands. The dogs ran inside, their chains dragging on the floor. Zipnick's mother called from within the cabbage-fragrant apartment below. "Marty! What are you doing out there? It's time for my sitz bath."

"Don't let me keep you, dear," said Zipnick, releasing Jane at last. "You go on ahead now, don't let me keep you."

She stumbled into the apartment, holding her hand over her throat like she was choking herself. In her other hand she held a suitcase. It was round and pink, like something Doris Day would carry. Jonah hadn't noticed it until now.

"Going on a trip?"

She was about to tell him that she was going to Europe on her honeymoon with Mark, or that they were moving to California, or maybe just following the president's orders and flying down to Disney World to keep the terrorists from winning. She'd come to say goodbye. But instead she said, "I thought you might invite me to stay here awhile. Since you have the extra room."

He was still holding the junk mail. He let it drop from his arms into the kitchen garbage can with a satisfying crash.

"You don't recycle?"

"Like roommates, you mean?"

"Like whatever," she said. "Roommates with benefits. I'm impulsive. Mark and I broke up. To tell the truth, I broke up with Mark. It's his apartment, so. I really, really don't want to have to move out to Queens. What do you say? I can pay rent, split the utilities. I promise not to, you know, eat all your peanut butter or leave dirty dishes in the sink. I'll buy toilet paper and I don't know. Stuff like that?"

"Roommates with benefits."

"I like you," she said, fluttering her hands, tugging at her skirt, like an antsy little girl. "Okay? This isn't just a thing about not wanting to move to Queens. This isn't a real estate thing. I liked you the first time we met."

Jonah moved behind her and closed the door, shutting out the smells of his neighbors' cigarettes and suppers, the noises of their televisions and radios. He locked the three deadbolts, enjoying the chunky metallic sound of the bolts clunking into their brushed brass strikes. He took the suitcase out of Jane's hand and carried it into his bedroom.

The window screens bellowed and howled. Jonah opened his eyes and looked at the glowing numbers on his clock. It was just after four in the morning. Miraculously, inexplicably, Jane Lipshitz (he only just learned her last name, and what a last name it was!) lay asleep beside him, the covers pulled up to her chin. They had gone to sleep naked in the swelter of sex and the sticky Bermuda High that had still hung over Manhattan in a mountain of heavy air, but the climate changed dramatically while they slept. Now an April chill gelled the room and hailstones pinged off the window ledges, peppering the street and sending up an incredible racket. He got up and closed the windows, then put on a pair of sweatpants and a flannel shirt. He stood in the kitchen holding himself and listening to the hail come down like a tremendous bag of marbles spilling onto a tile floor. He tried to remember what he'd been dreaming. Something about Rose. About being at Ground Zero and searching for her ashes, trying to sift the ashes that were Rose from the ashes that were everyone else. It was like trying to separate grains of sand on a beach. He looked around the apartment for her, in the shadowy corners where she liked to hide, but she wasn't there. She hadn't visited him since that day in Times Square when he'd failed to attack the happy family in the

Dodge Durango Living Window Display. Maybe she'd gotten tired of him. Maybe she'd just gotten tired.

He poured himself a glass of whiskey to help him sleep and stood looking at the table where the remains of his dinner with Jane had solidified into crust on the unwashed dishes, the same dishes his parents had been bringing to New York on the day of the accident. Normally, he would have been compelled to wash them right away, running them under hot soapy water before he even finished chewing the food in his mouth, but tonight the untidiness did not compel him. Over dinner he and Jane had been talking about ashes, his mother's and Rose's, and about the distressing sensation of being covered in particulate human remains last September. Jane recalled reading something in the news about a devout Jewish woman who was unwilling to clean the dust from her windows because it could contain human remains. She asked her rabbi what to do and he told her to pick up the dust with wet paper towels and deliver it to a Jewish funeral home for proper burial, like they do in Israel with the smallest body fragments of suicide-bomb victims. "Then there's human shrapnel to think about," Jane said. "Can you imagine living with bits of terrorist bone under your skin? I guess it eventually works its way out, like splinters." Jonah told Jane about his carbon-atom fantasy, imagining the particles of strangers drifting over Manhattan and Brooklyn, over Jersey and the ocean, imagining parts of Rose herself mingling with the oxygen he breathed last fall, becoming part of his own bones. But Jane said it was farfetched. How could human remains be in that dust? So they got online and did some research. Now he looked at the piece of paper where they'd written down the calculations of everything that had been pulverized and burned:

- Total weight of towers (inc. concrete, steel, glass, furnishings, etc.) plus two Boeing 767s: 2 million tons (approx.)
- Total weight of all people lost in towers @ 150 pounds average: 210 tons
- Subtract 75% of human weight for water (evaporation) = 53 tons of non-aqueous human components
- 2 million tons of inanimate matter – 53 tons of human matter = a lot more inanimate matter

Researchers, they discovered, found no carbon in the ash at Ground Zero. Samples contained mostly aluminum, calcium, and silicon (from concrete, glass, and dirt); sulfur and nickel (from the burning of fuel oil); along with trace amounts of mercury and lead. Some of the calcium and sulfur could have been human, Jonah reasoned, but the human body didn't have much of those elements. A report from another group of scientists with expertise in volatile organic compounds said they tested the dust, but there was no mention of carbon.

"In each human body lost in the World Trade Center," said Jonah, as they finished their meal, "there would have been about thirty pounds of carbon. That means that approximately forty tons of carbon from humans burned, but none of it ended up in the ash. So where did forty tons of carbon go? That's like losing six elephants, or a brontosaurus, or a sperm whale. In that giant dust cloud of 43,000 vaporized windows and 40,000 gallons of jet fuel, what happened to the human element?"

Jane said, "Maybe it went up in the smoke and never settled. At least not at Ground Zero where the researchers were taking samples. Probably most of it settled on the water, in the harbor, and drifted out to sea."

"Even then," said Jonah, "when you think about it, it comes to almost nothing. There are billions of carbon atoms in the human body but 99.9% of each atom is empty space."

"The *Zwischenraum.*"

"My father was right. We are only the foam on the ocean."

It was so easy, he thought now, standing in his cold kitchen, to lose a single human being. Of that forty tons of lost carbon, twenty-two pounds would have come from Rose Oliveri's slender body. But what remained? In the tiny packet of ash that the City of New York had given to Vivian, there surely was no trace of Rose, not a single particle. Only pulverized glass and concrete, pieces of the shaken Earth. Vivian knew this. She had given the urn to Jonah like it was nothing because it *was* nothing. But his mother's ashes were something. That box was not filled with the dust of office furniture and Jumbo Jets. That ash was undeniably her.

He swallowed the rest of the whiskey and took Rose's urn in one hand, weighing it against the box of his mother's cremains. His mother wanted her ashes to be scattered in the ocean, but the idea disturbed him, to think of her lost at sea. Here, he always knew where she was. Holding her in his palm, with Rose's urn in the other, he seesawed his hands like a pair of scales seeking balance.

"What's going on?" Jane squinted at him from the bedroom doorway, messy headed and wrapped in his wool bathrobe. "What are you, juggling?"

She took his arm and rested her head against him, yawning. He was not sorry that he'd woken her and felt glad for the company. The dogs opened their eyes and looked up from the couch where they slept, but did not otherwise stir, as if late-night cremains juggling were an everyday event.

"I think it's time to let these go," Jonah said.

They pushed the dogs aside and sat down on the couch. A Google search informed them that there were many methods for disposing of a loved one's ashes. Wide awake now, buzzing with anticipation for a "closure ritual," Jane narrated from her keyboard.

"Eternal Reefs will mix the ashes with concrete and mold them into a synthetic Memorial Reef, which they will then drop into the ocean to provide safe harbor for countless marine life, both flora and fauna, for the next five hundred years. That sounds good."

"Too weird. Fish are going to live inside my mother?"

"Okay. How about this one? Eternally Yours will mix the remains with oil paint and provide you with a truly personalized gold-framed landscape of trees, mountains, and clouds that you can hang on your wall and contemplate for generations."

"Sounds a little tacky."

"You don't want that one anyway," she said, clicking backward through the web pages. "You've contemplated these ashes long enough. Okay, here's another. The Mementos Company will swirl the remains into molten glass to make reliquary touchstones, bud vases, or paperweights."

"Is there anything more like scattering? She told me once she might like to have her ashes scattered on the ocean."

"This is very impressive, look at this. The Celestis Group will seal the ashes into a capsule and shoot them out into space, where they will orbit the Earth ad infinitum. They've already done Gene Roddenberry and Timothy Leary."

"My dad would probably go for that one, but not my mom."

"Celebrate Life!, Inc. will secure the remains in specially modified fireworks shells, then light up the night with your loved one to the rousing tunes of John Philip Sousa.

And look. The package comes complete with an engraved commemorative plaque that includes your loved one's name and a color photograph of the fireworks display. Come on, that's a good one. It's perfect."

"Too violent."

"You're hard to please. I think you're just avoiding this whole thing because you don't want to let your mother go."

"I'm not avoiding it. Find another one."

Jane continued the search, clicking from page to page, dismissing ideas before even running them by Jonah.

"This is the one," she finally announced. "It's another memento kind of thing, but Jeez Louise, it's incredible. The LifeGem company will extract all of the carbon from your loved one, either during the cremation process or from existing ashes, and compress it into real, synthetic diamonds that you can wear in any number of elegant settings, as rings, bracelets, pendants, you name it. 'Like the memory of a loved one,' it says here, 'a diamond lasts forever.' Oh, do it. You're into the whole carbon thing."

"No," he said, putting his arm around her and kissing her cheek. They searched a while longer, Jonah taking the helm, surfing through the vast oceans of the Internet, until Jane fell asleep on the couch beside him. He closed the laptop and set it aside. At the window, the hail turned to rain that sizzled as it struck the sill. He took the box of ashes off the coffee table and held them on his lap. Here was the dust of his mother's bones, a droning hive of atoms aswarm inside their box. He imagined her mitochondria twirling in colorful ribbons, entwined in clustered helixes. The jittery building blocks of Jonah's own tissues seemed to pulse inside the box. It was a vital, organic thing, this ash his mother had become. To scatter it in the ocean would be like opening the lid on a jar of fireflies: liberation and loss. All that's left is an empty jar, with all the lights gone out.

He carefully unfolded the cardboard flaps to find a plastic bag sealed with a twist-tie. He untwisted it like a loaf of bread, letting it spin itself open, and pulled the cinched plastic apart. The cremated remains were light gray, the color of smoke. He expected them to smell of White Shoulders, his mother's favorite scent, but they had no odor. He dipped a finger inside and swirled the ash, which was not soft, but coarse like sand on a rocky beach. He pushed his finger in deeper and the ash parted roughly, packed in tight and resisting him as he pressed. He felt a chill, his hand shaking, as he sensed a presence inside the ash. He thought of those scenes in sci-fi movies, where the desert sand covers up a monstrous mouth, a bottomless, sucking mucosal tube. One false move, and you'll be swallowed up forever. But this was his mother's body. This bag of dust was the place he came from. Nothing would hurt him here.

He pressed another finger inside, then another, then his thumb. He opened his hand and wiggled his fingers, loosening the ash enough to allow his entire hand to enter, with a sibilant hush, until it was buried up to the wrist. His hand felt good, the way a hand feels when it burrows under the sand on a hot day at the beach. He let it be, for a while, inside his mother's body, mingling with her fingers and toes, her ribs and spine, her heart and lungs. Had he ever been so close to her? Not since his original departure, when he wavered in the briny sublittoral zone of fluid and amnion, unsure of his leaving. The doctor had to pull him out, his mother liked to tell him, because he didn't want to budge. Was everything that had come after nothing more than a continuation of his earliest apprehension? Moving forward was not a talent Jonah possessed. He would have preferred to stop time, to watch the dust settle on a spellbound, motionless world where nothing was ever forced to change, where everything remained the same, like the frozen universe after the great heat death. But now—it was different.

Next to him, Jane's nose whistled and her breasts rose and fell with the rhythm of breathing. Her body gave off a moist mammalian warmth, the sulfur smells of sleepy farts, and the lingering musk of humid sex. What he wanted was this.

He mashed his hand deeper into the ash, shifting his palm back and forth to force his way to the bottom, until he felt the plastic of the bag against his skin and he could go no further. He curled his hand into a fist, squeezing the dust between his fingers. It made a pleasant, ruffling sound that, again, reminded him of the beach, the feeling of holding a handful of sand, then letting it go, watching it run out from his fist with a long sigh, as if from an hourglass. Picking it up and letting it go.

Part Three

"I think of it as one, not two," she said. "Even though there are clearly two towers. It's a single entity, isn't it?"
"Very terrible thing but you have to look at it, I think."
"Yes, you have to look."
—Don DeLillo, from *Underworld*, 1997

17

Flowers bloomed in Vivian's front yard. Bruised by the heat wave and battered by the previous night's storm, hyacinth and narcissi survived in muddy squares, in the swan-shaped planter and the concrete donkey's wagon that several weeks ago, when Jonah had first stood on this doorstep, held only twigs and dead leaves. He was nervous about seeing Vivian. Though the morning weather was mild, late-April sweet, his back dripped with sweat.

"Thanks for coming with me," he said to Jane. "I don't think I could do this alone."

"You'll feel better once it's done."

He handed her the bouquet of roses he'd brought, and shrugged off his heavy backpack, letting the breeze cool his damp shirt.

"Stop procrastinating," Jane said, "and ring the bell."

The door of the house was open and music filtered through the screen. Easter Sunday felt like a long time ago and it seemed he was a stranger to this house all over again.

"Do you think the roses are too much? I could run back and get something simpler. Tulips maybe."

Ignoring him, Jane reached out and pressed the orange lozenge of the doorbell before he could stop her. He heard a familiar shift as Vivian came to answer.

"I knew you wouldn't miss this day. Get in here," she said, opening the aluminum door. She regarded Jane coldly over his shoulder as she hugged him. "Who's this?"

"This is Jane," he said, moving out of Vivian's embrace. "My friend."

"It's a pleasure to meet you," Jane said boldly. "These are for you."

Vivian took the roses and pressed them to her face to breathe them in. "Thank you. Jane. All right, well, hurry before the flies get in."

Jonah watched while Vivian put the roses in water and prepared a pot of coffee, taking out milk and sugar, setting spoons onto the flannel-backed vinyl tablecloth with efficient clicks. He could tell she was angry. It was a familiar feeling from his own mother: the cold, brisk movements, a sideways set to the jaw.

"I invited my sister and her husband," Vivian said while she took bakery cookies out of their white box and arranged them on a serving plate. "But forget it. Should they come all the way from Bay Ridge? They can't be bothered. Not for nothing, but it *is* their niece's birthday. My sister thinks it's ridiculous to have a cake. 'Time to move on,' she says. 'Stop dwelling in the past,' she says. 'You got to get back to your life or else you'll moan and groan forever.' She thinks who she is, my sister. What does she know? She's *got* her kids. They're all she ever talks about. 'Oh, did you hear Ricky got a promotion?' Big deal. He works at Circuit City. And the other one sells pool supplies. It ain't brain surgery. So, anyways. You're friends, you two?"

"Roommates," Jonah said. "And friends."

"Roommates and friends," Vivian repeated, turning away to focus on the coffee as it dripped into its pot. "You don't return my calls for weeks."

"I know. I'm sorry."

"Now I see why. You've been busy with other things."

"I had work and—"

Vivian stopped him with a raised hand. Turning to her guests, she said, "You seem like a nice girl, miss, but he could've picked up the phone, asked for an invitation. I wasn't expecting another mouth." She pulled a cigarette out of its pack on the counter and lit it.

"I'm sorry," Jonah said again, lamely. He wasn't used to seeing Vivian so angry.

"I knew you'd move on eventually. I just didn't think it'd be so soon," she said. "She's coming with us to Ground Zero, too?"

"If that's okay," said Jane.

"We don't have to," Jonah said. "We can leave if it's too much."

"What difference does it make? You're here now. I already started the coffee, so," Vivian interrupted, waving her cigarette in the air dismissively. "I had a dream about her last night. I thought the dreams were over, but they came back."

"What did you dream?" Jane asked, pushing up her glasses, shrink-like.

"What was your name again?"

"Jane."

"Jane, my daughter passed on 9/11."

"I know. Jonah told me."

"He did?"

"Jane's a therapist," Jonah offered, as if her profession justified the disclosure of any intimate detail, as long as it went into the locked vault of a therapist's ear.

"You're sending me to a shrink now?"

"I'm in training," said Jane.

"A trainee," said Vivian. "Not even a real shrink. Well. I probably need one. Do you know what dreams mean? There was a boat and I think that means travel, like a vacation."

"Dreams mean different things to different people," Jane explained. "There's no one way to interpret them. For you, a boat might mean travel while to another dreamer it could mean something else entirely. It's all in the associations. It's not like there's a big book where you can just look up 'boat' and get an answer."

"I had a book like that once," Vivian said, sitting down at the table. "I wish I had it now because this dream was a real winner. It didn't make no sense. I was on a boat. I think it was a cruise ship because I was eating chocolate, a lot of chocolate, like at the Chocoholic Buffet? And Rose was there. We were out on the deck, except the deck looked just like my living room. Isn't that stupid? What's my living room doing on the deck of a ship? All of a sudden, the sky goes black and a big wave starts coming right at us. Big as a building. Just as it's about to crash onto the boat—which isn't even a boat anymore, now it's my house—the wave freezes, like one of those glaciers up in Alaska, and I can see inside it, right through the ice. I can see all kinds of fish and whales and sharks. All dead. You know what it reminded me of? That part in *The Wizard of Oz* where Judy Garland's house is swept up in the twister and all those people go by—the guys in the rowboat, the old lady in the rocking chair, and that witch on her broom. It was like that. Only fish. And dead. Then I see Rose in there. She's caught up in the wave of ice. Frozen right inside. And she's alive. Before I even have time to *think* about what to do, the boat pulls away—it's a boat again now—and I'm eating chocolate just like before. Rose is frozen in some giant wave and I'm stuffing my face at the Chocoholic Buffet. Now tell me what *that* means."

Vivian stopped and relit the cigarette that had gone out in her hand.

"Can I bum one of those? I've been trying to quit," said Jane, "but it's no use."

"I tried quitting a hundred times. I tried the patch, the gum. I even got hypnotized," Vivian said, handing Jane one of her long, slender cigarettes. "What do you think of this weird dream? Am I crazy?"

"If I had to guess, and I don't know you at all, but if I had to guess. First, let me say that it's a wonderful dream. Very evocative. Your unconscious is really working. And if I had to guess I would say that the dream is about moving on in life. There's the pain of leaving your daughter behind, yes, but you're going to continue. And you're going to enjoy life and, you know, keep eating chocolate, savoring the pleasures—the *sweetness*—of life. You might *feel* stuck, but you're not. You're not frozen in ice."

Vivian took a drag from her cigarette and squinted at Jane through the smoke, contemplating the interpretation. She wasn't going to like it, Jonah thought. He never should have brought Jane, uninvited, on her dead daughter's birthday. This was a bad idea. He never should have come back here.

"I'm not frozen," Vivian quietly considered. She had her plump elbows on the table and the cigarette raised in one hand. Absentmindedly, she began scratching an itch on her bare arm, under the brand of a smallpox vaccination scar, her fingernails leaving pale trails in dry skin, her gold bracelets chiming on her wrist. Jonah followed her gaze down to the tablecloth, to the blistered brown wound of a cigarette burn in the floral-patterned vinyl.

"You're not frozen," Jane repeated gently. "If you were frozen, you wouldn't have planted all those flowers in the yard. People who are stuck don't look to the future. They don't have hope. And what could be more hopeful than a garden?"

Vivian put her fist to her mouth, tears coming to her eyes. Jane placed her hand on Vivian's arm and Vivian let her, nodding. It would be all right, Jonah thought. He would be forgiven—for being a bad son, for killing and destroying, for telling the lies he would soon confess. Feeling the tang of salt rising to his own eyes, he excused himself and went to the bathroom in the front hall, where he filled the cups of his hands with cold water and rinsed his face. He let the water run, making its pleasing, distracting sound in the pink marbleized sink. The bathroom had a beach theme, with seashells everywhere—embroidered on the towels, pressed into mini soaps, shading the ceiling light. A cork-stoppered jar held a collection of starfish and sand dollars. Above the toilet, perfume bottles in the shapes of ladies' shoes walked across a glass shelf. The sight of those glass shoes, more than anything, made Jonah sorry. Vivian was an innocent, he thought, a woman who collected glass shoes. He wanted to tell her the truth, but it might break her. He imagined a heart attack, a stroke, blood vessels shattering like delicate spun-glass filaments in the brain.

The moth in his throat began to flutter with anxiety. Today he'd left home without checking the stove for the first time in months. Jane wouldn't let him. She said everything would be all right. But as he thought of confessing to Vivian, he imagined his apartment exploding. He could see his street splashed red with fire truck light, the sky turned black with smoke. It was all his fault. Everything. All of it. But Jane had explained it— how it was just magical thinking, repressed rage, a deep wish to be a boy again. There was nothing, she said, to be afraid of. Slightly shaking, he dried his face and opened the bathroom door. He was going to tell the truth.

"What are you doing here?"

It was Frank.

Jonah slipped against the wall and Frank caught him, grabbing his shoulder with his porterhouse hand, the bluebird of happiness a fluttering smudge on his arm.

"You betrayed me," Frank hissed in his ear. "You were supposed to stick around. That was our deal."

"I have to tell her."

"No, you don't. You don't have to tell her nothing. She thinks her fucked-up little girl was an angel, a real sweetheart. You want to take that away from her?"

"It's the right thing to do."

"You want to kill her? That's the right thing?"

"I can't be around her and not tell her."

"Then quit coming around. But don't tell her this thing just so you can ease your guilty conscience. You made this shit sandwich and now you gotta eat it."

"I brought back the urn," Jonah said, grabbing his backpack from the floor and pulling out the reliquary. Frank snatched it from him.

"You stole this."

"She gave it to me."

"Bullshit she did. She'd never part with this."

Jonah slipped away and headed back to the kitchen, leaving Frank staring at the urn in his hands. Vivian poured the coffee into her good cups. She, Jonah, and Jane sat quietly together. They added the milk and sugar, their spoons ringing musically as they stirred. Jonah listened for the sound of Frank in the hall. He could feel him there, breathing, listening, waiting.

Vivian looked at Jonah and asked, "Are you over her?"

"Over her," he echoed, rattled by his encounter with Frank, unsure of what to say, trying to find a way to the truth.

"They were going to get married," Vivian said to Jane. "Did he tell you that?"

"He did."

"Six, seven months isn't that long," said Vivian. "Not with someone you were going to marry. What happens now? What happens to us?"

"Tell her," said Jane.

"Vivian," Jonah began when Frank stepped into the kitchen.

"You gave this to him," Frank said, raising the urn like a weapon.

"Don't ruin this now, Frank. We're here to celebrate Rosie's birthday and have some cake." Vivian braced herself on the table and got to her feet. She pulled a cardboard box from the refrigerator, plunked it on the countertop, and snipped the red-and-white-striped string that tied it.

"Tell her," Jane said again.

"Tell me, don't tell me," said Vivian, opening a packet of pink candles. "Some things are better left unsaid. I don't gotta know everything."

Frank walked over to his wife and put a hand on the edge of the counter. In his other hand, he held the wooden urn. He stared at her, willing her to look at him. She didn't.

"She loved frosting roses," said Vivian. "Remember when she was little how she made me save all the roses from her birthday cakes? She wouldn't let any of the other kids have them."

"She was selfish, that's why."

"Don't, Frank."

"You could never face it," he said. "You still got your head in the goddamn sand."

"Don't ruin this."

"Years of heartache with that girl and your head in the sand! The boys, the drugs, the mean and nasty way she talked to you.

For years. She *stole* from you and you looked the other way. She stole from your sister, from your mother. And you never faced it. You thought you were protecting her? You protected yourself! And then you just give her away? To some stranger?"

"Shut up, willya, I'm losing count," Vivian said, placing the candles. "Was she thirty already?"

"I'm the one that cleaned up the messes," Frank continued.

"Or thirty-one? That's awful. Why can't I remember?"

"I'm the one that bailed her out, that picked her up at Jimmy's, when she was too fucked up to walk home. I'm the one that got the scumbags off her ass, three in the morning and I'm banging on doors. But you don't remember that, do you? 'Cause you never had to look at none of it. Then you just give her away? She was my daughter, too."

Frank's voice boomed across the kitchen. Vivian stood still, looking down at the cake.

"You never faced the truth, but you're gonna face it now," Frank said. "You listen and you listen good. It's all lies. He didn't even know her. He didn't work with her, didn't date her, and he sure as hell wasn't going to marry her. He's just some fucking loser that lived on her block. It's all a big story. He's a goddamn liar. Just like her. You hear me? He made it up!"

Vivian stood still at the counter, her back to the room. Jonah waited for the pop of breaking glass, for Vivian to fall to the floor in a sprawl. But she didn't. She made the soft sound of air escaping from a deflating balloon, then finished counting the candles and placing them in a circle around the white cake. She licked the frosting from her fingers and wiped her hands on a dishtowel.

"I know," she said, facing her husband.

"Like fun," said Frank. "You don't know shit. He fooled you. He made a fool out of you."

"You really think I'm that stupid? Please."

"He's been telling you nothing but stories."

"And they were beautiful stories," she said, turning to Jonah. "I loved hearing them."

She looked at Jonah the way a mother looks at a boy who has just destroyed her new carpets in his tender efforts to bring her the most beautiful mud pie in the world. He felt unraveled and held all at once, a confused feeling that made his face burn and his stomach ring tight like a wet rag. He had been exposed, but not condemned. If she had known all along, he wondered, were his lies still lies?

"You knew he was bullshitting you, and you gave her away to him," Frank said, waving the urn in Vivian's face. "What right did you have? She wasn't yours to give. She was ours."

"There's nothing in there," Vivian stated, turning to light the candles with a match.

"How can you call her nothing?"

"Our daughter's not in there. There's nothing in there but dirt. It's a cheap souvenir. Come on, now. Everybody sing." She lifted the frothy cake into the air, candles ablaze.

With one swipe of his paw, Frank knocked it halfway across the kitchen, white frosting spattering the cabinets and walls, wilted pink sugar roses weeping down the refrigerator door. With his other hand, he raised the urn and brought it down hard onto the tile floor. The wood split like the seam of a nesting doll cracked open and the glassine packet of ash jumped out. Frank snatched it and held it up for Vivian to see.

"This is all I have left," he said, his voice fracturing under the weight of these words.

Vivian closed her hand around Frank's and the scant spoonful of ash in his fist.

"We have a lot more than this, Francis. A lot more."

18

The wrought-iron gate around St. Paul's Chapel looked like a cyclone fence after a cyclone, cluttered with the flotsam of tattered newspapers and fast-food wrappers all caught in the chaos of rain-ruined flags and fire department t-shirts, drooping memorial banners and posterboard signs spelling out the slogans: God Bless, Trust in Jesus, United We Stand, You'll Never Be Forgotten, Our Tears Are Endless, We Ache in Albuquerque, and Osama! The U.S. Wants You and Your Mama!

A stream of slow-moving tourists shuffled past, posing for pictures, making the V sign with their fingers for peace or for victory or for saying nothing more than "I was here." Jonah watched while Vivian added a bouquet of roses and a tattered teddy bear to the pile, wishing Rose a happy birthday. She had wanted to leave a slice of cake, but it had proven unsalvageable and was heaped in the trash at home, where she'd left Frank to clean up the mess. By now, Jonah thought, he'd be on the roof with his pigeons, with his own way of grief.

Vivian had trouble finding a spot for the teddy bear and Jane helped her, wedging its plushy bulk between two fence posts, upsetting a t-shirt signed by the men of the Turkeytown Volunteer Fire Department. Tourists bumped against Jonah, trying to view the next thing. They were like a single organism, pressing all around him, their breath smelling of coffee and chewing gum. He could feel their hunger for it, all their urgent need for this scene of death.

As they inched through the line to mount the Ground Zero viewing platform, the tourists followed, dressed in t-shirts and windbreakers announcing local allegiances to Springfield Softball and Annunciation Basketball, the Ascension Eagles and the Penn State Lions. One woman claimed to belong to "Team Ralph Lauren." Jane whispered, "Look at the terror tourists," pointing out the ones completely outfitted in patriotic Ground Zero gear—FDNY baseball caps and Twin-Towered "Remember Forever" t-shirts, God-Bless-America leather jackets with flag-waving Mickey Mouses pinned to the lapels, 9/11 "Never Forget" shoelaces looped through their sneakers. "Terror tourists" was a good term for them, Jonah thought, quickly sketching a couple into his book.

A security guard took their time-stamped tickets and they stepped onto the unpainted plywood ramp that led to the viewing platform. Below, St. Paul's cemetery lay green and cleaned of the dust that had once made it gray. It was quiet except for a rhythmic ticking of metal, like the soft flutter of pie plates that Jonah remembered his mother used to hang in the garden to frighten the birds. He looked up. All across the cemetery, in the branches of every leafless sycamore, a strange foliage bloomed. Clumps of fabric, matted tablecloths and window drapes, hung dark and limp, but the sounds came from the twisted remains of Venetian blinds. Painted a dull corporate eggshell, they ticked and clucked in the breeze, moving softly on tangled strings like weird wind chimes. On 9/11 they had rained down into the trees, down from sky-high offices, from conference rooms and kitchenettes, their cords once pulled by hands now turned to dust. With slats twisted and bent together into spiral shapes, they looked like Spanish moss, as if they had simply taken root and grown there, a new species of flowering plant.

"When are they going to clear all this junk away?" Jonah wondered out loud, raising the eyebrows of nearby tourists, people who had come grieving from somewhere in the vastness of the middle country, who came to Ground Zero like pilgrims to scrawl their messages on the platform's plywood walls with ballpoint pens and felt-tip markers, telling New York about their own suffering.

"Look at this one," Jonah said to Jane as Vivian moved ahead and out of earshot. "'In Smile City, Nebraska we're crying too NYC.' Really? It's twisted. Don't forget about *us*, say the tourists. We're suffering, too. We watched it on our televisions and it made us afraid to go out of our houses, afraid to get into our cars and take a quick run down to Linens-N-Things to buy new hand towels for the bathroom, even though, Lord knows, we desperately needed new hand towels. We were afraid someone might blow up our local post office, so we stopped buying stamps. We were afraid someone might drop an airplane on our favorite Pizza Hut, so we started ordering delivery. We stayed away from the mall for an entire week. It wasn't easy. This tragedy is our tragedy, too, New York. We ache in Albuquerque. We weep in Wichita. We hunger for revenge in Rapid City."

"Everyone wants a piece of this grief," said Jane. "You should understand that."

"They're stealing it."

"Like you stole Rose."

"But I was here," he said. "I breathed it in. I felt the ground shake. I lived in the smoke."

Jonah still wasn't sure if he could include himself in the roster of the legitimately bereaved. Did his mother count?

Plucked unbelted from her passenger seat on the Jersey Turnpike as the skyline flowered into flame, ejected through the windshield while a planeload of people burst, her ruined cheek meeting the cool steel of car hood, crumpling while bodies sailed down from the withering heights across the river—did any of her pain count in the final tally of death from that day? The name Teresa Marie Soloway did not appear on the laminated list thumb-tacked to the plywood platform above Ground Zero, nor would it be carved in black granite on any Maya Lin-style memorial, where Jonah could never go with paper and crayon to create a souvenir rubbing. On future 9/11s, her name would not be read over the airwaves with all the rest. She was not included in the *New York Times'* "Portraits of Grief." The people of Smile City, Nebraska, would not cry for her. The citizens of Albuquerque would not ache.

Where the gray hole in the ground opened below, Jonah leaned on the plywood barrier for a better look, squeezed by tourists with cameras in hand. He imagined the hole filled with wandering ghosts. Was Rose down there? Was his mother? Had she found her way to this celebrated grave? He remembered the day, soon after 9/11, when he'd come to this place in air still thick with granular smoke, gritty enough to make him cough for a week. It was just after his mother's funeral and he'd come straight down from the bus terminal with her box of ashes in his backpack, just as he carried them now, literally holding the weight of her on his shoulders. He had imagined scattering her then, in that place, to mix her ashes with the ashes of the other victims from that day, but he could not get close enough. She belonged there, but was not allowed. He had ducked down side streets and climbed overpasses, had gotten near enough to glimpse orange fires still burning in lesser buildings, to stare at the remaining tower skin standing like a medieval choir screen, but the police barricades kept him back and he carried his mother's dust home to his bookshelf.

Now the hole just looked like a hole. "The pit," they called it, though it was first known more elegantly as "the bathtub," the original basement of the two towers, where the slurry walls held back the Hudson River from flowing in, an engineering feat. Jonah leaned on the wooden railing and looked down into the World Trade Center's beginnings, to the portholes of severed water lines and rusty sleeves of tieback anchors, to the ancient openings of the long-abandoned Hudson tunnels, down past the Manhattan schist and quartzite rock, into the silt of glacial outwash and soft organic river mud, where the jetsam of bygone generations once lay in a Colonial garbage dump.

"The men who dug the bathtub in the late 1960s," Jonah explained aloud in his PBS narrator voice, "hauled up an American historian's treasure trove of clay pipes and hand-blown bottles, the hulls of sailing ships and shoes, and the animal bones of countless New Amsterdam suppers. Some of those same men, years later, spent the past winter searching for more recent artifacts: airplane turbines and chunks of landing gear, wristwatches and wedding rings, house keys and driver's licenses, human bones and teeth."

"Jonah," Jane warned him, but he was on a roll. As long as he kept talking, he didn't have to feel the thing that bubbled up inside of him as the cameras clicked around his head like biting insects.

"They took everything out to Staten Island, to the Fresh Kills landfill," he continued. "Along with the Great Wall of China, the Fresh Kills landfill is one of two man-made structures visible from outer space. *Kills* means *stream*. From the Dutch. It's an unfortunate choice of words, considering.

They hauled it all out on garbage scows, straight across the harbor. Piles of steel. Sculptures from Cantor Fitzgerald's "Museum in the Sky." Figures from Auguste Rodin's "The Three Shades," inspired by Dante, the guardians of the Gates of Hell. Abandon all hope, you who enter here. Imagine the piles of eyeglasses and shoes. Who could see them and not think of those photographs from Auschwitz? And there were body parts, of course. Twenty thousand body parts, the newspapers said, some no larger than an aspirin."

Jane squeezed his hand hard to stop him.

"Let's move along now," said the security guard, taking Jonah by the elbow. "Other folks are waiting their turn to see the site."

"Did that guard say *site* or *sight*," Jonah asked Jane, "as in *see the sights?*"

"Does it matter?" Jane said, steering him down the ramp on the other side of the platform.

"Wait." Jonah stopped and grabbed a blue Sharpie from the wall, left behind by a note-writing tourist. He looked at the security guard and quickly added his mother's name to the laminated poster, alongside the S column, between Solomon and Song, in blue indelible ink. The guard didn't stop him. He knew his mother would be erased from the records of that day, but for now, her death counted.

The atmosphere on the streets bordering Ground Zero was a flea market, like Orchard Street on a Sunday afternoon, filled with milling shoppers and vendors hawking cheap wares. "Check it out, check it out," the salesmen called as Jonah, Jane, and Vivian wandered by the tables that lined the curb. "Souvenir! Souvenir!" they shouted when the threesome stopped to examine the Ground Zero baseball hats, t-shirts, and vanity license plates. Jane picked up one of a dozen identical "Collector's Edition" snow globes and gave it a shake. Inside the sphere, a miniature diorama of disaster showed the Twin Towers standing tall, their gray tops painted an urgent red, while tiny toy fire engines gathered at their feet. Jane shook the globe again, making the white plastic shavings swirl. It looked like ash.

"Eight dollars, eight dollars," said the vendor, barking over the racket of a CD-ROM playing on a laptop where Ray Charles sang "America the Beautiful" over images of death and a woman's voice screaming, "I can see people jumping!"

Jane put the globe back on the table, shaking her head. She said, "Vivian, are you sure you want to be here?"

"I want to see it all."

At every table, shoppers grabbed souvenir photo collections, slick "book-azines" entitled *Tragedy*, *Attack on New York*, and *Terror in America*. Jonah picked one up and paged through its full-color photos of people running through the streets covered in ash, tumbling out of buildings, lying dead on stretchers. As he stood gaping at the pictures, the tourists elbowed him out of the way, handing over their ten-dollar bills to gobble up the souvenirs. He surveyed the shoppers' faces. A few were smiling. Others seemed bored and weary. Many had that hungry expression of desperation, wide-eyed and almost frantic, the bloodlust inspired by the sudden accumulation of goods. What would they do with the postcard photos of falling men and women tumbling silhouetted and upside down, splayed against the tower's pinstriped skin, shirts fluttering and flying off, some holding hands, as they reached terminal velocity before breaking on the street? Maybe they would thumb-tack the postcards to cork walls above computer terminals, next to "Hang in There" cat posters and pictures from fishing trips. Maybe they would hide them in desk drawers, taking them out like pornographic images to be savored in secret gasps of seeing. A little boy held a lenticular poster of the World Trade Center and his father showed him how to turn it back and forth in his hands to make the towers burst into flames, then return to normal, then burst into flames again, again. Did they all crave these souvenirs of death as *memento mori*, to remind them of their own mortality? Remember you will die, said the postcards and the t-shirts and the snow globes.

Behind the vendor's table, gleaming in the sun, stood the Brooks Brothers store, formerly a makeshift morgue. Not so long ago, National Guardsmen hauled in body bags, filled not with bodies, but with parts—a spleen, a piece of lung, a hunk of buttock attached to a leg. Horrible human fragments reduced to meat. Since then, the shattered windows had been replaced and the ash-covered clothing removed. There were no dead bodies behind the Windexed window of Brooks Brothers, just a cleaning woman on her hands and knees with a dust rag and a can of Lemon Pledge, polishing the bare white feet of a mannequin dressed in madras and chinos, a sweater the color of cantaloupe flesh draped over its shoulders, ready for a weekend in the Hamptons. Jonah couldn't decide which was worse: the insistent mementos of death or this stark erasure.

"Let's go," he said, dropping *Terror in America* on the table. "I want to get this over with."

On the way to the Staten Island Ferry terminal, they crossed Battery Park. The cherry trees were all in blossom, riotous and pink, matching the bags of cotton candy that mustached men sold from umbrella-shaped contraptions carried on their shoulders. Africans, used to equatorial heat, wore knit winter caps as they held open briefcases filled with glittering counterfeit watches. Here it was business as usual, no signs of 9/11, until they came to Fritz Koenig's "Sphere," the bronze sculpture that had once stood in the World Trade Center's courtyard surrounded by a fountain of flowers. Battered and shredded, stained with paint from the heavy machines that had hauled it out of the wreckage, the Sphere hunkered on a bed of mulch surrounded by a plot of grass and a white plastic chain fence that did little to deter people from stepping over it to leave their offerings: bouquets of flowers still in their cellophane wrappers, teddy bears, garlands of origami peace cranes, American flags, prayer cards, photos of the dead.

The Parks Department had stuck signs on skewers in the grass that said, "Please Do Not Touch the Sphere" and "Por Favor No Toque El Sphere," but people made a special point to touch the Sphere, like Christians fingering the toes of sainted icons and Jews pressing their hands to the Wailing Wall. They came from all over the world and could not stop themselves from touching the Sphere, this thing that had survived, beaten and bruised, this thing that had been There, where it all happened. This witness that had risen from the ashes, now polished by the sun, could tell them secrets, could tell them how and why. Or so they hoped. Jonah debated sharing a fact he had read somewhere about how recovery workers, when they first unearthed the broken sphere and climbed inside, found three items: a King James Bible, an airplane seat, and an uncoiled human intestine. He decided to keep his mouth shut this time. He stood back and watched as a family of tourists, wearing green foam-rubber Lady Liberty crowns on their heads, stepped over the plastic fence to pose, their palms flat against the warm metal of the Sphere, while the dad scanned his camcorder over the scene.

Vivian and Jane smoked their cigarettes and looked out at the harbor. Jonah walked over to them. It was strange, with his back turned to the Sphere, to witness how the whole city went on with it, despite all the signs of death. The ferries kept going in and out, the pretzel men continued selling hot pretzels, half a dozen living Statues of Liberty kept standing still, frozen atop their milk crates waiting for tips. Things happened, terrible things and not so terrible things, and it all just went on.

He used to have this feeling on days when he stayed home sick from school. He remembered, in detail, the very first time that it hit him. He was lying in bed with the flu and looking out the window. It was a sunny winter day and the snow was melting. A sparrow landed on a branch of the lilac tree outside and began rubbing its beak on the bark. He saw other kids, kids he knew, walking home from school along the sidewalk. This was before he was bused to the junior high, so he was young, maybe ten. He watched the kids scooping up sloppy snowballs and tossing them, the way they all did together when he walked with them, only he wasn't with them. He hadn't been with them all day, and yet these other kids still showed up for school and did the things they always did. They sat at their desks and sharpened their pencils. The teachers showed up, too, and taught their lessons without him. They wrote on the chalkboards and handed out quizzes. The boys shoved each other in the halls on the way to lunch where the girls blew bubbles into waxy cartons of milk. They all went on without him—the kids, the teachers, the sparrows, the melting snow. That's when he had the most horrible thought: "When I die, everyone will go on without me." And it pissed him off. It didn't seem fair. Something, someone, should stop when a person dies.

It was the thought of a ten-year-old, but Jonah thought it again now, twenty years after first thinking it, and it still made him angry and sad. He thought that he would never not be angry and sad about these things and that was all right. Someone had to be serious in a world full of terror tourism and fifty-cent suicide souvenirs, patriotic shopping and engineered grief, a world full of pretenders like himself.

He wanted then to know something true. He turned to Vivian and asked, "What was she really like?"

Vivian sighed, exhaling smoke, and thought a moment before answering, "She was tough. Like Frank said. To tell you the truth, she was a troubled girl. From the beginning, I didn't know what to do with her. She was willful. Threw tantrums like you wouldn't believe. And then as a teenager, forget about it. We went through the horrors of hell. But girls are tough, everyone says so. She was boy crazy, and then she got into those stupid drugs. I knew she was stealing, I'm not an idiot, but what did he want me to do, reject my own child? It killed me when she left. I wanted her home where I could keep an eye on her. But she did all right in the city. She got it together so she worked, paid her rent. She never asked us for nothing. Oh, Frank gave her money. He thought I didn't know but I know *everything*."

Jonah wondered what Vivian knew and didn't know about Rose. It was possible, he thought, that Rose resembled his version—maybe she had changed for the better. Who really could have known? But this was the sort of thinking he was trying to move away from. He watched the army of living Statues of Liberty, unmoving, a tableau vivant of nothing from life, except maybe a souvenir shop's still life, the clutter of green ladies on a shelf. Only one living statue wasn't Liberty, a man dressed as a soldier and spray-painted copper from helmet to boots. He held his rifle in both hands and stood frozen in mid-step like a man making his way across a hostile landscape. Jonah recalled playing Swing the Statue as a kid, how easy it was for him to be quiet and still, to hold a difficult position even with insects buzzing his face and the grass itching his bare feet. There was a peacefulness to it and he could stay that way for a long time. *Stillness*, he thought now, *is not the same as inertia.* Muscles strain and the mind works in ways no one can see to keep things fixed, to hold it all cemented in place. That's the backbreaking hard work. Movement is easy. It's getting from rest to motion that's difficult. Another of his father's favorite sayings came to mind: A body at rest tends to stay at rest—unless acted upon by some external force. He watched Jane walk over to the living soldier statue and rummage in her purse.

He asked Vivian, "When did you know about me?"

"Oh," she said, the air going out from her. "From the beginning, I think. The first time you called me on the phone, I heard something, in your voice, but I wasn't sure. I didn't know I knew. Then when you said you were getting married, I knew. But I didn't want to know. You understand? It's stupid but sometimes it feels good to be fooled."

"I've never been much of a liar."

"I wouldn't say that."

Jane dropped a dollar in the living soldier statue's tip jar and he came alive, briefly, marching in place, taking a few steps before he froze again.

"Did anything I tell you about Rose ring true?"

"She wasn't a bad girl," Vivian said. "She was very smart. And she could paint. She was very independent, too. She didn't need nobody. I admired that about her. I loved her, without a doubt, but. Maybe I'm a terrible mother for saying this, and God forgive me, but I didn't *like* her all that much. I wanted to. I tried. It sounds crazy, but I liked your Rose better than mine."

"I'm sorry," was all Jonah could think to say. He wished Jane would put another dollar in the soldier's jar so he would come to life again, but she just stood there, staring at the motionless man as if daring him to falter from his pose.

"I was jealous of you, too," Vivian continued, "for having her. Isn't that stupid? I knew in my gut you were making it up, but I was jealous. You could think of her in ways I never could. She was real. And now she's gone again."

He tried to picture this Rose, the woman of his sentimental invention, recalling all the stories he'd told, but that wasn't Rose. He imagined the ghost who'd haunted his thoughts, another fictional Rose, and the girl in Soyer's "Office Girls," but that wasn't Rose either. He remembered the anonymous neighbor who walked her dog and dropped her glove, who seemed lonely and cool, impossible to access. That might have been Rose, in some way, the real Rose. But he could never be sure. There was no way to know. She was scattered into bits and everyone who'd ever encountered her had their own hard piece to hold.

"I'm really mad at you for that," said Vivian, matter-of-fact. "For making me have to lose her all over again."

He wanted to make it right, to conjure something that would take a bit of the sting out of Vivian's grief, the one story that could have been true, and he said, "One winter morning, I was walking to work behind her, on the sidewalk, and she dropped a glove. I picked it up and ran to catch her. When I handed it to her, she thanked me. It wasn't a big deal, really, but she was so gracious about it. Another person might have said nothing, or just muttered a quick 'Thanks' as they rushed off. You know how people are. But Rose gave me this really nice thank you, with a warm smile, and I could tell, right then, that she was good person. I think that's when I fell in love with her. That part was true."

Vivian nodded and put her arm around him. He felt forgiven, if not entirely believed. The living statue climbed down off his milk crate to take a break, bending his knees and stretching his coppery arms to the sky. He sat on a park bench and counted his tips. Jane gave him another dollar before she walked back over to Vivian and Jonah. He watched her approach, this real, live girl with sunlight glinting off the rhinestones on her eyeglasses, and he felt something that might have been not so bad.

19

Inside the Staten Island Ferry terminal, the long wooden benches were filled with people, sitting back to back, their legs stretched out before them. They had a tired, used-up look. The sun slanted in over the harbor, through the dusty windows, and lit their faces in cubist geometries of light and shadow. In the ceiling beams, a pigeon clapped its wings, sending a single gray feather floating to the floor where it landed in a puddle of light.

Jane and Vivian found a seat while Jonah wandered over to browse the newsstand, a shack laden with merchandise: candy bars and pain relievers, international calling cards and cough drops, plastic combs, disposable cameras, God-Bless-America cigarette lighters, and Lady Liberty foam-rubber crowns. *There should be something here to help make the occasion more festive*, he thought, considering the assortment of champagne party poppers, a yellowed box of sparklers leftover from last July Fourth, and Pop Pop Snappers, but none of it was quite right.

A patter of energy sailed through the terminal as one knowing commuter gathered her bags and rose from the bench. Another followed, sending a domino ripple through the crowd. People, one by one, shuffled over to the big sliding metal doors, responding to some telepathic signal that told them the next ferry would soon be arriving. Jonah joined Jane and Vivian in the crowd as they jockeyed for position. Men stood up close to the doors, peering through the little square windows. A girl nibbled from a bag of salted peanuts. A woman carried a Mylar balloon that said, "It's a Boy!" The air smelled of dirty harbor water and hot popcorn. At the clang of a bell, the doors slid open, and like racehorses out of the starting gate, the crowd surged down the ramp, streaming onto the ferry.

"How do you want to do this?" Jane asked Jonah as they headed for the front of the boat.

"I think I want to do it alone. On the way back in. I'll go downstairs, close to the water, and just do it."

"You sure you don't want company?" Vivian asked.

"No, thanks. You two stay up top and watch the scenery. I'll join you before we dock back in Manhattan."

He left them and found a place to be as alone as he could be. The Statue of Liberty sailed past, inspiring the tourists to lift their cameras to the sky in unison. She looked to Jonah like a female titan just emerged from the sea, her wet garments clinging, a green colossus of the deep. Farther out, where the water widened into New York Bay, they roared past tugs and tankers, bulkers carrying bananas and coffee, and deep-drafted container ships headed for Red Hook hauling corrugated steel boxes filled with coal, wheat, bagged flour, and (Jonah imagined) more nefarious cargo like human slaves and ballistic missiles.

"Attention please. We'll be docking shortly at Saint George," the speakers crackled. Soon the ferry bumped into Staten Island's wooden slip, splintering the boards with a series of painful cracks. Jonah hefted his backpack onto one shoulder and headed down the stairs, to the urine-stinking belly of the boat where he would not be found during the turnaround. There were other riders hiding here, too, people who spent the whole day going back and forth across the harbor, with nothing else to do. In the dank aquamarine corridor of that lower deck, he passed a young mother breastfeeding her baby in a graffitied corner. She was a heavy girl and her big gallon jug of a breast was the color of milk, so white it was almost blue, as if it were transparent and showing off its creamy unhomogenized contents. He tried not to look plainly at the breast, watching it from the corner of his eye, and in his effort to look and not look, he tripped on something in the aisle, the weight of his backpack pushing him face-first into a wooden bench scrawled with the names of Staten Island's most ardent lovers. He felt his lip split and tasted the warm metallic tang of blood.

"Watch your step," said a voice, scratched and brown as the wood of the bench he was lying on, resting under a dirty green Army blanket. It was the Cross Man, his wooden crucifix sticking out into the aisle. "Take these, son. You're bleeding."

He handed Jonah a wrinkled stack of clean paper napkins branded with the Starbucks logo.

"Thanks," Jonah said, wiping his mouth. He looked into the man's blue-white eyes. "For years now, I've seen you all over town. I've always wanted to ask. Why do you carry that cross?"

"It's the first thing in my life I ever wanted to do," said the Cross Man. "I don't know why I picked up the cross. It just happened. I'm happy when I carry my cross. Some mornings, I wake up on the street and I hurt, and I feel weak, and the thing I look for is my cross. When I pick it up, all the pain is gone away. I feel strong. Some days, I carry my cross from downtown all the way up to Harlem. Some days, like today, I carry it out to Staten Island and back again."

"And you never preach? Never tell anyone to repent, that the end is near?"

"I'm not trying to shame anybody, son. Some people think I'm making a statement. I'm not making a statement. Some think the cross is nothing. All right, the cross is nothing, but it's my nothing. That's what I want to do with my life. Nothing. It's the first thing I ever really wanted to do."

"I envy you."

"Don't be stupid. You got your own nothing to do."

With that, the Cross Man pulled the Army blanket up over his head and lay back down on the bench. The ferry bucked and jerked its way out of the slip, heading back to Manhattan. Jonah didn't have much time. He stood and waited for the Cross Man to say something more, something he could use, a golden piece of folk wisdom that people like the Cross Man gave out to people like Jonah all the time in the movies. But the Cross Man only snored, already deep in sleep.

Jonah stepped out onto the stern, down below where the cars parked and no one came except the teenagers of the suburban-style island, leaning on their bicycles, leaving home for the city. He liked being close to the cool spray, inhaling the organic, salty essence of the Atlantic. As they picked up speed, Staten Island receded before him. In the hazy distance, the Verrazano Bridge shimmered like a mirage on the horizon, vaporous and blue over the Narrows. If he was going to do it, he'd better do it now, while they were still close to the open ocean.

He dropped his backpack onto the floor and took out the cardboard box. The edge of the deck was guarded by a low rust-colored accordion gate. He looked around, then lifted the latch and rolled the gate open just enough so he could slip through. Holding onto the gate with one hand and gripping the box of ashes with the other, he lowered himself into a seated position on the tread-plate floor. He sat Indian-style, the box tucked into the donut hole between his legs, leaning back with his hands flat on the steel plate beneath him, the diamond-shaped treads digging into his palms, leaving their indentations. The boat bounced, sloshing water onto the deck, wetting his hands. The water was just beneath him, a sizzling, marbled mass so gelatinous it seemed he could scoop it up and it would not run through his fingers. He stared into the wake, a pus-colored slush of carbonated salt water and slime sizzling out in front of him, trailing across the dirty harbor. Maybe he should wait, he thought. Take a boat from Long Island, motor out to a distant spot where the water was clean and deep. But his mother did have good feelings for polluted New York Harbor. Her father's father's name was carved into the wall at Ellis Island. Her mother's mother's battered suitcase was preserved there behind a sheet of glass. She grew up hearing stories about the boat that carried her ancestors past the Statue of Liberty, that cinematic scene where the peasants, in their dark hats and shawls, look up with tired eyes, those huddled masses yearning to breathe free, reeking of olives and Romano cheese. She had traveled over this water once, a cellular thing secreted deep inside the bodies of her predecessors. Now these waters would carry her out again.

He opened the box and unwrapped the plastic bag. He closed his eyes and felt the thrumming of the boat beneath him, listened to the loud hush of the water, its deep and vibratory cadence rising and falling as the waves folded one on top of the other, pushing down and surging up. In each trough, between the peaks, there was silence. A nanosecond of silence. He could hear the eloquence of the spaces in between. The interstitial messages. The *Zwischenraum*. He opened his eyes to see them: empty troughs among the swells, bubbles of air that formed and, just as quickly, burst again. Above, a seagull glided, a physical presence pressed into the backdrop of nothing sky. This close, he could see the feathers rippling like waves themselves, white against the blue. The wings shifted, blue on blue, then white again. Something, nothing, something, nothing. He reached inside the bag and took a handful of ash. He held his clenched fist out over the churning water and let go. In an instant, the dust disappeared, sucked back and out over the glaucous green foam. He grabbed a second handful and watched as it vanished in the salty stir.

He felt his heart seize then, a catch in his throat. He thought to jump in after her. What would it be like to hug the box like a stone and drop into the sea? Would he feel like those people who stepped out of the burning towers? Would he swim or sink? Swirling into the aqueous silence, his arms forever locked about his lost first love, their bodies would become a reef down in the dark, calcified and permanent, a moveless monument beyond the reach of light and time. He could hear the siren singing, calling him down into the murk. There was no mast on this ship, no sturdy pillar to which he could lash himself. The mouth of the waters opened at his feet. It would be so easy. He put his fist to his mouth to stop himself from making a sound, and he could taste her, a grit like sand on his lips. He looked at his hand. Damp when it went into the bag, it was coated with ash. He held it out to see the grains and flakes of his mother's body and, in between, the pink flesh of his own, mapping a muddled geography of darkness and light. She would forever cling to him. No matter what. The past could never really be shucked.

He took a breath, lifted the box, and tossed the whole of it in. The waters closed around it, whipping the ash into lather, and then it was gone, sucked under the wake. The currents and tides would take her now, in a million directions at once.

Jonah stood and climbed back onto the deck, safe behind the chains. He took a last look before going up to the topmost bow of the ferry where Jane and Vivian were waiting. In the commotion of wind, they were quiet. Jane took his hand, Vivian put her arm in his, and they stood like that, not saying anything. Up ahead, its glass and steel glinting in sunlight, the city came back to Jonah. It looked the way it had that day when he blotted out the towers with his thumb, they way he'd wanted it to look. But he knew this had nothing to do with him. He felt an excitement in returning as the harbor bounced beneath the boat, taking him home, and a sadness to think of his mother's ashes out there, rushing away from him. Like the burning dust of the Big Bang, they scattered in particles across the dark waters. Some were falling now to the black, flocculent harbor bottom, but many more were sailing along on the flood tide. Jonah consoled himself by imagining the many paths on which his mother was embarking.

In his PBS narrator voice, he thought: Up the tidal strait of the East River, the ashes pass through the gills of spawning striped bass and shad, through the shells of blue-claw crabs. Some stay swirling in the turbulent waters of Hell Gate, while more find their way into Flushing Bay and on into Long Island Sound, where they cling to the feet of wading herons and egrets, and lifted up, come to rest in the birds' lofty nests. Another group of ashes glides up the Hudson, riding on cool salty columns. At the piers they jockey with seahorses. At the George Washington Bridge they eddy about the gray steel pilings, crowding in with the suspended solid of plankton and the pollutants DDT and Agent Orange, mercury and arsenic. Some stay behind while others urge still northward, toward the river's source high in the Adirondacks, the summit waters of Lake Tear of the Clouds. Into every articular estuary, the ashes swim. Up the Harlem River and into stagnant Gowanus, choked by algal blooms. Into Newark Bay, Sawmill Creek, and Hackensack, deep in the Meadowlands' mud. Down the Kills and out to Sandy Hook. There, the ebb tide pushes them through the Narrows, under the silver Verrazano and out to sea, where the North Atlantic current sweeps them onto its cool conveyer belt and pulls them out into the blue expanses of the globe. Some sift through the bodies of whales and basking sharks, sink to the abyssal plain and are swallowed into the bellies of giant squids and luminescent lanternfish. At the spinning rotary of the weedy, eel-rich Sargasso Sea, the ashes separate again. Some go south to the Canary Islands and down through the turbulent waters off Cape Horn where the Pacific takes them into its volcanic vastnesses. Others go north to the Barents, cluttered with bergy bits, where they join phytoplankton in their springtime blossoming. And just a few of the ashes make it over the shallow sill of the Gibraltar strait to glide like water striders atop the warm and salty Mediterranean at last, home again, where the body began in another mother's shimmering dream on the blue banks of the Adriatic.

Acknowledgments

Thanks first and foremost to Rebecca Levi for her inspiring artwork, for reading drafts of this novel (early bad ones and later better ones), for bearing with my frustrations throughout the process, and for supporting me from beginning to end. Thanks to the friends who were helpful readers—Tia S., Catherine H., Josh M., and John E.—and to my parents for always encouraging my writing. Thanks to agents Philip Spitzer and Lukas Ortiz for seeing this book through to publication, and to my editor, Guy Intoci, for rescuing the manuscript from a forgotten pile and carrying it 3,000 miles, where he found it a home and helped get it into shape.

I also owe much gratitude to those who helped with my research. Jack Doyle, President of Ironworkers Local 40, kindly took time out of his busy day to meet with me and recall his time spent as raising gang foreman on the North Tower of the World Trade Center—his words helped to make Frank real. James Shackelford, Professor of Chemical Engineering at UC Davis and member of the DELTA Group (for Detection and Evaluation of Long-range Transport of Aerosols), informed me in detail about the particulate remains found and not found at Ground Zero. Christopher W. Stubbs, Professor of Physics and Astronomy at Harvard University, answered my questions about dark matter and massive compact halo objects (MACHOs). Finally, a special thank you to John Q. for talking with me about the beloved friend he lost on 9/11.

Author's Note

This book was originally written when it takes place, in the spring of 2002, when the number of New York casualties on 9/11 was estimated to be 2,801. That estimate was later reduced and eventually settled at 2,752. To be true to the time, I have left the number as it was known then.

The novel largely contains my own observations and memories of that spring in New York City, and I hope it will serve as a record of that time, between a dark winter and a new war. However, I have added a few events that came later. Also, throughout the writing and rewriting, I depended on a number of sources for inspiration and/or information, including: *The Monstrous-Feminine* by Barbara Creed; Don DeLillo's essay on terrorism and consumerism, "In the Ruin of the Future"; "The Mermaid," on the mythic history of the Starbucks logo, by Heinz Insu Fenkl; "On Whales and Adventures Therein: Loss as a Mutative Experience in Psychoanalytic Treatment," a talk by Robert Fischl, MD; Sigmund Freud's "The Uncanny"; Malcolm Gladwell's essay on the SUV, "Big and Bad"; *Regarding the Pain of Others* by Susan Sontag; *The Devil's Playground* by James Traub. I read too many newspaper articles to enumerate, but Dan Barry at the *New York Times* and Michael McLeod at the *Orlando Sentinel* both provided great details about the Dodge Durango SUV living window display in Times Square, facts from which I borrowed liberally. As Philip Roth has written of the American writer, we have our "hands full trying to understand, and then describe, and then make *credible* much of the American reality. It stupefies, it sickens, it infuriates, and finally it is even a kind of embarrassment to one's meager imagination. The actuality is continually outdoing our talents, and the culture tosses up figures almost daily that are the envy of any novelist…The daily newspapers then fill one with wonder and awe; is it possible? Is it happening?"